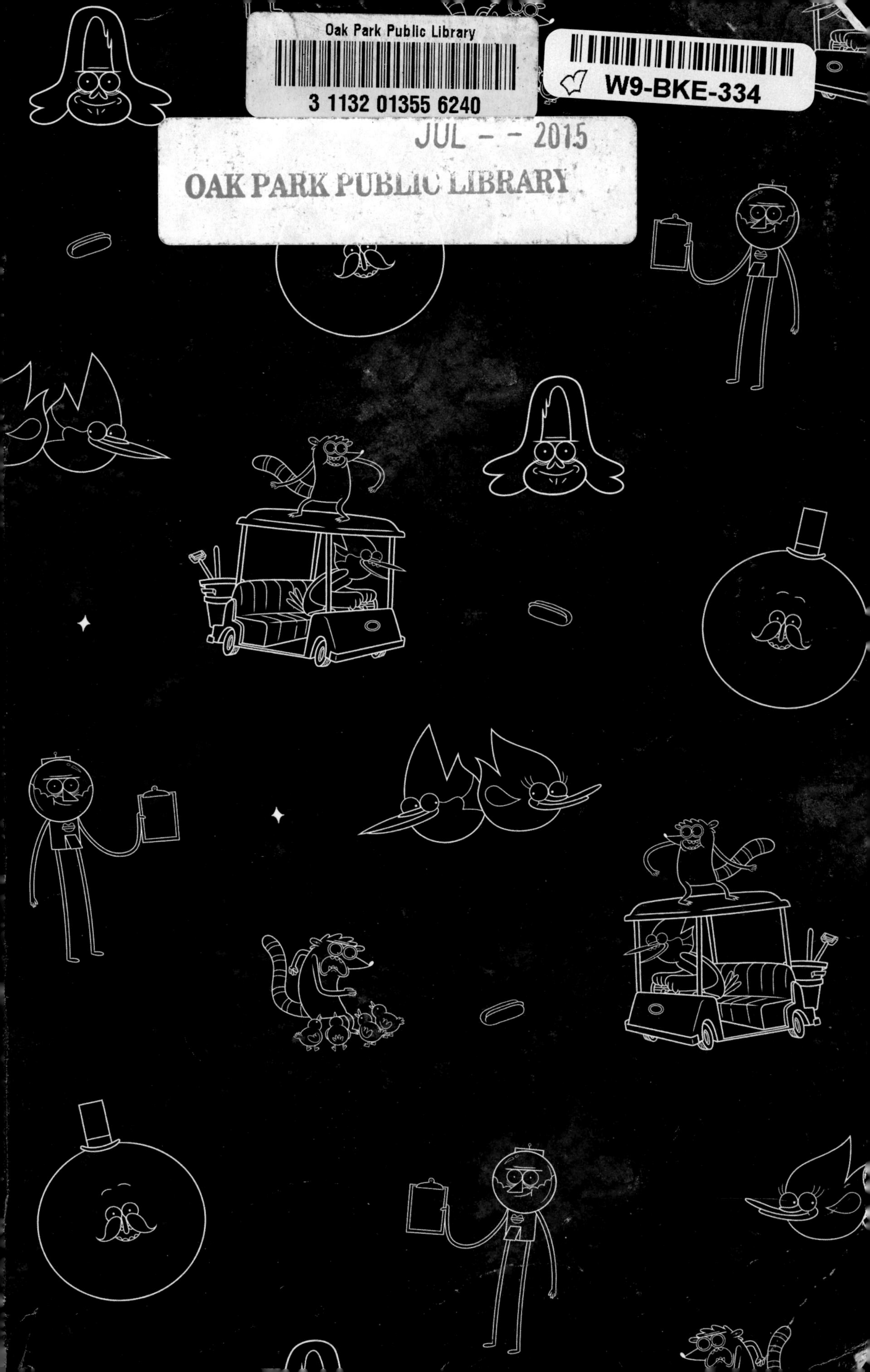

REGULAR SHOW™

VOLUME FOUR

ROSS RICHIE CEO & Founder • MARK SMYLIE Founder of Archaia • MATT GAGNON Editor-in-Chief • FILIP SABLIK President of Publishing & Marketing • STEPHEN CHRISTY President of Development
LANCE KREITER VP of Licensing & Merchandising • PHIL BARBARO VP of Finance • BRYCE CARLSON Managing Editor • MEL CAYLO Marketing Manager • SCOTT NEWMAN Production Design Manager
IRENE BRADISH Operations Manager • CHRISTINE DINH Brand Communications Manager • DAFNA PLEBAN Editor • SHANNON WATTERS Editor • ERIC HARBURN Editor • REBECCA TAYLOR Editor • IAN BRILL Editor
WHITNEY LEOPARD Associate Editor • JASMINE AMIRI Associate Editor • CHRIS ROSA Assistant Editor • ALEX GALER Assistant Editor • CAMERON CHITTOCK Assistant Editor • MARY GUMPORT Assistant Editor
KELSEY DIETERICH Production Designer • JILLIAN CRAB Production Designer • KARA LEOPARD Production Designer • MICHELLE ANKLEY Production Design Assistant • DEVIN FUNCHES E-Commerce & Inventory Coordinator
AARON FERRARA Operations Coordinator • JOSÉ MEZA Sales Assistant • ELIZABETH LOUGHRIDGE Accounting Assistant • STEPHANIE HOCUTT PR Assistant • HILLARY LEVI Executive Assistant • KATE ALBIN Administrative Assistant

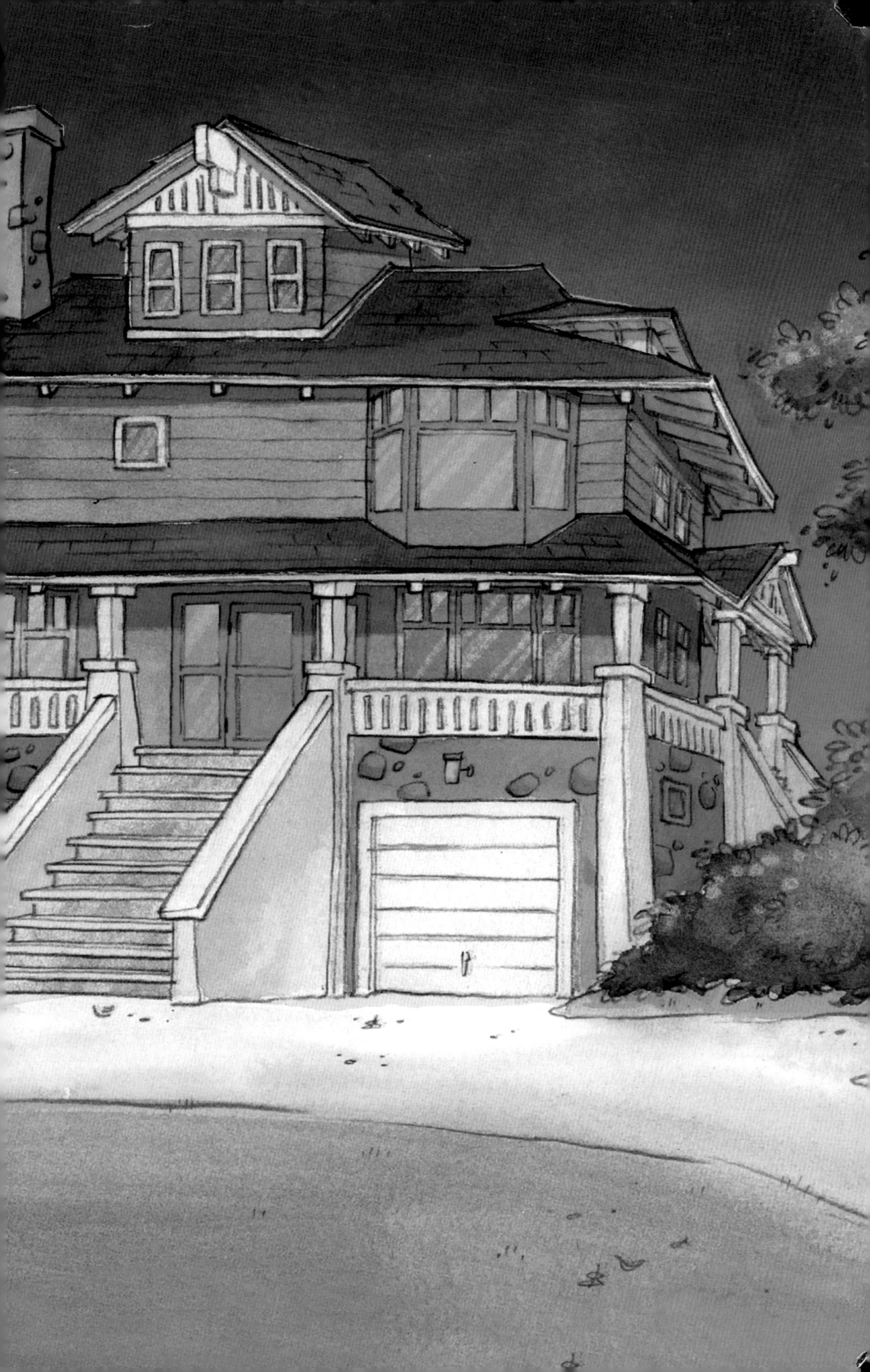

REGULAR

CREATED BY JG QUINTEL

WRITTEN BY **KC GREEN**

ART BY **ALLISON STREJLAU**

COLORS BY **LISA MOORE**

LETTERS BY **STEVE WANDS**

COVER BY
KYLE FEWELL

DESIGNER
KELSEY DIETERICH

ASSISTANT EDITOR
MARY GUMPORT

EDITOR
SHANNON WATTERS

SHOW™

"EILEEN DAY"

WRITTEN BY **MINTY LEWIS**
ILLUSTRATED BY **ALLISON STREJLAU**
COLORS BY **LISA MOORE**
LETTERS BY **STEVE WANDS**

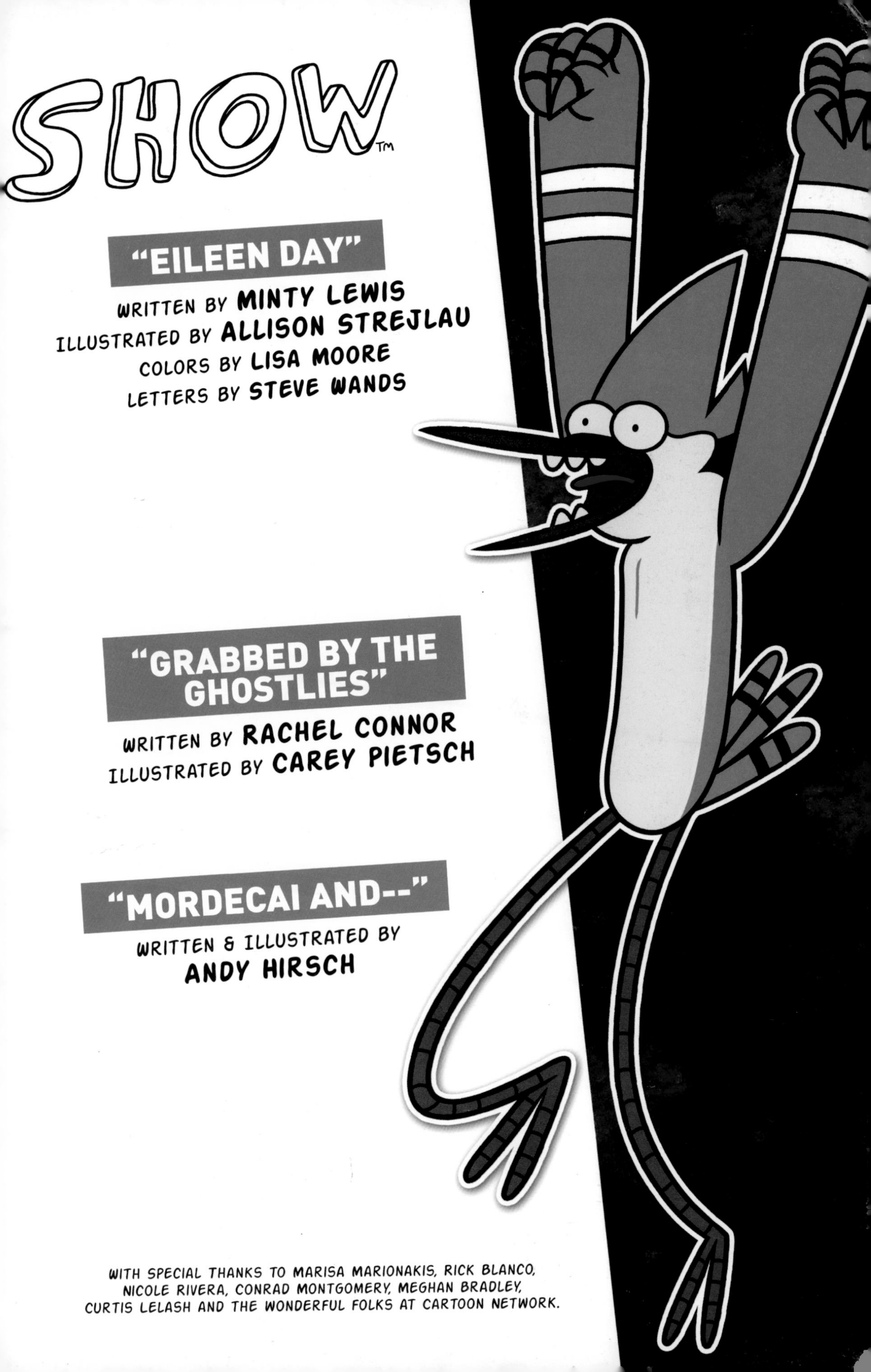

"GRABBED BY THE GHOSTLIES"

WRITTEN BY **RACHEL CONNOR**
ILLUSTRATED BY **CAREY PIETSCH**

"MORDECAI AND--"

WRITTEN & ILLUSTRATED BY
ANDY HIRSCH

WITH SPECIAL THANKS TO MARISA MARIONAKIS, RICK BLANCO, NICOLE RIVERA, CONRAD MONTGOMERY, MEGHAN BRADLEY, CURTIS LELASH AND THE WONDERFUL FOLKS AT CARTOON NETWORK.

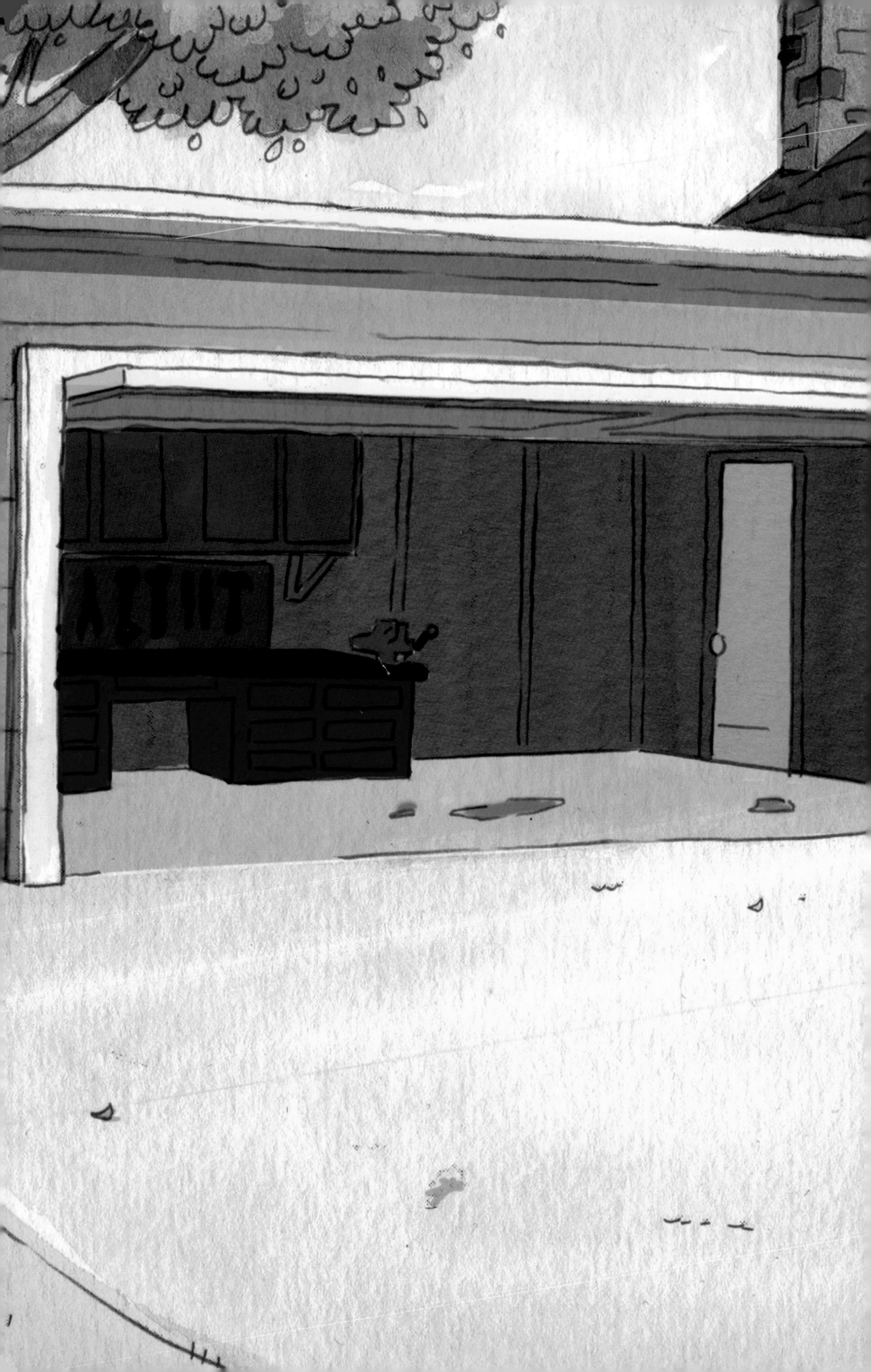

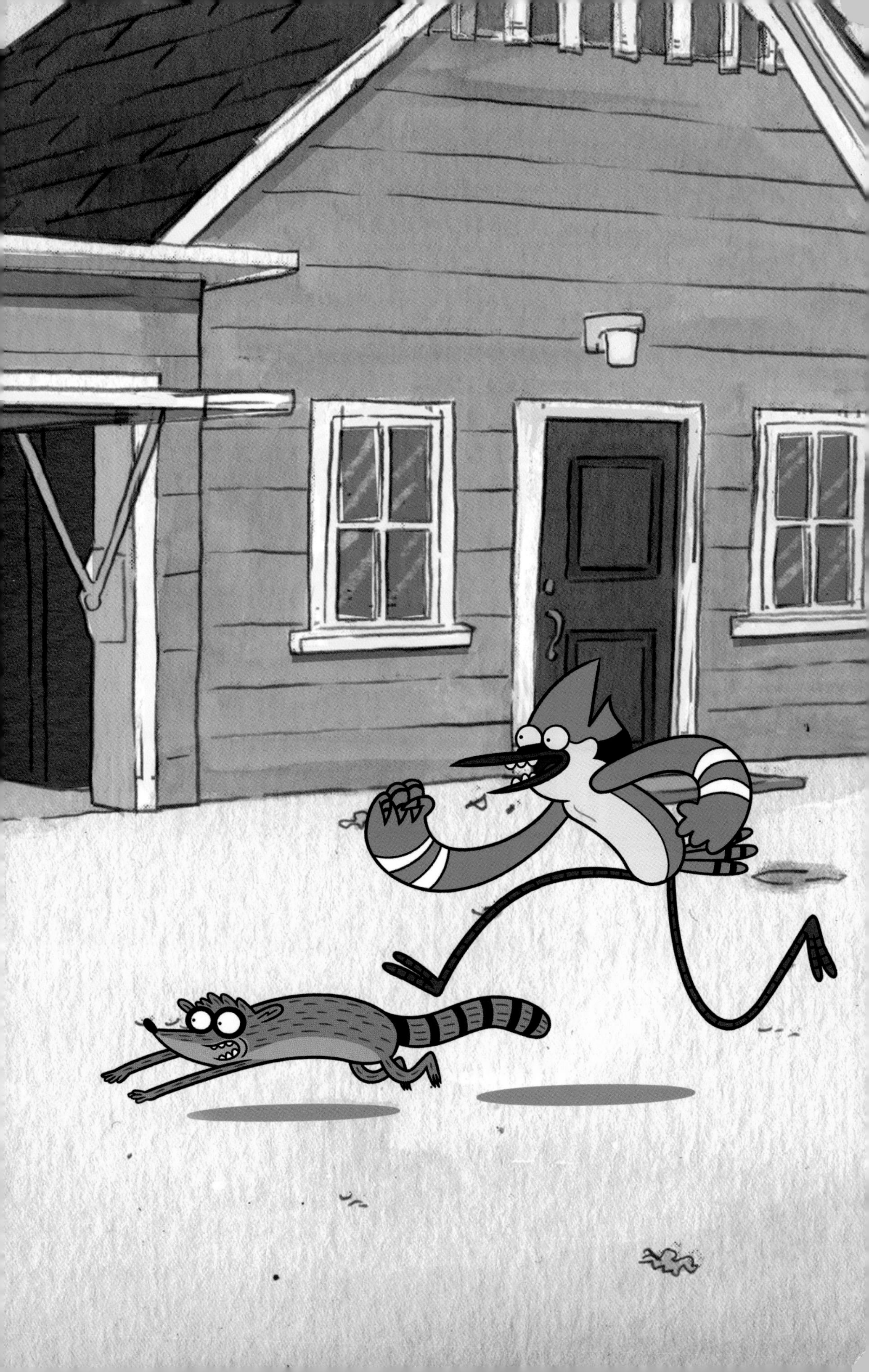

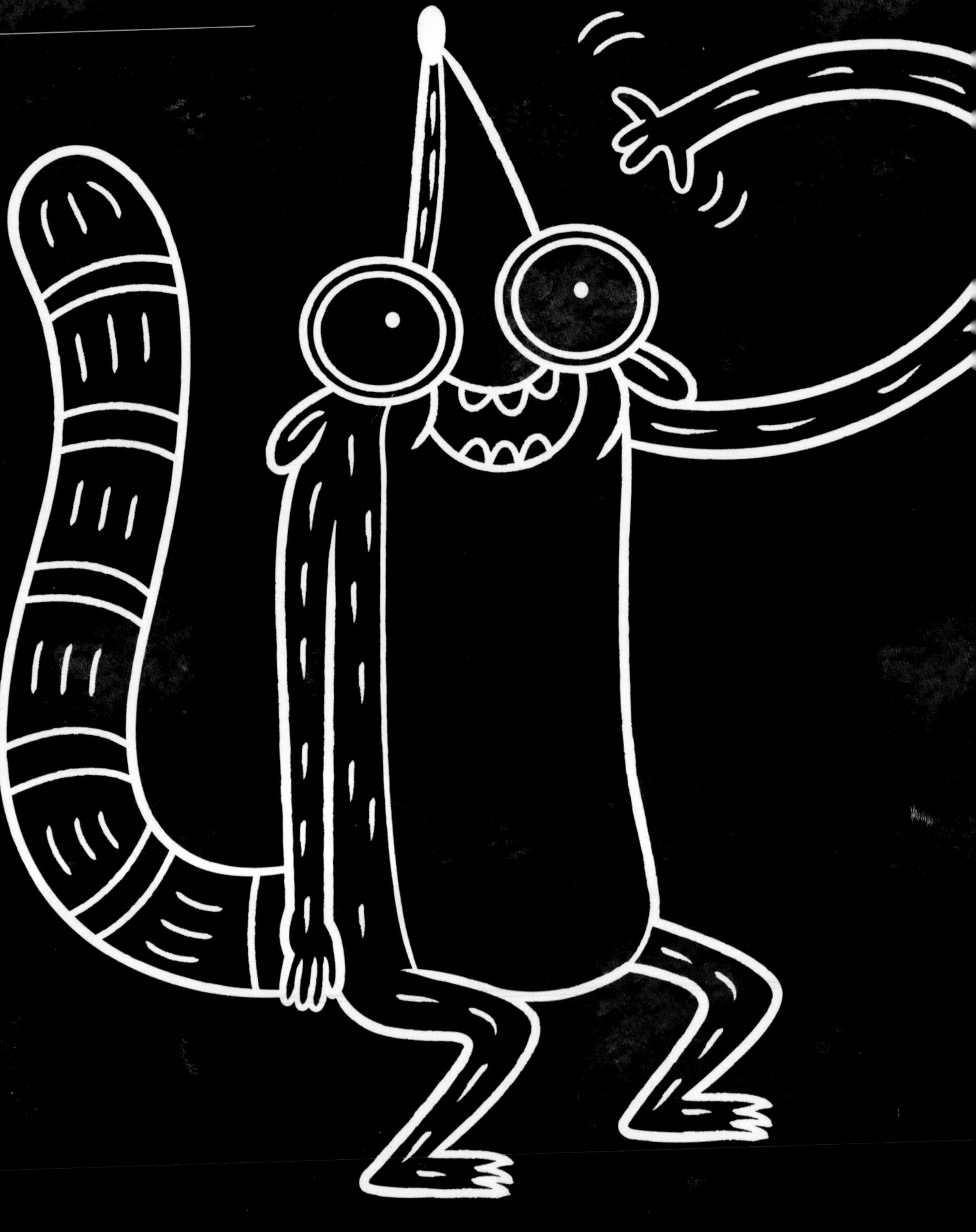

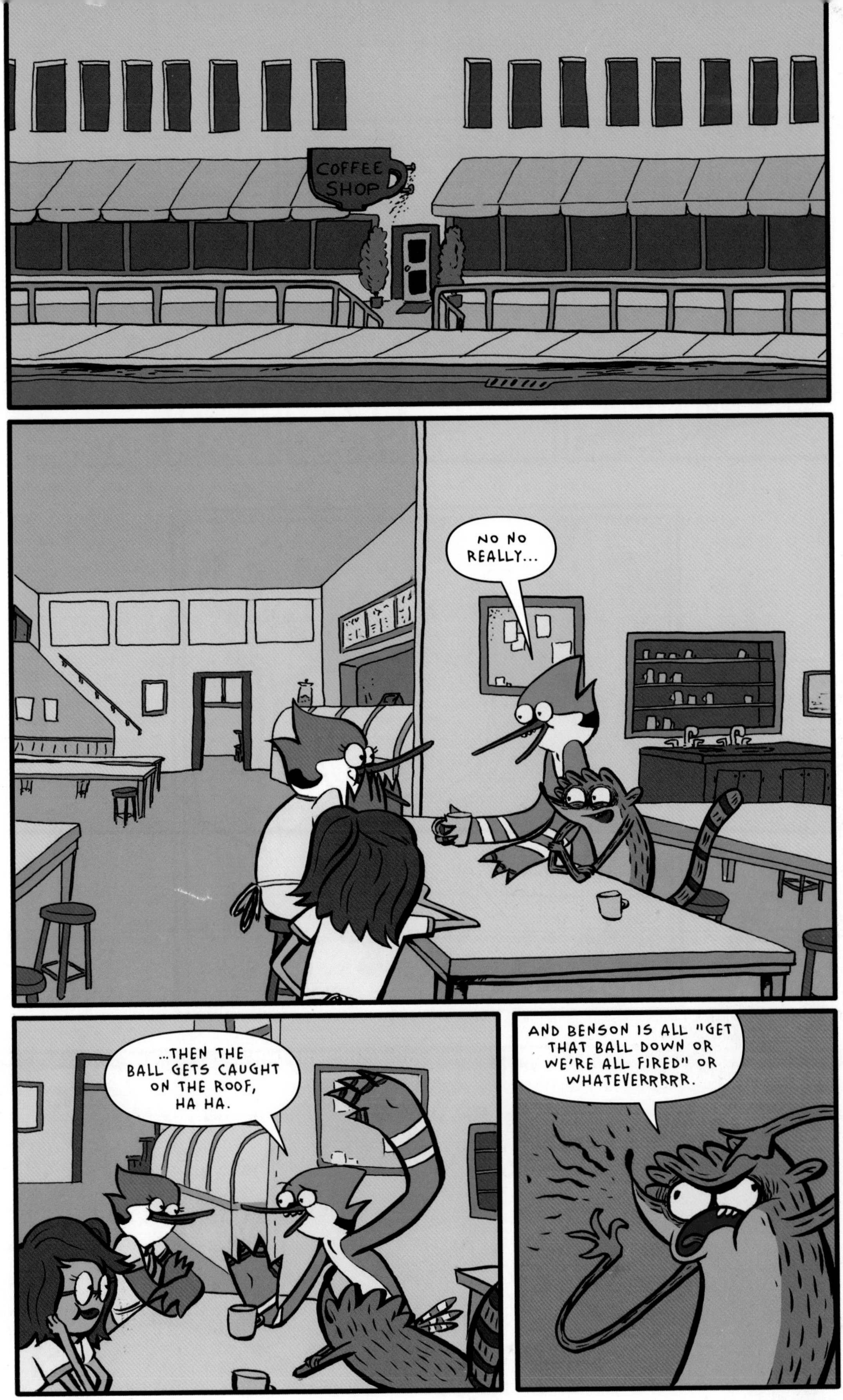
COFFEE SHOP
NO NO REALLY...
...THEN THE BALL GETS CAUGHT ON THE ROOF, HA HA.
AND BENSON IS ALL "GET THAT BALL DOWN OR WE'RE ALL FIRED" OR WHATEVERRRRR.

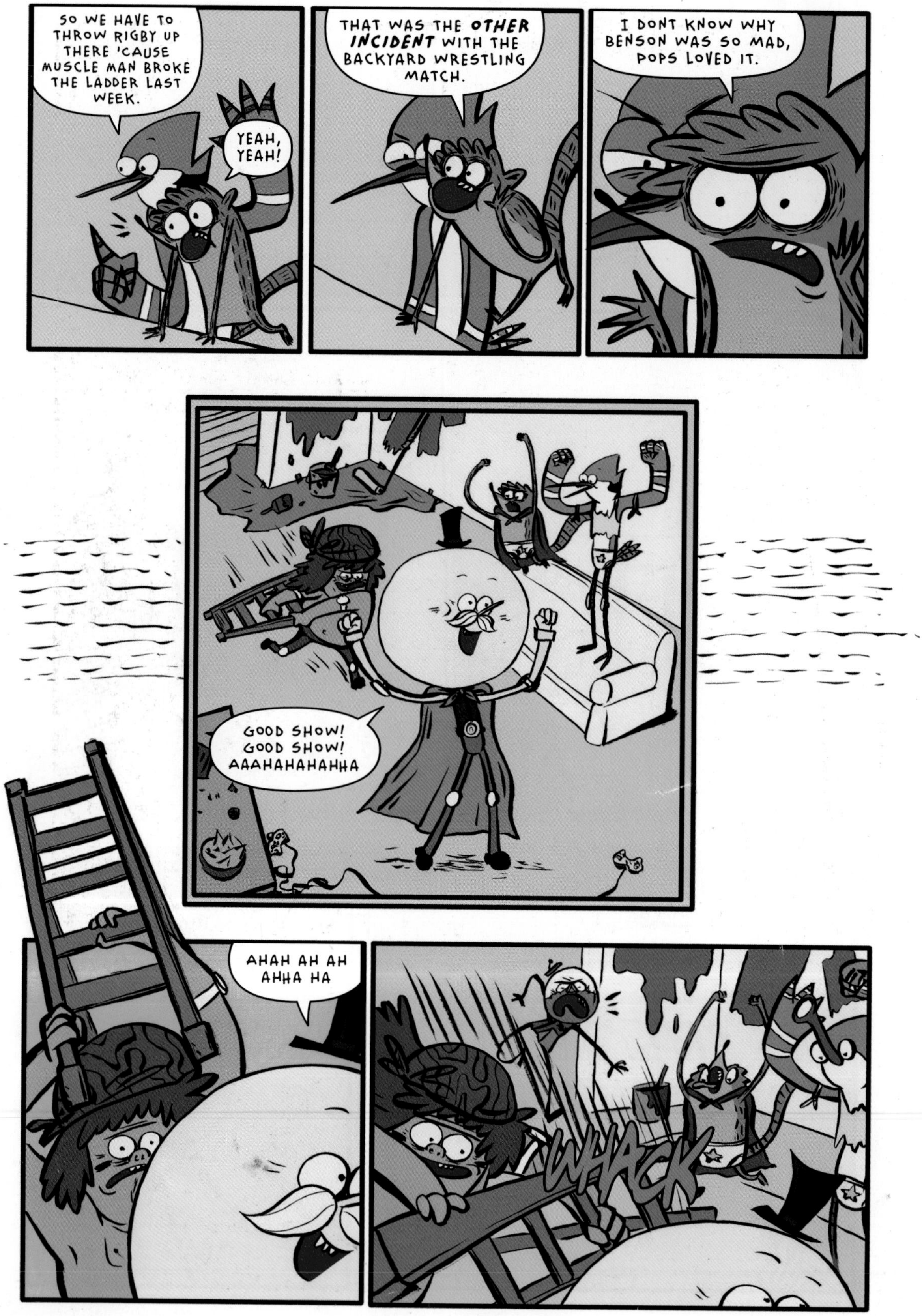
SO WE HAVE TO THROW RIGBY UP THERE 'CAUSE MUSCLE MAN BROKE THE LADDER LAST WEEK.
YEAH, YEAH!
THAT WAS THE OTHER INCIDENT WITH THE BACKYARD WRESTLING MATCH.
I DONT KNOW WHY BENSON WAS SO MAD, POPS LOVED IT.
GOOD SHOW! GOOD SHOW! AAAHAHAHAHHA
AHAH AH AH AHHA HA
WHACK

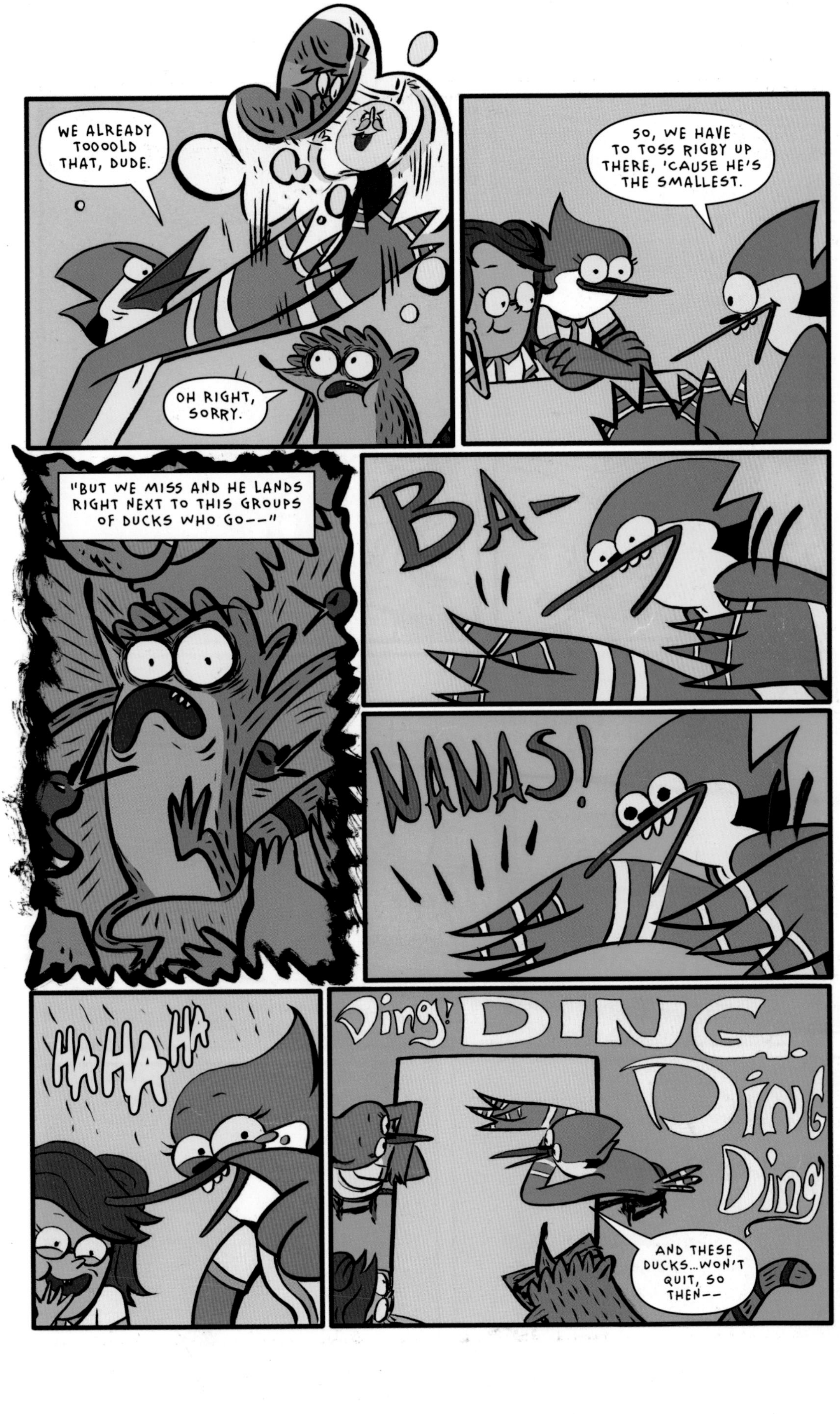
WE ALREADY TOOOOLD THAT, DUDE.
OH RIGHT, SORRY.
SO, WE HAVE TO TOSS RIGBY UP THERE, 'CAUSE HE'S THE SMALLEST.
"BUT WE MISS AND HE LANDS RIGHT NEXT TO THIS GROUPS OF DUCKS WHO GO--"
BA-
NANAS!
HAHAHA
Ding! DING. DING Ding
AND THESE DUCKS...WON'T QUIT, SO THEN--

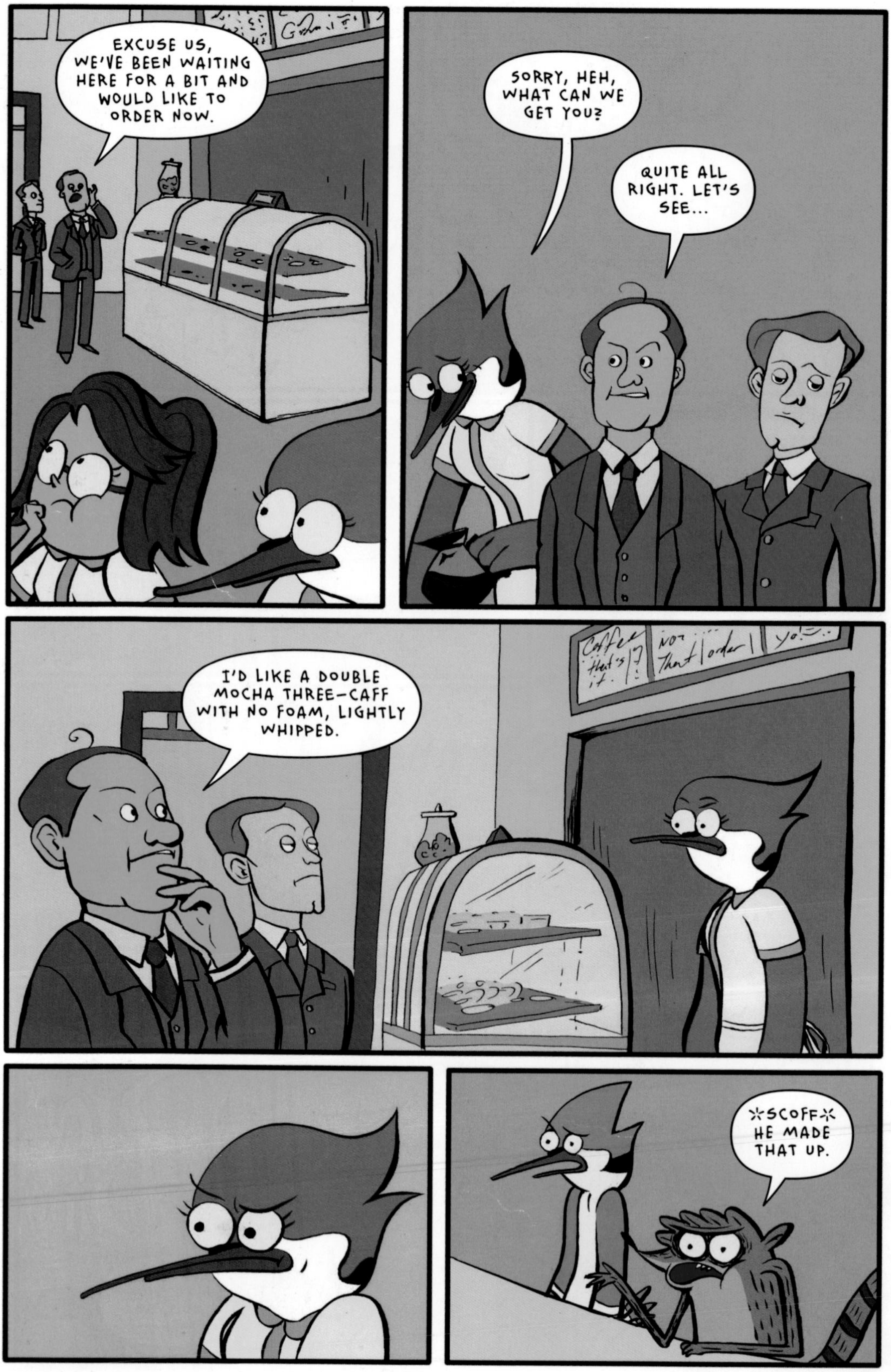
EXCUSE US, WE'VE BEEN WAITING HERE FOR A BIT AND WOULD LIKE TO ORDER NOW.
SORRY, HEH, WHAT CAN WE GET YOU?
QUITE ALL RIGHT. LET'S SEE...
I'D LIKE A DOUBLE MOCHA THREE-CAFF WITH NO FOAM, LIGHTLY WHIPPED.
SCOFF HE MADE THAT UP.

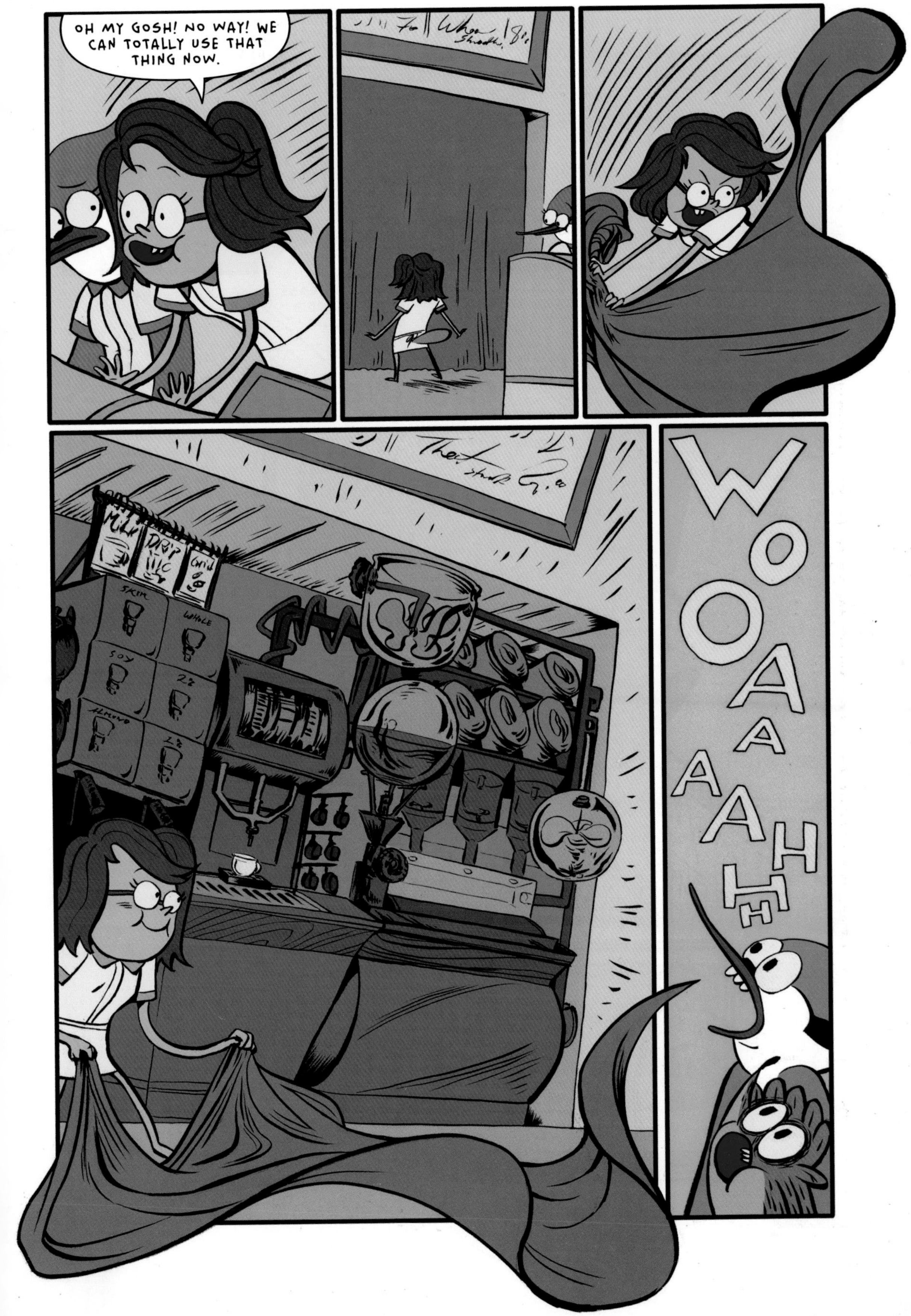
OH MY GOSH! NO WAY! WE CAN TOTALLY USE THAT THING NOW.
SKIM
WHOLE
SOY
ALMOND
WOOAAAAHHHH

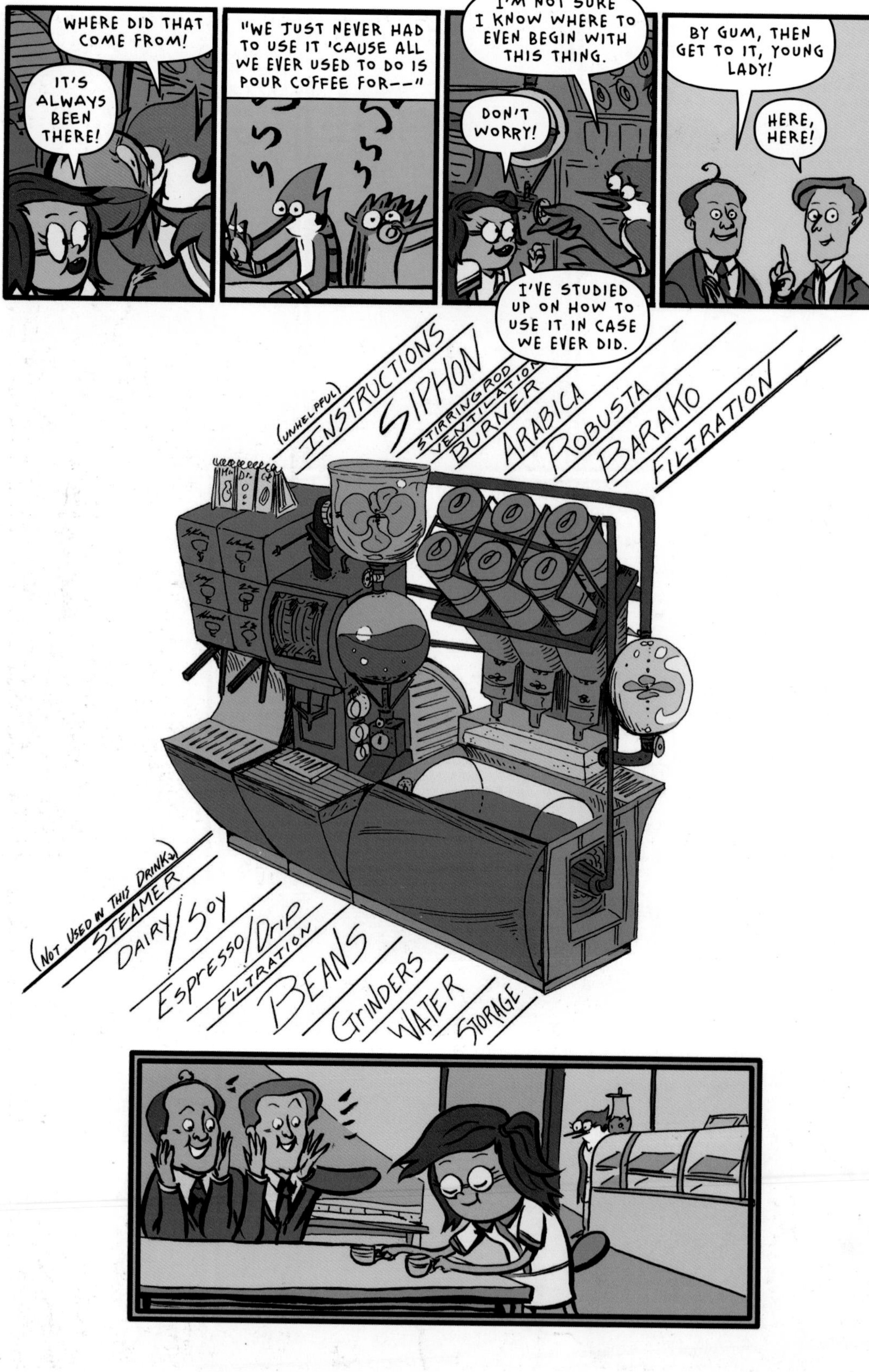
WHERE DID THAT COME FROM!
IT'S ALWAYS BEEN THERE!
"WE JUST NEVER HAD TO USE IT 'CAUSE ALL WE EVER USED TO DO IS POUR COFFEE FOR--"
I'M NOT SURE I KNOW WHERE TO EVEN BEGIN WITH THIS THING.
DON'T WORRY!
I'VE STUDIED UP ON HOW TO USE IT IN CASE WE EVER DID.
BY GUM, THEN GET TO IT, YOUNG LADY!
HERE, HERE!
(UNHELPFUL) INSTRUCTIONS
SIPHON
STIRRING ROD
VENTILATION
BURNER
ARABICA
ROBUSTA
BARAKO
FILTRATION
(NOT USED IN THIS DRINK)
STEAMER
DAIRY/SOY
ESPRESSO/DRIP
FILTRATION
BEANS
GRINDERS
WATER
STORAGE

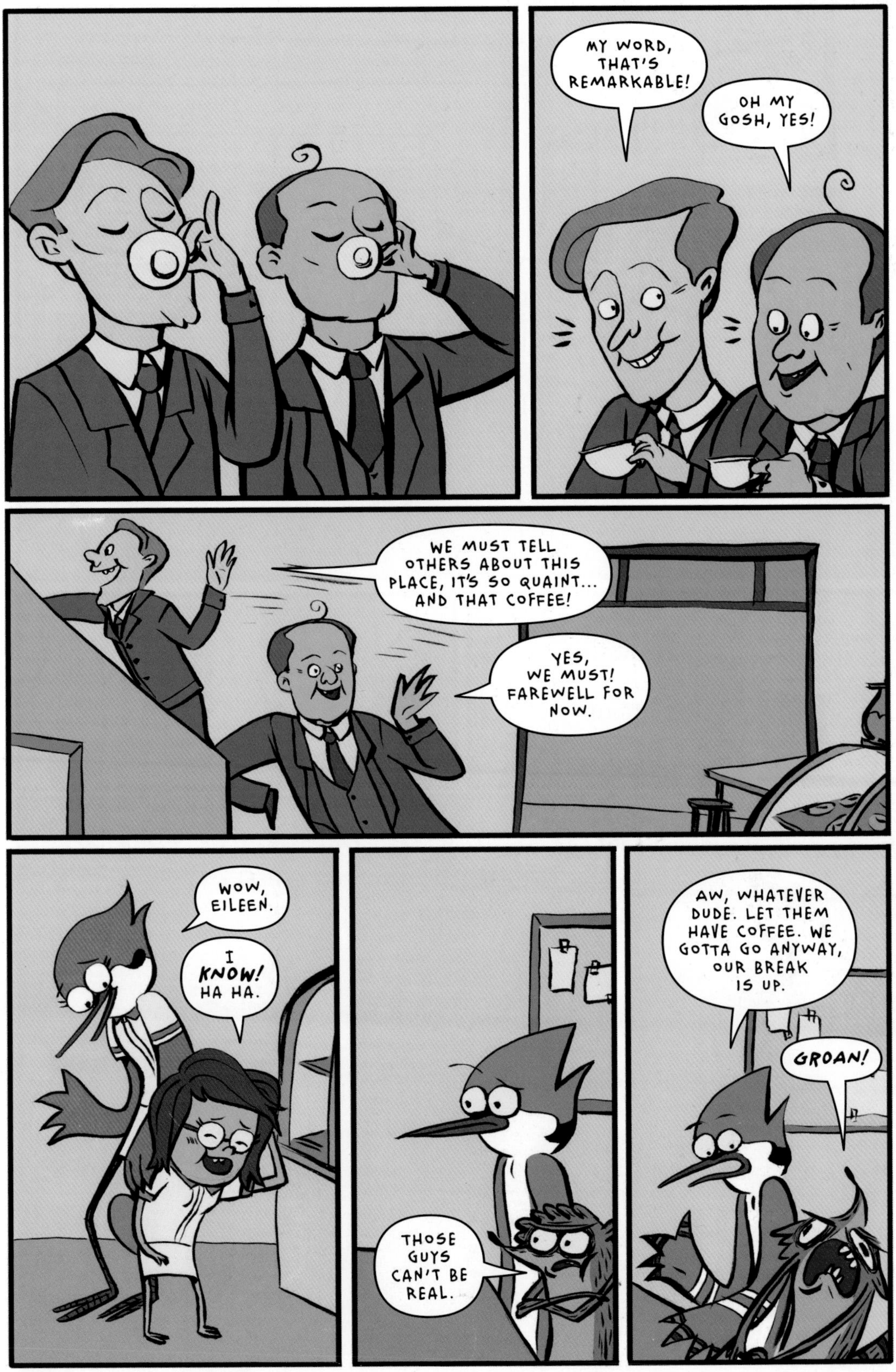
MY WORD, THAT'S REMARKABLE!
OH MY GOSH, YES!
WE MUST TELL OTHERS ABOUT THIS PLACE, IT'S SO QUAINT... AND THAT COFFEE!
YES, WE MUST! FAREWELL FOR NOW.
WOW, EILEEN.
I KNOW! HA HA.
THOSE GUYS CAN'T BE REAL.
AW, WHATEVER DUDE. LET THEM HAVE COFFEE. WE GOTTA GO ANYWAY, OUR BREAK IS UP.
GROAN!

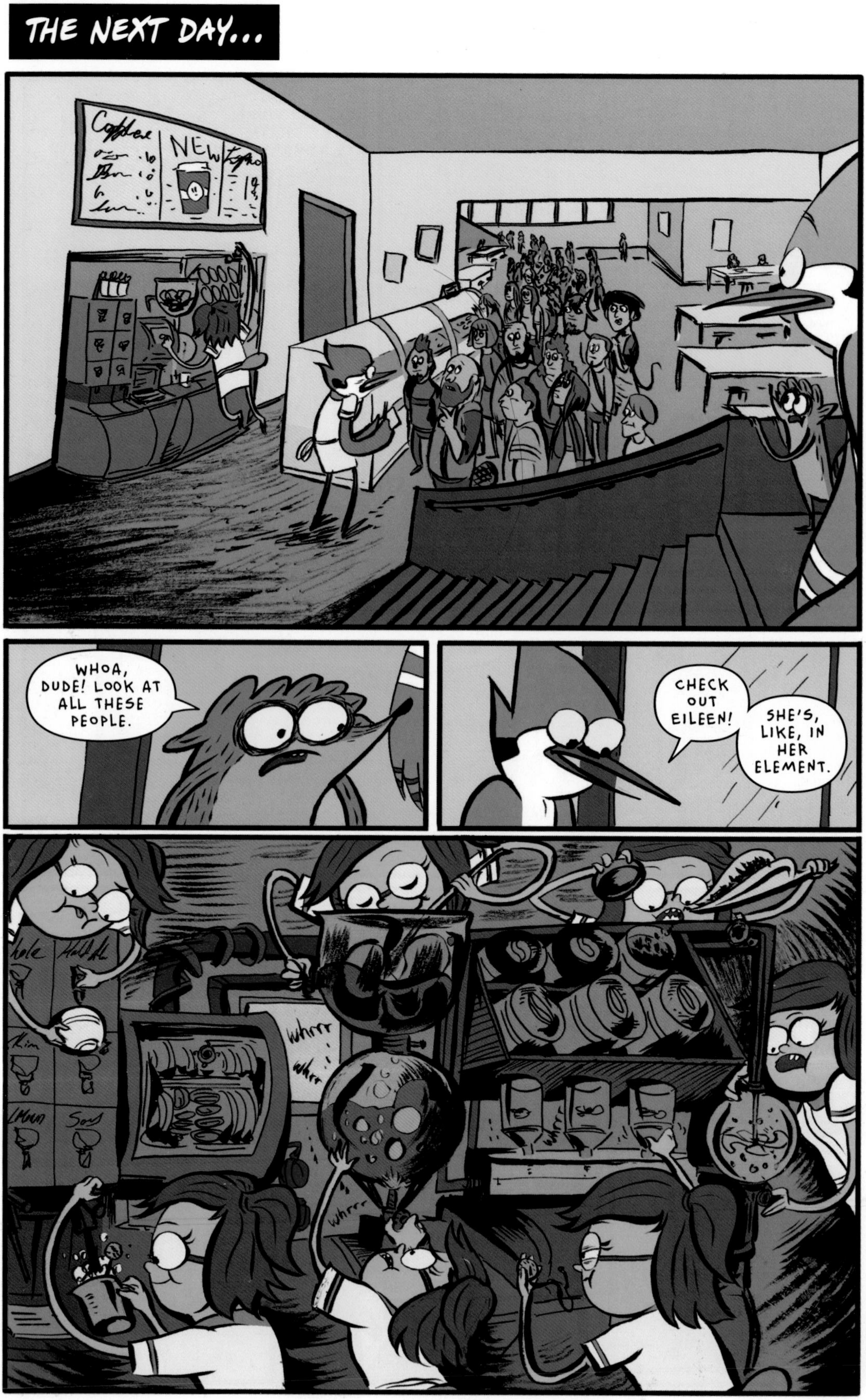
THE NEXT DAY...
NEW
WHOA, DUDE! LOOK AT ALL THESE PEOPLE.
CHECK OUT EILEEN!
SHE'S, LIKE, IN HER ELEMENT.
whrrr
whrrr
whrrr

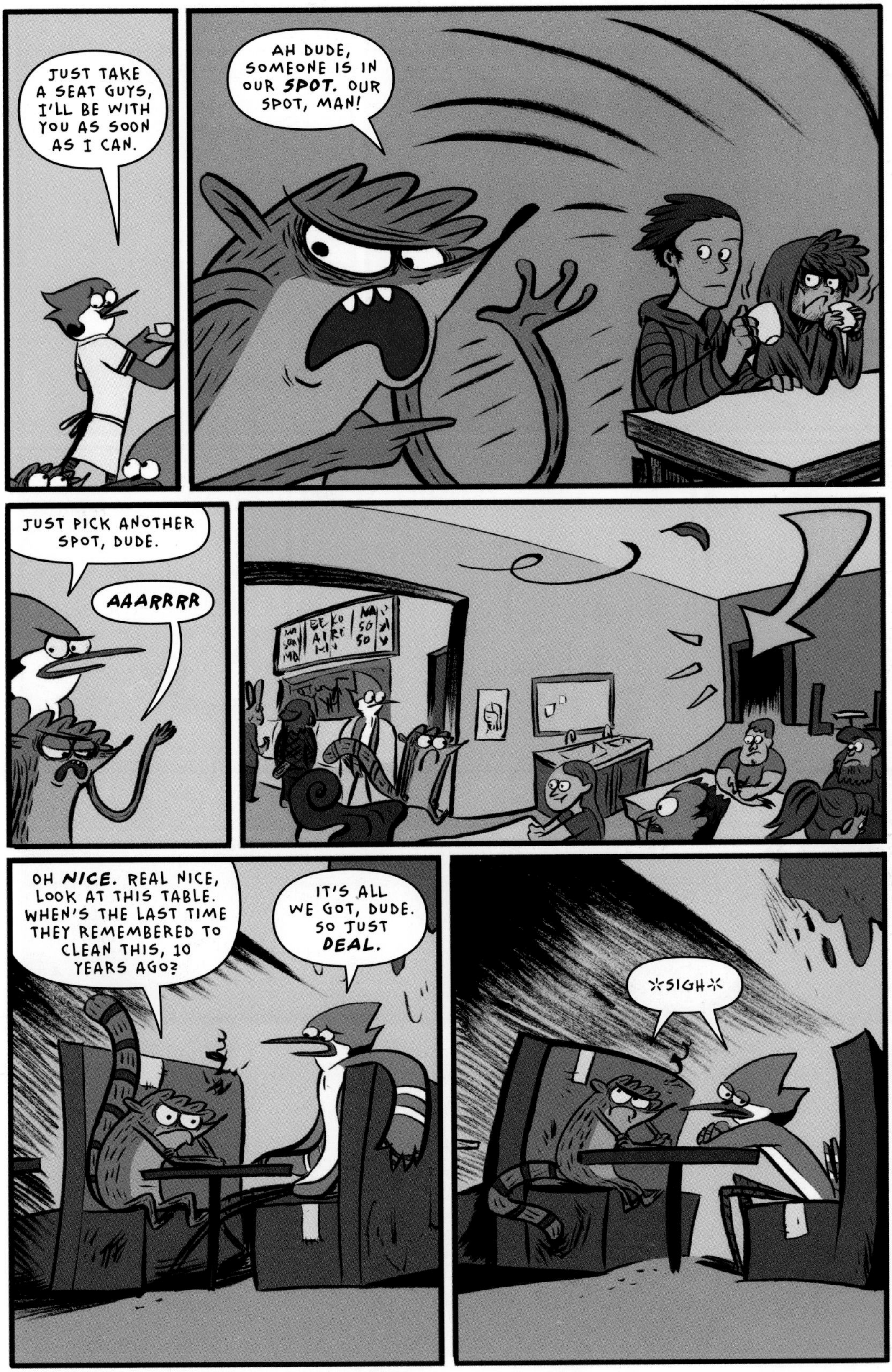
JUST TAKE A SEAT GUYS, I'LL BE WITH YOU AS SOON AS I CAN.
AH DUDE, SOMEONE IS IN OUR SPOT. OUR SPOT, MAN!
JUST PICK ANOTHER SPOT, DUDE.
AAARRRR
OH NICE. REAL NICE, LOOK AT THIS TABLE. WHEN'S THE LAST TIME THEY REMEMBERED TO CLEAN THIS, 10 YEARS AGO?
IT'S ALL WE GOT, DUDE. SO JUST DEAL.
SIGH

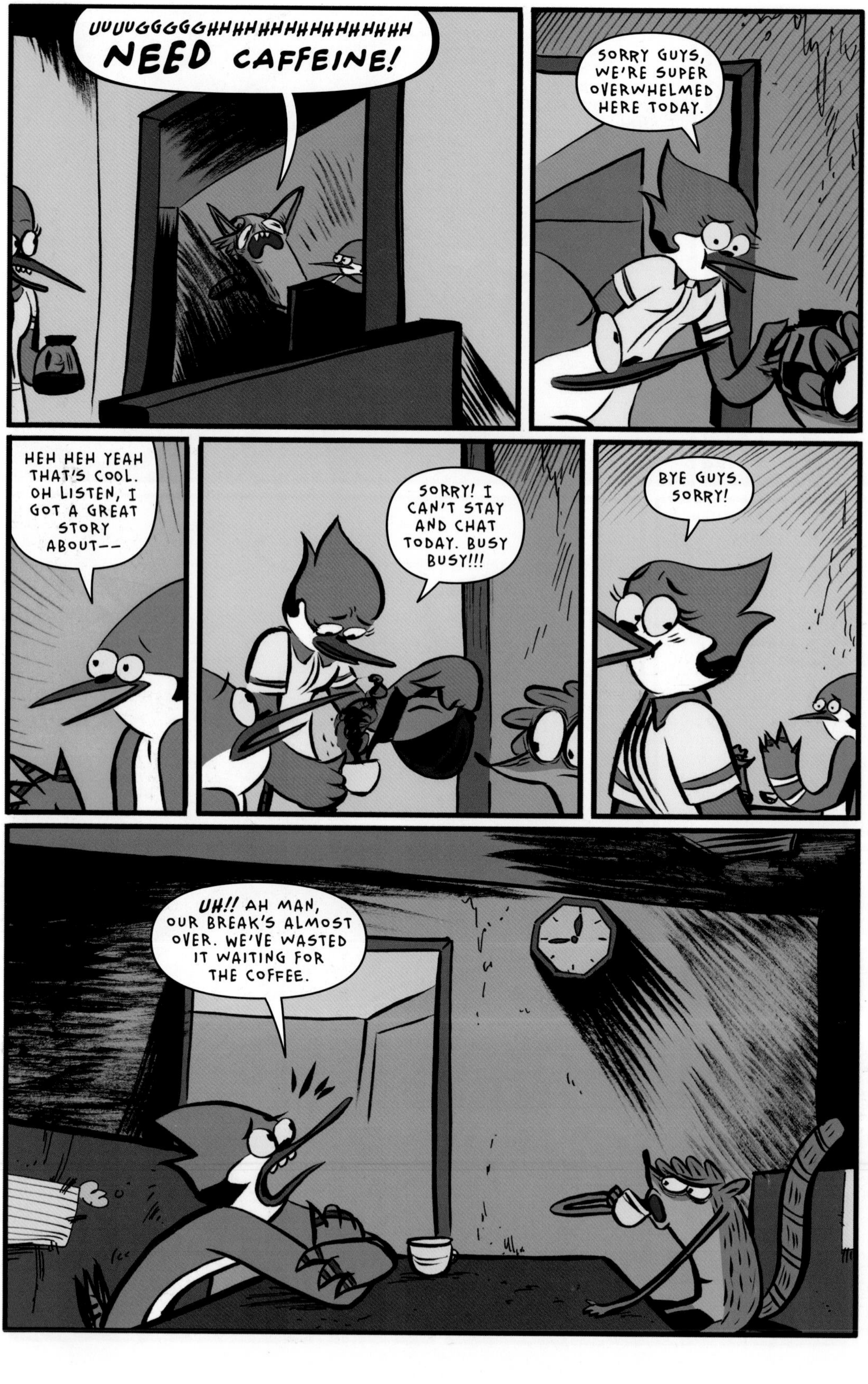
UUUUGGGGGHHHHHHHHHHHHHHHH NEED CAFFEINE!
SORRY GUYS, WE'RE SUPER OVERWHELMED HERE TODAY.
HEH HEH YEAH THAT'S COOL. OH LISTEN, I GOT A GREAT STORY ABOUT--
SORRY! I CAN'T STAY AND CHAT TODAY. BUSY BUSY!!!
BYE GUYS. SORRY!
UH!! AH MAN, OUR BREAK'S ALMOST OVER. WE'VE WASTED IT WAITING FOR THE COFFEE.

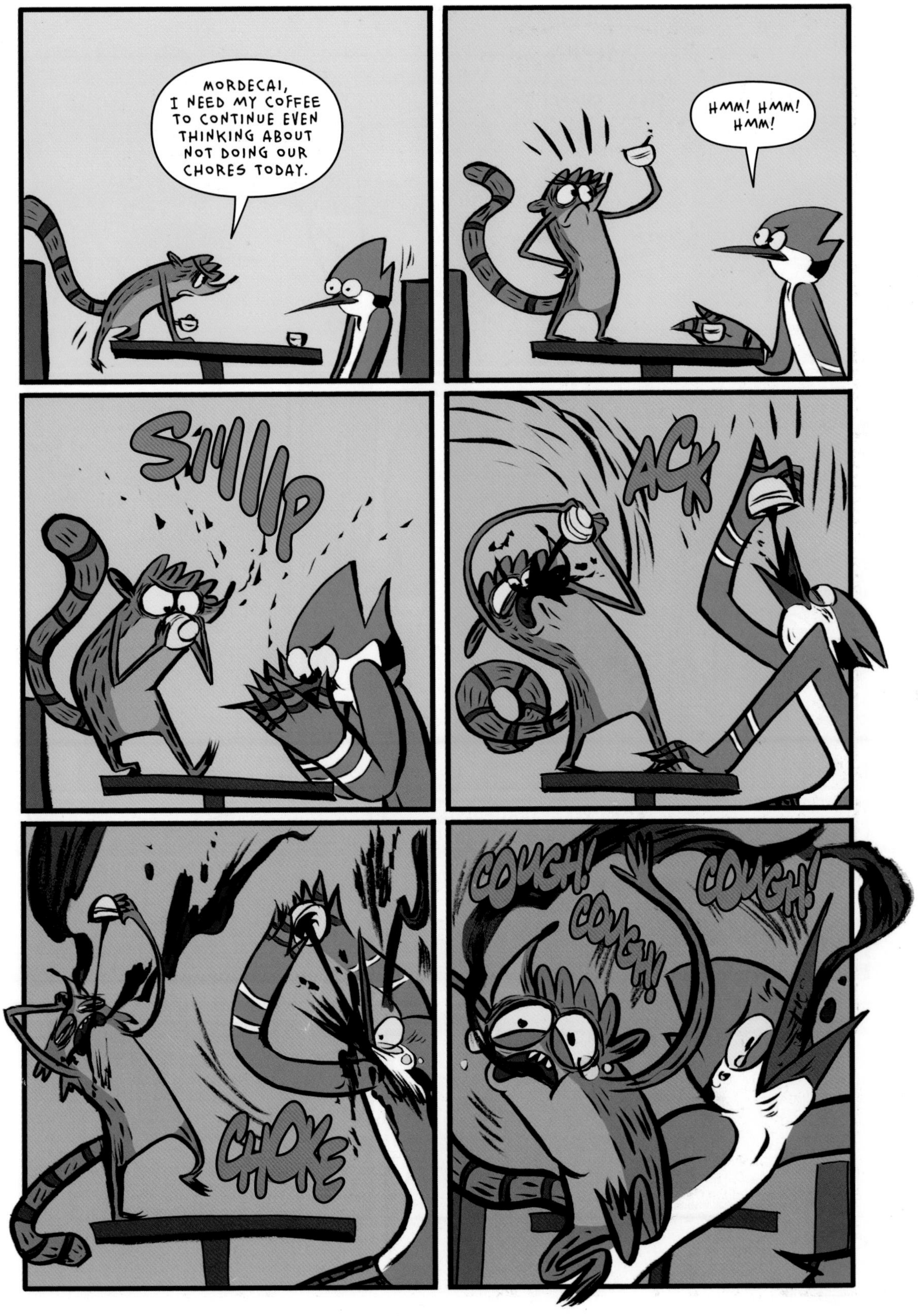
MORDECAI, I NEED MY COFFEE TO CONTINUE EVEN THINKING ABOUT NOT DOING OUR CHORES TODAY.
HMM! HMM! HMM!
SLLLLP
ACK
CHOKE
COUGH!
COUGH!
COUGH!

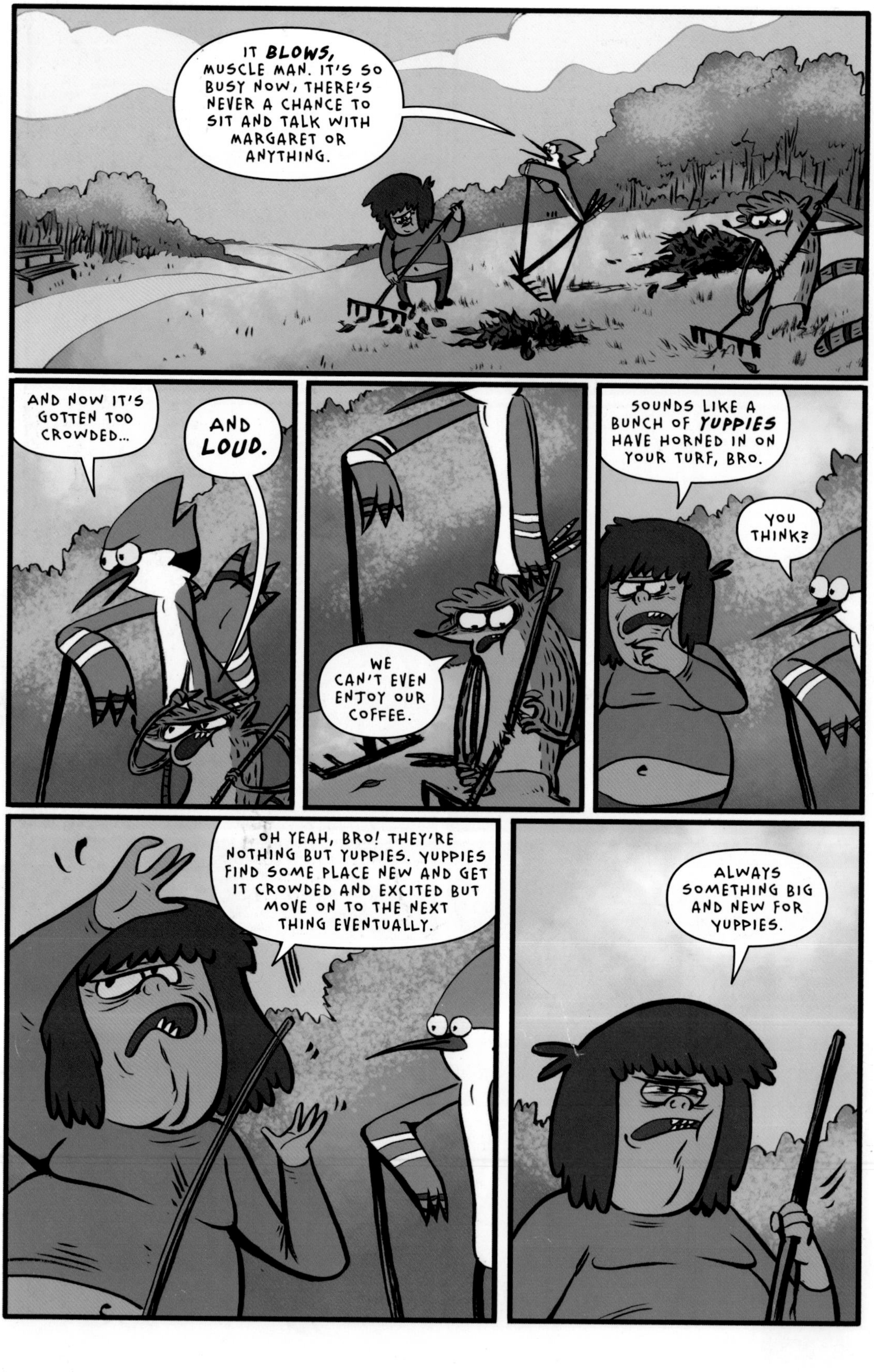
IT BLOWS, MUSCLE MAN. IT'S SO BUSY NOW, THERE'S NEVER A CHANCE TO SIT AND TALK WITH MARGARET OR ANYTHING.
AND NOW IT'S GOTTEN TOO CROWDED...
AND LOUD.
WE CAN'T EVEN ENJOY OUR COFFEE.
SOUNDS LIKE A BUNCH OF YUPPIES HAVE HORNED IN ON YOUR TURF, BRO.
YOU THINK?
OH YEAH, BRO! THEY'RE NOTHING BUT YUPPIES. YUPPIES FIND SOME PLACE NEW AND GET IT CROWDED AND EXCITED BUT MOVE ON TO THE NEXT THING EVENTUALLY.
ALWAYS SOMETHING BIG AND NEW FOR YUPPIES.

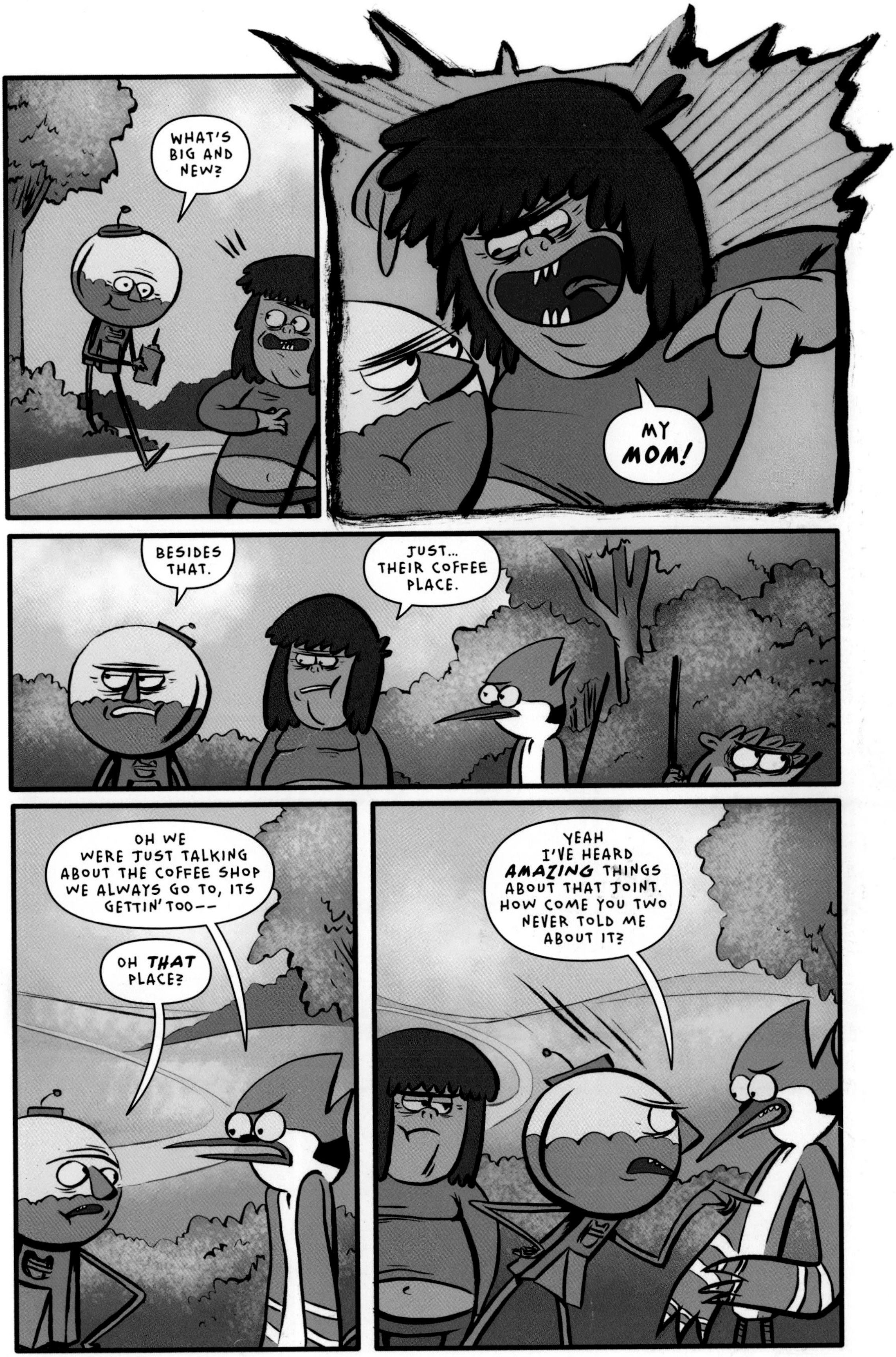
WHAT'S BIG AND NEW?
MY MOM!
BESIDES THAT.
JUST... THEIR COFFEE PLACE.
OH WE WERE JUST TALKING ABOUT THE COFFEE SHOP WE ALWAYS GO TO, ITS GETTIN' TOO--
OH THAT PLACE?
YEAH I'VE HEARD AMAZING THINGS ABOUT THAT JOINT. HOW COME YOU TWO NEVER TOLD ME ABOUT IT?

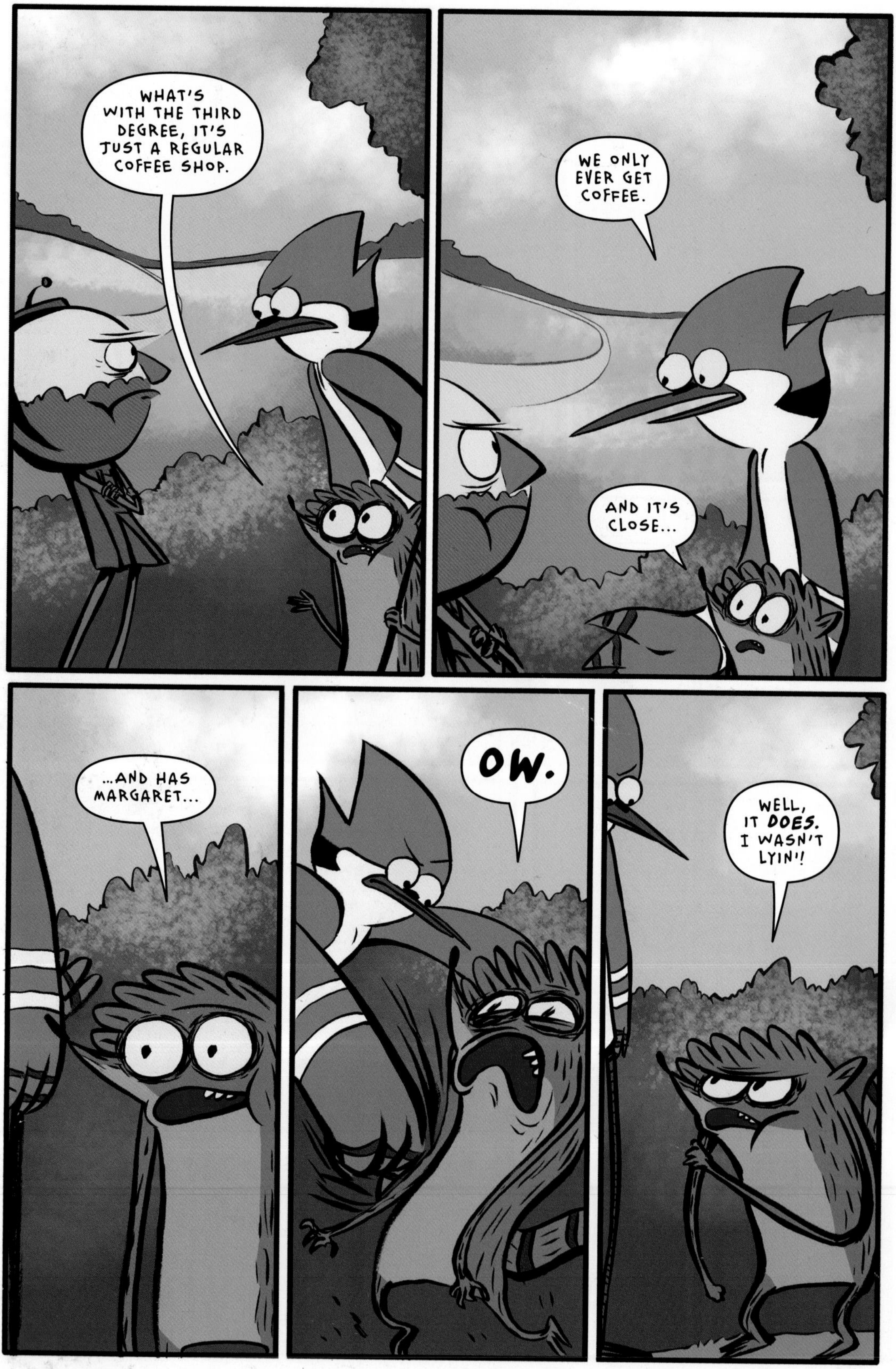
WHAT'S WITH THE THIRD DEGREE, IT'S JUST A REGULAR COFFEE SHOP.
WE ONLY EVER GET COFFEE.
AND IT'S CLOSE...
...AND HAS MARGARET...
OW.
WELL, IT DOES. I WASN'T LYIN'!

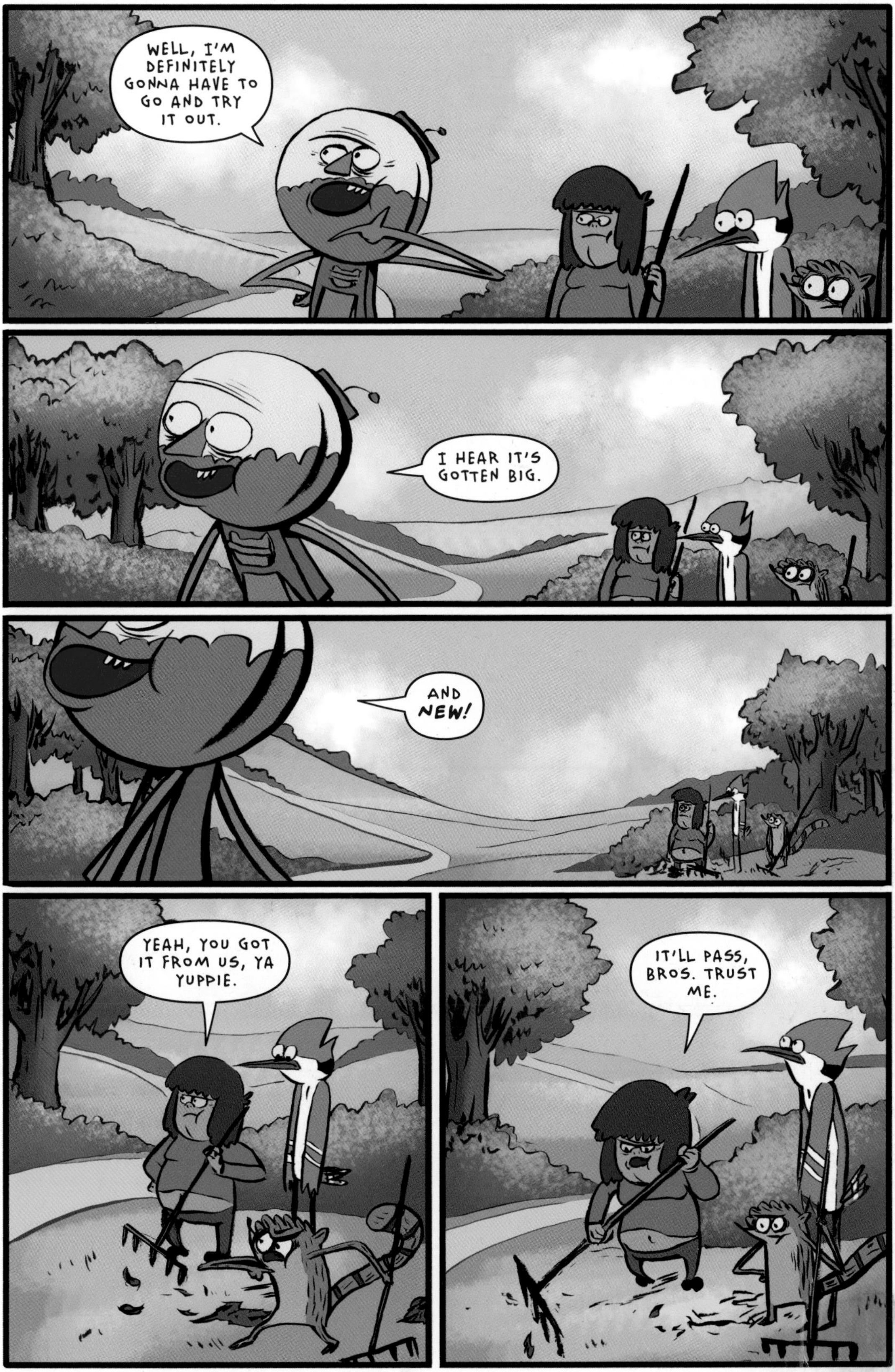
WELL, I'M DEFINITELY GONNA HAVE TO GO AND TRY IT OUT.
I HEAR IT'S GOTTEN BIG.
AND NEW!
YEAH, YOU GOT IT FROM US, YA YUPPIE.
IT'LL PASS, BROS. TRUST ME.

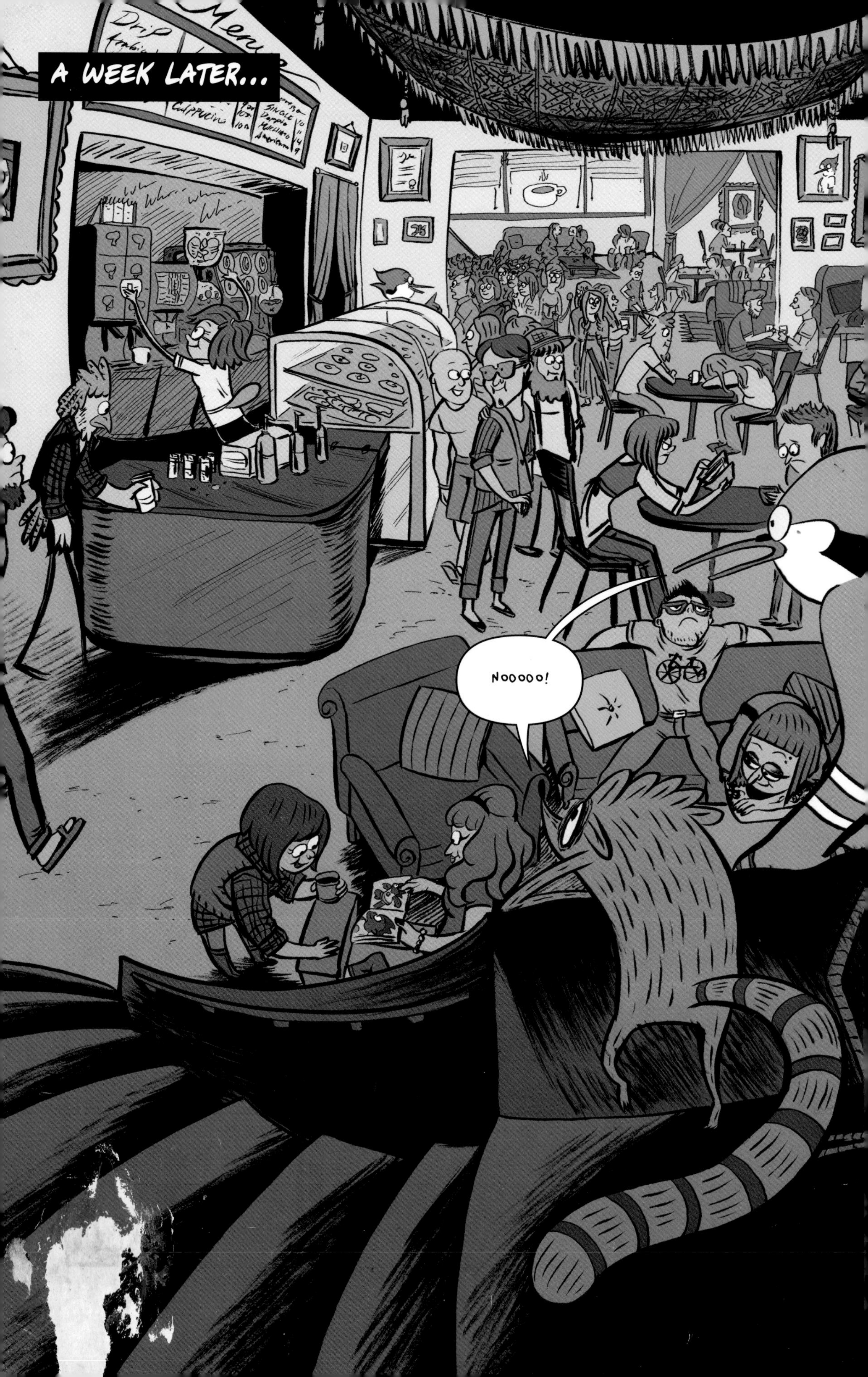
A WEEK LATER...
NOOOOO!

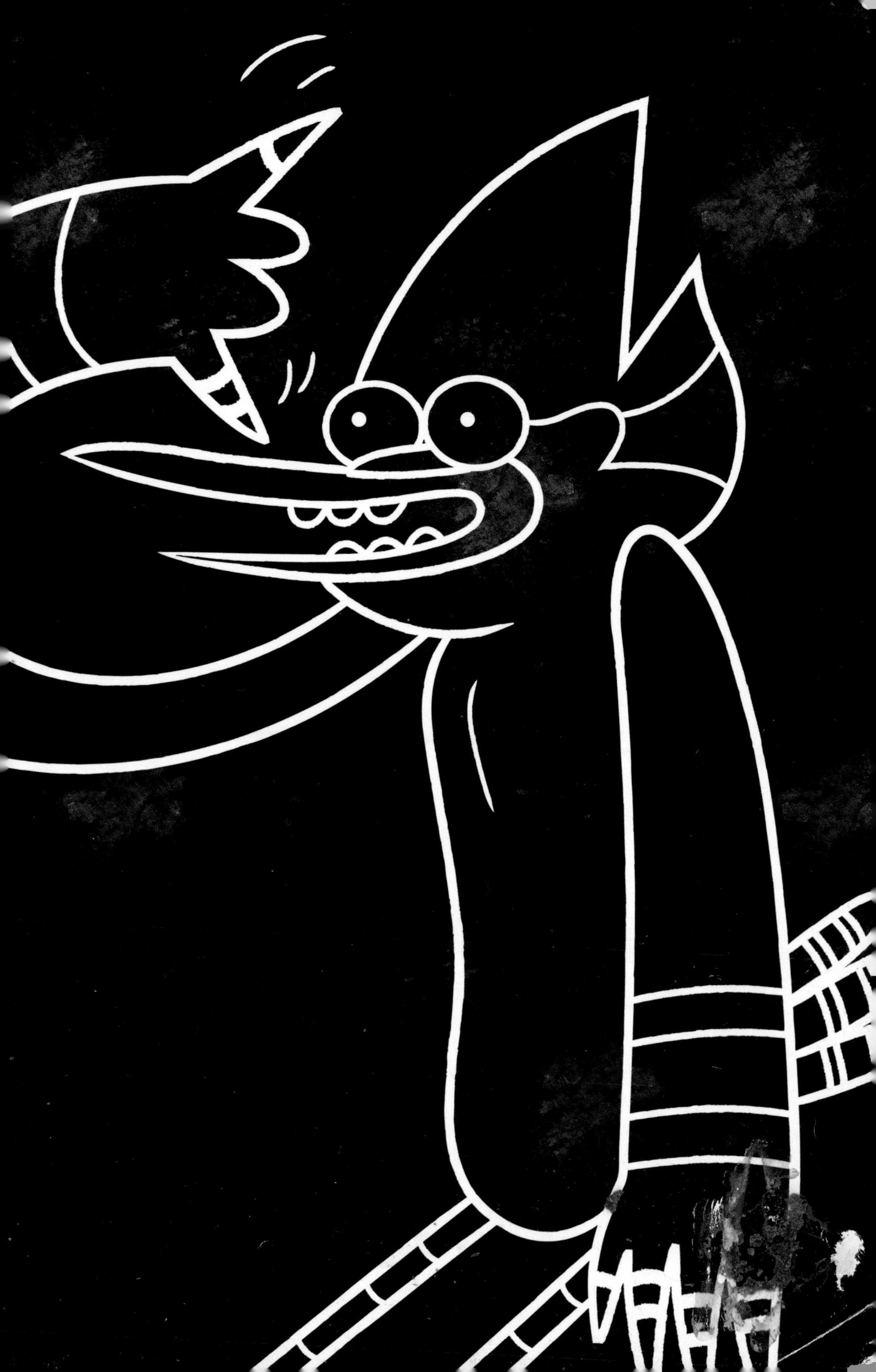

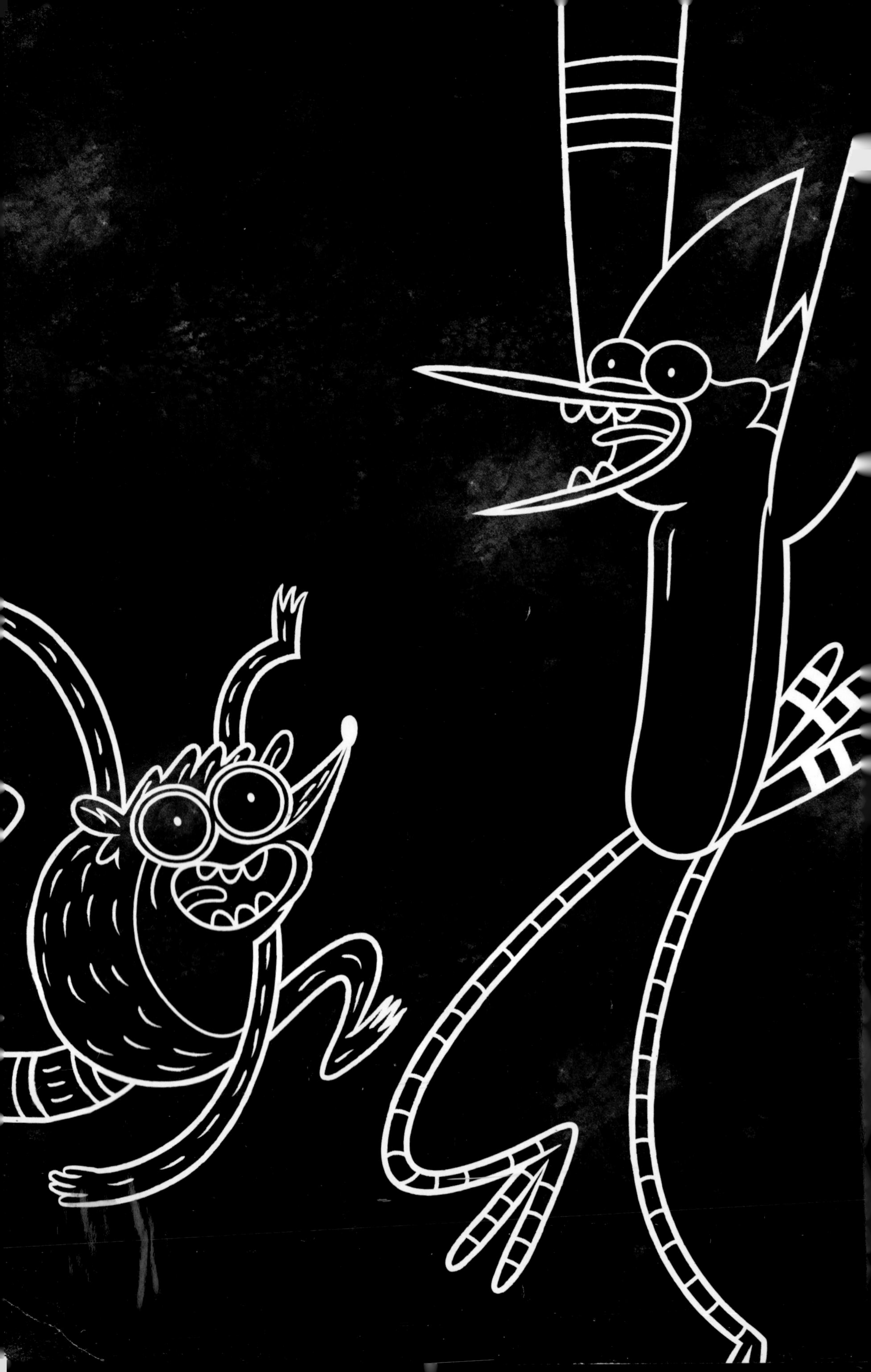

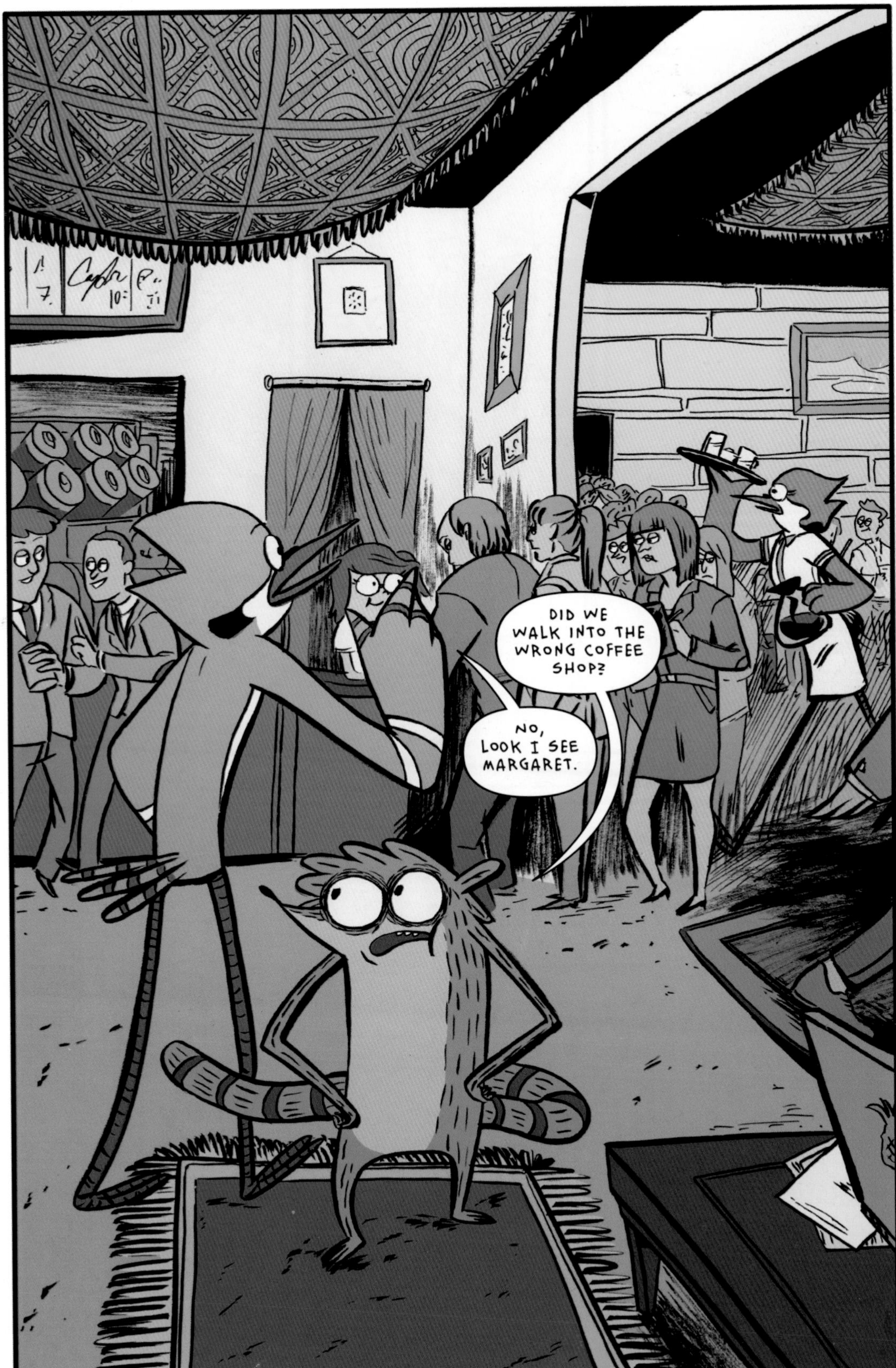
DID WE WALK INTO THE WRONG COFFEE SHOP?
NO, LOOK I SEE MARGARET.

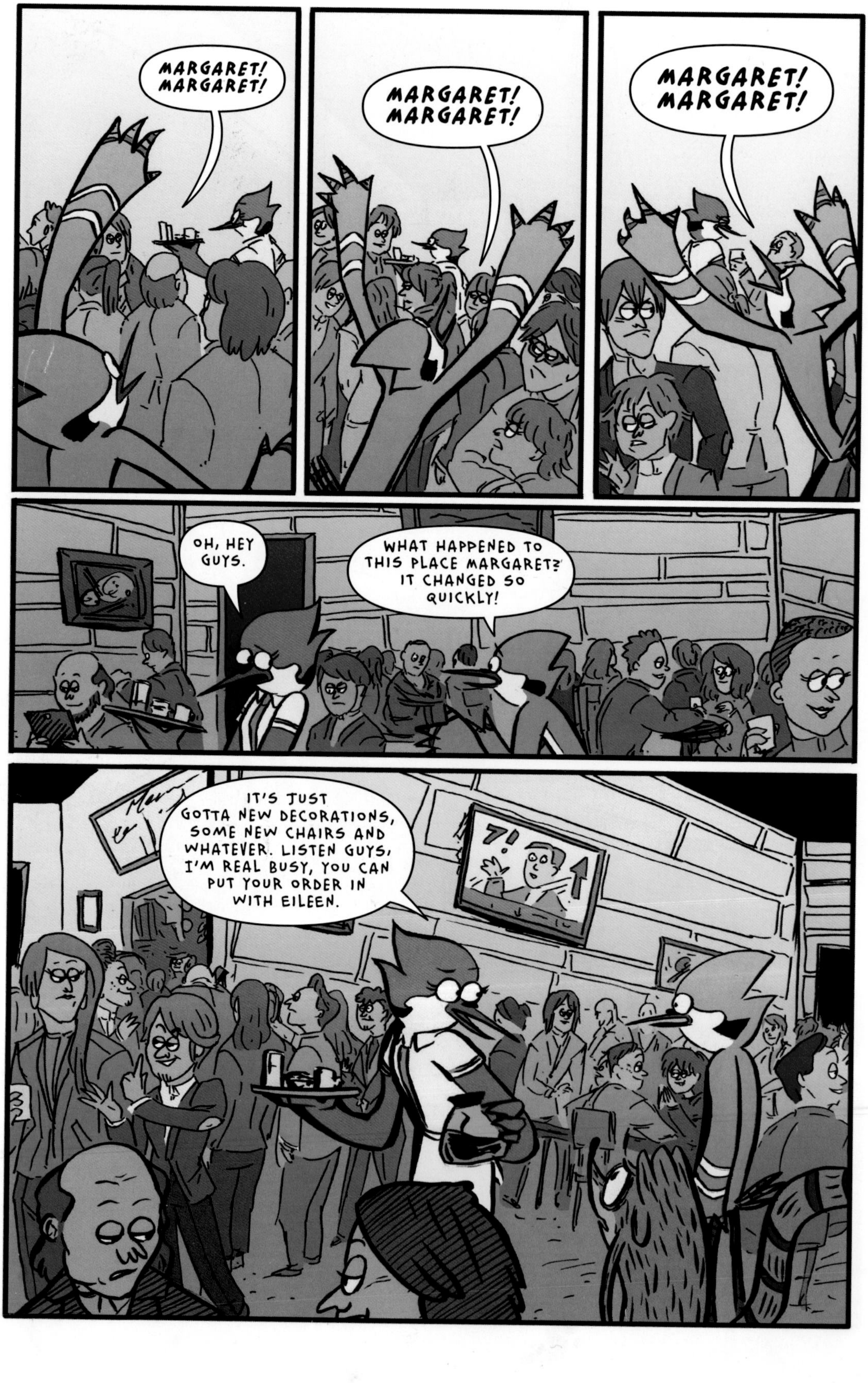
MARGARET! MARGARET!
MARGARET! MARGARET!
MARGARET! MARGARET!
OH, HEY GUYS.
WHAT HAPPENED TO THIS PLACE MARGARET? IT CHANGED SO QUICKLY!
IT'S JUST GOTTA NEW DECORATIONS, SOME NEW CHAIRS AND WHATEVER. LISTEN GUYS, I'M REAL BUSY, YOU CAN PUT YOUR ORDER IN WITH EILEEN.
7!

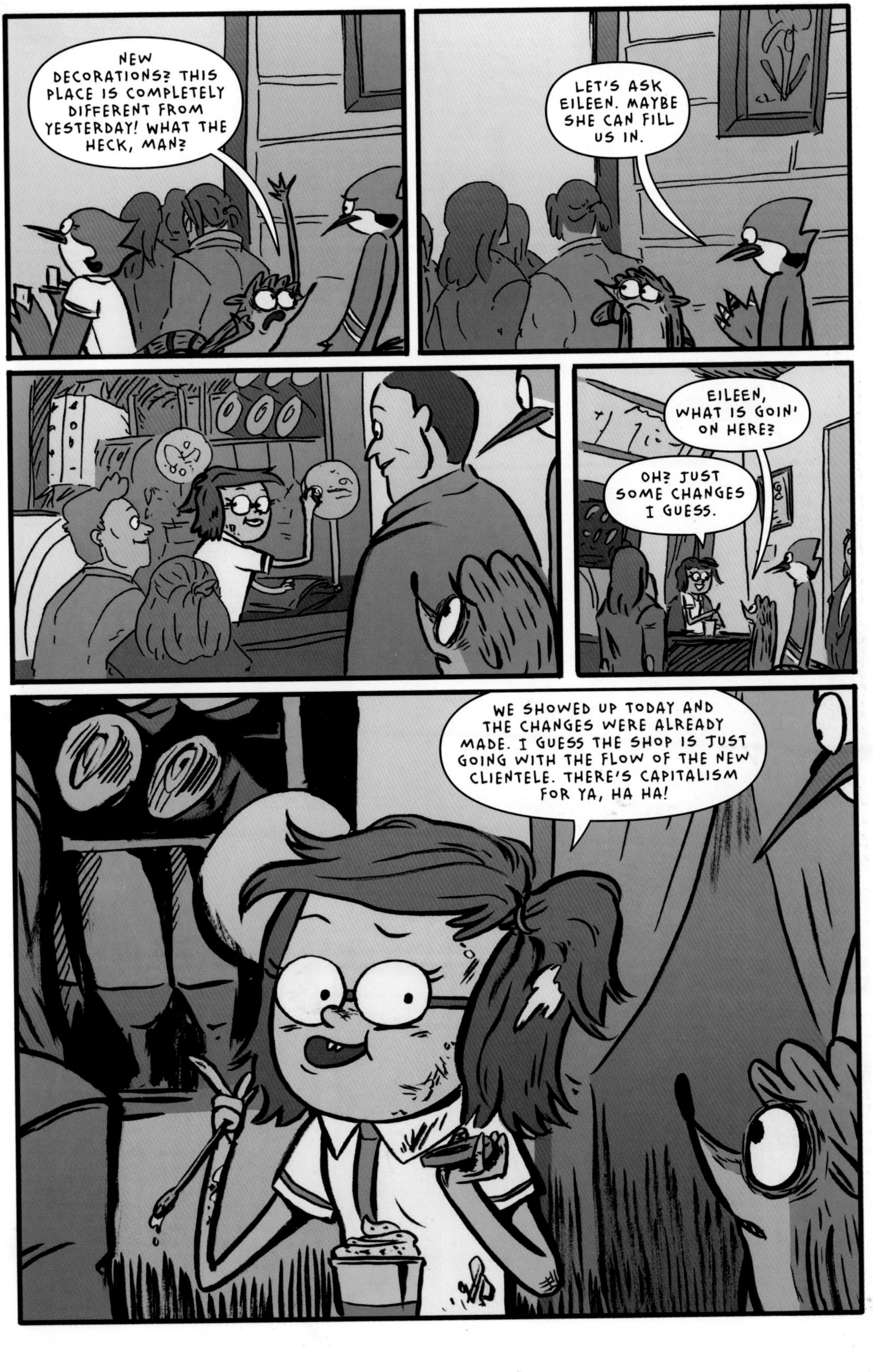
NEW DECORATIONS? THIS PLACE IS COMPLETELY DIFFERENT FROM YESTERDAY! WHAT THE HECK, MAN?
LET'S ASK EILEEN. MAYBE SHE CAN FILL US IN.
EILEEN, WHAT IS GOIN' ON HERE?
OH? JUST SOME CHANGES I GUESS.
WE SHOWED UP TODAY AND THE CHANGES WERE ALREADY MADE. I GUESS THE SHOP IS JUST GOING WITH THE FLOW OF THE NEW CLIENTELE. THERE'S CAPITALISM FOR YA, HA HA!

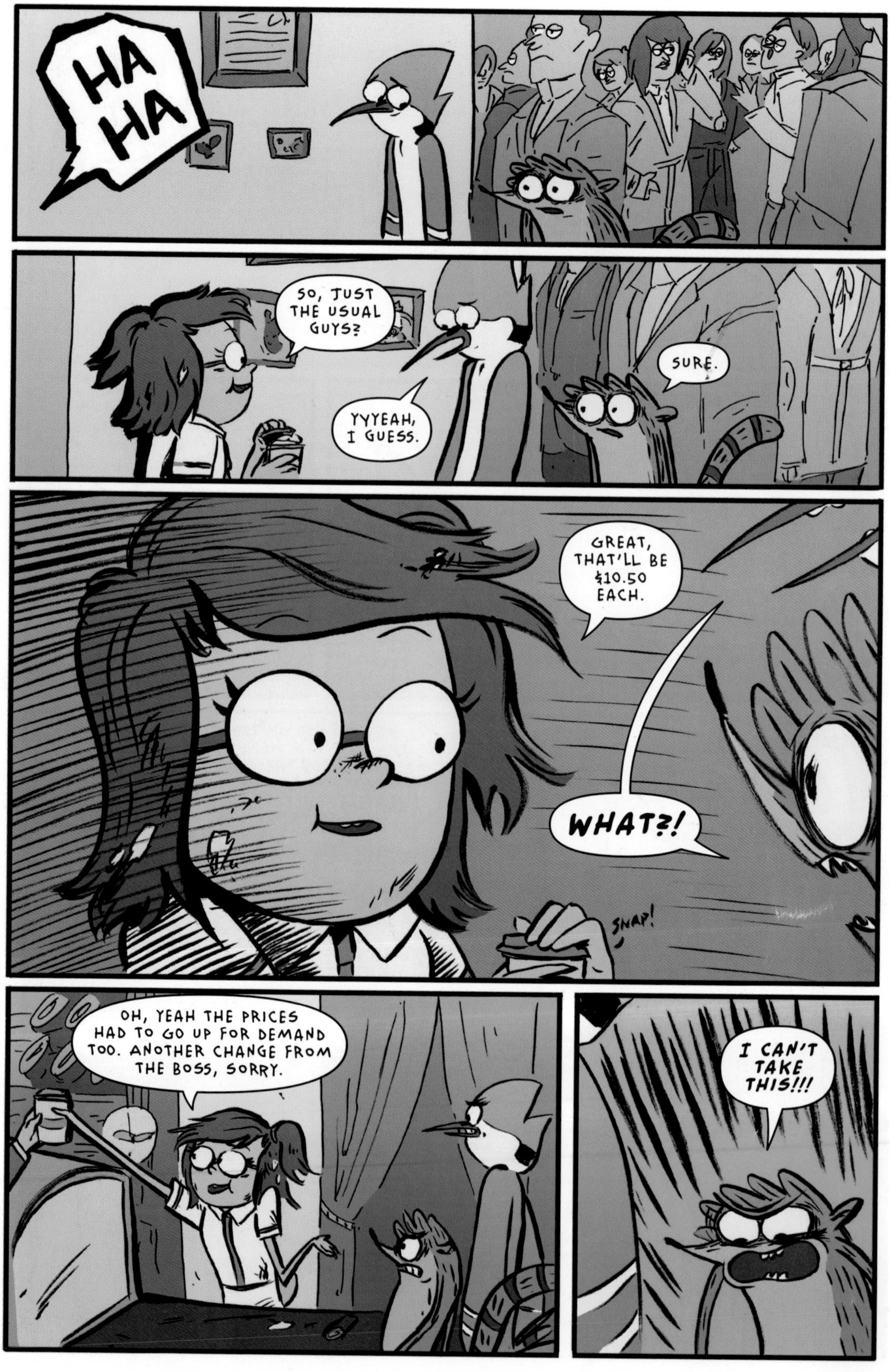

HA HA
SO, JUST THE USUAL GUYS?
YYYEAH, I GUESS.
SURE.
GREAT, THAT'LL BE $10.50 EACH.
WHAT?!
SNAP!
OH, YEAH THE PRICES HAD TO GO UP FOR DEMAND TOO. ANOTHER CHANGE FROM THE BOSS, SORRY.
I CAN'T TAKE THIS!!!

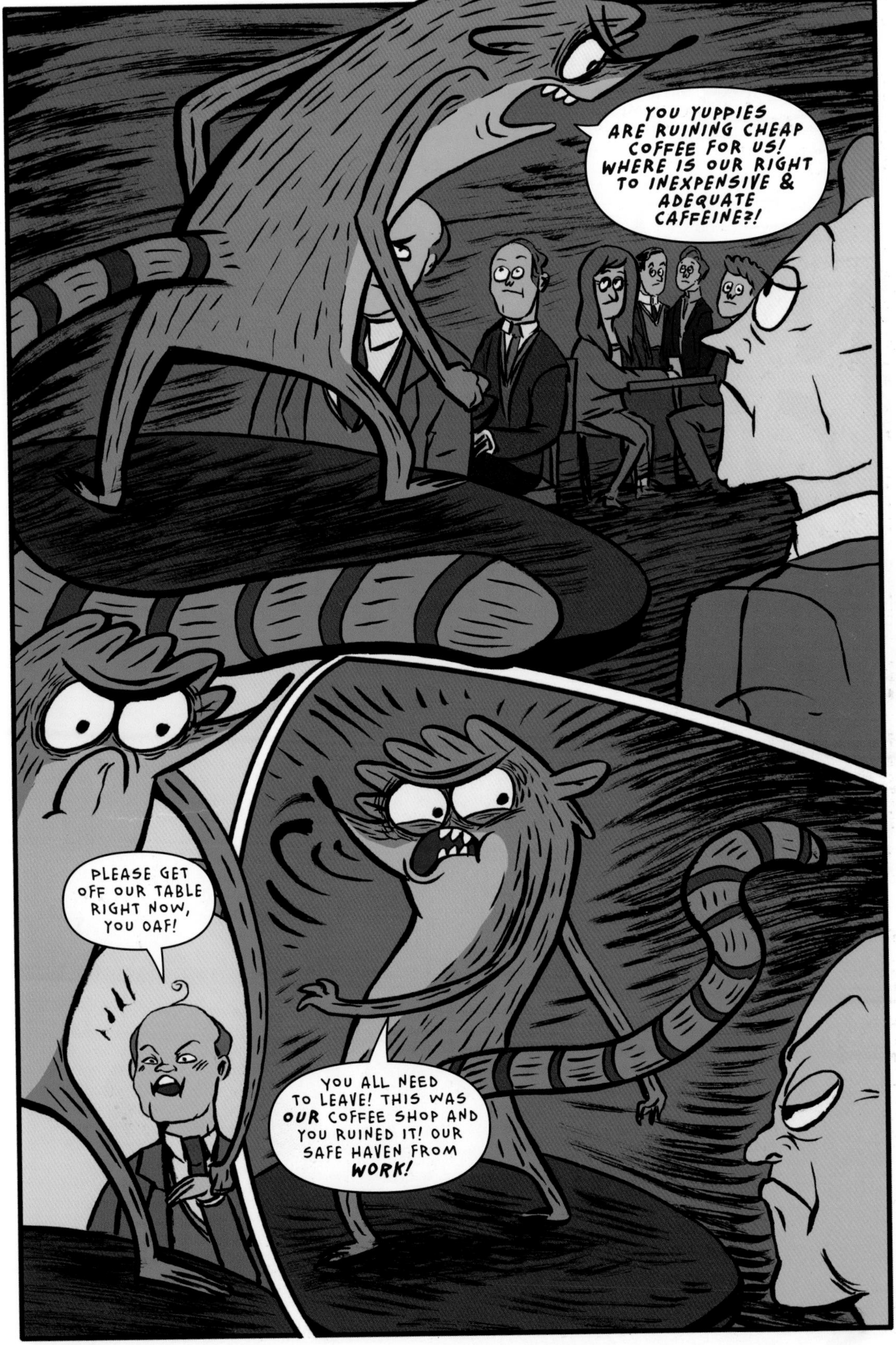
YOU YUPPIES ARE RUINING CHEAP COFFEE FOR US! WHERE IS OUR RIGHT TO INEXPENSIVE & ADEQUATE CAFFEINE?!
PLEASE GET OFF OUR TABLE RIGHT NOW, YOU OAF!
YOU ALL NEED TO LEAVE! THIS WAS OUR COFFEE SHOP AND YOU RUINED IT! OUR SAFE HAVEN FROM WORK!

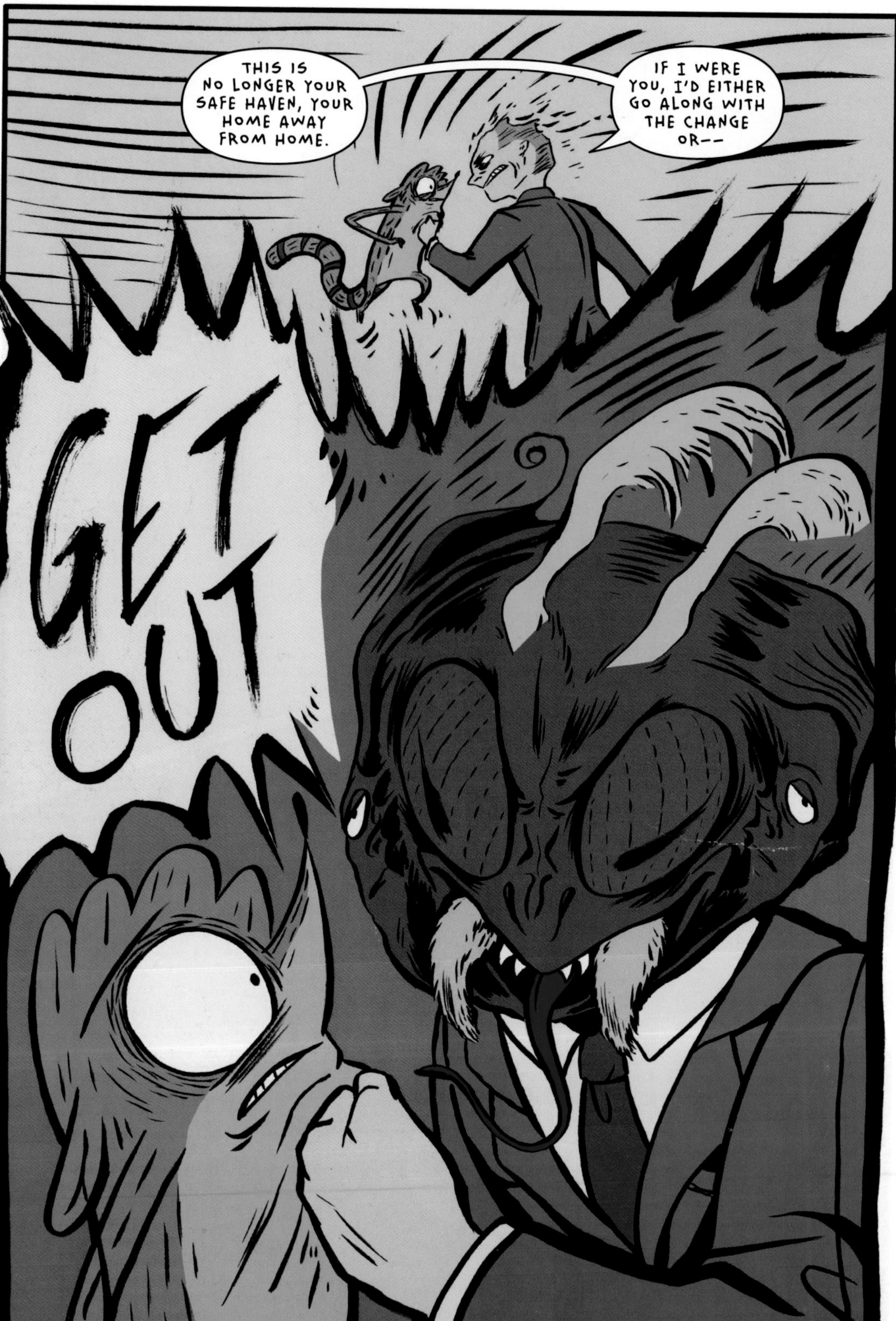
THIS IS NO LONGER YOUR SAFE HAVEN, YOUR HOME AWAY FROM HOME.
IF I WERE YOU, I'D EITHER GO ALONG WITH THE CHANGE OR--
GET OUT

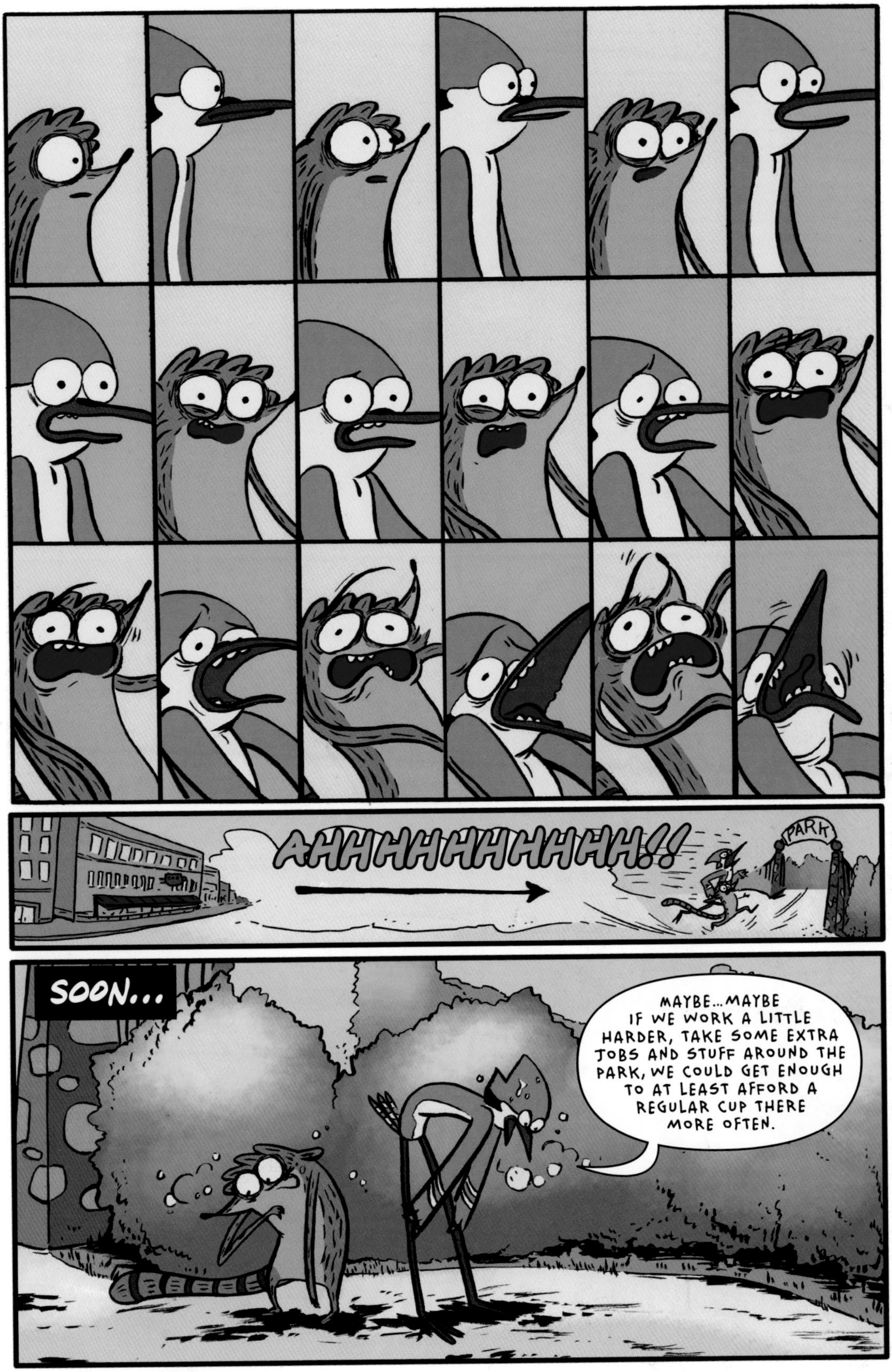
AHHHHHHHHHHHH!!
PARK
SOON...
MAYBE...MAYBE IF WE WORK A LITTLE HARDER, TAKE SOME EXTRA JOBS AND STUFF AROUND THE PARK, WE COULD GET ENOUGH TO AT LEAST AFFORD A REGULAR CUP THERE MORE OFTEN.

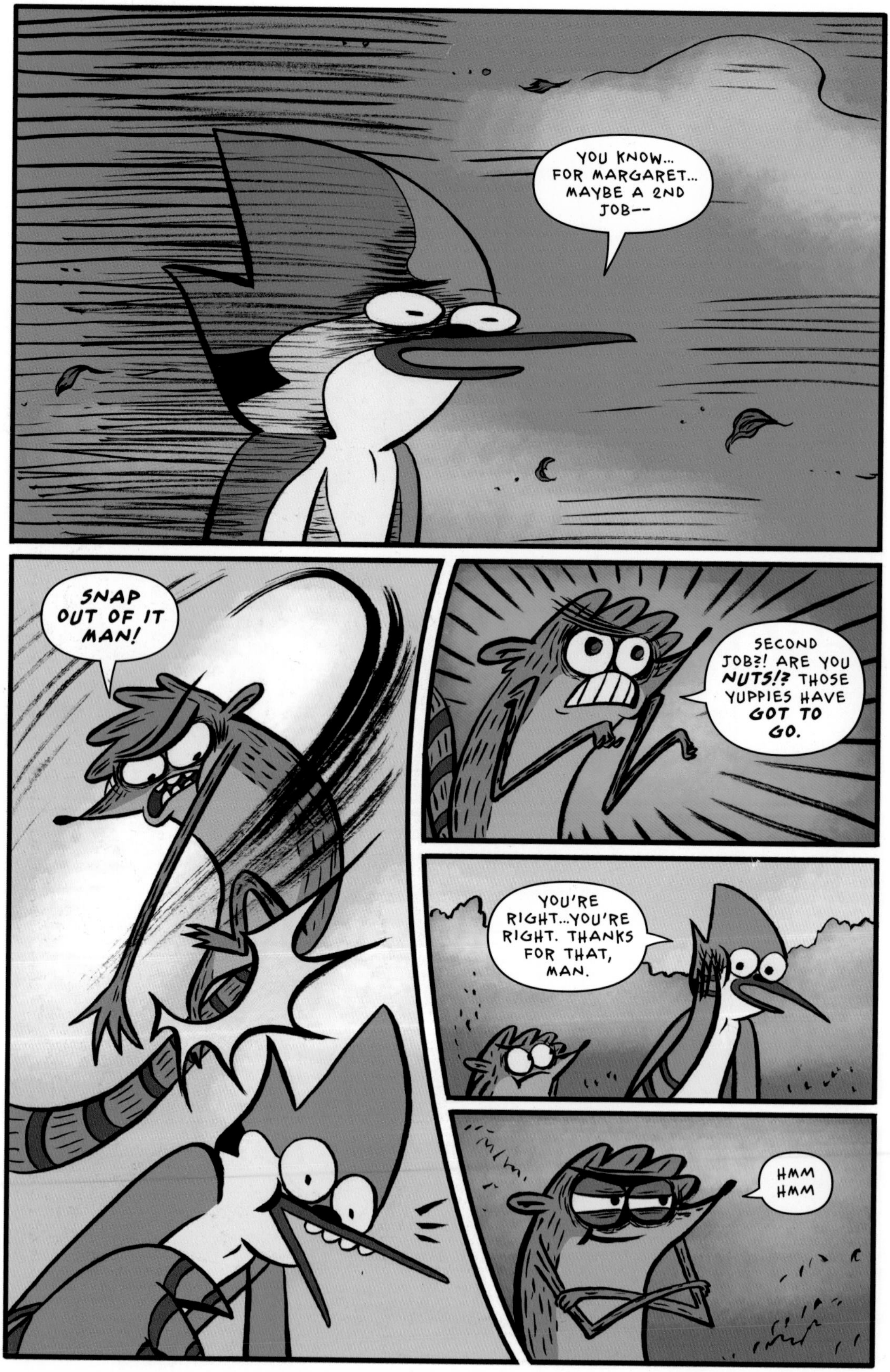
YOU KNOW... FOR MARGARET... MAYBE A 2ND JOB--
SNAP OUT OF IT MAN!
SECOND JOB?! ARE YOU NUTS!? THOSE YUPPIES HAVE GOT TO GO.
YOU'RE RIGHT...YOU'RE RIGHT. THANKS FOR THAT, MAN.
HMM HMM

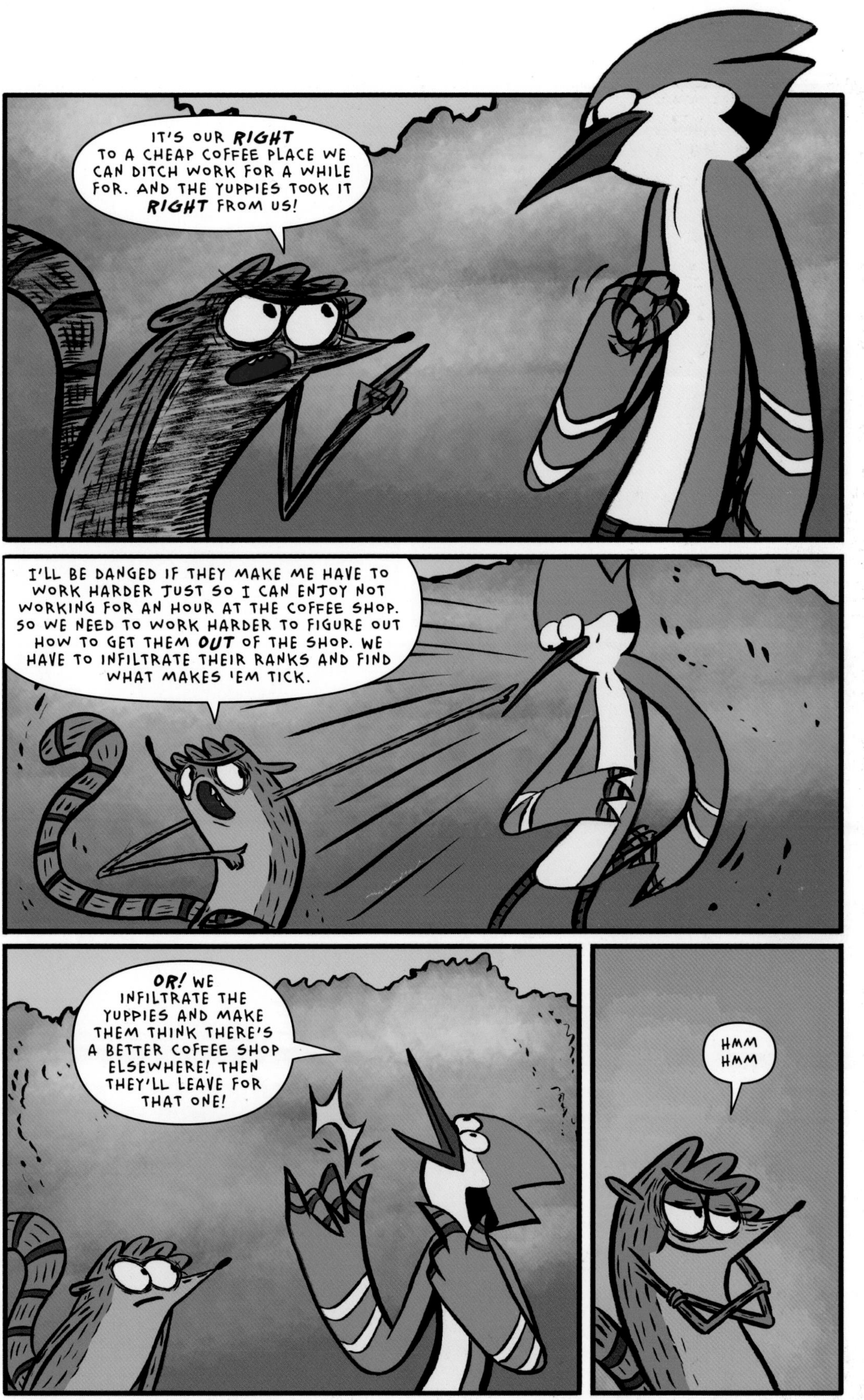
IT'S OUR RIGHT TO A CHEAP COFFEE PLACE WE CAN DITCH WORK FOR A WHILE FOR. AND THE YUPPIES TOOK IT RIGHT FROM US!
I'LL BE DANGED IF THEY MAKE ME HAVE TO WORK HARDER JUST SO I CAN ENJOY NOT WORKING FOR AN HOUR AT THE COFFEE SHOP. SO WE NEED TO WORK HARDER TO FIGURE OUT HOW TO GET THEM OUT OF THE SHOP. WE HAVE TO INFILTRATE THEIR RANKS AND FIND WHAT MAKES 'EM TICK.
OR! WE INFILTRATE THE YUPPIES AND MAKE THEM THINK THERE'S A BETTER COFFEE SHOP ELSEWHERE! THEN THEY'LL LEAVE FOR THAT ONE!
HMM HMM

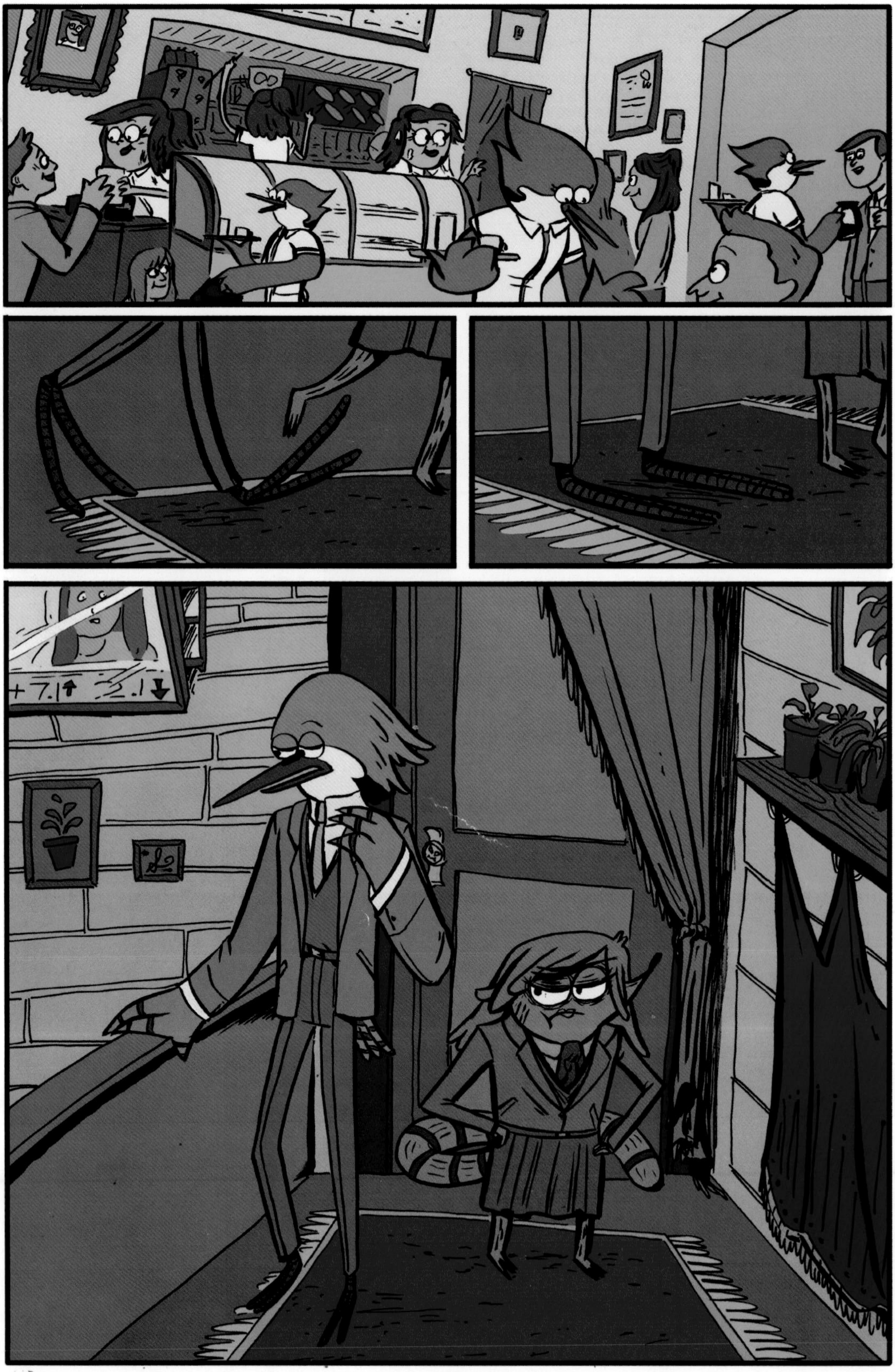

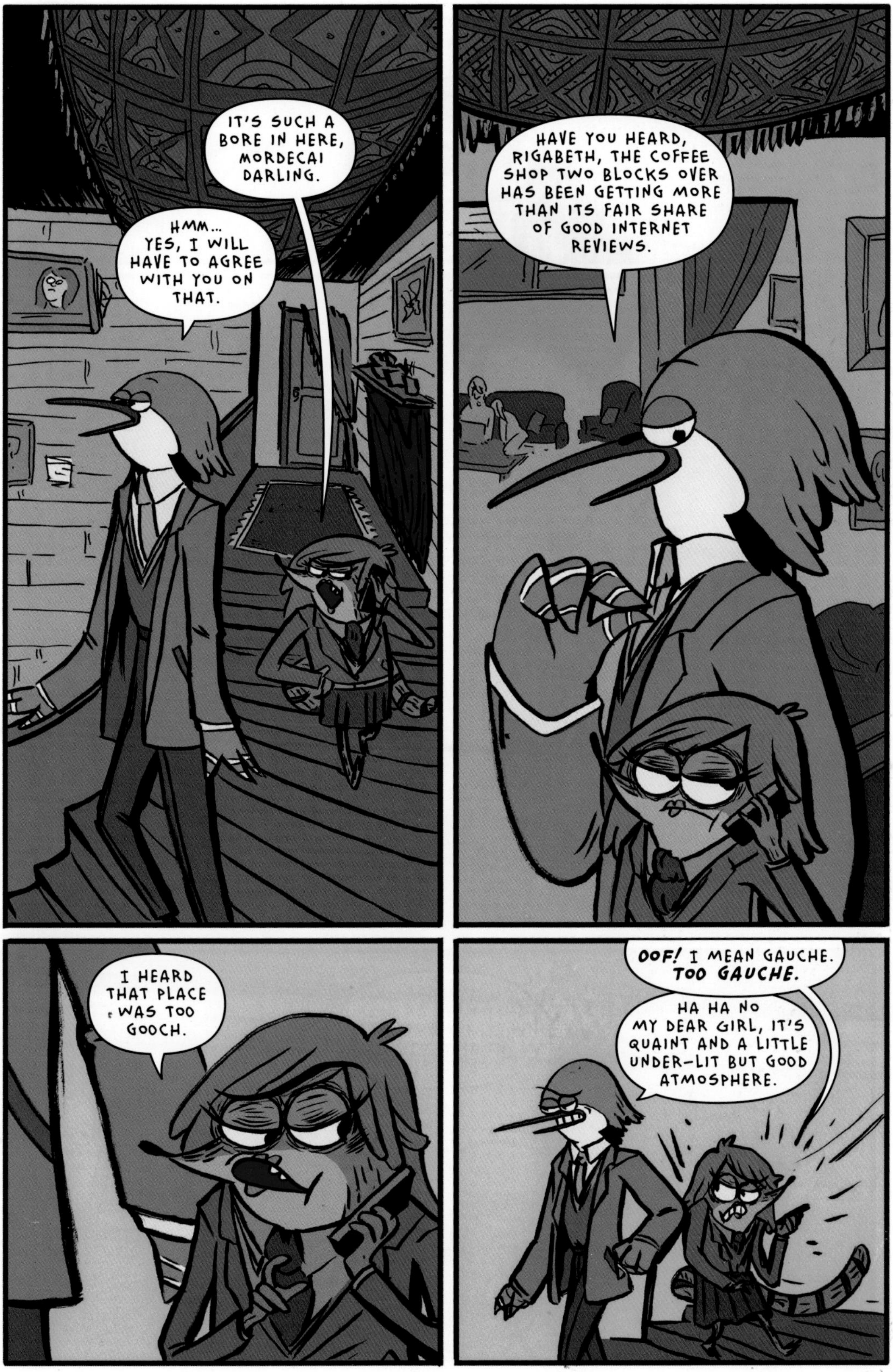
IT'S SUCH A BORE IN HERE, MORDECAI DARLING.
HMM... YES, I WILL HAVE TO AGREE WITH YOU ON THAT.
HAVE YOU HEARD, RIGABETH, THE COFFEE SHOP TWO BLOCKS OVER HAS BEEN GETTING MORE THAN ITS FAIR SHARE OF GOOD INTERNET REVIEWS.
I HEARD THAT PLACE WAS TOO GOOCH.
OOF! I MEAN GAUCHE. TOO GAUCHE.
HA HA NO MY DEAR GIRL, IT'S QUAINT AND A LITTLE UNDER-LIT BUT GOOD ATMOSPHERE.

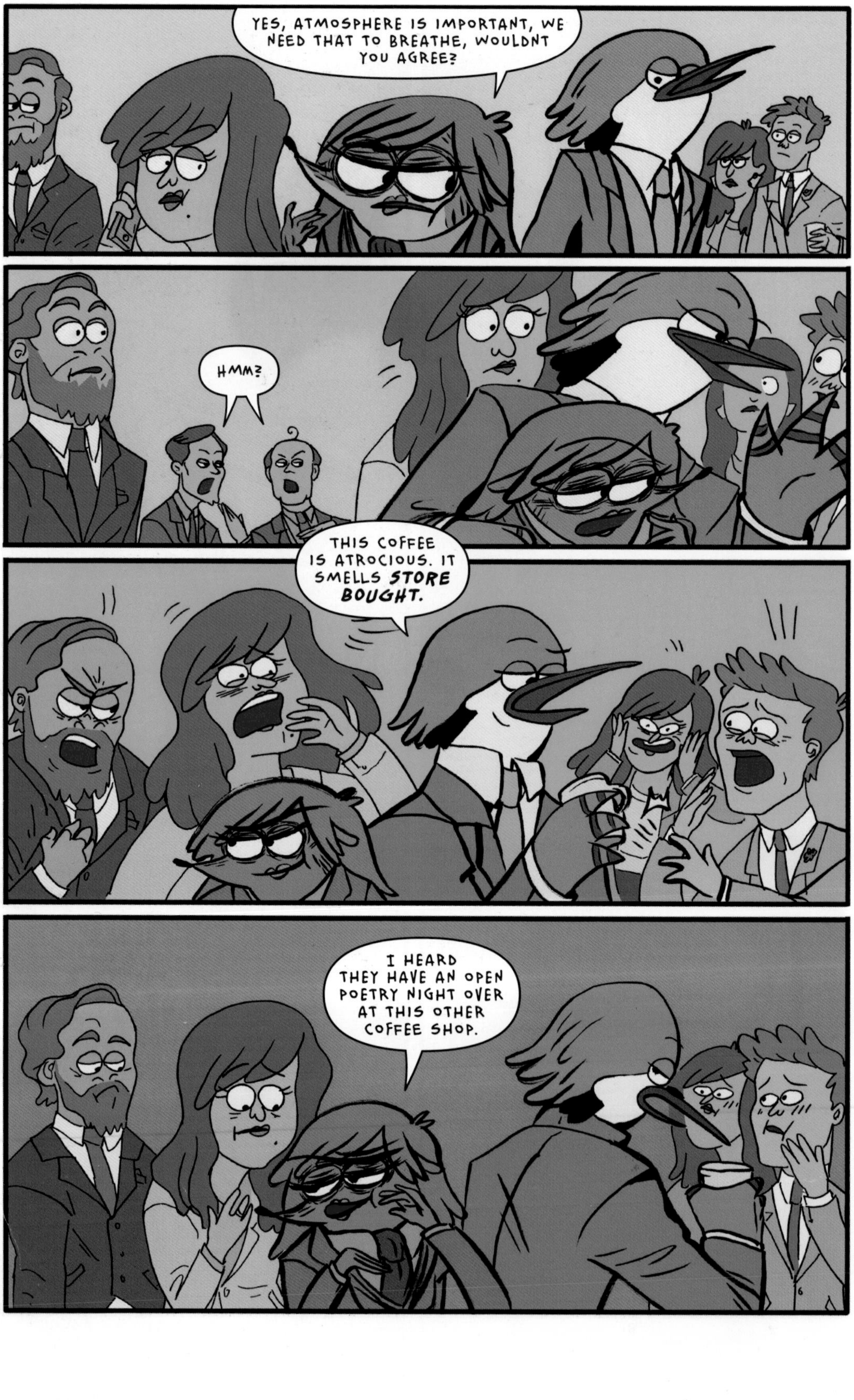
YES, ATMOSPHERE IS IMPORTANT, WE NEED THAT TO BREATHE, WOULDNT YOU AGREE?
HMM?
THIS COFFEE IS ATROCIOUS. IT SMELLS **STORE BOUGHT.**
I HEARD THEY HAVE AN OPEN POETRY NIGHT OVER AT THIS OTHER COFFEE SHOP.

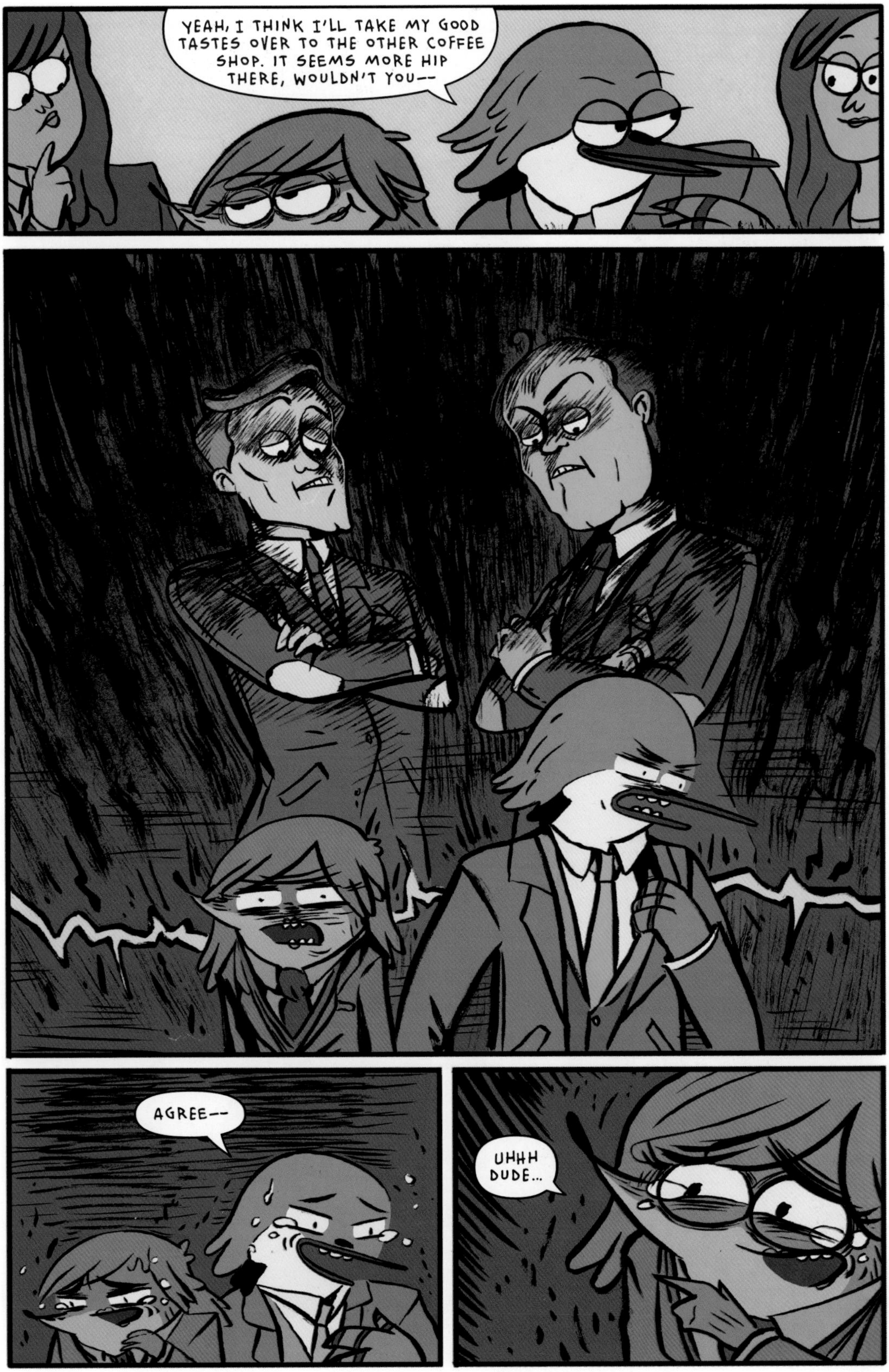
YEAH, I THINK I'LL TAKE MY GOOD TASTES OVER TO THE OTHER COFFEE SHOP. IT SEEMS MORE HIP THERE, WOULDN'T YOU--
AGREE--
UHHH DUDE...

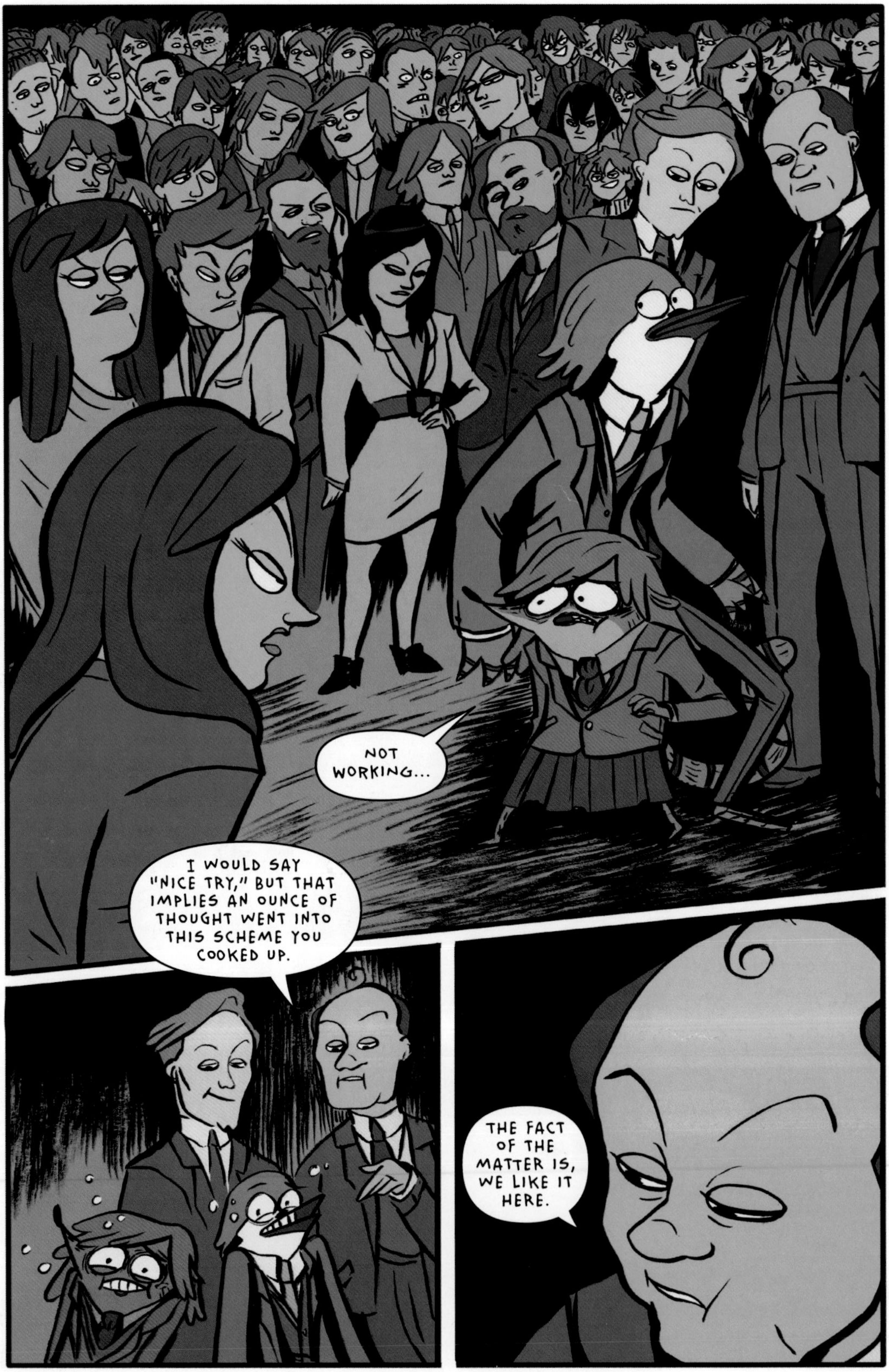
NOT WORKING...
I WOULD SAY "NICE TRY," BUT THAT IMPLIES AN OUNCE OF THOUGHT WENT INTO THIS SCHEME YOU COOKED UP.
THE FACT OF THE MATTER IS, WE LIKE IT HERE.

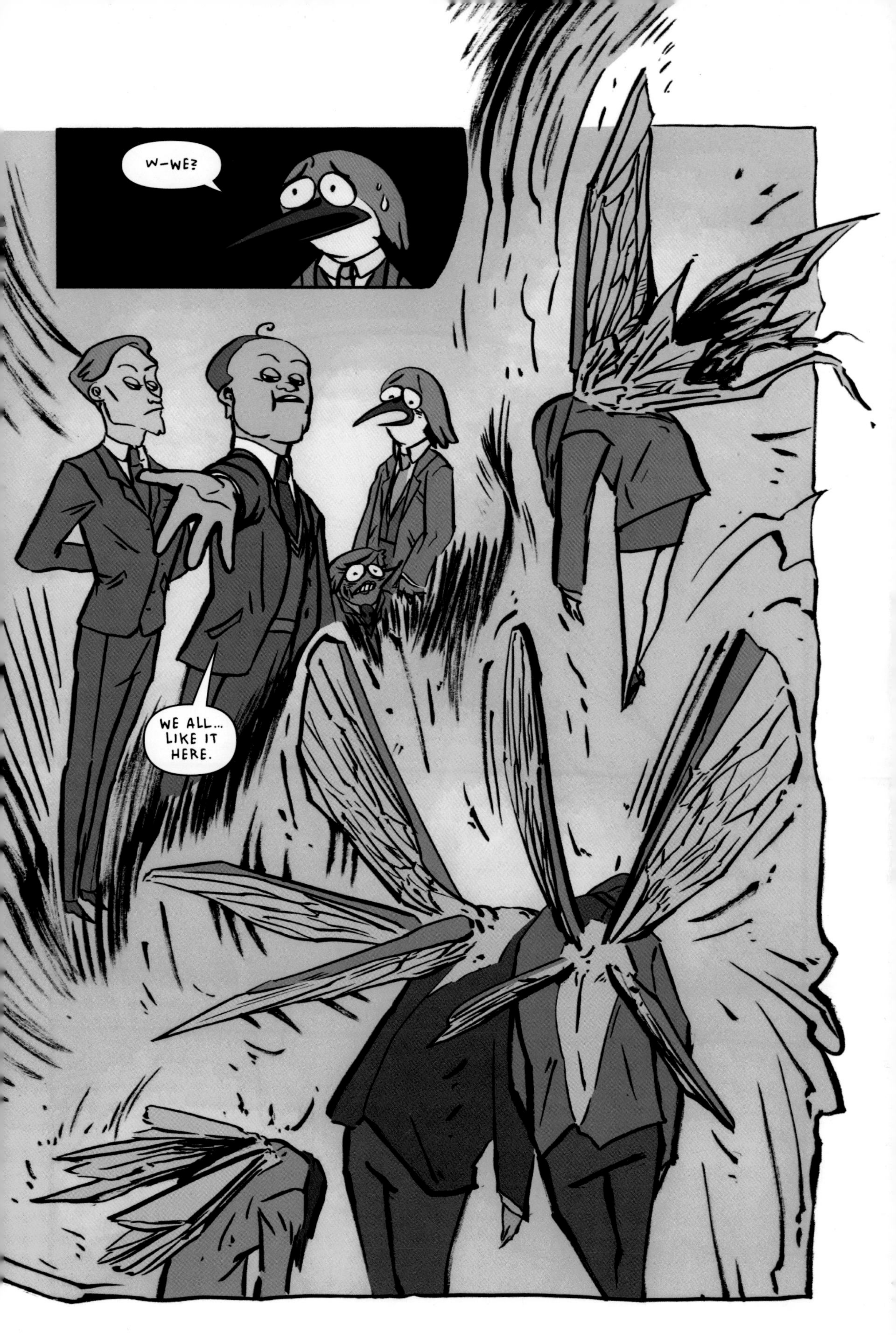
W-WE?
WE ALL... LIKE IT HERE.

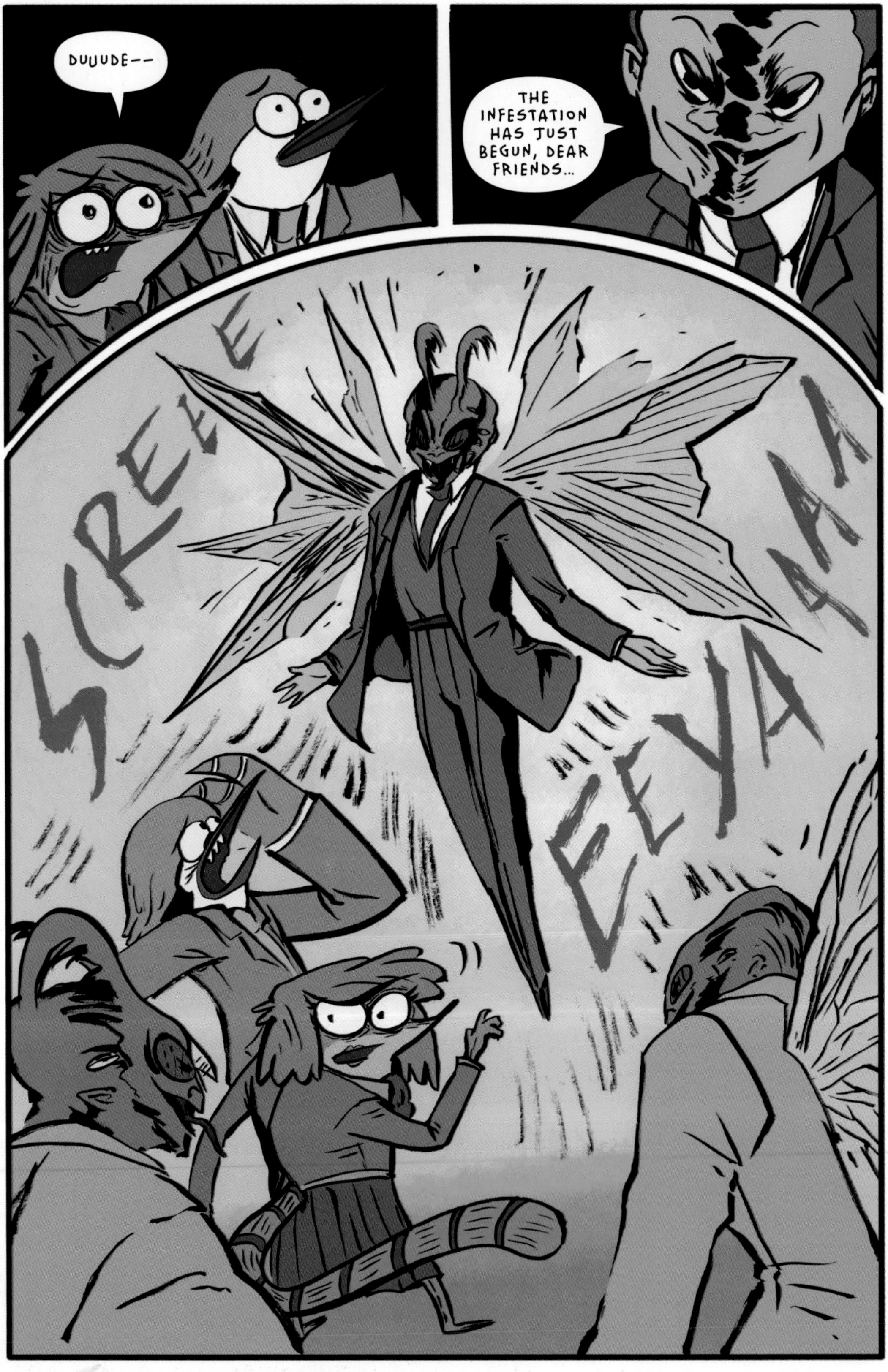
DUUUDE--
THE INFESTATION HAS JUST BEGUN, DEAR FRIENDS...
SCREEE
EEYAAA

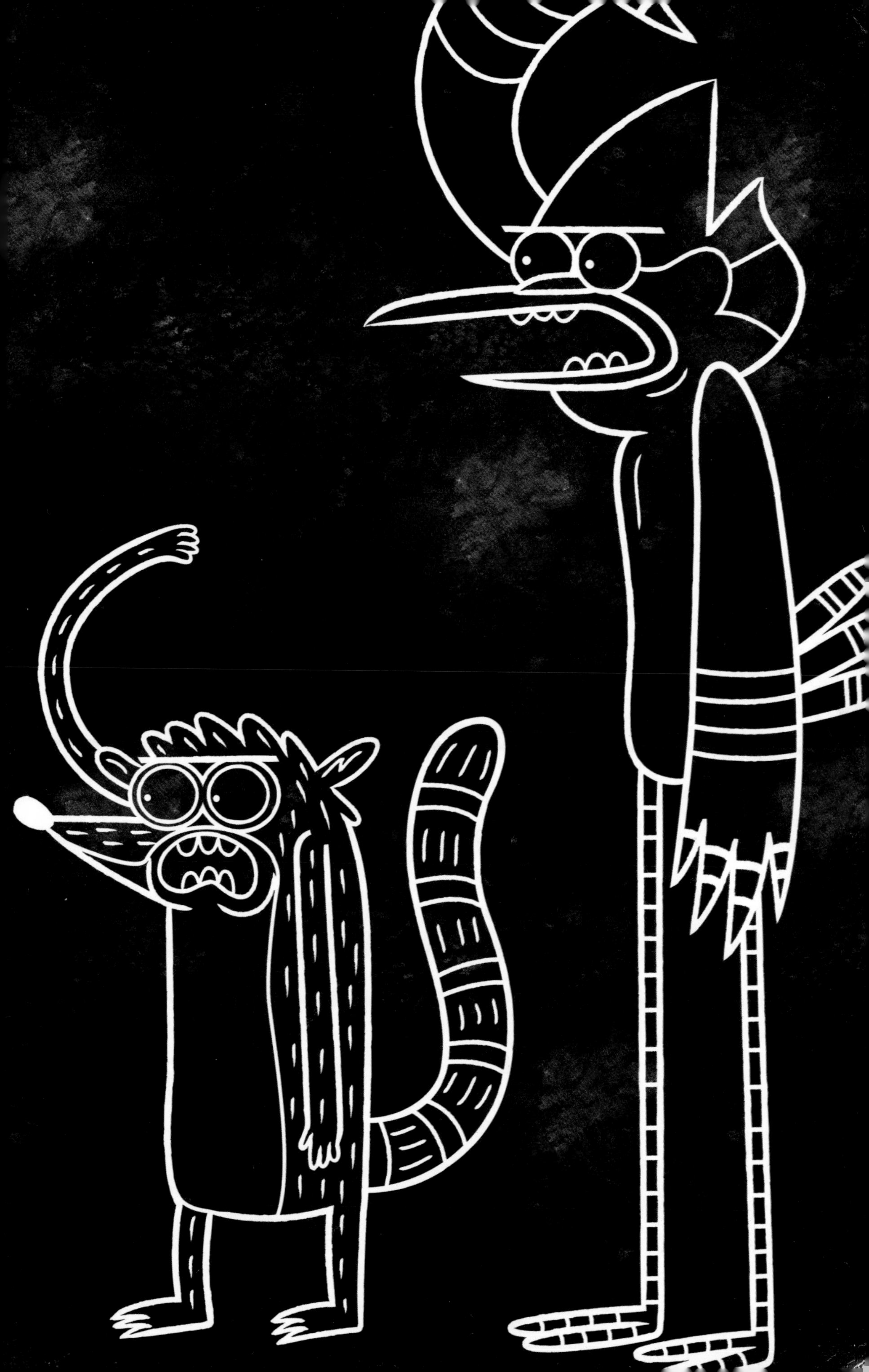

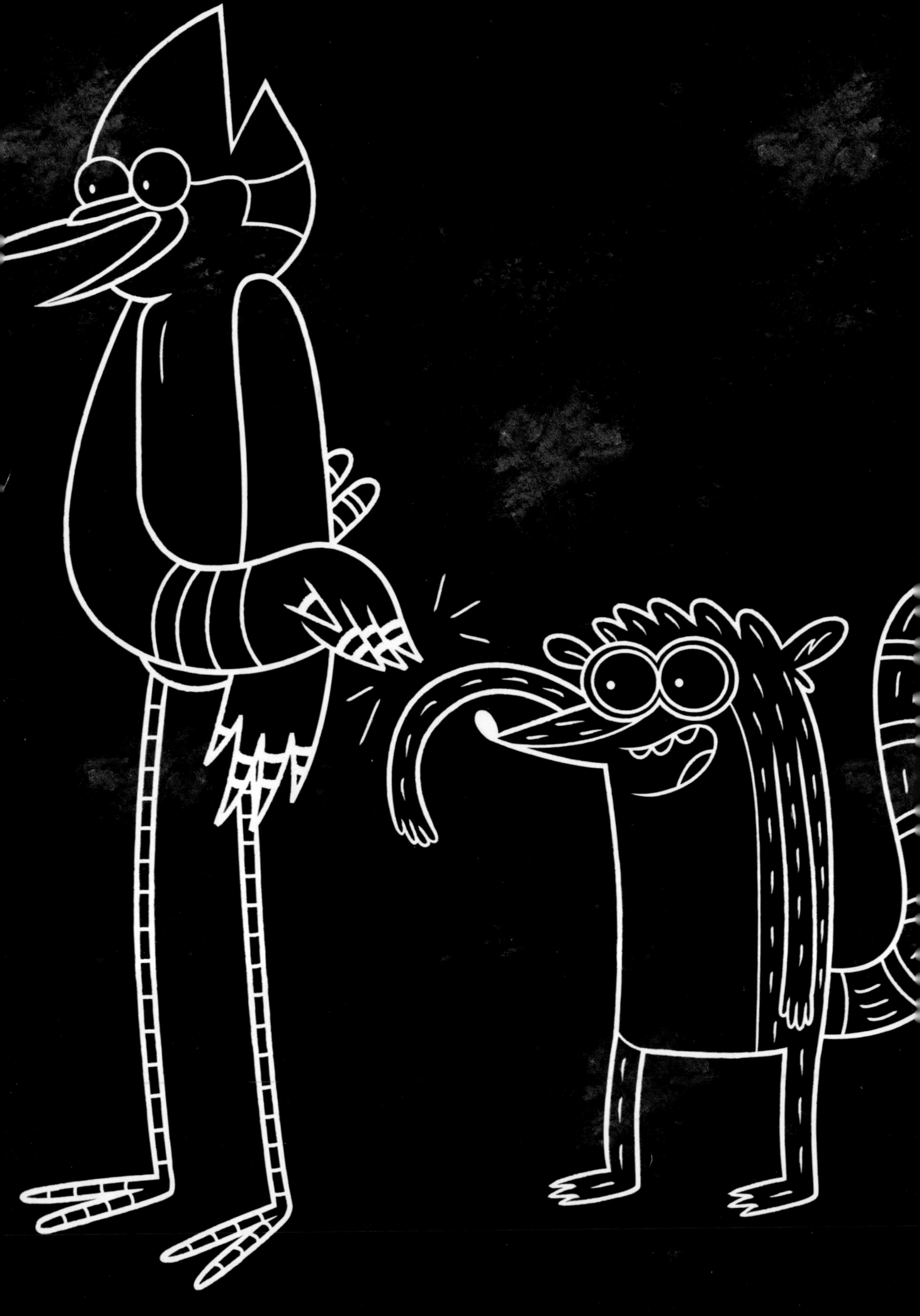

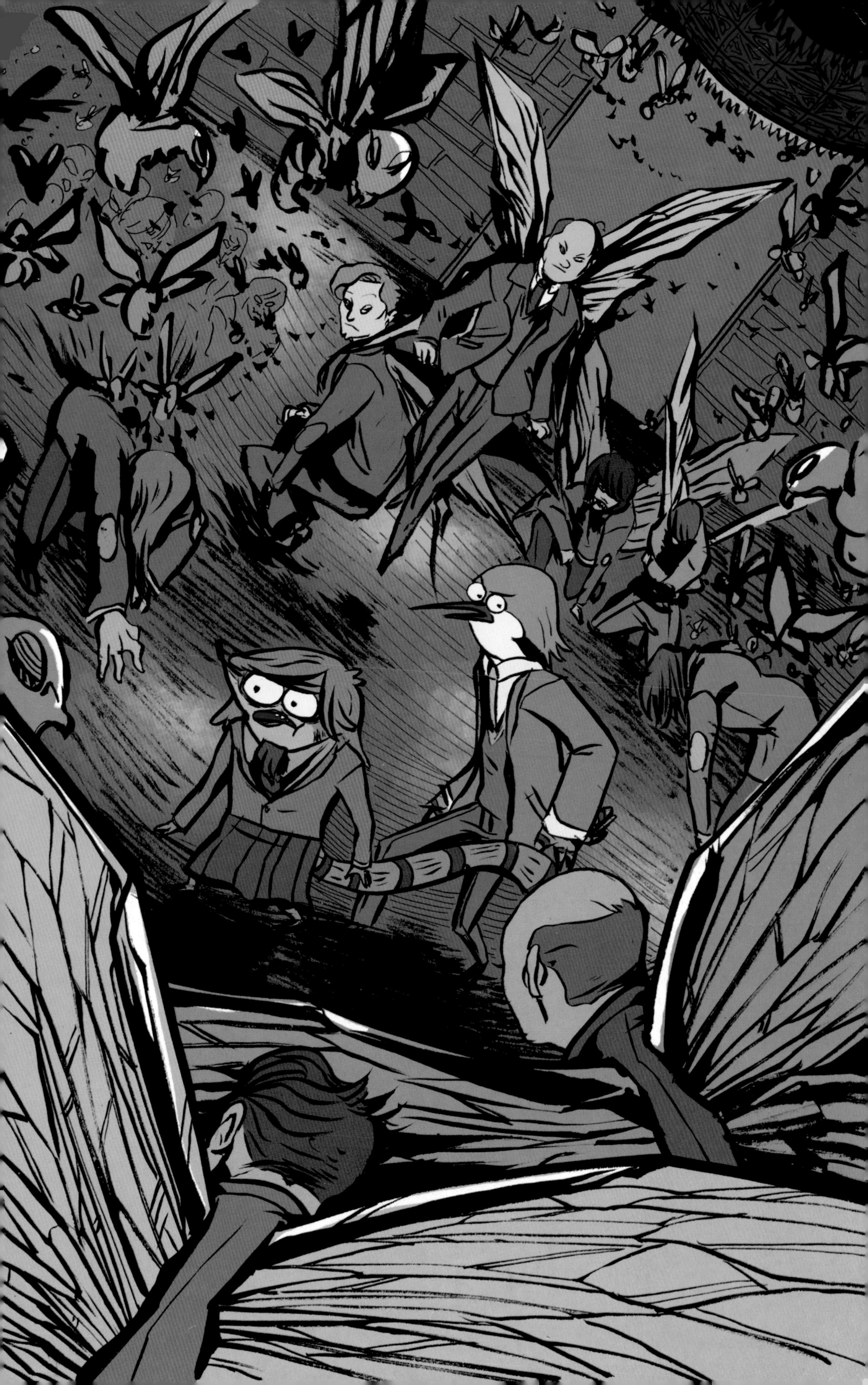

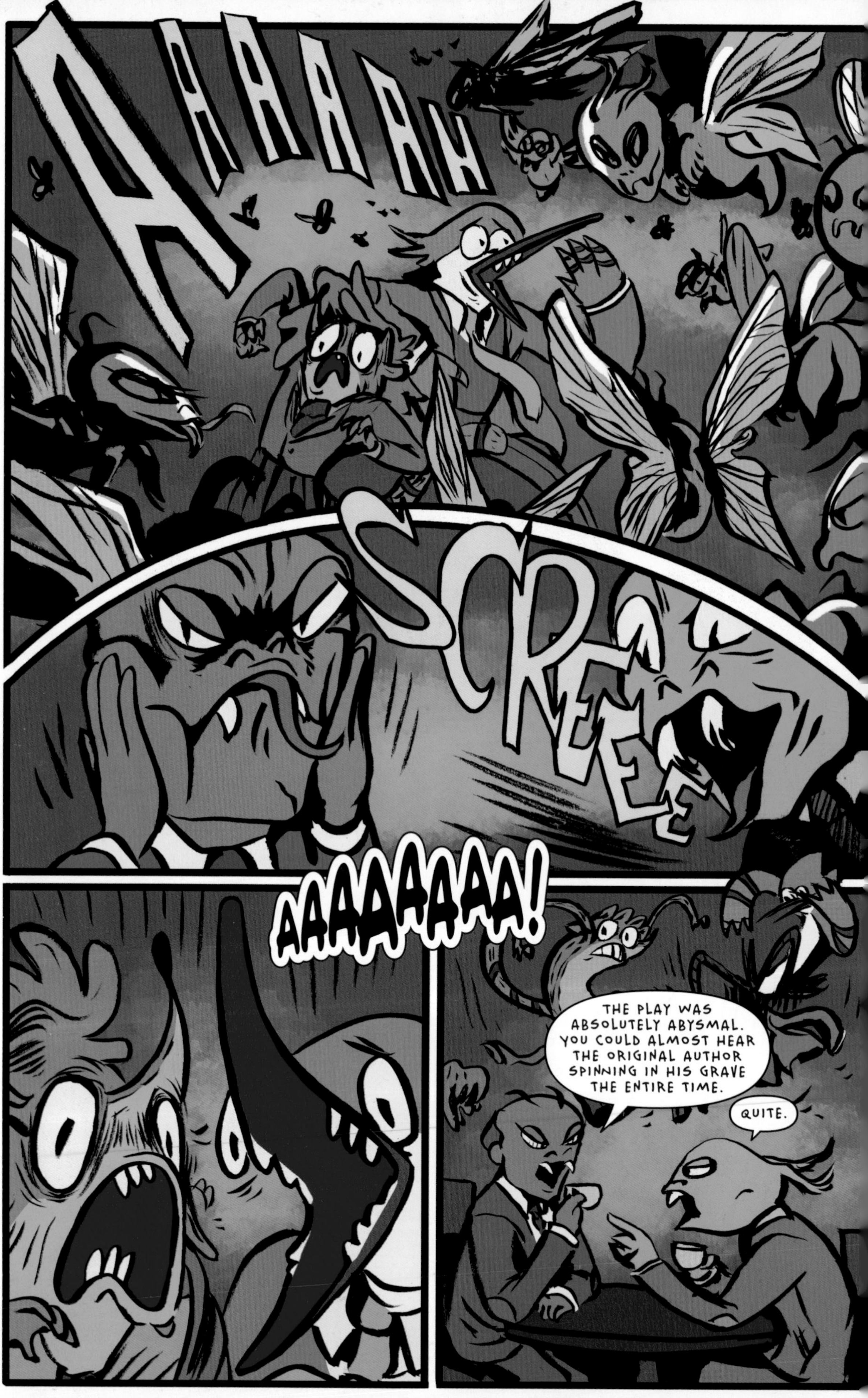
AAAAAAH
SCREEEE
AAAAAAAA!
THE PLAY WAS ABSOLUTELY ABYSMAL. YOU COULD ALMOST HEAR THE ORIGINAL AUTHOR SPINNING IN HIS GRAVE THE ENTIRE TIME.
QUITE.

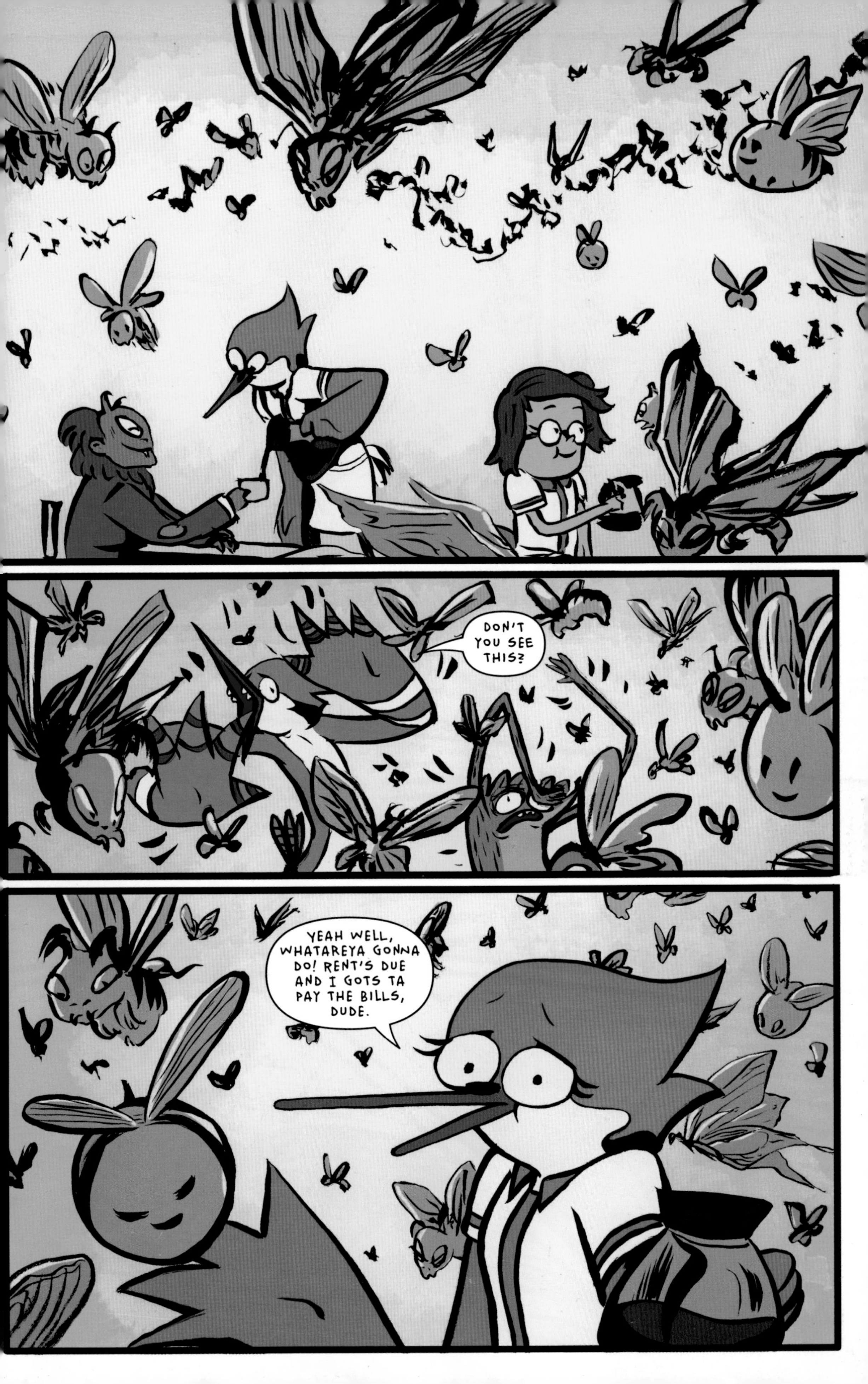
DON'T YOU SEE THIS?
YEAH WELL, WHATAREYA GONNA DO! RENT'S DUE AND I GOTS TA PAY THE BILLS, DUDE.

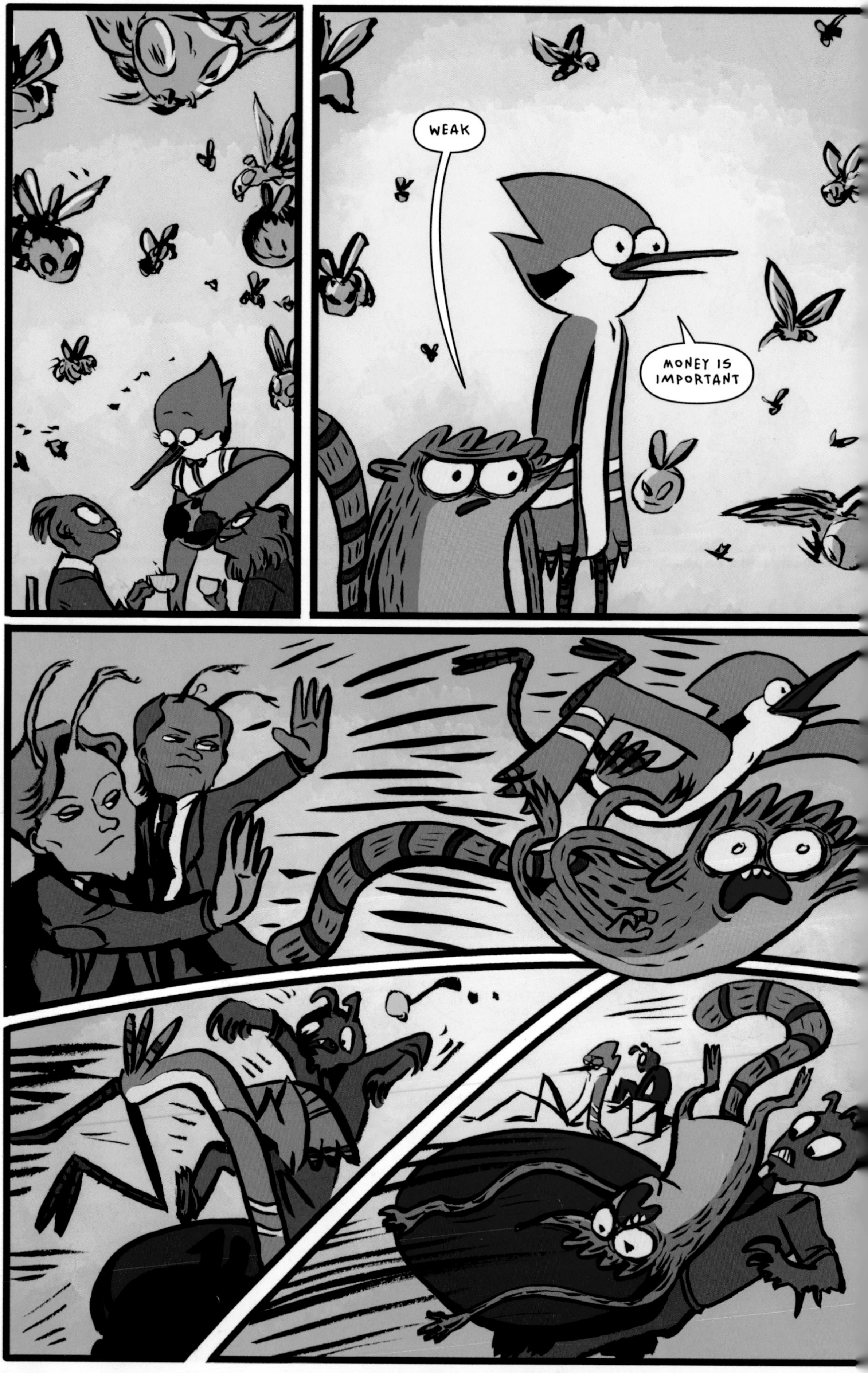
WEAK
MONEY IS IMPORTANT

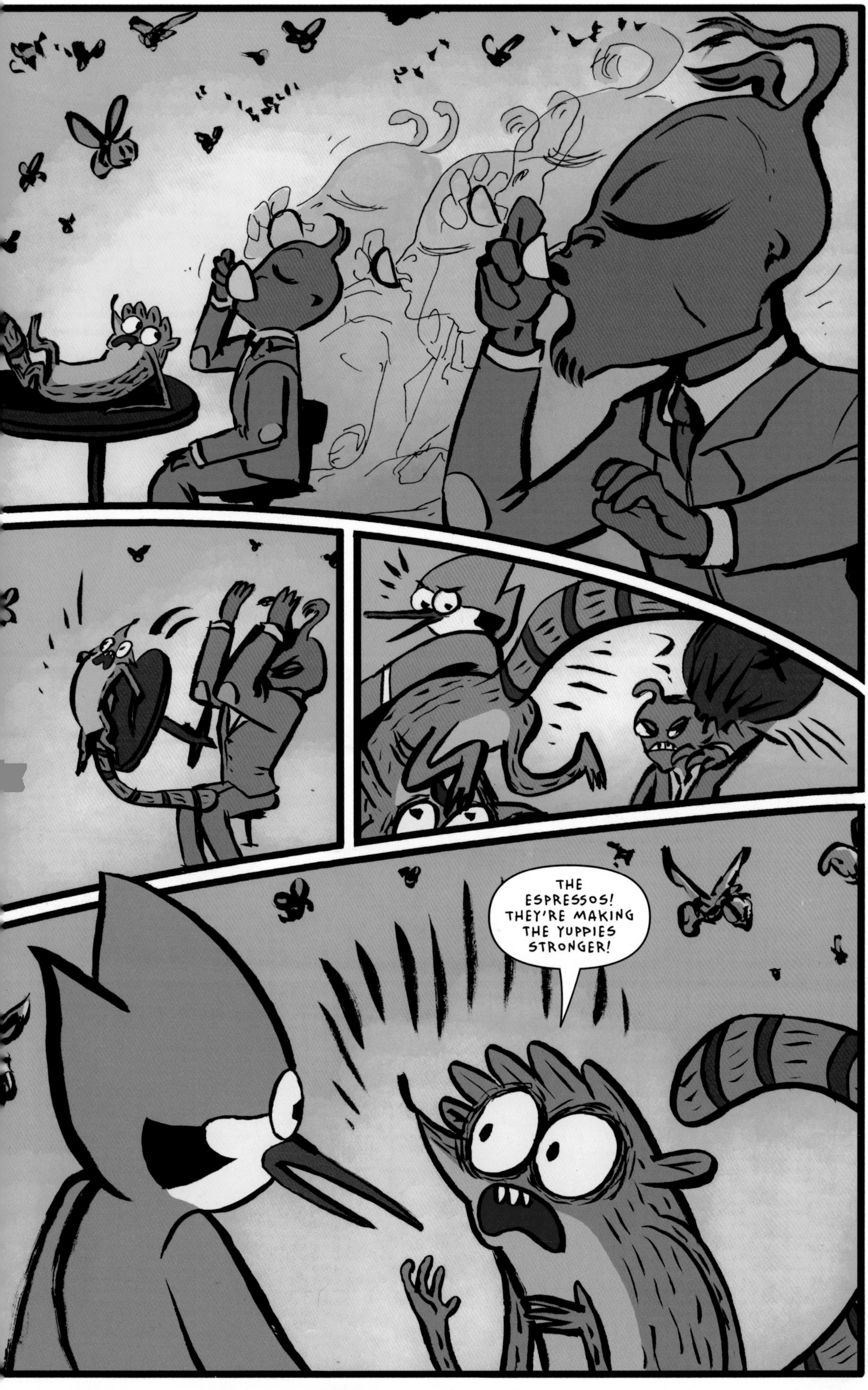
THE ESPRESSOS! THEY'RE MAKING THE YUPPIES STRONGER!

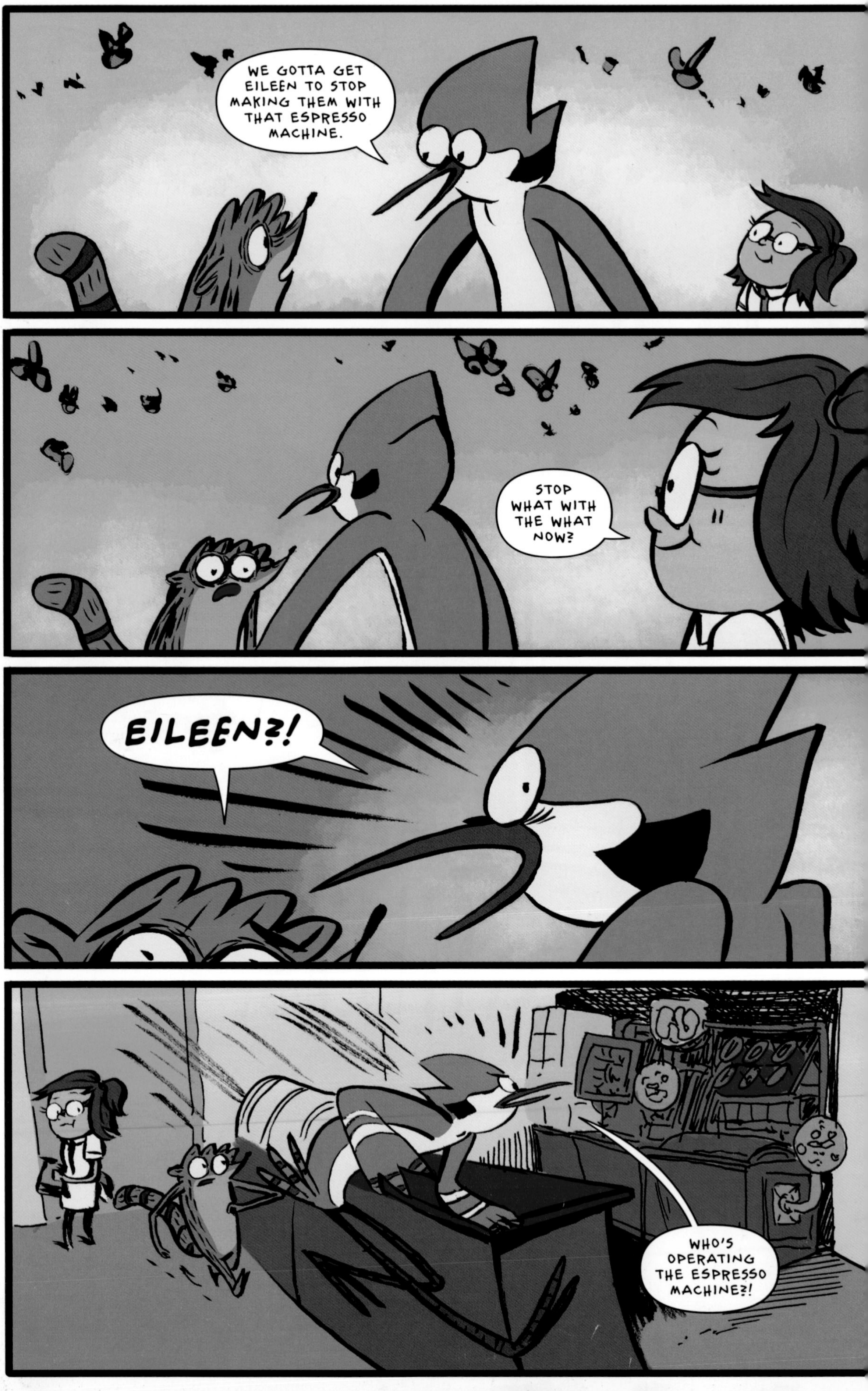
WE GOTTA GET EILEEN TO STOP MAKING THEM WITH THAT ESPRESSO MACHINE.
STOP WHAT WITH THE WHAT NOW?
EILEEN?!
WHO'S OPERATING THE ESPRESSO MACHINE?!

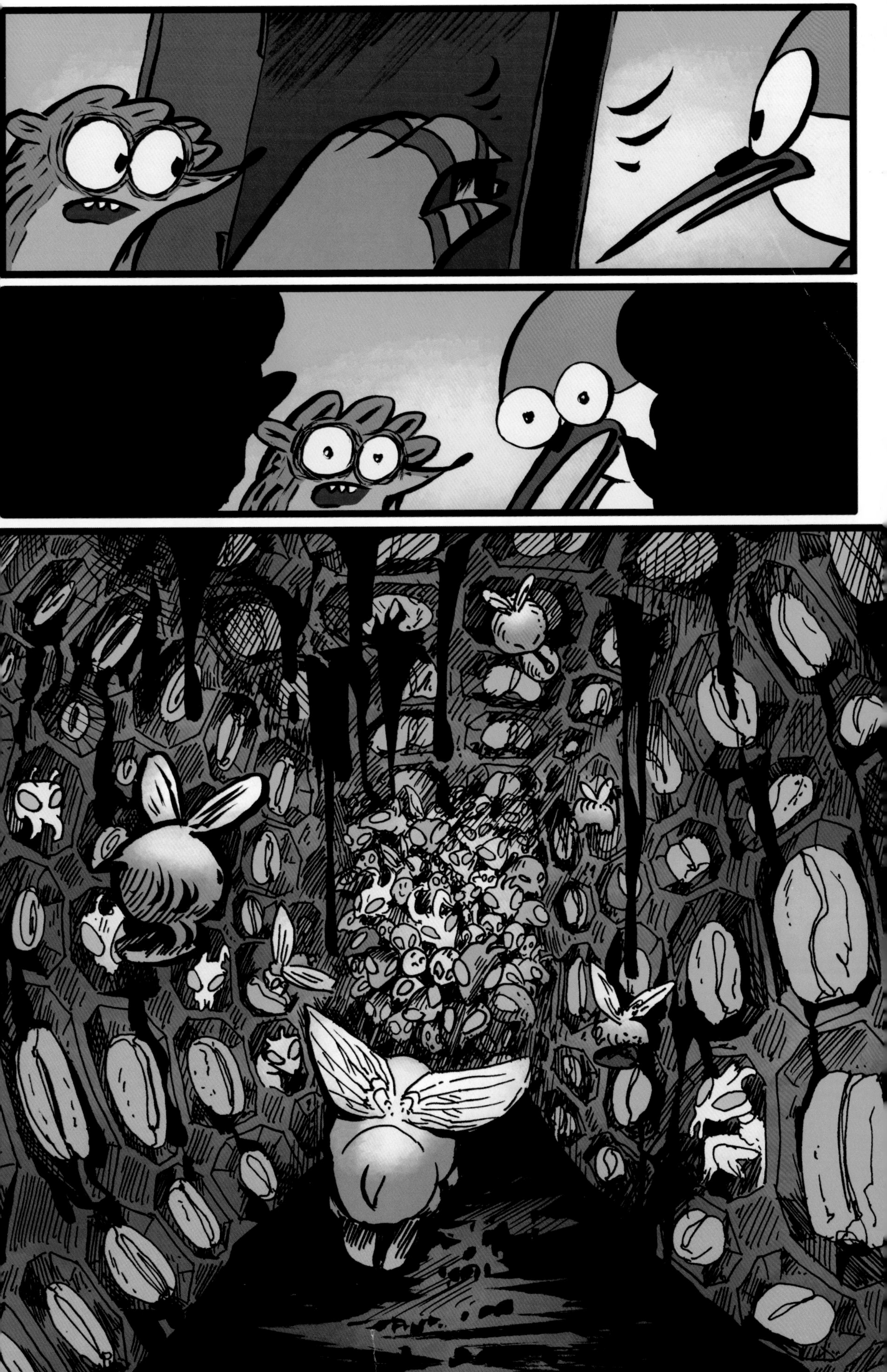

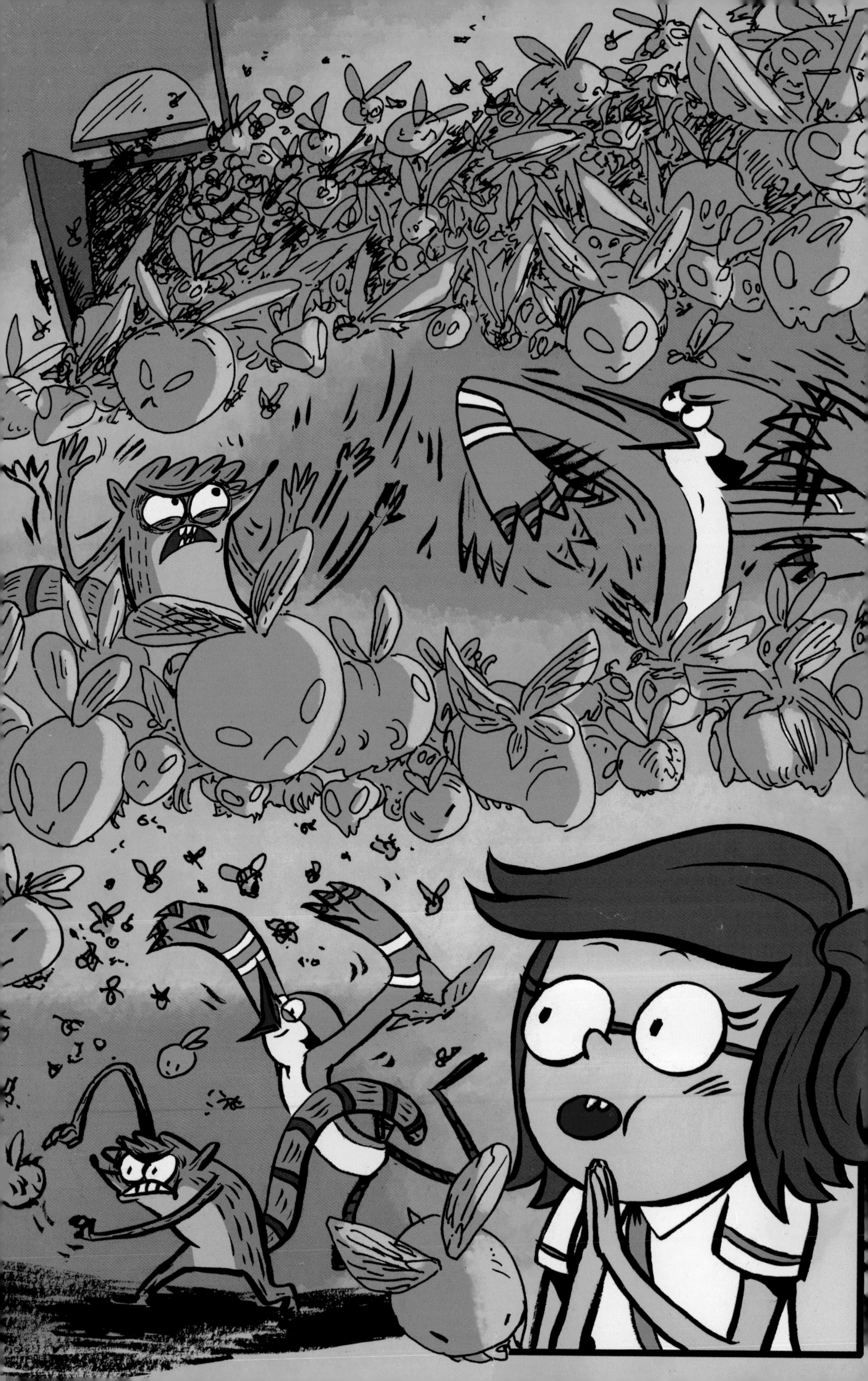

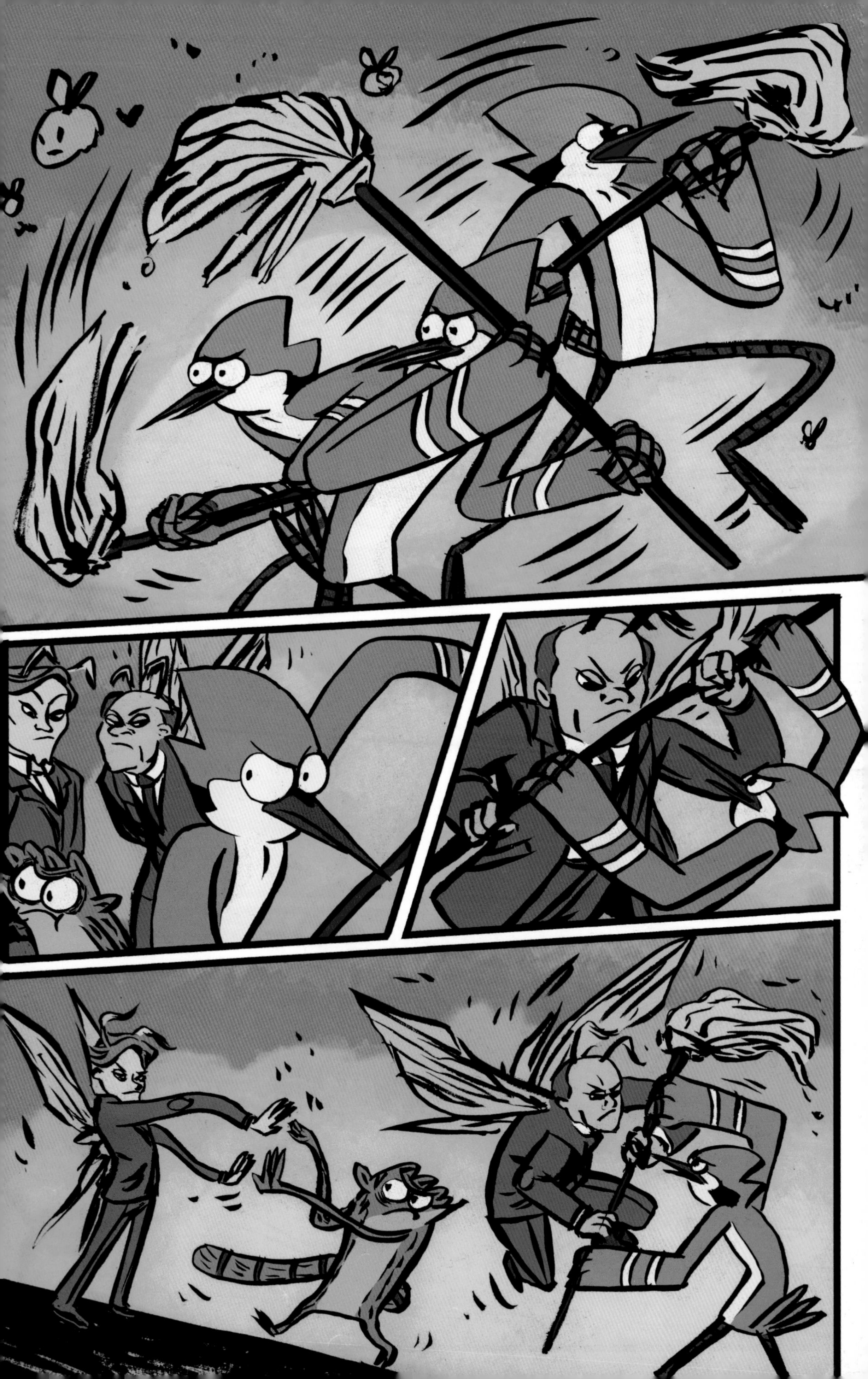

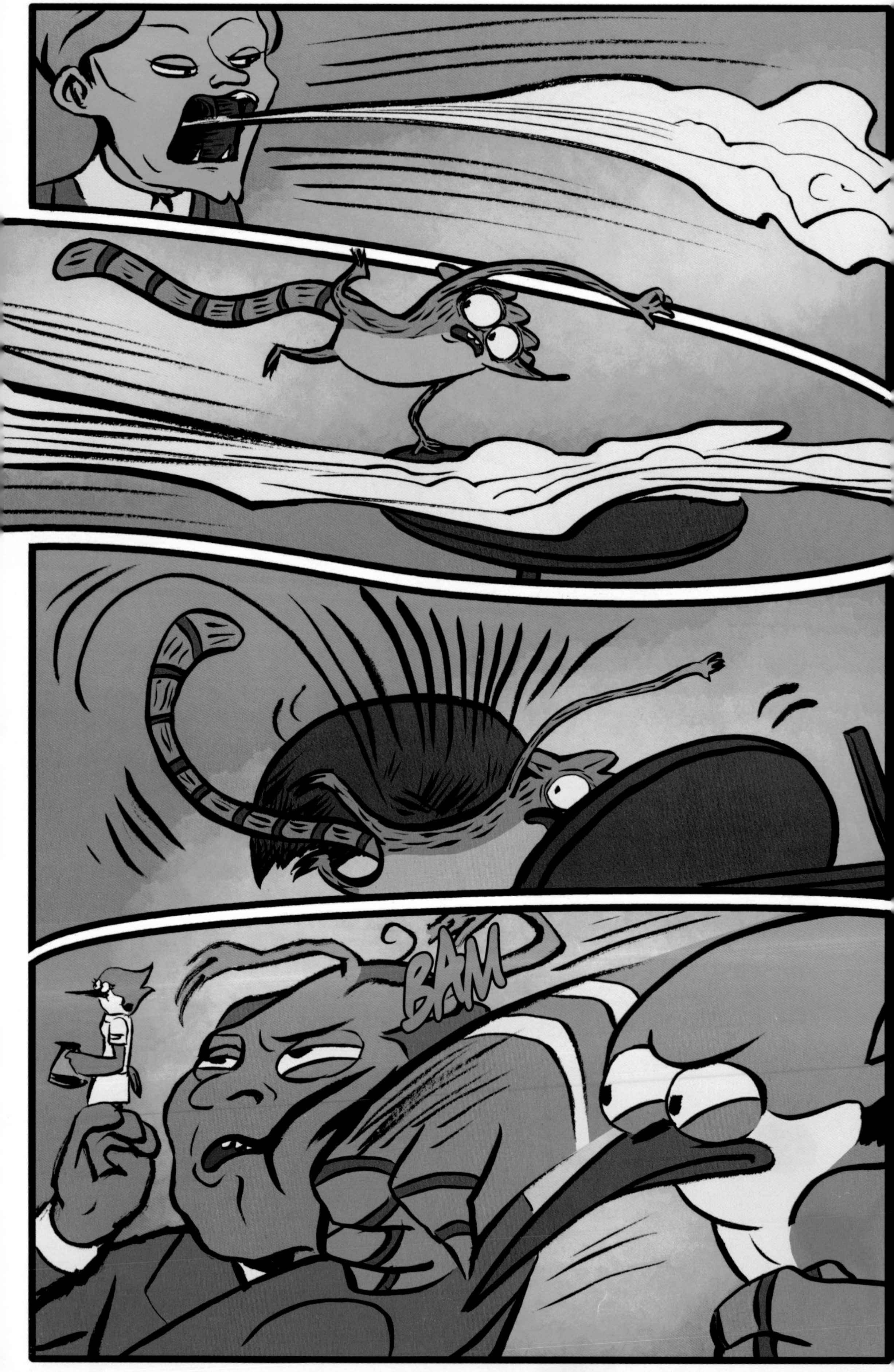
BAM

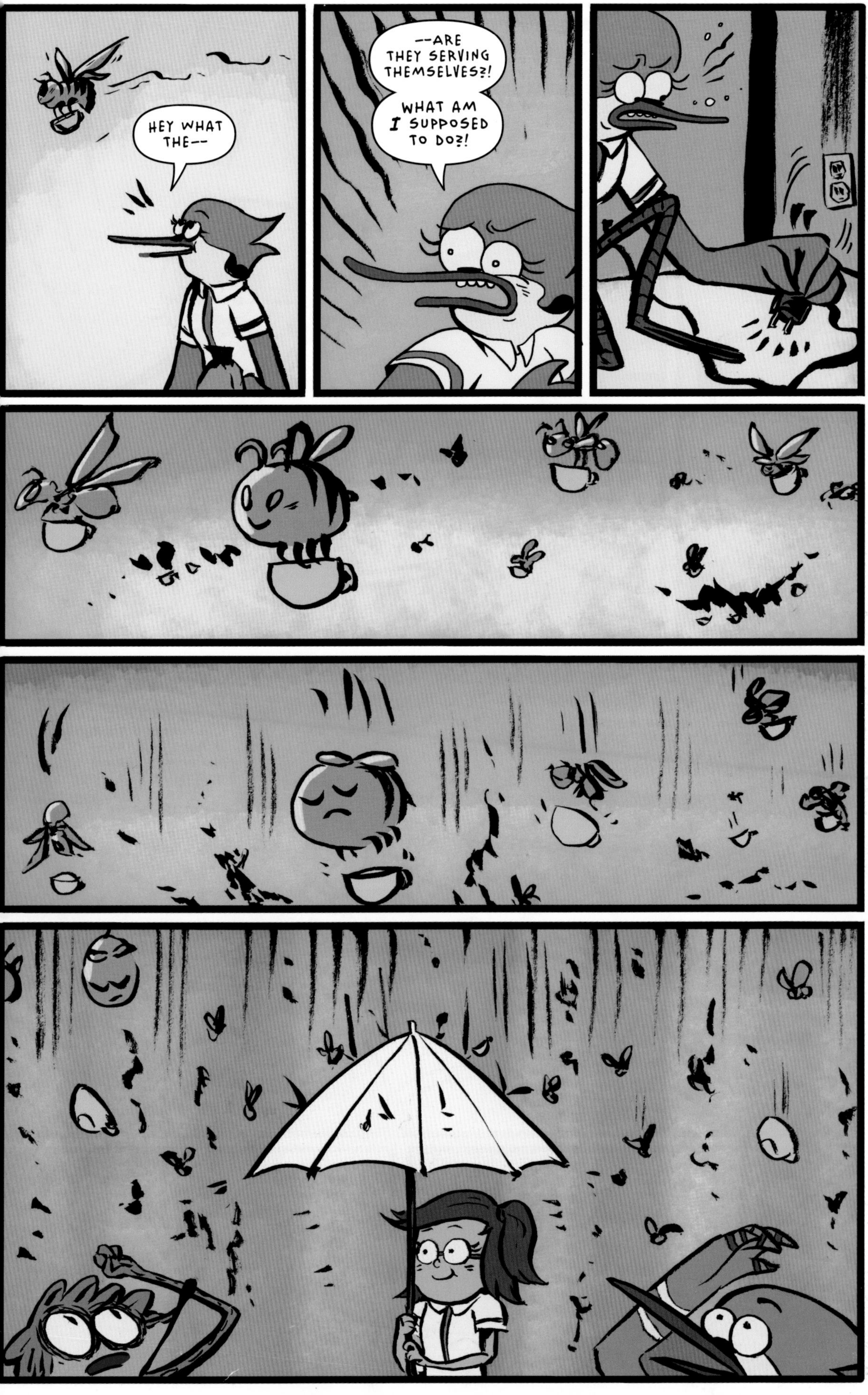
HEY WHAT THE--
--ARE THEY SERVING THEMSELVES?!
WHAT AM I SUPPOSED TO DO?!

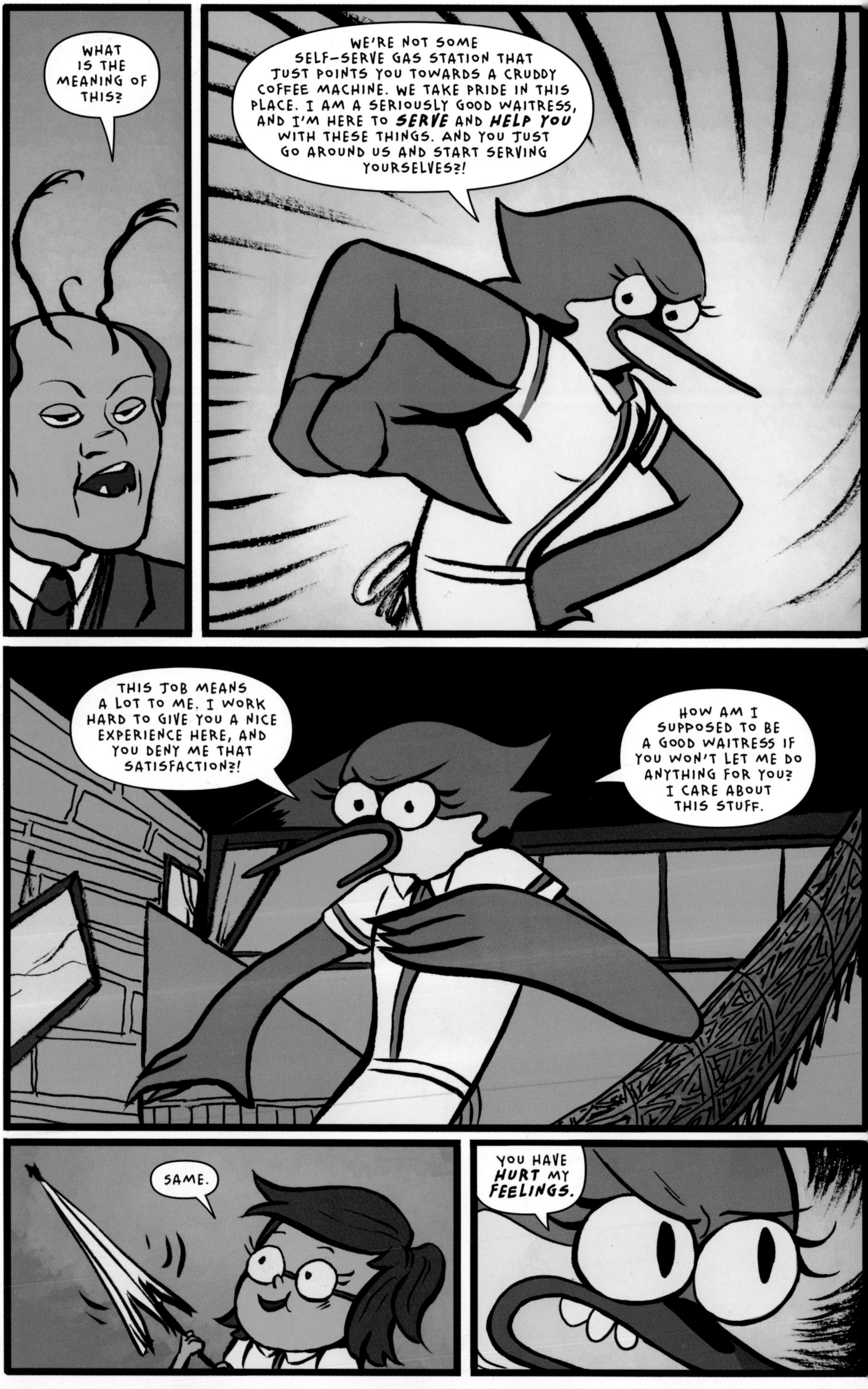
WHAT IS THE MEANING OF THIS?
WE'RE NOT SOME SELF-SERVE GAS STATION THAT JUST POINTS YOU TOWARDS A CRUDDY COFFEE MACHINE. WE TAKE PRIDE IN THIS PLACE. I AM A SERIOUSLY GOOD WAITRESS, AND I'M HERE TO SERVE AND HELP YOU WITH THESE THINGS. AND YOU JUST GO AROUND US AND START SERVING YOURSELVES?!
THIS JOB MEANS A LOT TO ME. I WORK HARD TO GIVE YOU A NICE EXPERIENCE HERE, AND YOU DENY ME THAT SATISFACTION?!
HOW AM I SUPPOSED TO BE A GOOD WAITRESS IF YOU WON'T LET ME DO ANYTHING FOR YOU? I CARE ABOUT THIS STUFF.
SAME.
YOU HAVE HURT MY FEELINGS.

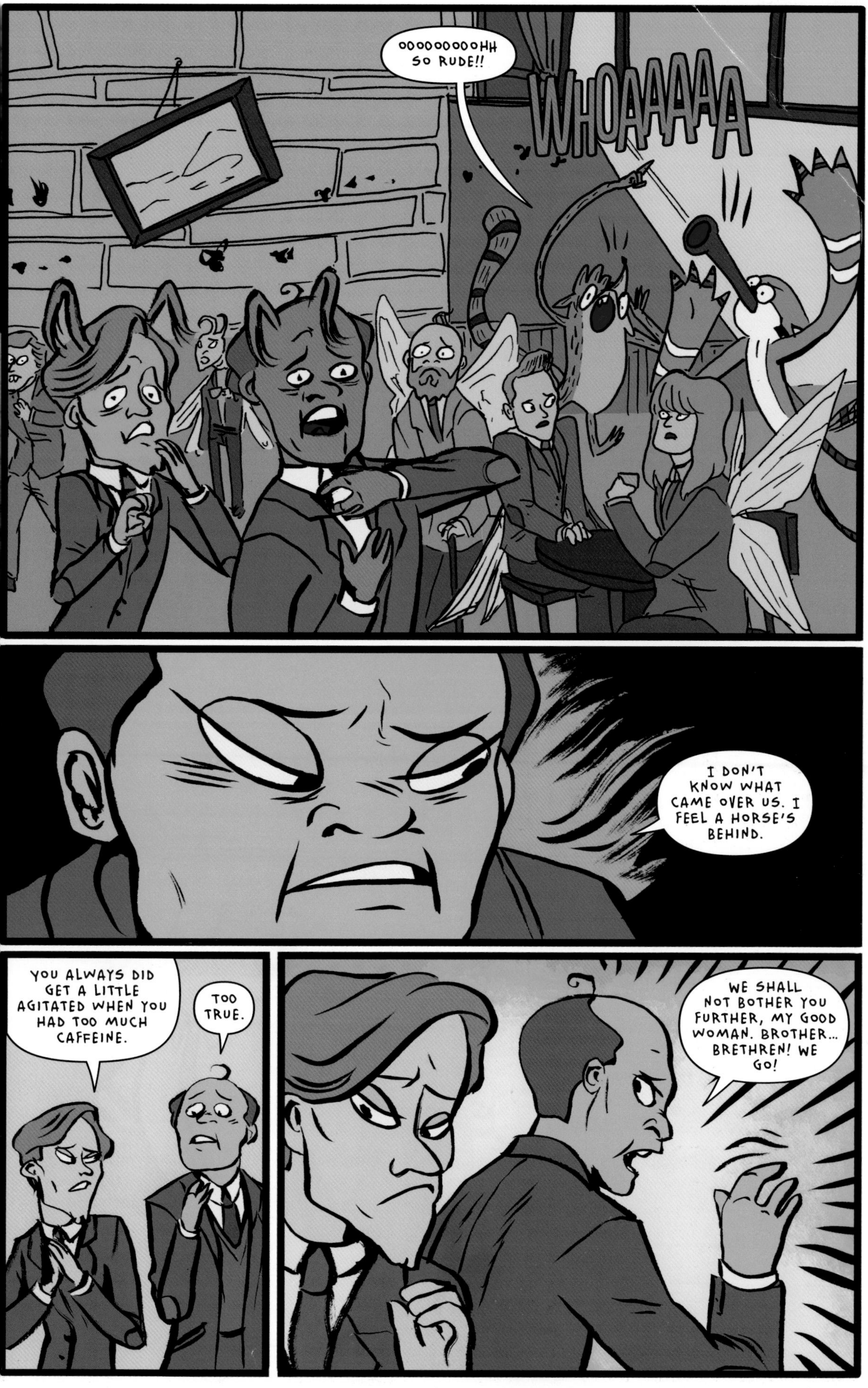
OOOOOOOOOHH SO RUDE!!
WHOAAAAAA
I DON'T KNOW WHAT CAME OVER US. I FEEL A HORSE'S BEHIND.
YOU ALWAYS DID GET A LITTLE AGITATED WHEN YOU HAD TOO MUCH CAFFEINE.
TOO TRUE.
WE SHALL NOT BOTHER YOU FURTHER, MY GOOD WOMAN. BROTHER... BRETHREN! WE GO!

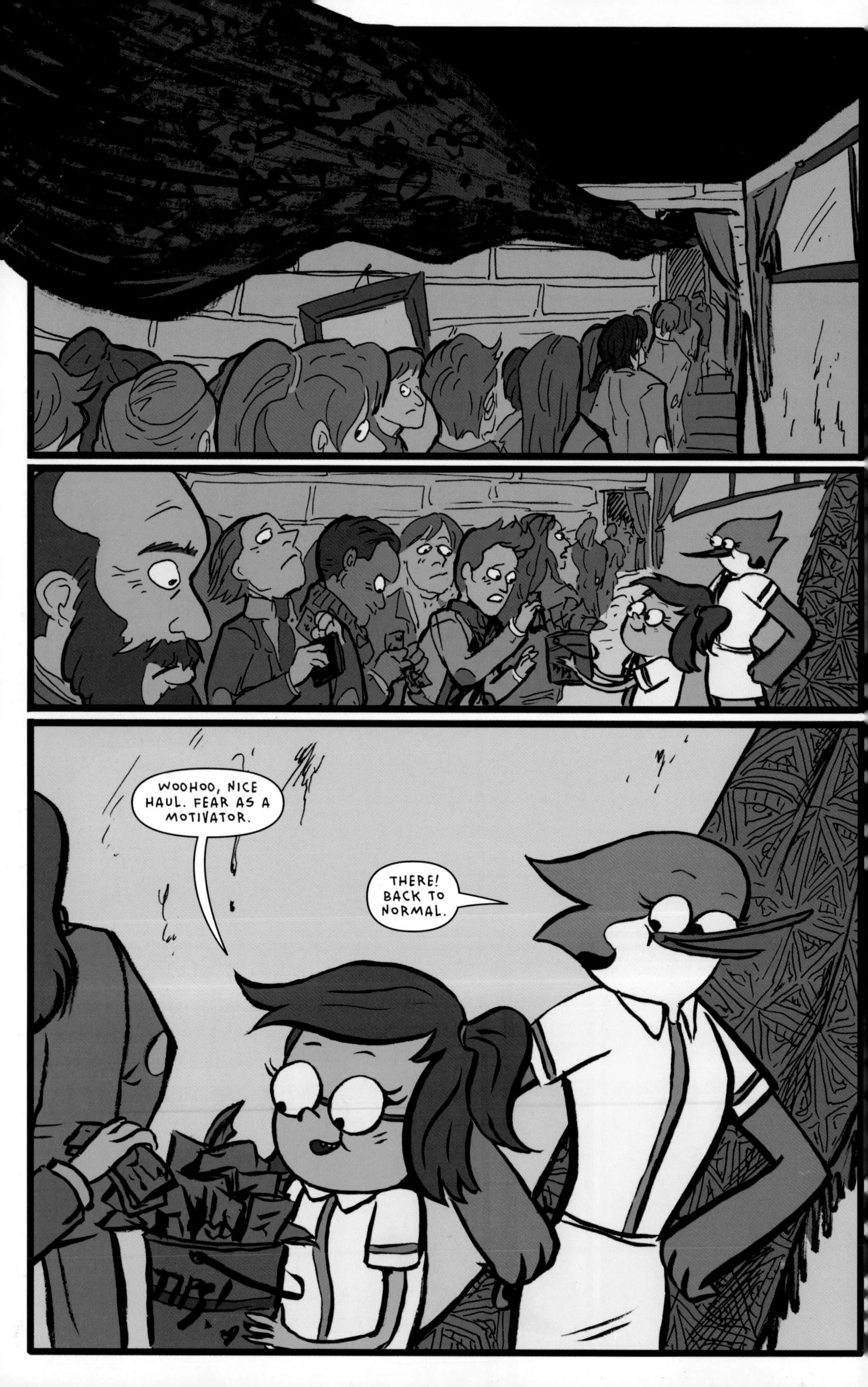
WOOHOO, NICE HAUL. FEAR AS A MOTIVATOR.
THERE! BACK TO NORMAL.

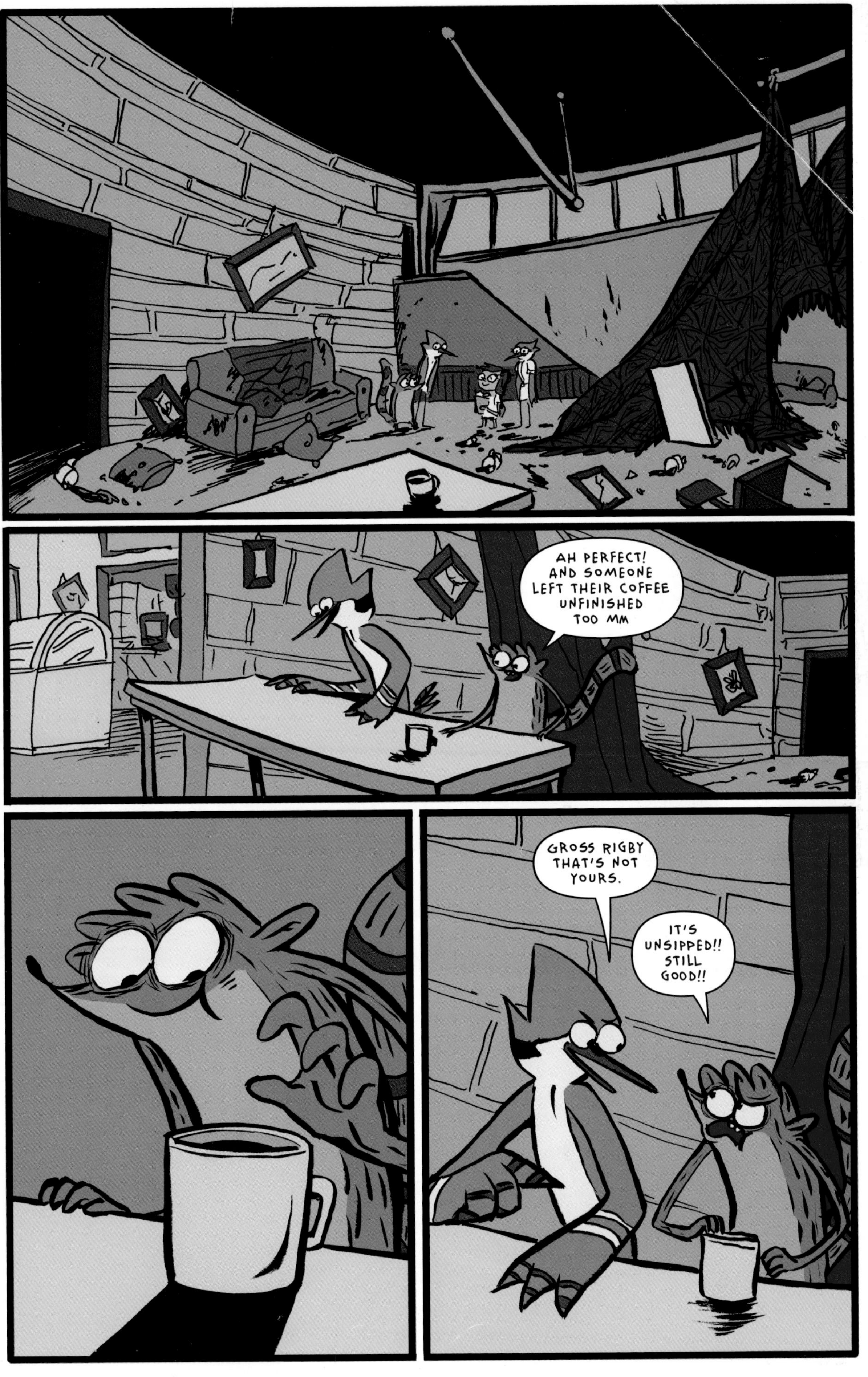
AH PERFECT! AND SOMEONE LEFT THEIR COFFEE UNFINISHED TOO MM
GROSS RIGBY THAT'S NOT YOURS.
IT'S UNSIPPED!! STILL GOOD!!

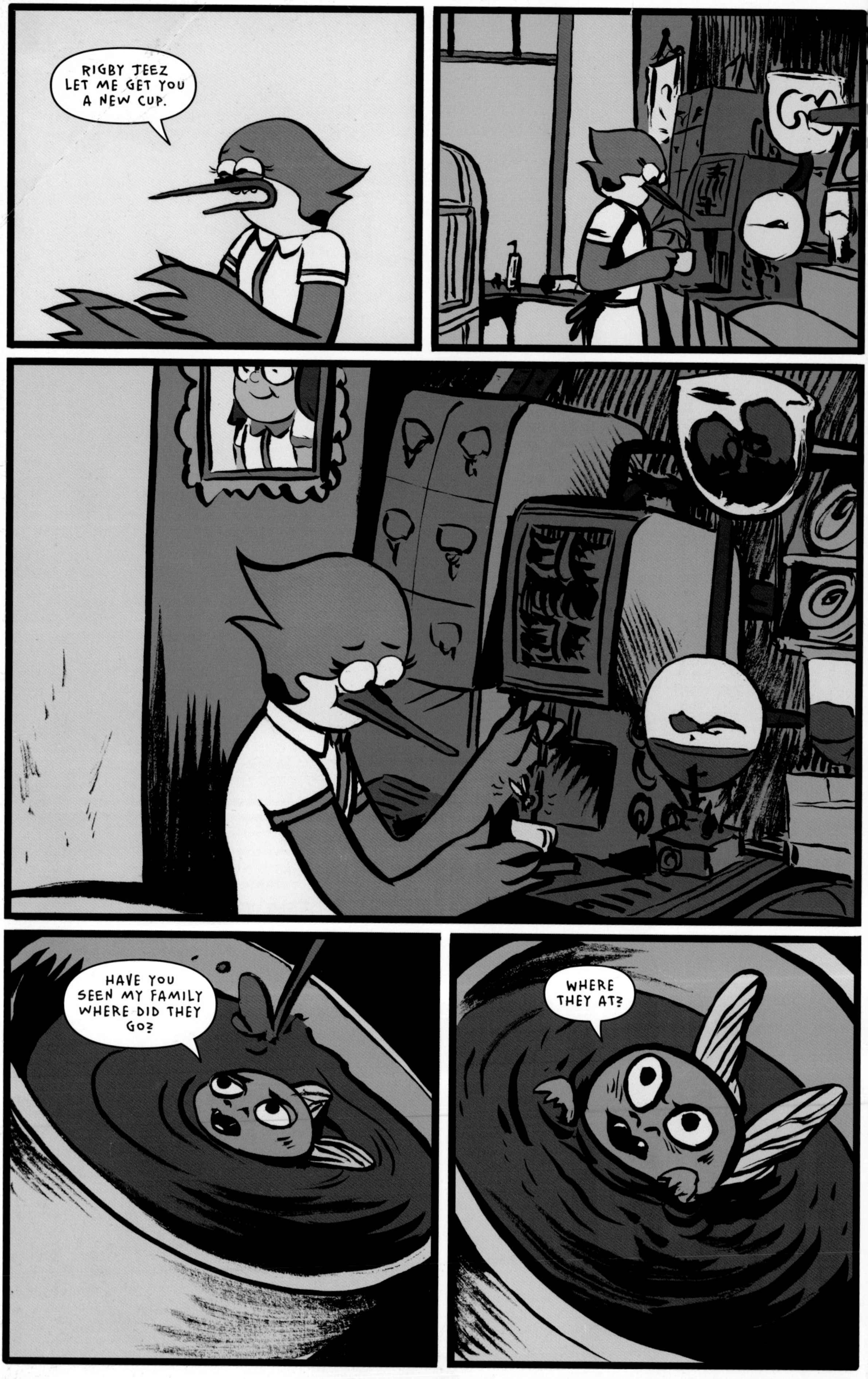
RIGBY JEEZ LET ME GET YOU A NEW CUP.
HAVE YOU SEEN MY FAMILY WHERE DID THEY GO?
WHERE THEY AT?

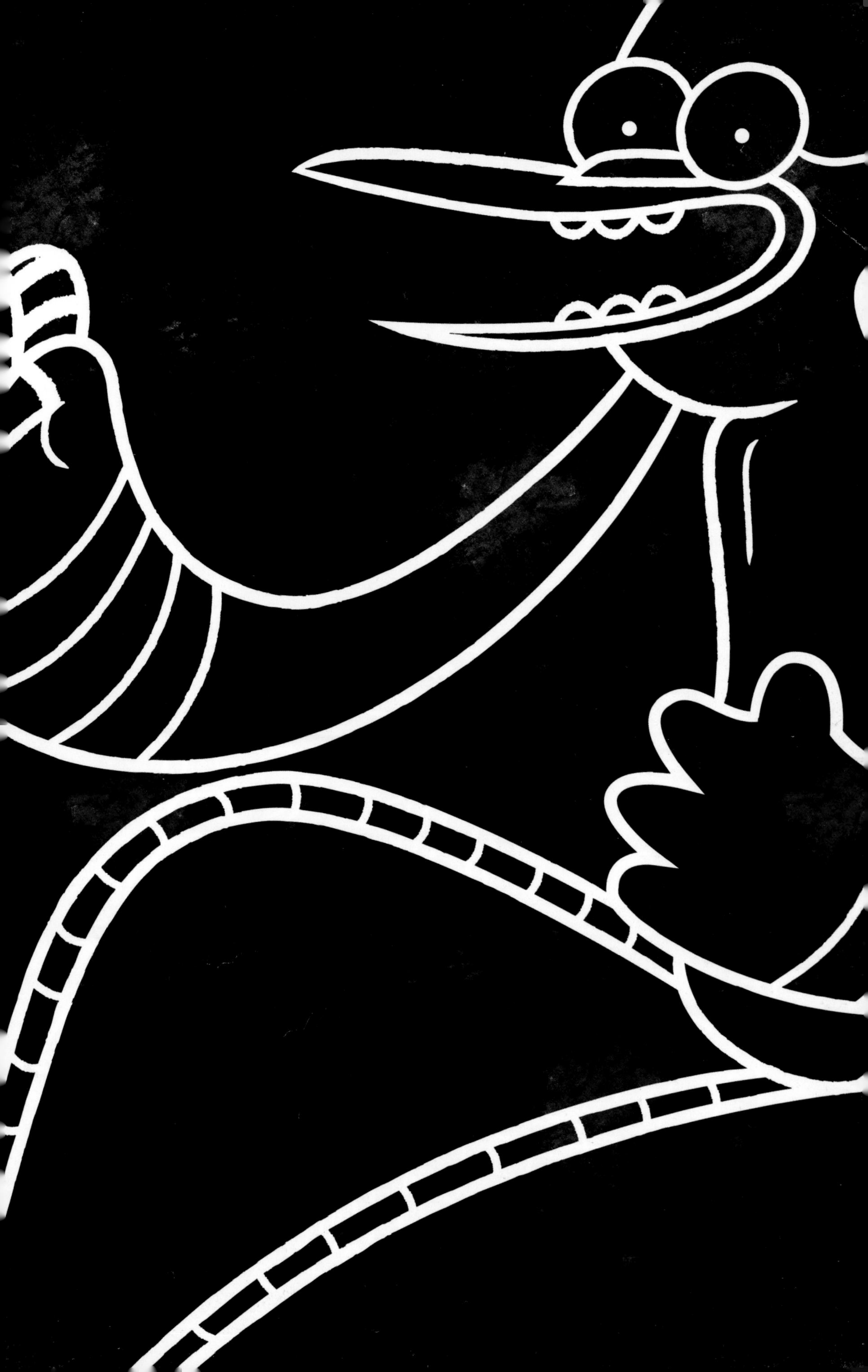

"EILEEN DAY"

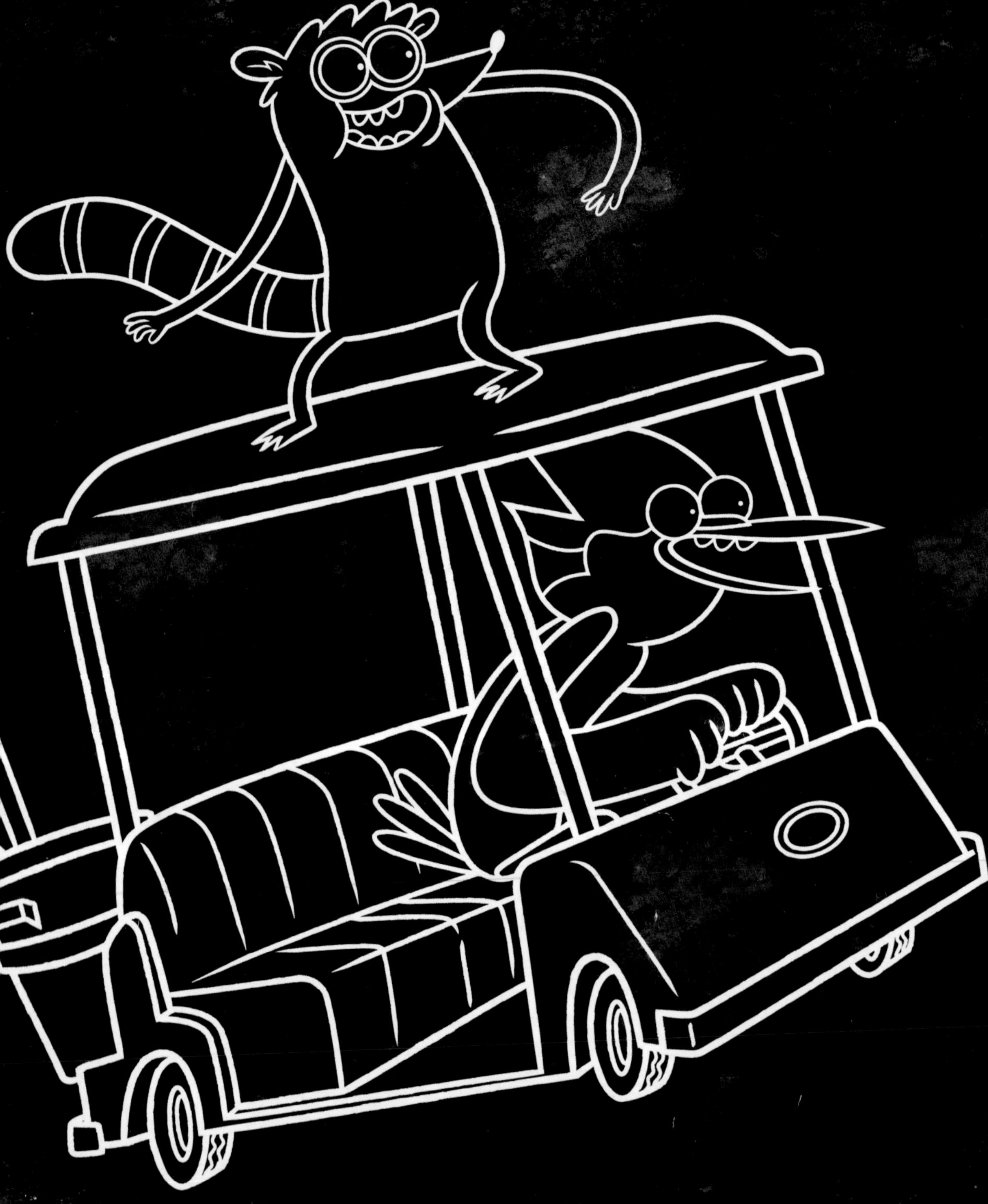

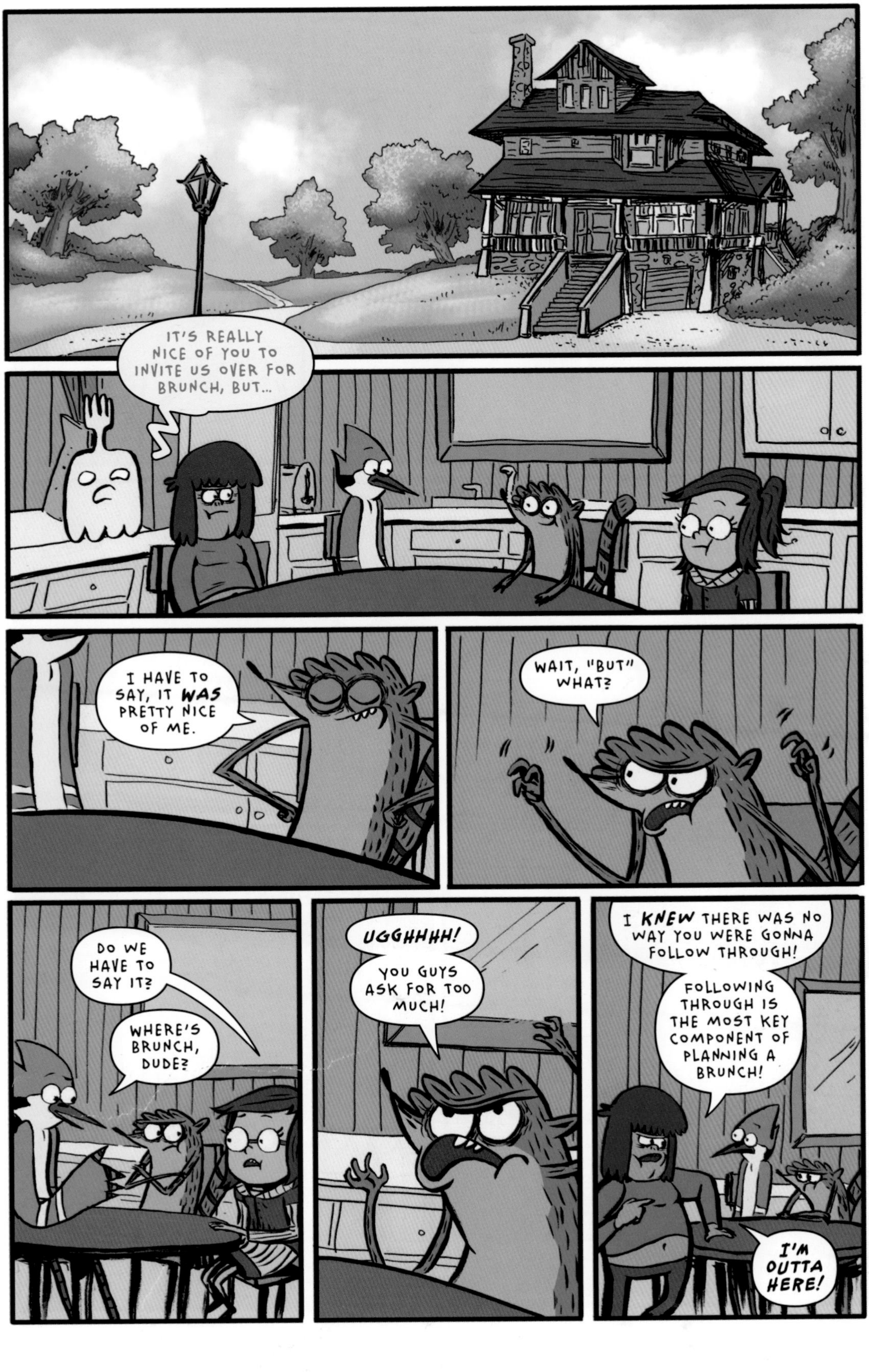
IT'S REALLY NICE OF YOU TO INVITE US OVER FOR BRUNCH, BUT...
I HAVE TO SAY, IT WAS PRETTY NICE OF ME.
WAIT, "BUT" WHAT?
DO WE HAVE TO SAY IT?
WHERE'S BRUNCH, DUDE?
UGGHHHH!
YOU GUYS ASK FOR TOO MUCH!
I KNEW THERE WAS NO WAY YOU WERE GONNA FOLLOW THROUGH!
FOLLOWING THROUGH IS THE MOST KEY COMPONENT OF PLANNING A BRUNCH!
I'M OUTTA HERE!

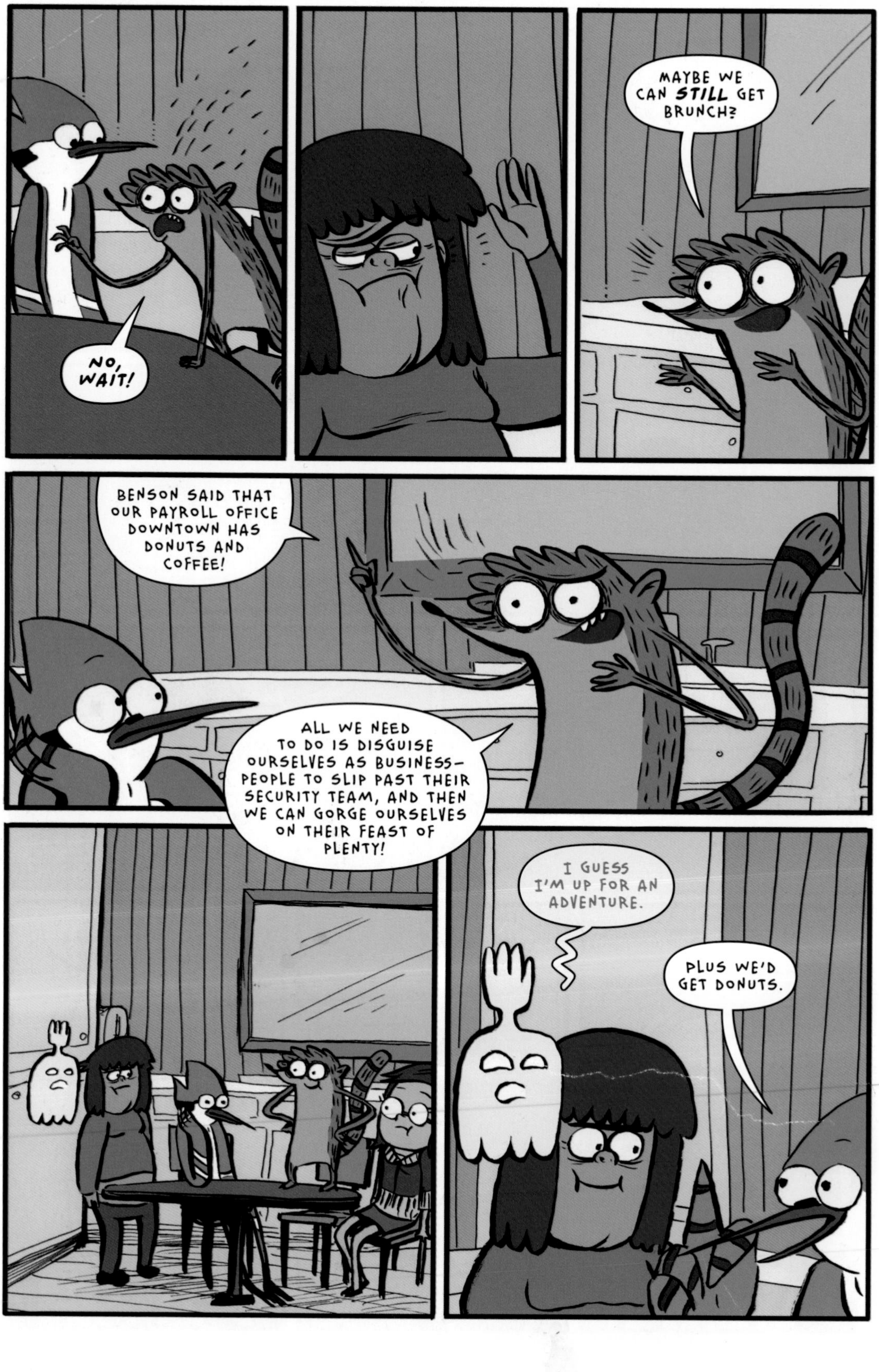
NO, WAIT!
MAYBE WE CAN STILL GET BRUNCH?
BENSON SAID THAT OUR PAYROLL OFFICE DOWNTOWN HAS DONUTS AND COFFEE!
ALL WE NEED TO DO IS DISGUISE OURSELVES AS BUSINESS-PEOPLE TO SLIP PAST THEIR SECURITY TEAM, AND THEN WE CAN GORGE OURSELVES ON THEIR FEAST OF PLENTY!
I GUESS I'M UP FOR AN ADVENTURE.
PLUS WE'D GET DONUTS.

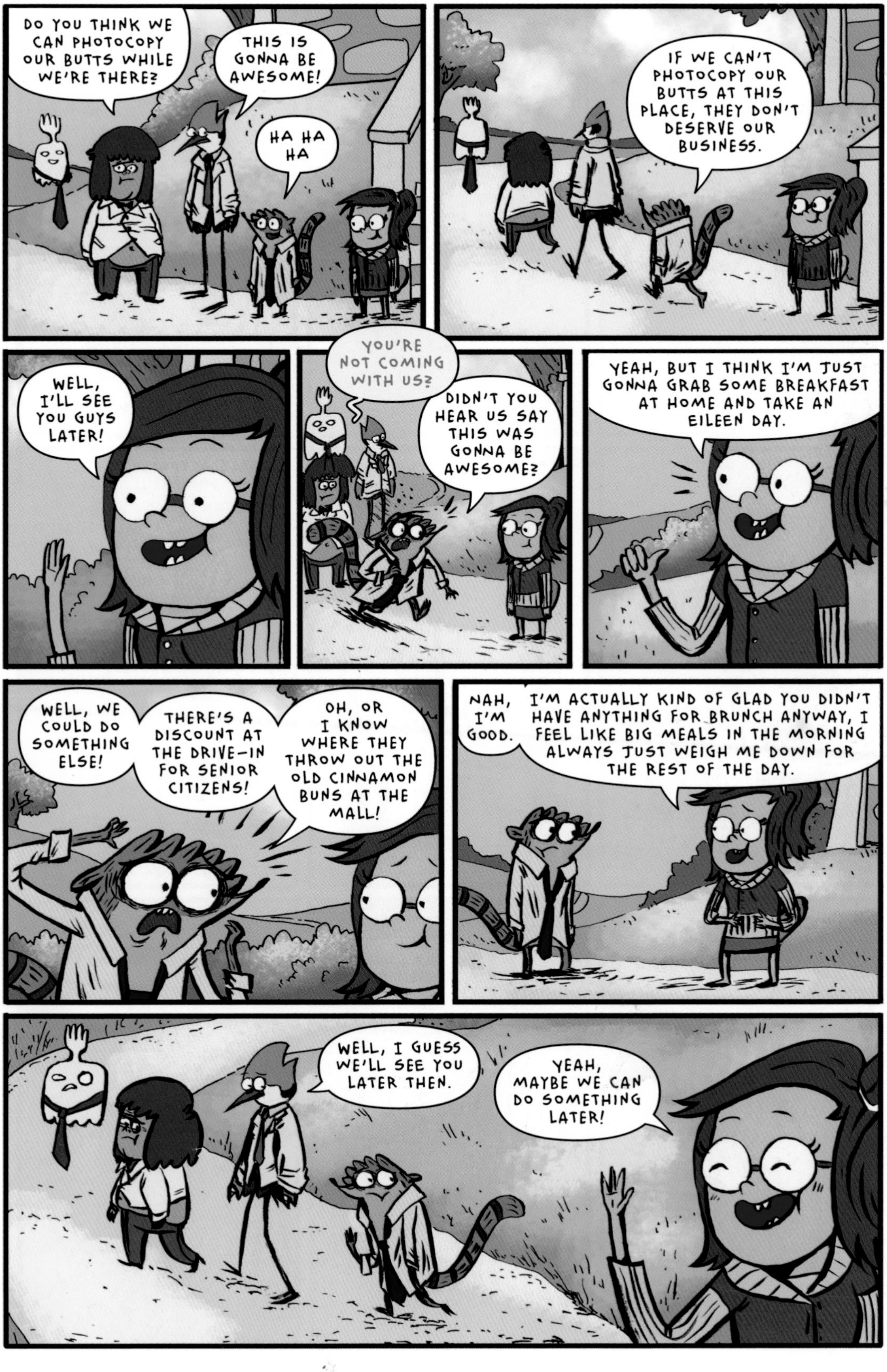
DO YOU THINK WE CAN PHOTOCOPY OUR BUTTS WHILE WE'RE THERE?
THIS IS GONNA BE AWESOME!
HA HA HA
IF WE CAN'T PHOTOCOPY OUR BUTTS AT THIS PLACE, THEY DON'T DESERVE OUR BUSINESS.
WELL, I'LL SEE YOU GUYS LATER!
YOU'RE NOT COMING WITH US?
DIDN'T YOU HEAR US SAY THIS WAS GONNA BE AWESOME?
YEAH, BUT I THINK I'M JUST GONNA GRAB SOME BREAKFAST AT HOME AND TAKE AN EILEEN DAY.
WELL, WE COULD DO SOMETHING ELSE!
THERE'S A DISCOUNT AT THE DRIVE-IN FOR SENIOR CITIZENS!
OH, OR I KNOW WHERE THEY THROW OUT THE OLD CINNAMON BUNS AT THE MALL!
NAH, I'M GOOD.
I'M ACTUALLY KIND OF GLAD YOU DIDN'T HAVE ANYTHING FOR BRUNCH ANYWAY, I FEEL LIKE BIG MEALS IN THE MORNING ALWAYS JUST WEIGH ME DOWN FOR THE REST OF THE DAY.
WELL, I GUESS WE'LL SEE YOU LATER THEN.
YEAH, MAYBE WE CAN DO SOMETHING LATER!

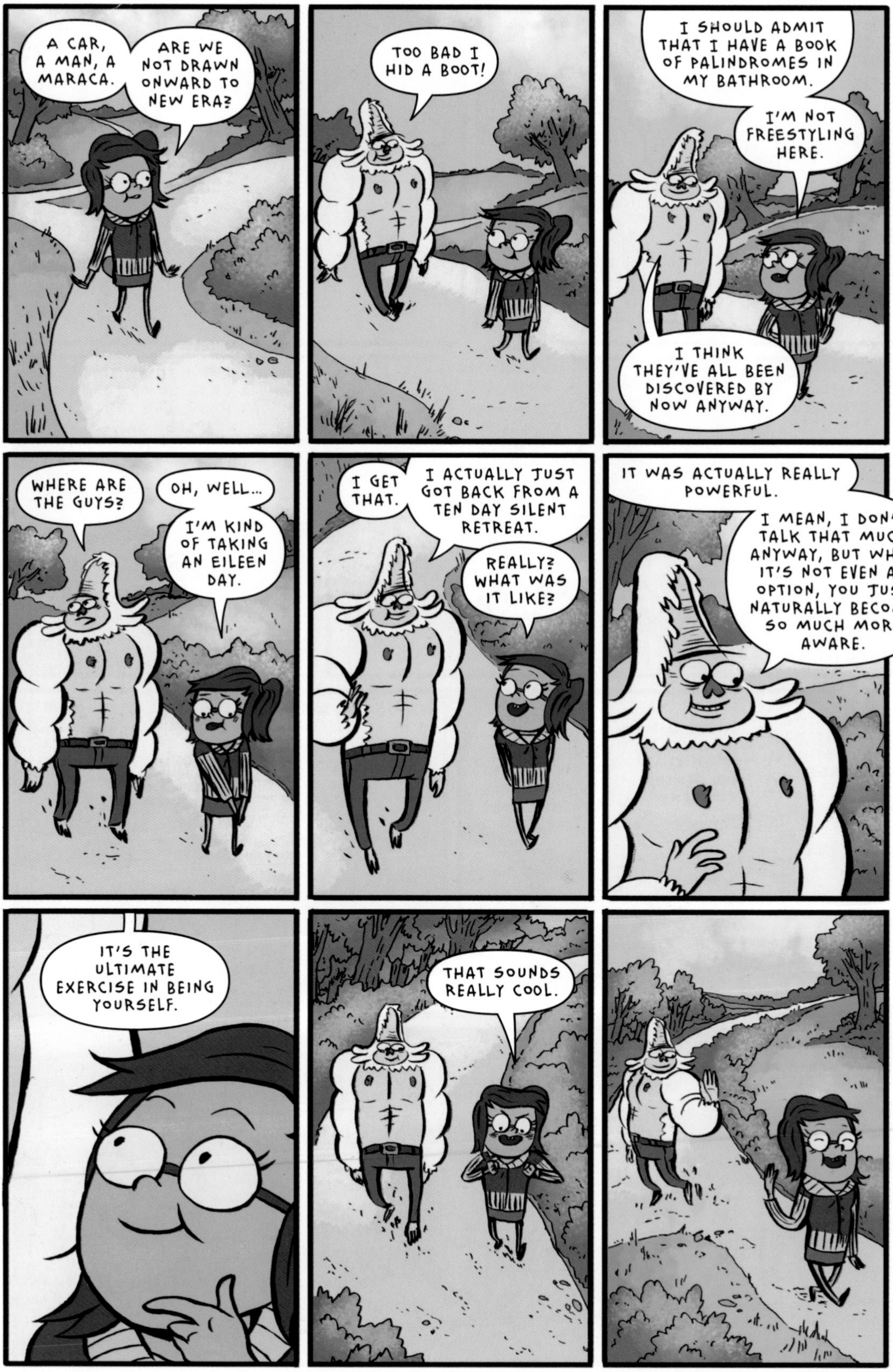
A CAR, A MAN, A MARACA.
ARE WE NOT DRAWN ONWARD TO NEW ERA?
TOO BAD I HID A BOOT!
I SHOULD ADMIT THAT I HAVE A BOOK OF PALINDROMES IN MY BATHROOM.
I'M NOT FREESTYLING HERE.
I THINK THEY'VE ALL BEEN DISCOVERED BY NOW ANYWAY.
WHERE ARE THE GUYS?
OH, WELL...
I'M KIND OF TAKING AN EILEEN DAY.
I GET THAT.
I ACTUALLY JUST GOT BACK FROM A TEN DAY SILENT RETREAT.
REALLY? WHAT WAS IT LIKE?
IT WAS ACTUALLY REALLY POWERFUL.
I MEAN, I DON'T TALK THAT MUCH ANYWAY, BUT WHEN IT'S NOT EVEN AN OPTION, YOU JUST NATURALLY BECOME SO MUCH MORE AWARE.
IT'S THE ULTIMATE EXERCISE IN BEING YOURSELF.
THAT SOUNDS REALLY COOL.

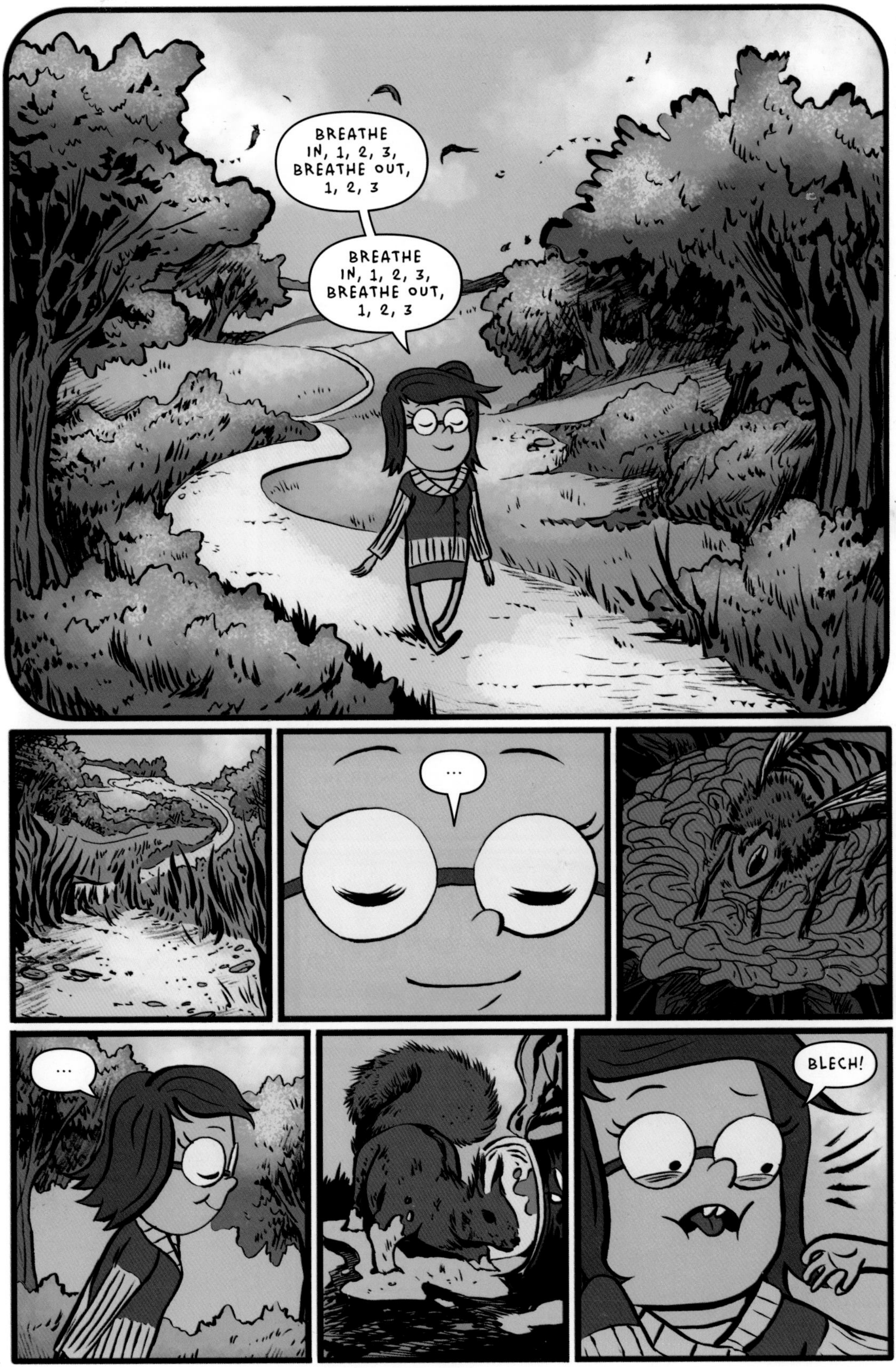
BREATHE IN, 1, 2, 3, BREATHE OUT, 1, 2, 3
BREATHE IN, 1, 2, 3, BREATHE OUT, 1, 2, 3
...
...
BLECH!

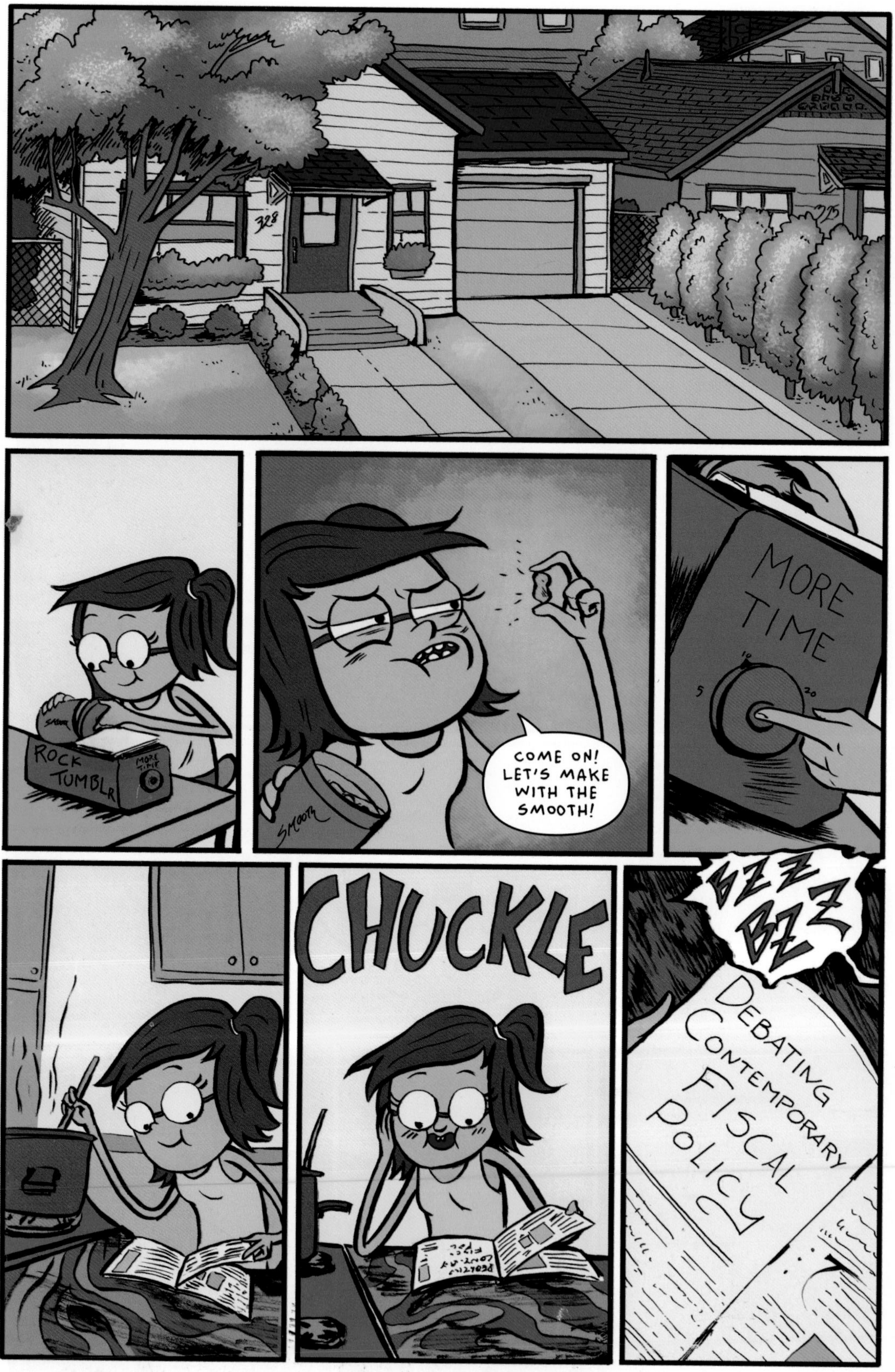

328
ROCK TUMBLR
COME ON! LET'S MAKE WITH THE SMOOTH!
MORE TIME
CHUCKLE
BZZ BZZ
DEBATING CONTEMPORARY FISCAL POLICY

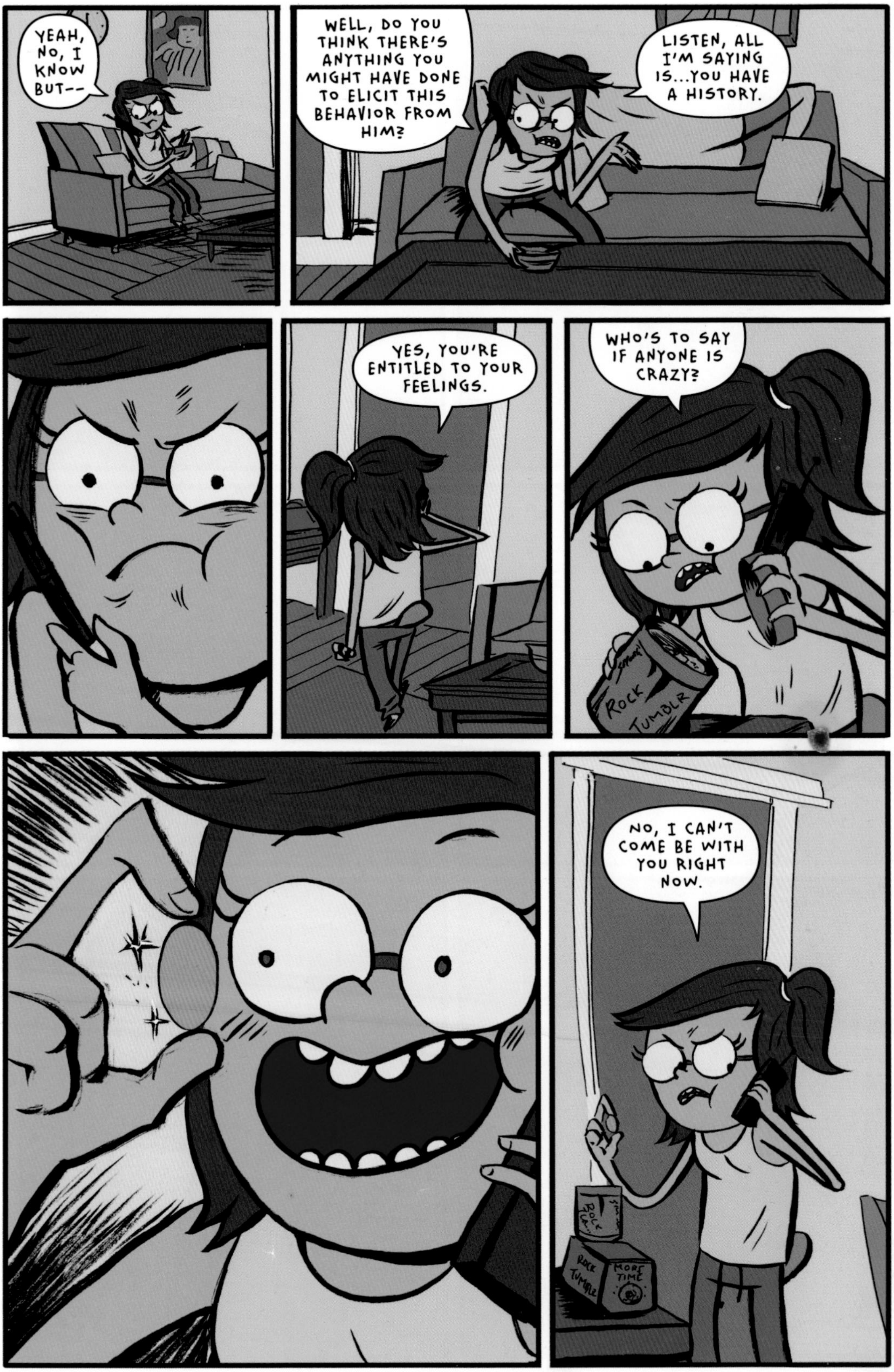
YEAH, NO, I KNOW BUT--
WELL, DO YOU THINK THERE'S ANYTHING YOU MIGHT HAVE DONE TO ELICIT THIS BEHAVIOR FROM HIM?
LISTEN, ALL I'M SAYING IS...YOU HAVE A HISTORY.
YES, YOU'RE ENTITLED TO YOUR FEELINGS.
WHO'S TO SAY IF ANYONE IS CRAZY?
ROCK TUMBLR
NO, I CAN'T COME BE WITH YOU RIGHT NOW.
ROCK TUMBLR
MORE TIME

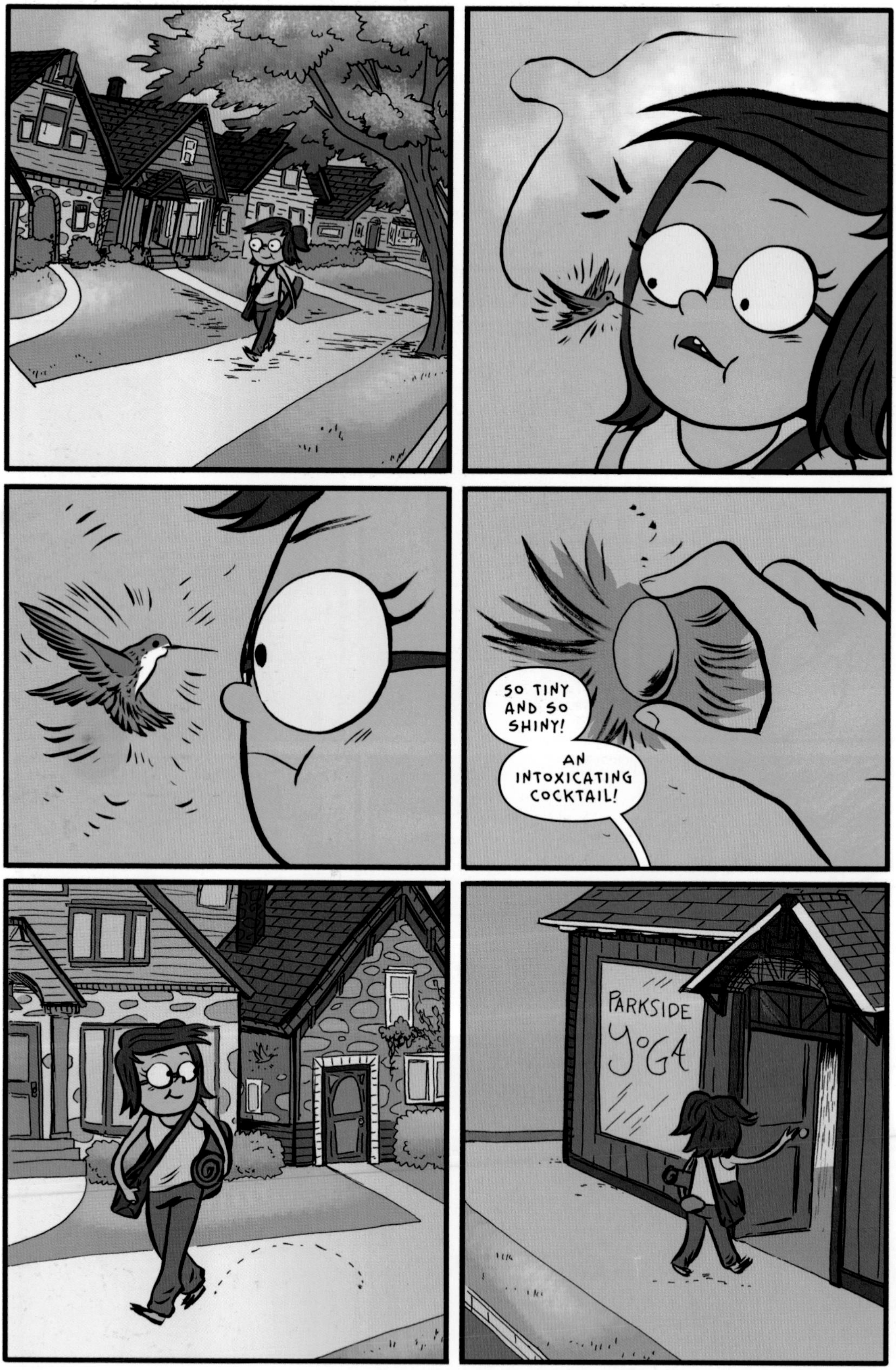
SO TINY AND SO SHINY!
AN INTOXICATING COCKTAIL!
PARKSIDE YOGA

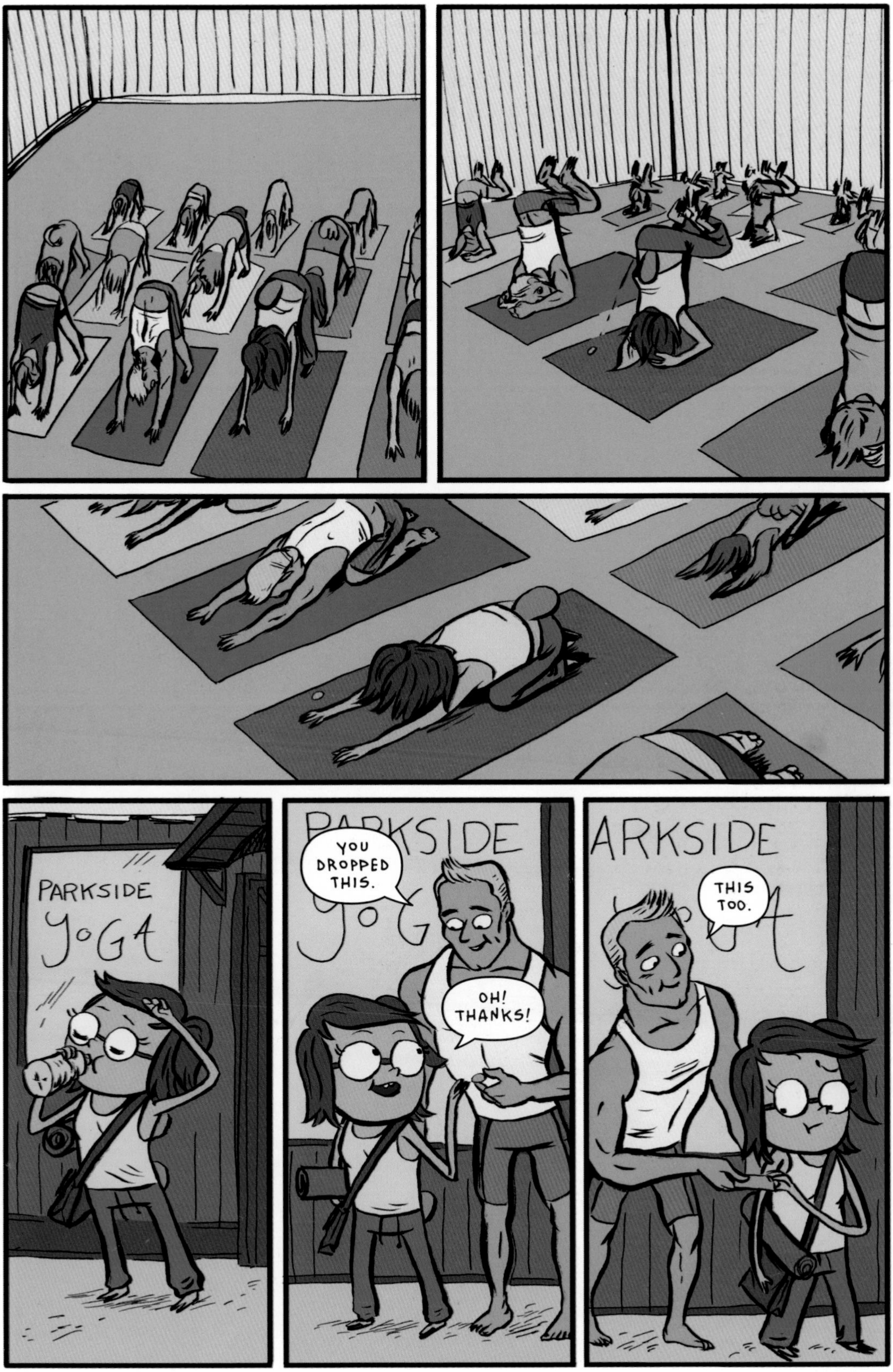
PARKSIDE
YoGA
PARKSIDE
YOU DROPPED THIS.
OH! THANKS!
ARKSIDE
THIS TOO.

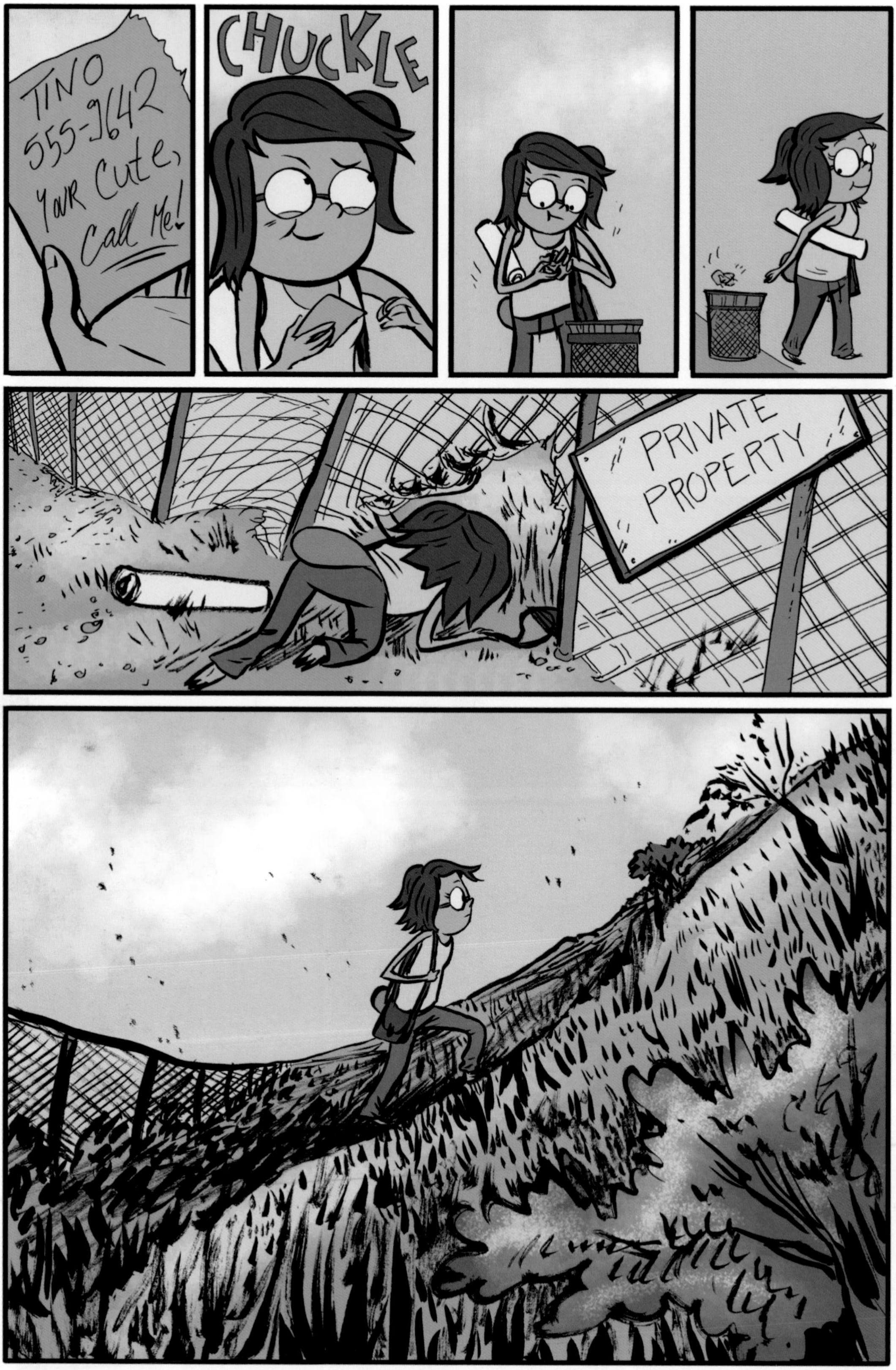

TINO
555-9642
Your Cute,
Call Me!
CHUCKLE
PRIVATE PROPERTY

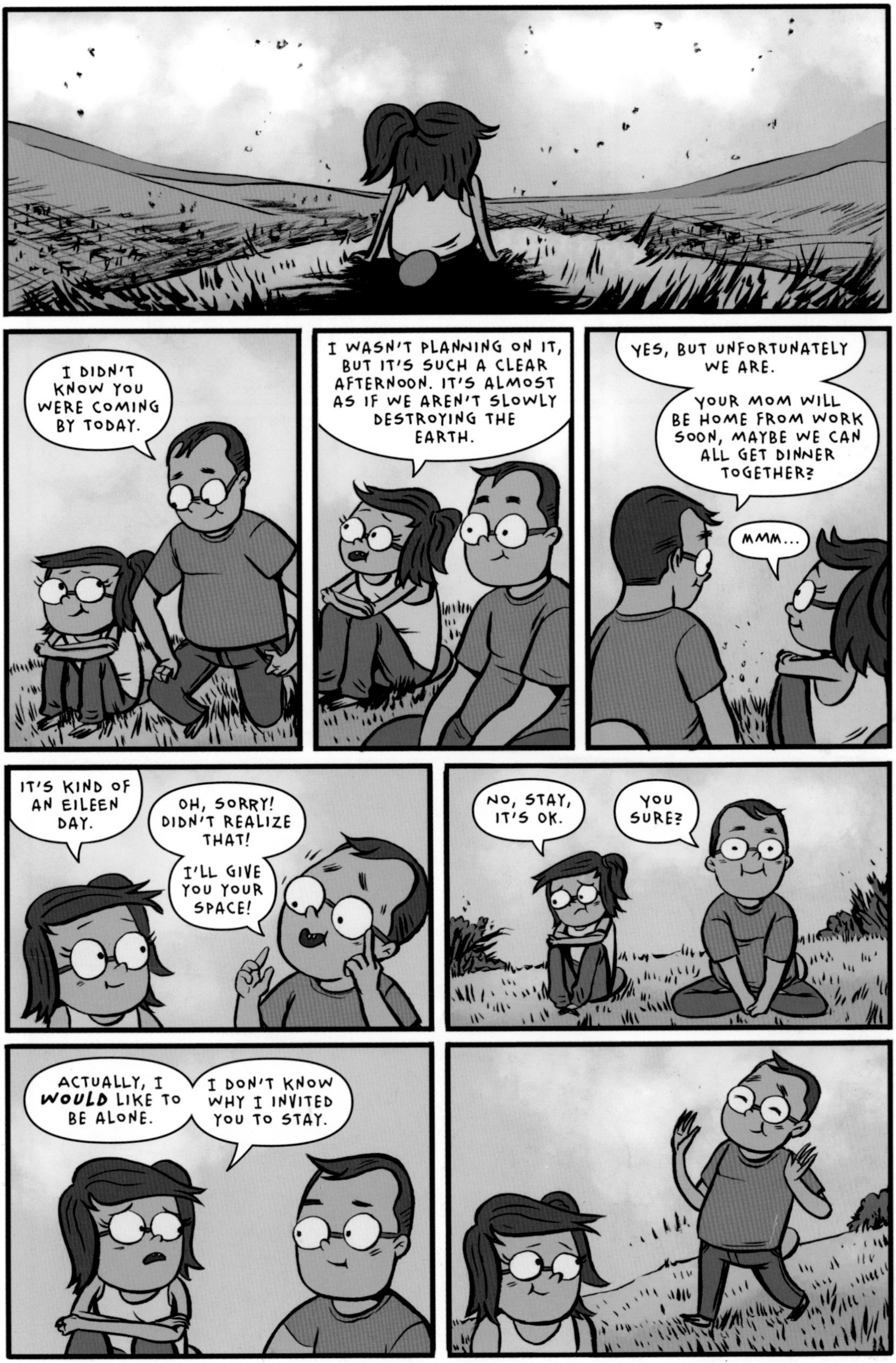
I DIDN'T KNOW YOU WERE COMING BY TODAY.
I WASN'T PLANNING ON IT, BUT IT'S SUCH A CLEAR AFTERNOON. IT'S ALMOST AS IF WE AREN'T SLOWLY DESTROYING THE EARTH.
YES, BUT UNFORTUNATELY WE ARE.
YOUR MOM WILL BE HOME FROM WORK SOON, MAYBE WE CAN ALL GET DINNER TOGETHER?
MMM...
IT'S KIND OF AN EILEEN DAY.
OH, SORRY! DIDN'T REALIZE THAT!
I'LL GIVE YOU YOUR SPACE!
NO, STAY, IT'S OK.
YOU SURE?
ACTUALLY, I **WOULD** LIKE TO BE ALONE.
I DON'T KNOW WHY I INVITED YOU TO STAY.

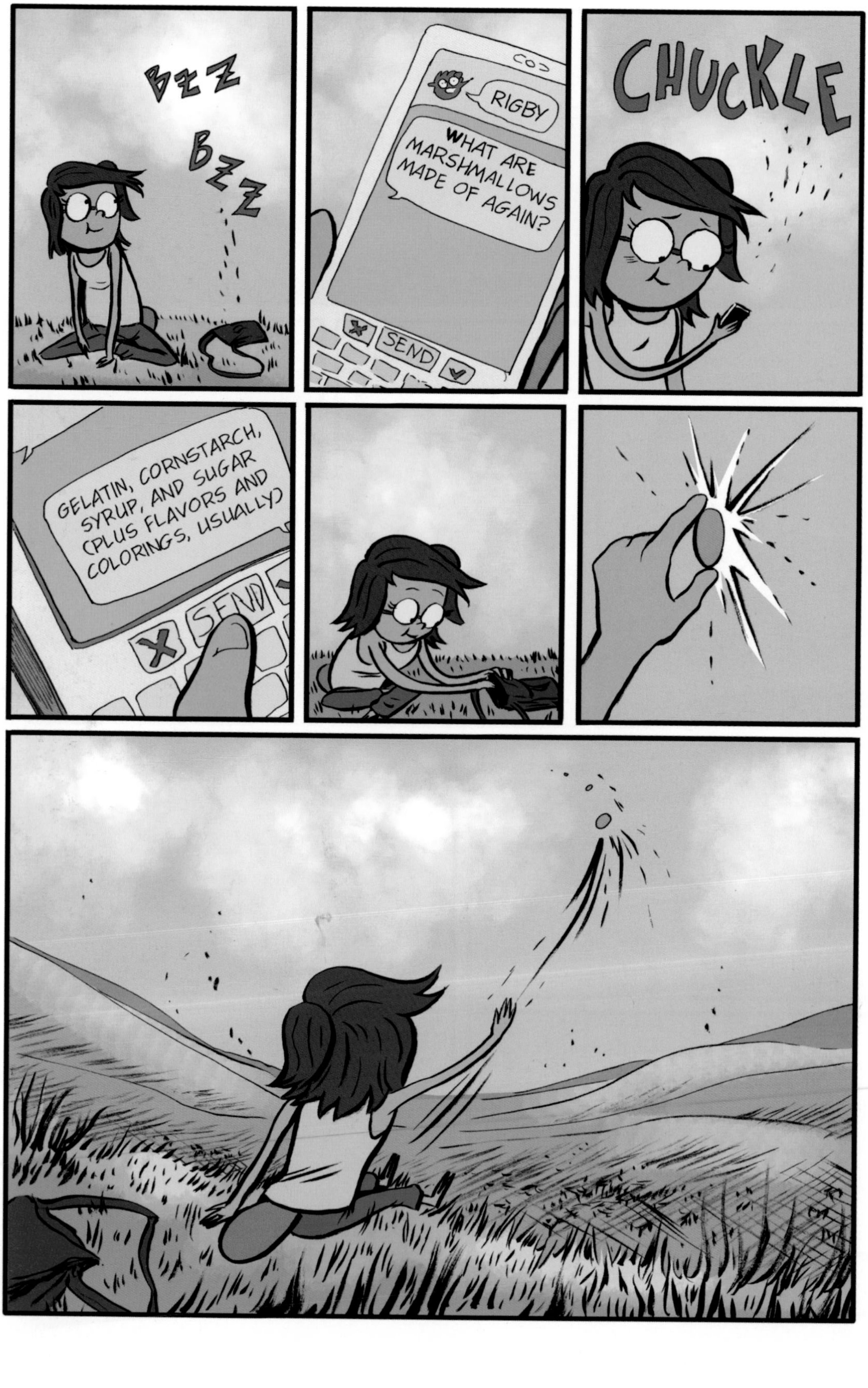
BZZ
BZZ
RIGBY
WHAT ARE MARSHMALLOWS MADE OF AGAIN?
SEND
CHUCKLE
GELATIN, CORNSTARCH, SYRUP, AND SUGAR (PLUS FLAVORS AND COLORINGS, USUALLY)
SEND

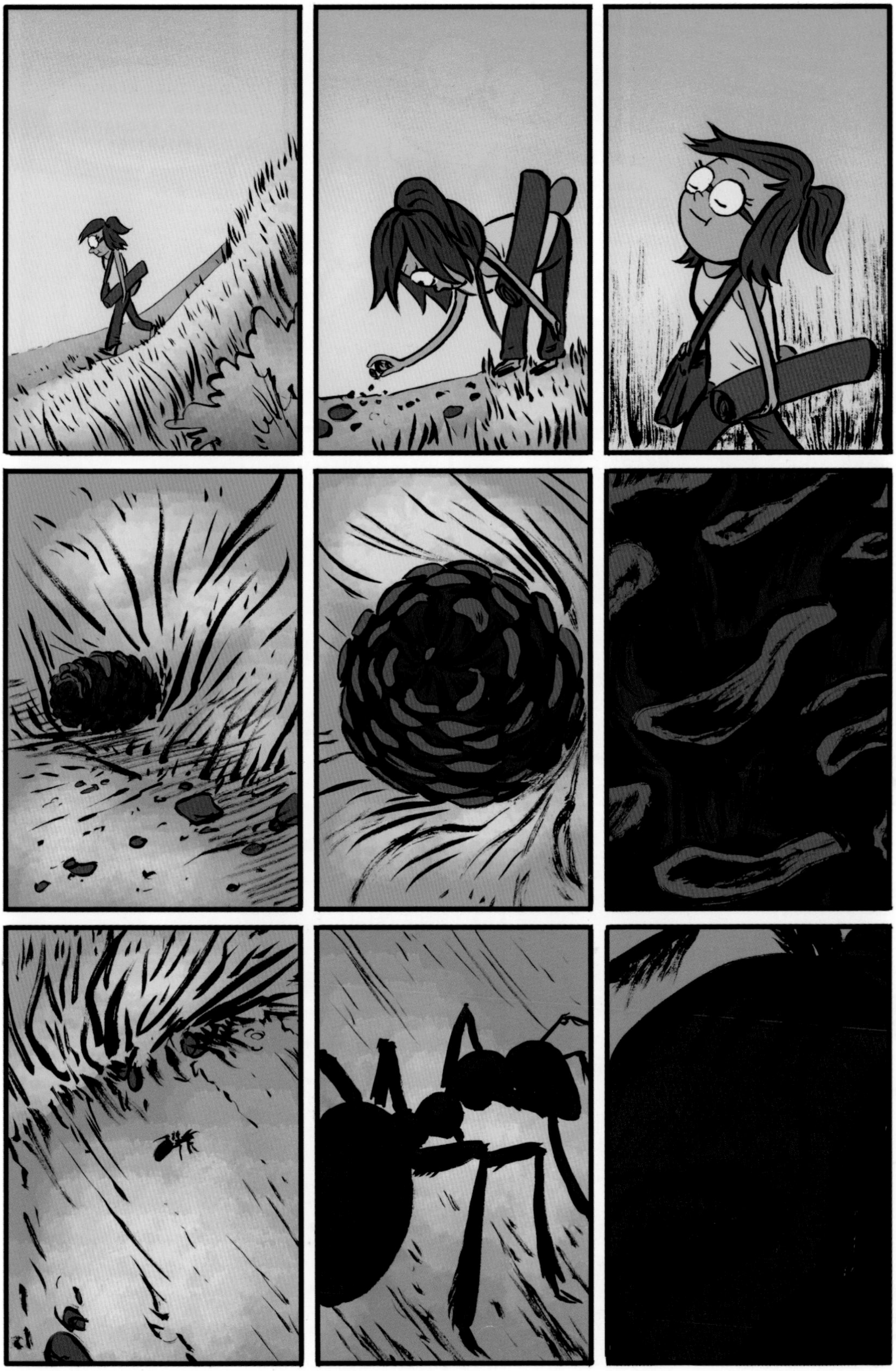

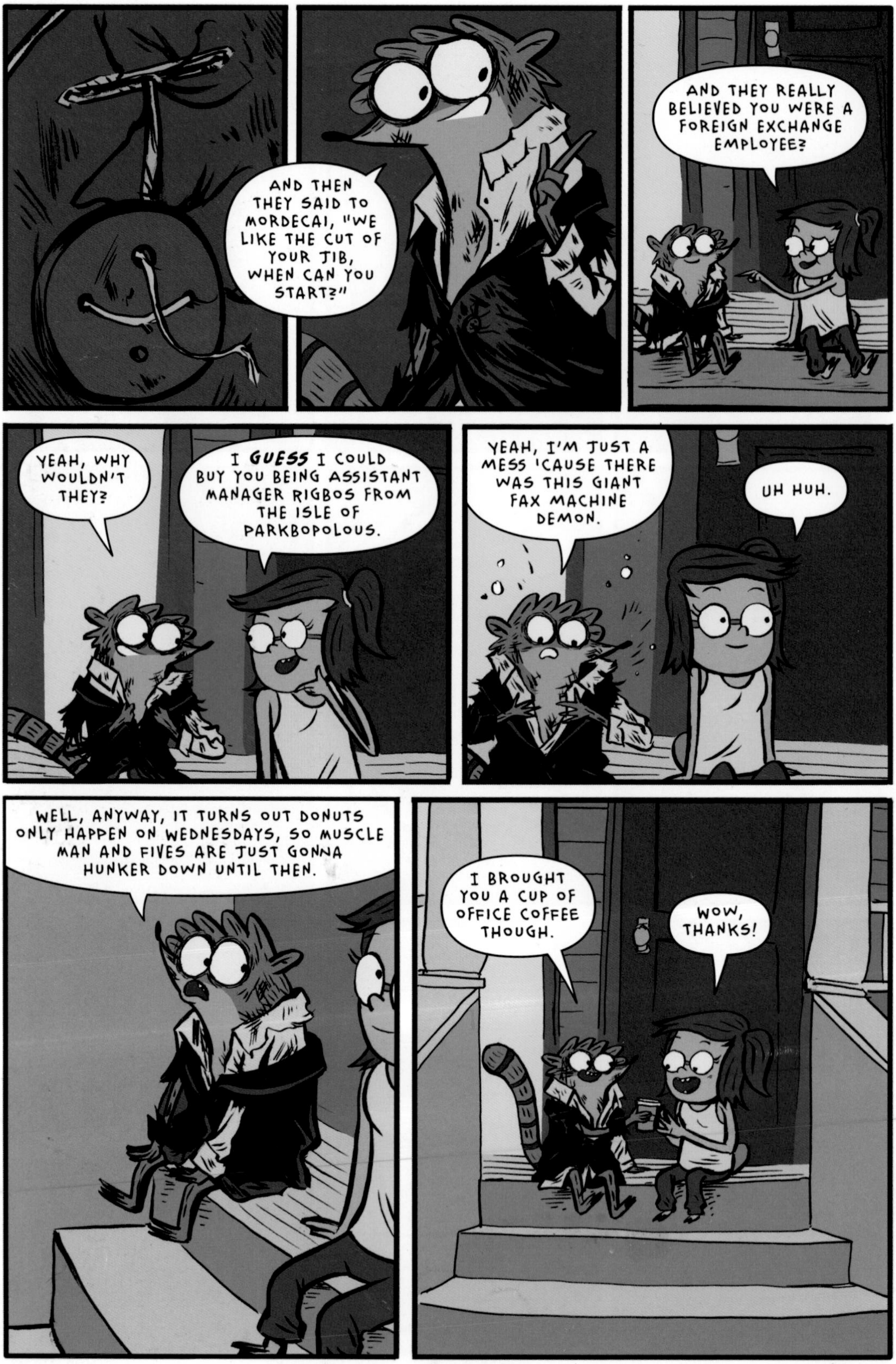
AND THEN THEY SAID TO MORDECAI, "WE LIKE THE CUT OF YOUR JIB, WHEN CAN YOU START?"
AND THEY REALLY BELIEVED YOU WERE A FOREIGN EXCHANGE EMPLOYEE?
YEAH, WHY WOULDN'T THEY?
I GUESS I COULD BUY YOU BEING ASSISTANT MANAGER RIGBOS FROM THE ISLE OF PARKBOPOLOUS.
YEAH, I'M JUST A MESS 'CAUSE THERE WAS THIS GIANT FAX MACHINE DEMON.
UH HUH.
WELL, ANYWAY, IT TURNS OUT DONUTS ONLY HAPPEN ON WEDNESDAYS, SO MUSCLE MAN AND FIVES ARE JUST GONNA HUNKER DOWN UNTIL THEN.
I BROUGHT YOU A CUP OF OFFICE COFFEE THOUGH.
WOW, THANKS!

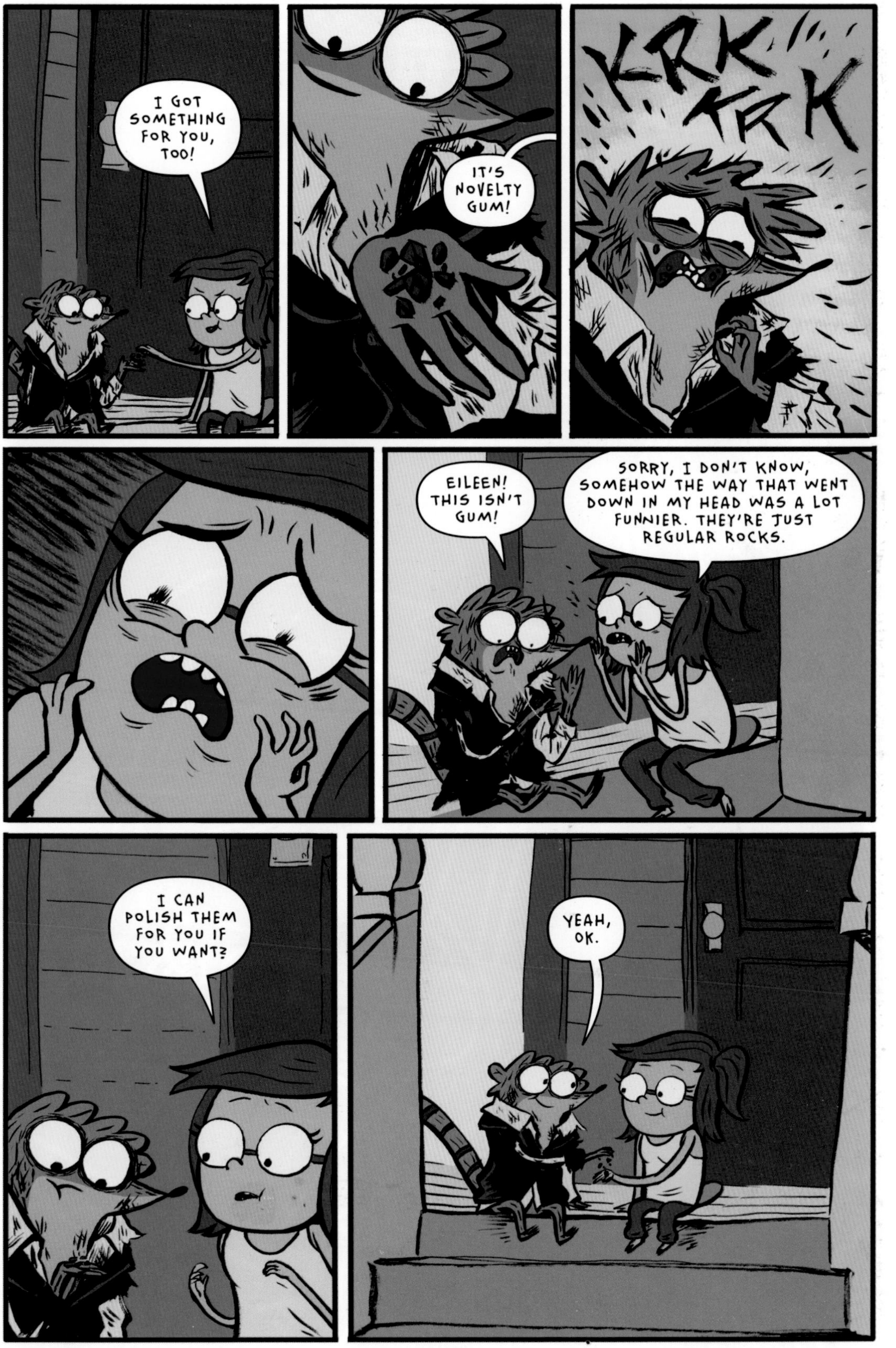
I GOT SOMETHING FOR YOU, TOO!
IT'S NOVELTY GUM!
KRK KRK
EILEEN! THIS ISN'T GUM!
SORRY, I DON'T KNOW, SOMEHOW THE WAY THAT WENT DOWN IN MY HEAD WAS A LOT FUNNIER. THEY'RE JUST REGULAR ROCKS.
I CAN POLISH THEM FOR YOU IF YOU WANT?
YEAH, OK.

GRABBED BY THE GHOSTLIES

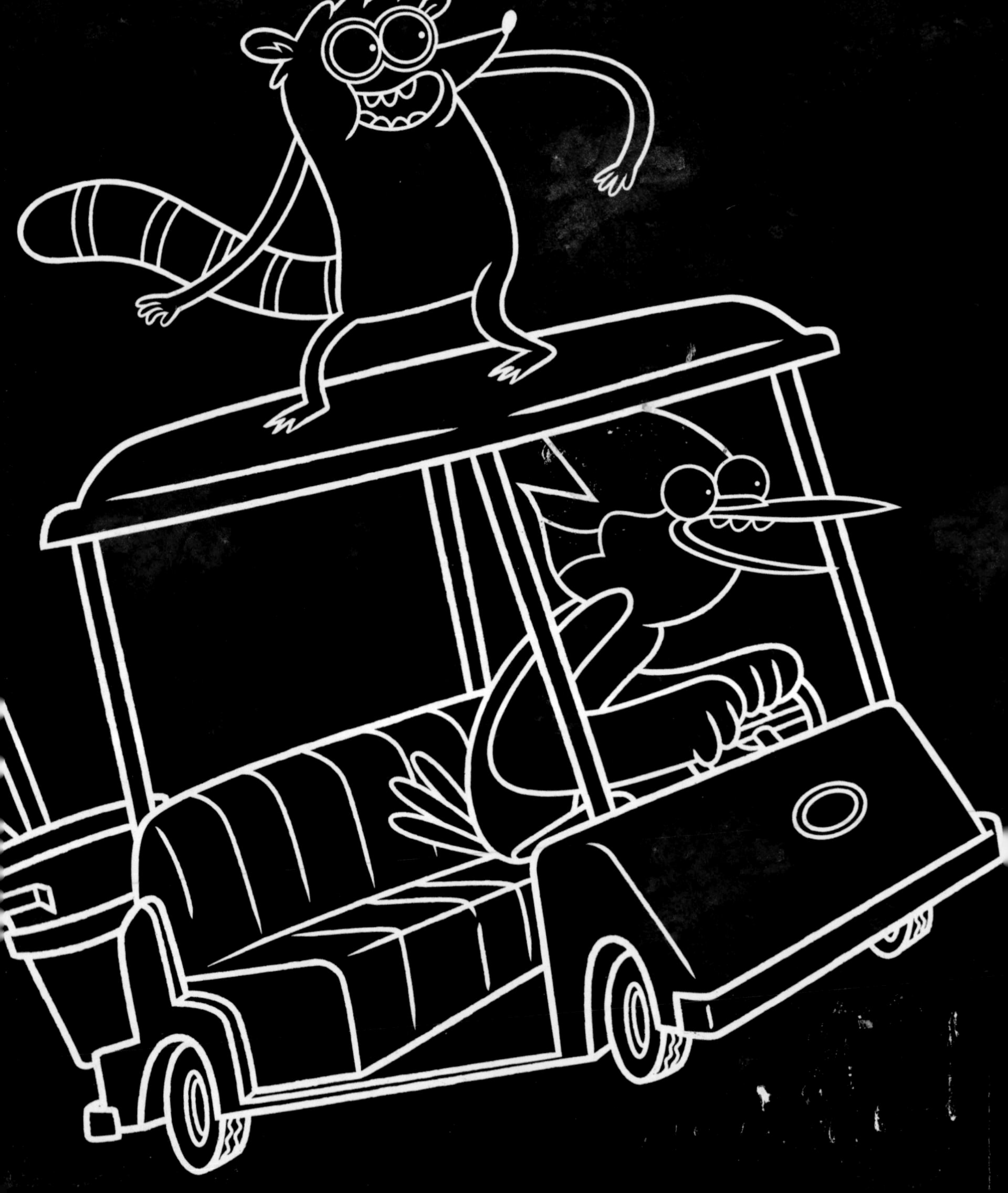

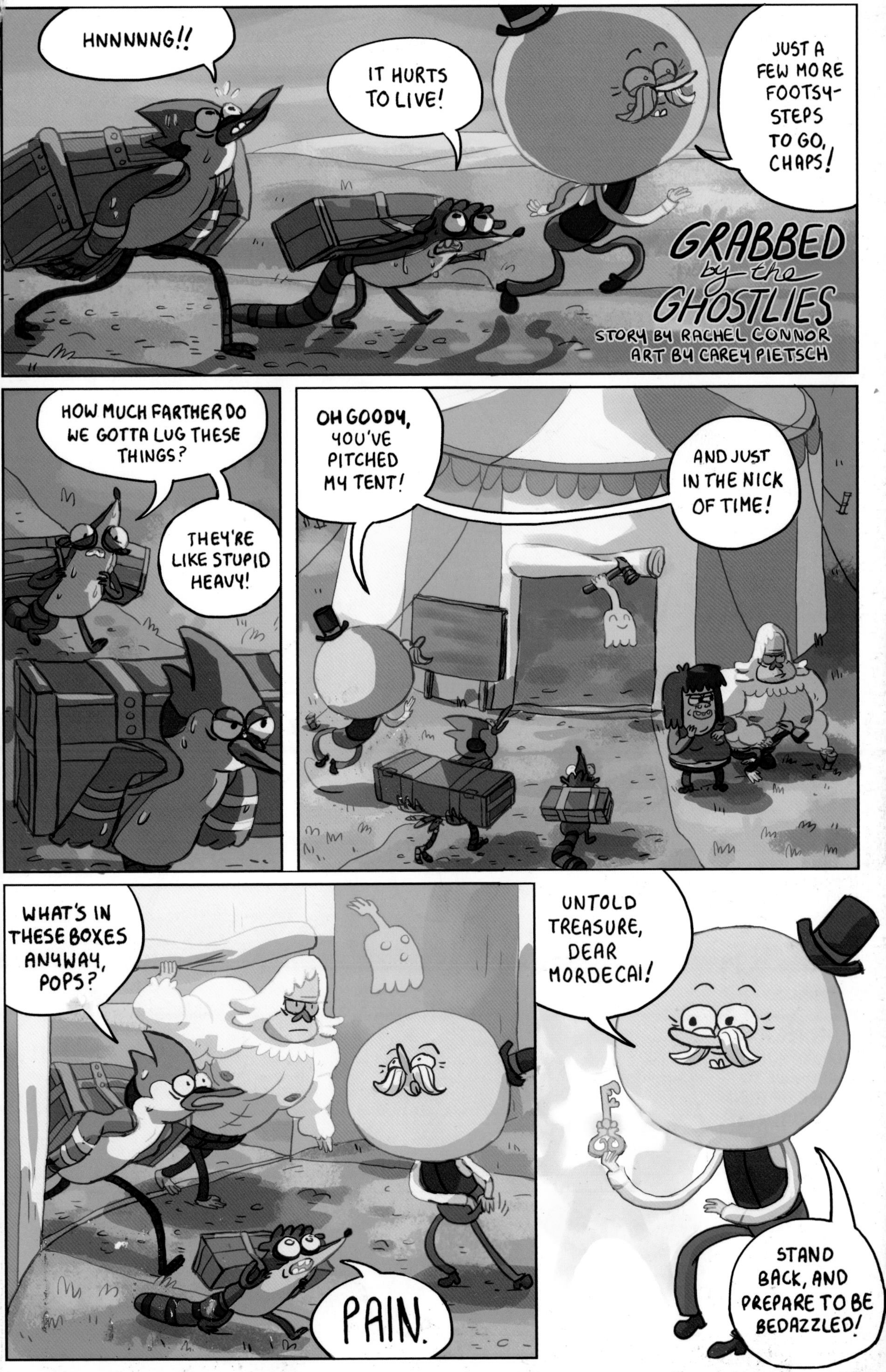
HNNNNNG!!
IT HURTS TO LIVE!
JUST A FEW MORE FOOTSY-STEPS TO GO, CHAPS!
GRABBED by the GHOSTLIES
STORY BY RACHEL CONNOR
ART BY CAREY PIETSCH
HOW MUCH FARTHER DO WE GOTTA LUG THESE THINGS?
THEY'RE LIKE STUPID HEAVY!
OH GOODY, YOU'VE PITCHED MY TENT!
AND JUST IN THE NICK OF TIME!
WHAT'S IN THESE BOXES ANYWAY, POPS?
PAIN.
UNTOLD TREASURE, DEAR MORDECAI!
STAND BACK, AND PREPARE TO BE BEDAZZLED!

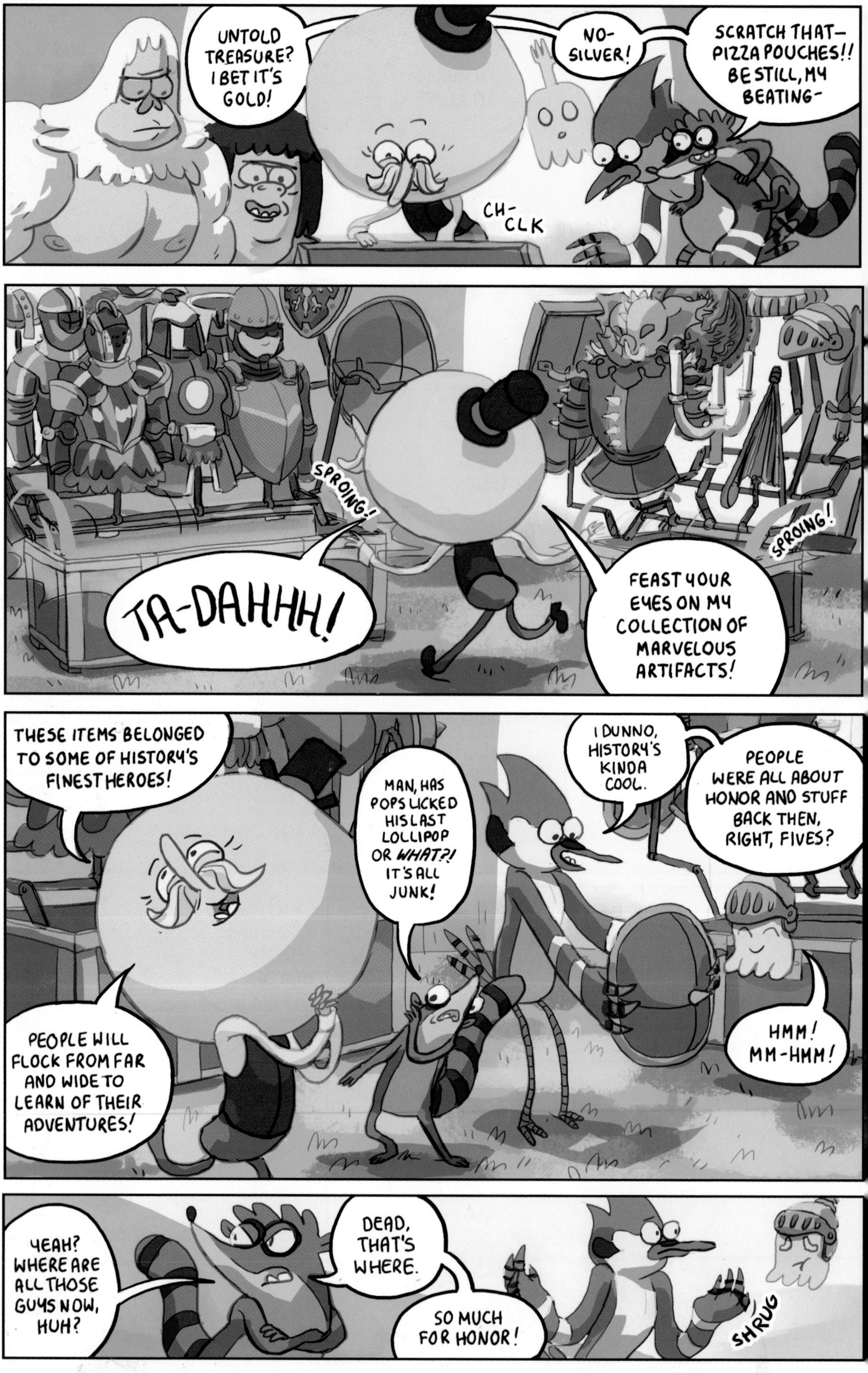
UNTOLD TREASURE? I BET IT'S GOLD!
NO- SILVER!
SCRATCH THAT- PIZZA POUCHES!! BE STILL, MY BEATING-
CH- CLK
SPROING!
TA-DAHHH!
FEAST YOUR EYES ON MY COLLECTION OF MARVELOUS ARTIFACTS!
SPROING!
THESE ITEMS BELONGED TO SOME OF HISTORY'S FINEST HEROES!
PEOPLE WILL FLOCK FROM FAR AND WIDE TO LEARN OF THEIR ADVENTURES!
MAN, HAS POPS LICKED HIS LAST LOLLIPOP OR WHAT?! IT'S ALL JUNK!
I DUNNO, HISTORY'S KINDA COOL.
PEOPLE WERE ALL ABOUT HONOR AND STUFF BACK THEN, RIGHT, FIVES?
HMM! MM-HMM!
YEAH? WHERE ARE ALL THOSE GUYS NOW, HUH?
DEAD, THAT'S WHERE.
SO MUCH FOR HONOR!
SHRUG

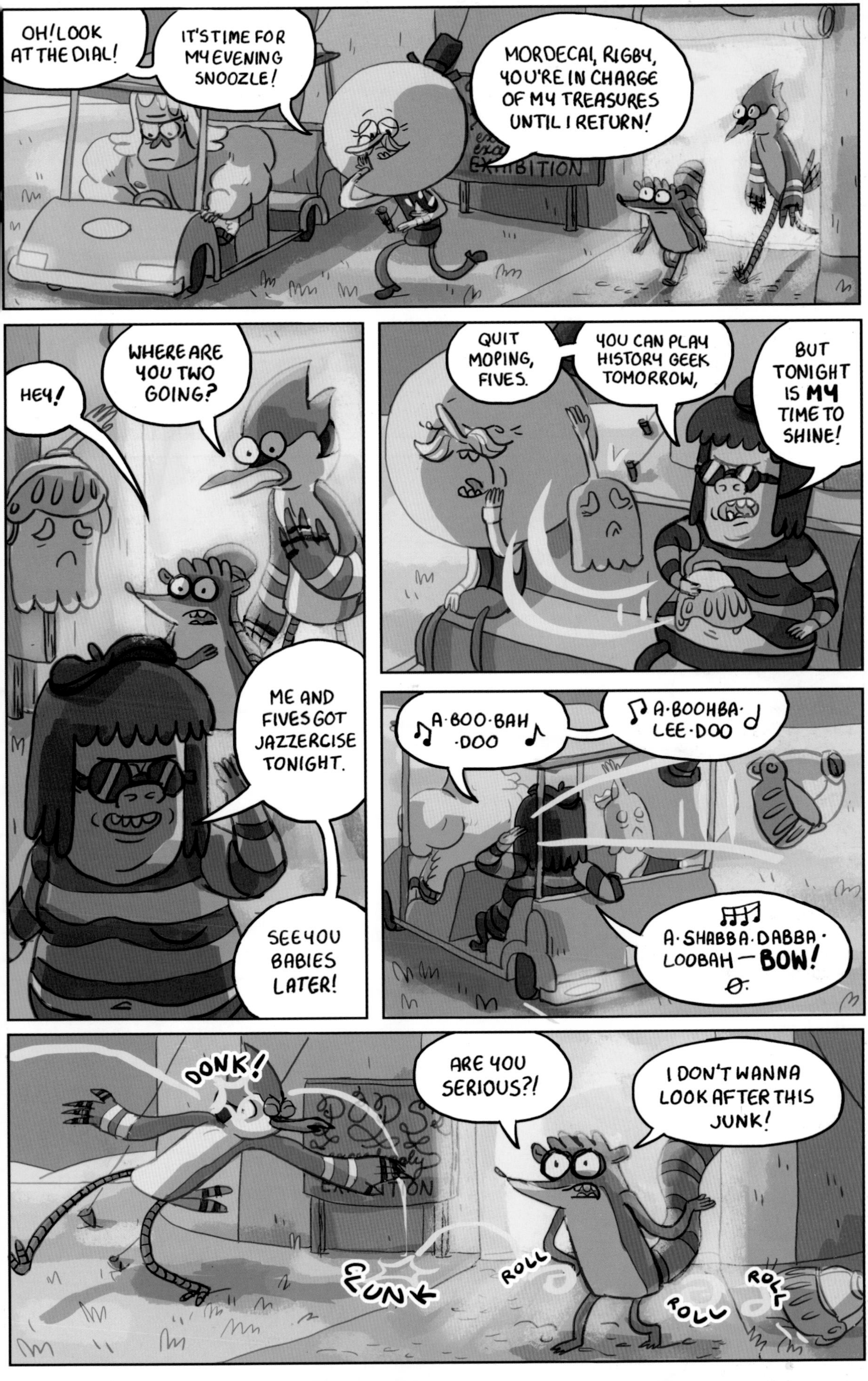
OH! LOOK AT THE DIAL!
IT'S TIME FOR MY EVENING SNOOZLE!
MORDECAI, RIGBY, YOU'RE IN CHARGE OF MY TREASURES UNTIL I RETURN!
EXHIBITION
HEY!
WHERE ARE YOU TWO GOING?
ME AND FIVES GOT JAZZERCISE TONIGHT.
SEE YOU BABIES LATER!
QUIT MOPING, FIVES.
YOU CAN PLAY HISTORY GEEK TOMORROW,
BUT TONIGHT IS **MY** TIME TO SHINE!
A·BOO·BAH ·DOO
A·BOOHBA· LEE·DOO
A·SHABBA·DABBA· LOOBAH—**BOW!**
DONK!
ARE YOU SERIOUS?!
I DON'T WANNA LOOK AFTER THIS JUNK!
CLUNK
ROLL
ROLL
ROLL

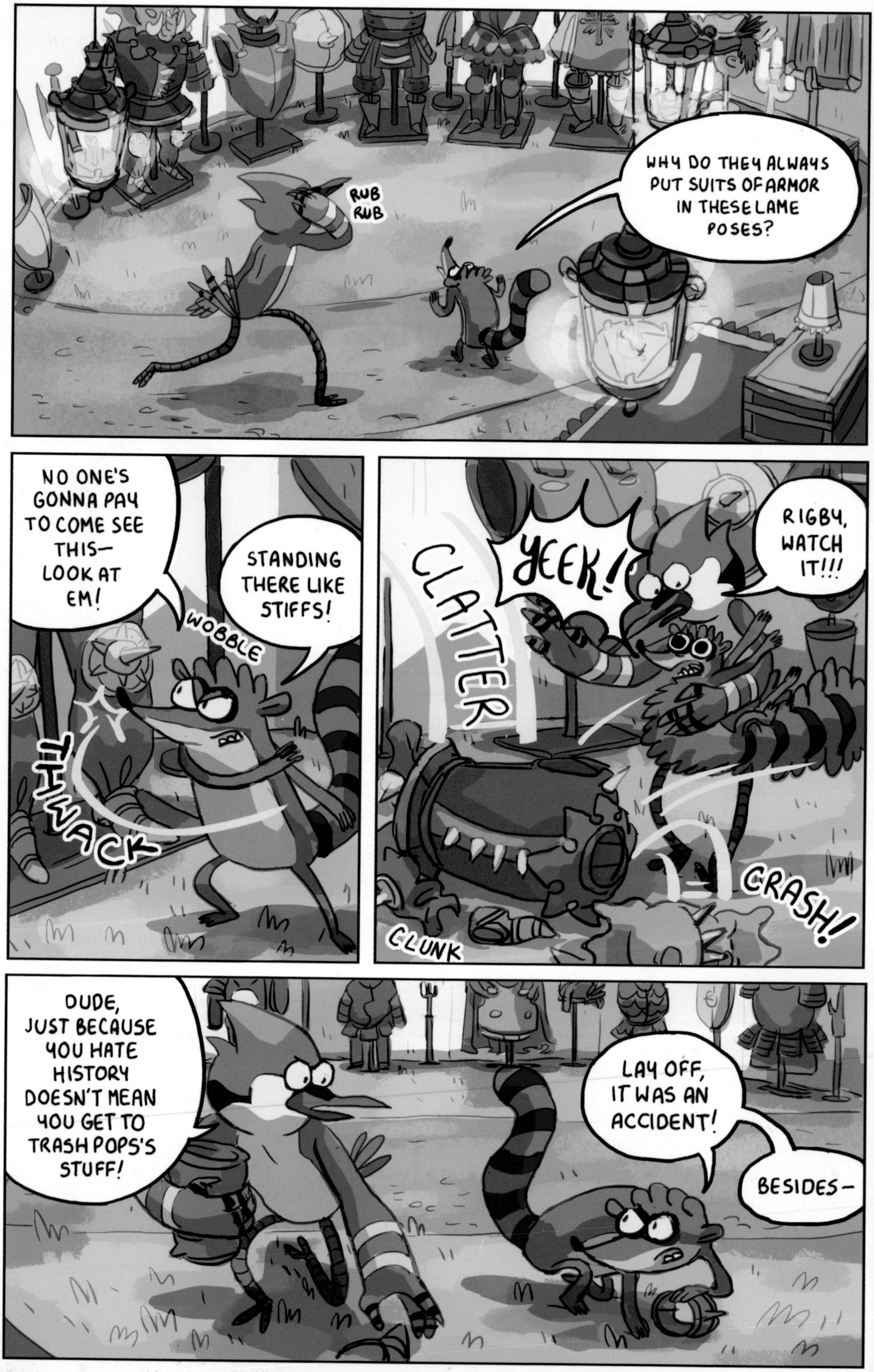
RUB RUB
WHY DO THEY ALWAYS PUT SUITS OF ARMOR IN THESE LAME POSES?
NO ONE'S GONNA PAY TO COME SEE THIS— LOOK AT EM!
STANDING THERE LIKE STIFFS!
WOBBLE
THWACK
CLATTER
YEEK!
RIGBY, WATCH IT!!!
CRASH!
CLUNK
DUDE, JUST BECAUSE YOU HATE HISTORY DOESN'T MEAN YOU GET TO TRASH POPS'S STUFF!
LAY OFF, IT WAS AN ACCIDENT!
BESIDES—

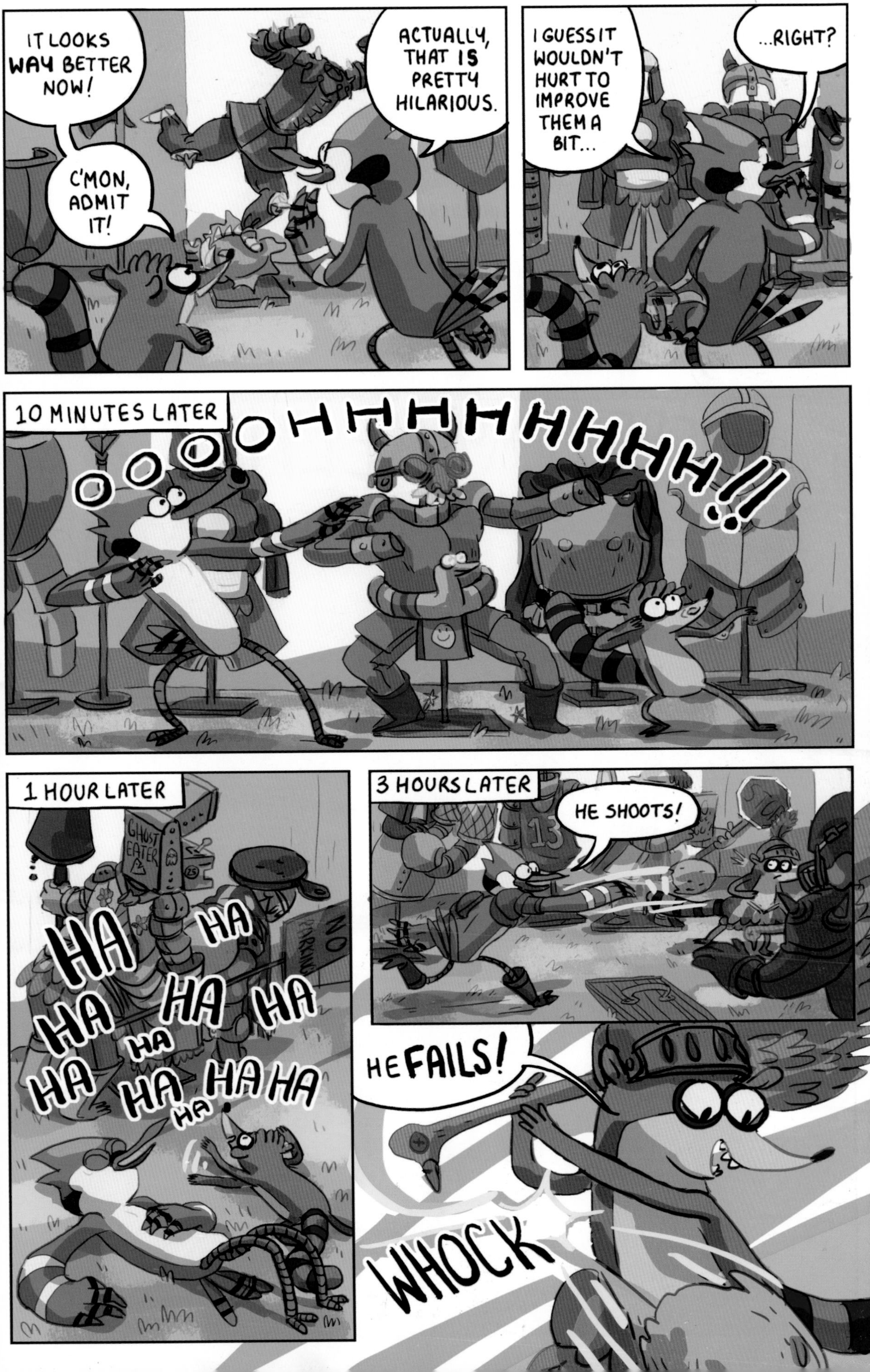
IT LOOKS WAY BETTER NOW!
C'MON, ADMIT IT!
ACTUALLY, THAT IS PRETTY HILARIOUS.
I GUESS IT WOULDN'T HURT TO IMPROVE THEM A BIT...
...RIGHT?
10 MINUTES LATER
OOOOOHHHHHHHHHH!!!
1 HOUR LATER
GHOST EATER
NO PARKING
HA HA HA HA HA HA HA HA HA HA HA HA
3 HOURS LATER
HE SHOOTS!
13
HE FAILS!
WHOCK

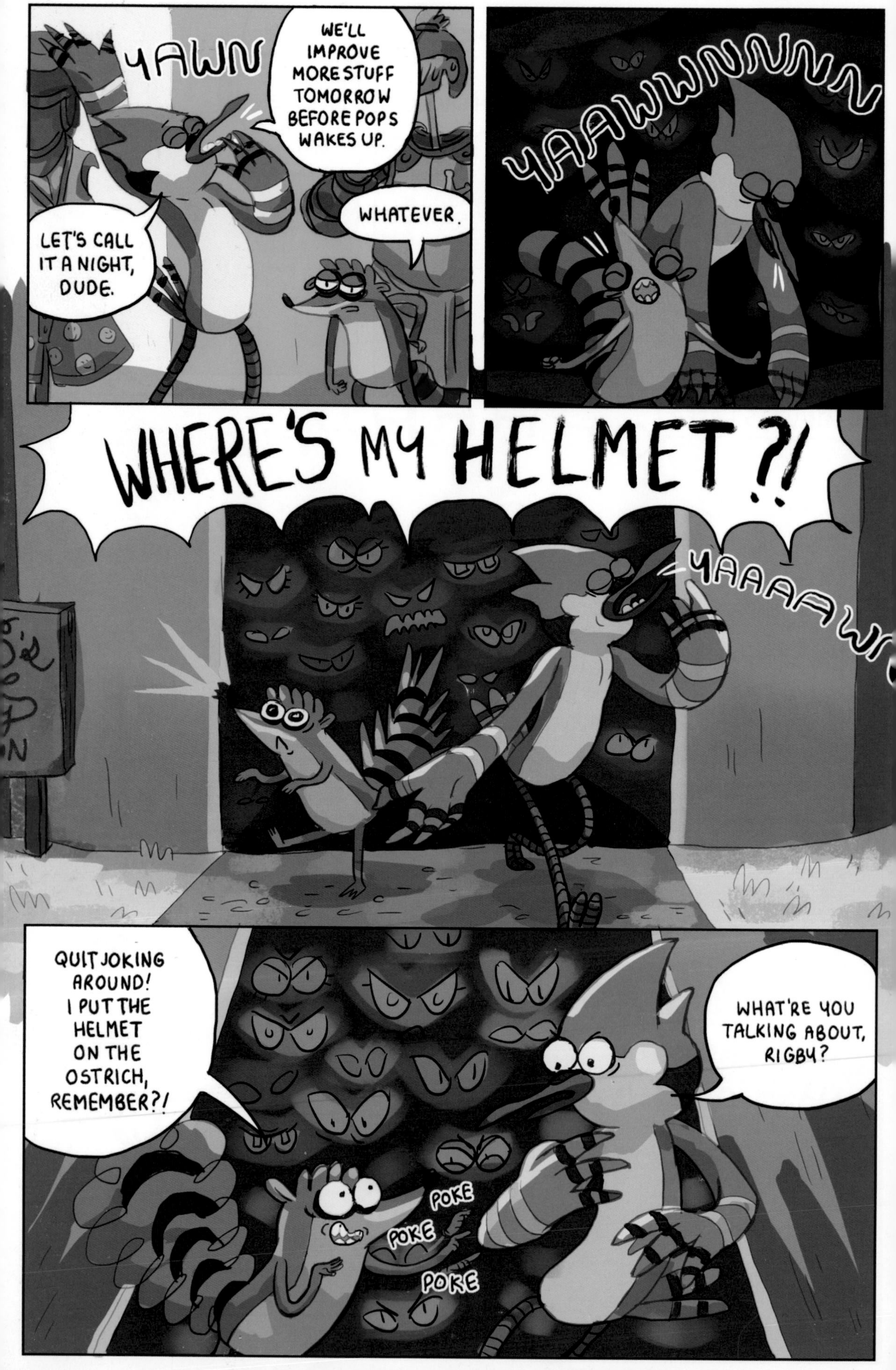
YAWN
WE'LL IMPROVE MORE STUFF TOMORROW BEFORE POPS WAKES UP.
LET'S CALL IT A NIGHT, DUDE.
WHATEVER.
YAAWWNNNNN
WHERE'S MY HELMET?!
YAAAAAWN
QUIT JOKING AROUND! I PUT THE HELMET ON THE OSTRICH, REMEMBER?!
WHAT'RE YOU TALKING ABOUT, RIGBY?
POKE
POKE
POKE

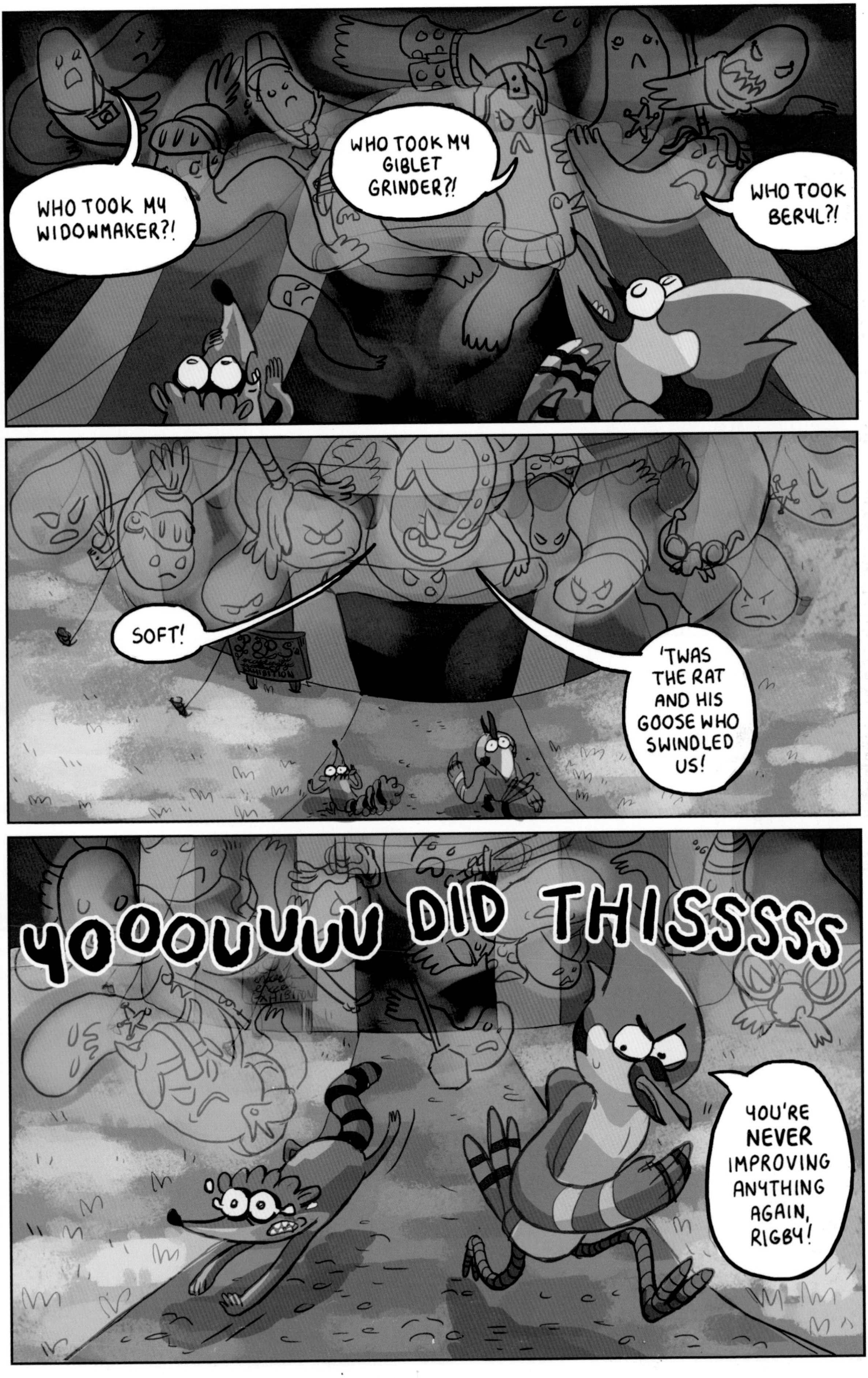
WHO TOOK MY WIDOWMAKER?!
WHO TOOK MY GIBLET GRINDER?!
WHO TOOK BERYL?!
SOFT!
'TWAS THE RAT AND HIS GOOSE WHO SWINDLED US!
YOOOUUUU DID THISSSSS
YOU'RE NEVER IMPROVING ANYTHING AGAIN, RIGBY!

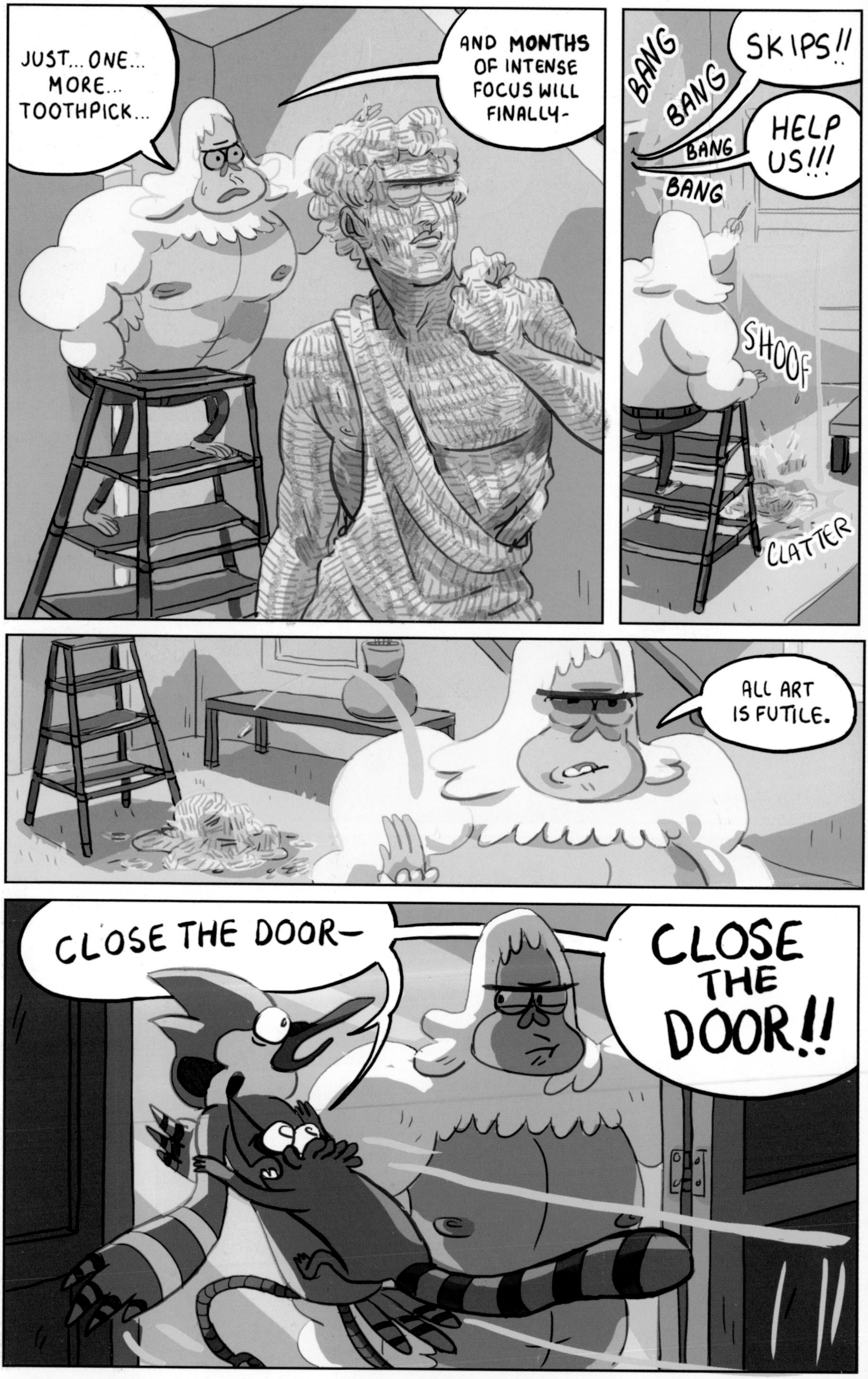
JUST... ONE... MORE... TOOTHPICK...
AND MONTHS OF INTENSE FOCUS WILL FINALLY-
BANG
BANG
BANG
BANG
SKIPS!!
HELP US!!!
SHOOF
CLATTER
ALL ART IS FUTILE.
CLOSE THE DOOR-
CLOSE THE DOOR!!

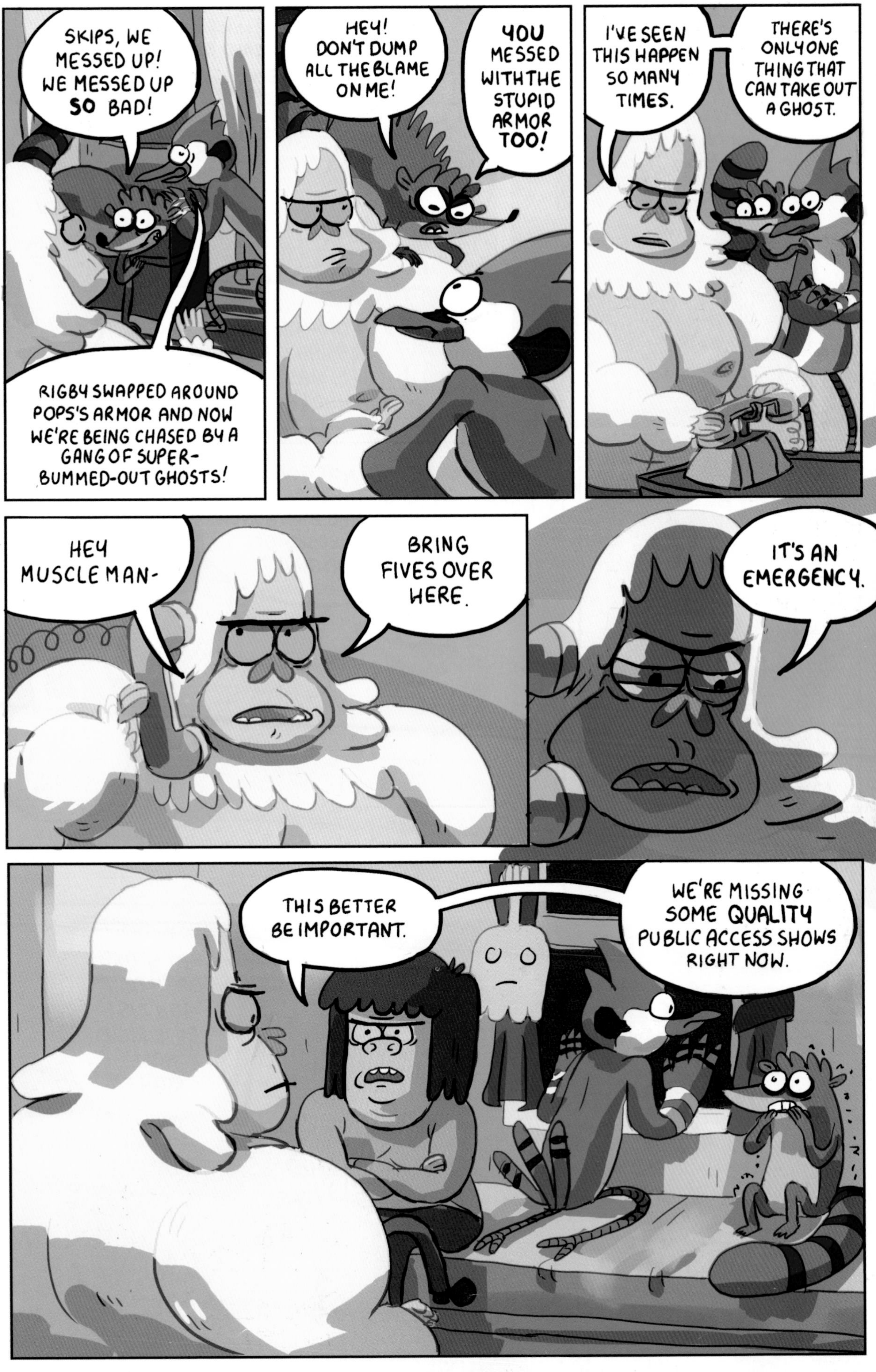
SKIPS, WE MESSED UP! WE MESSED UP SO BAD!
RIGBY SWAPPED AROUND POPS'S ARMOR AND NOW WE'RE BEING CHASED BY A GANG OF SUPER-BUMMED-OUT GHOSTS!
HEY! DON'T DUMP ALL THE BLAME ON ME!
YOU MESSED WITH THE STUPID ARMOR TOO!
I'VE SEEN THIS HAPPEN SO MANY TIMES.
THERE'S ONLY ONE THING THAT CAN TAKE OUT A GHOST.
HEY MUSCLE MAN-
BRING FIVES OVER HERE.
IT'S AN EMERGENCY.
THIS BETTER BE IMPORTANT.
WE'RE MISSING SOME QUALITY PUBLIC ACCESS SHOWS RIGHT NOW.

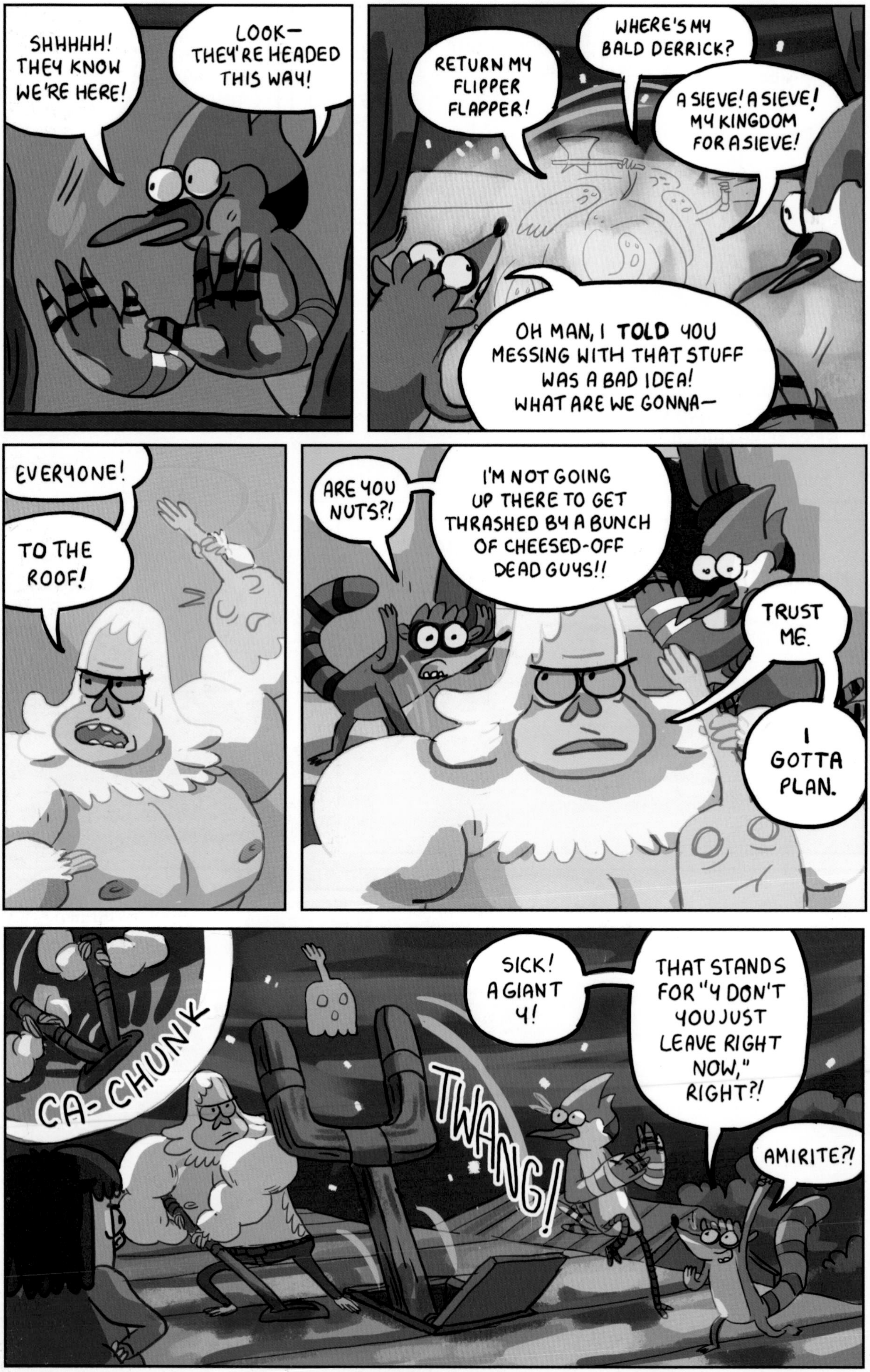
SHHHHH! THEY KNOW WE'RE HERE!
LOOK— THEY'RE HEADED THIS WAY!
RETURN MY FLIPPER FLAPPER!
WHERE'S MY BALD DERRICK?
A SIEVE! A SIEVE! MY KINGDOM FOR A SIEVE!
OH MAN, I **TOLD** YOU MESSING WITH THAT STUFF WAS A BAD IDEA! WHAT ARE WE GONNA—
EVERYONE!
TO THE ROOF!
ARE YOU NUTS?!
I'M NOT GOING UP THERE TO GET THRASHED BY A BUNCH OF CHEESED-OFF DEAD GUYS!!
TRUST ME.
I GOTTA PLAN.
CA-CHUNK
TWANG!
SICK! A GIANT Y!
THAT STANDS FOR "Y DON'T YOU JUST LEAVE RIGHT NOW," RIGHT?!
AMIRITE?!

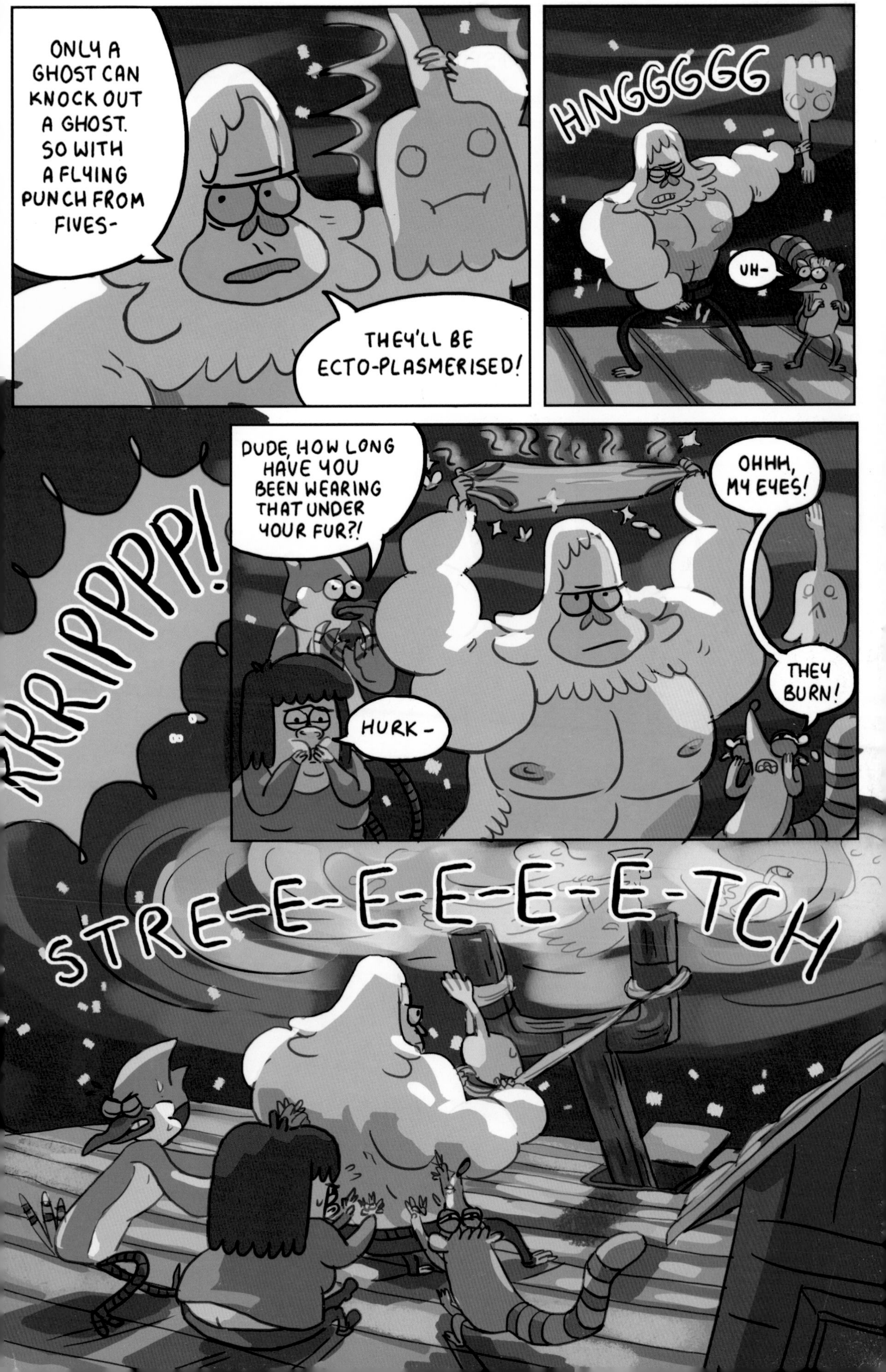
ONLY A GHOST CAN KNOCK OUT A GHOST. SO WITH A FLYING PUNCH FROM FIVES-
THEY'LL BE ECTO-PLASMERISED!
HNGGGGG
UH-
KRRIPPPP!
DUDE, HOW LONG HAVE YOU BEEN WEARING THAT UNDER YOUR FUR?!
OHHH, MY EYES!
THEY BURN!
HURK-
STRE-E-E-E-E-E-TCH

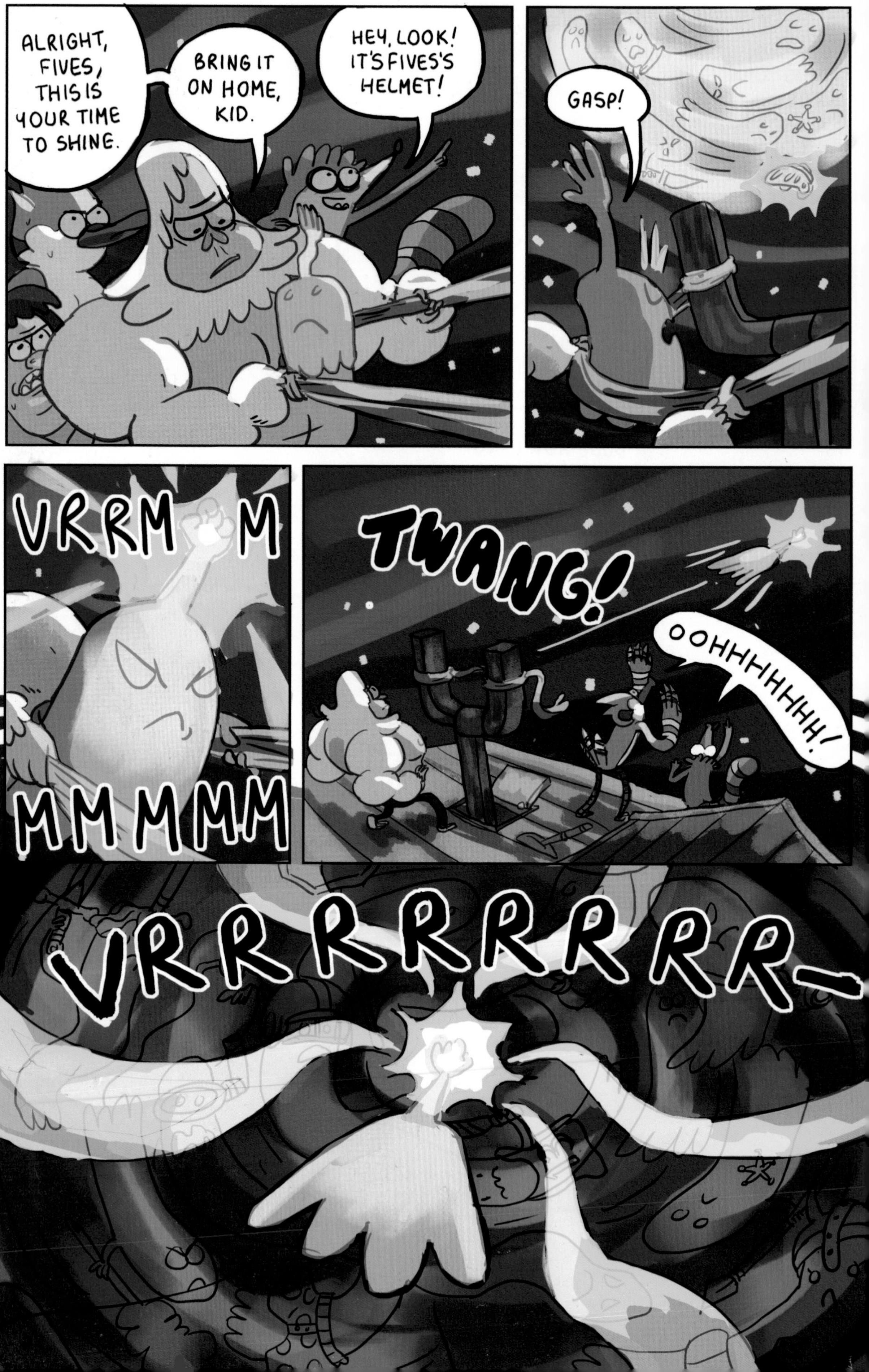
ALRIGHT, FIVES, THIS IS YOUR TIME TO SHINE.
BRING IT ON HOME, KID.
HEY, LOOK! IT'S FIVES'S HELMET!
GASP!
VRRM M
MMMMM
TWANG!
OOHHHHHHH!
VRRRRRRRR—

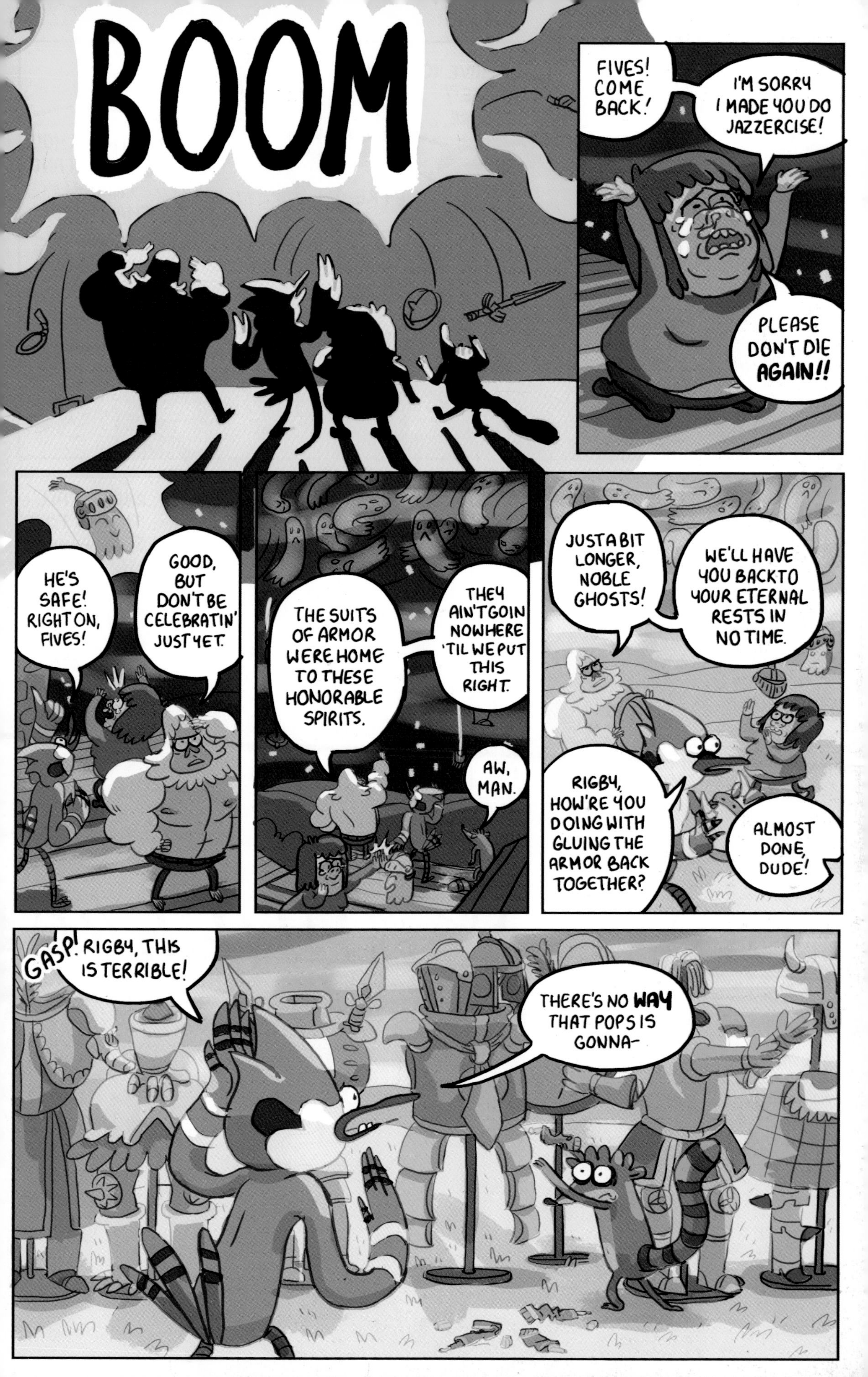
BOOM
FIVES! COME BACK!
I'M SORRY I MADE YOU DO JAZZERCISE!
PLEASE DON'T DIE **AGAIN!!**
HE'S SAFE! RIGHT ON, FIVES!
GOOD, BUT DON'T BE CELEBRATIN' JUST YET.
THE SUITS OF ARMOR WERE HOME TO THESE HONORABLE SPIRITS.
THEY AIN'T GOIN NOWHERE 'TIL WE PUT THIS RIGHT.
AW, MAN.
JUST A BIT LONGER, NOBLE GHOSTS!
WE'LL HAVE YOU BACK TO YOUR ETERNAL RESTS IN NO TIME.
RIGBY, HOW'RE YOU DOING WITH GLUING THE ARMOR BACK TOGETHER?
ALMOST DONE, DUDE!
GASP! RIGBY, THIS IS TERRIBLE!
THERE'S NO **WAY** THAT POPS IS GONNA-

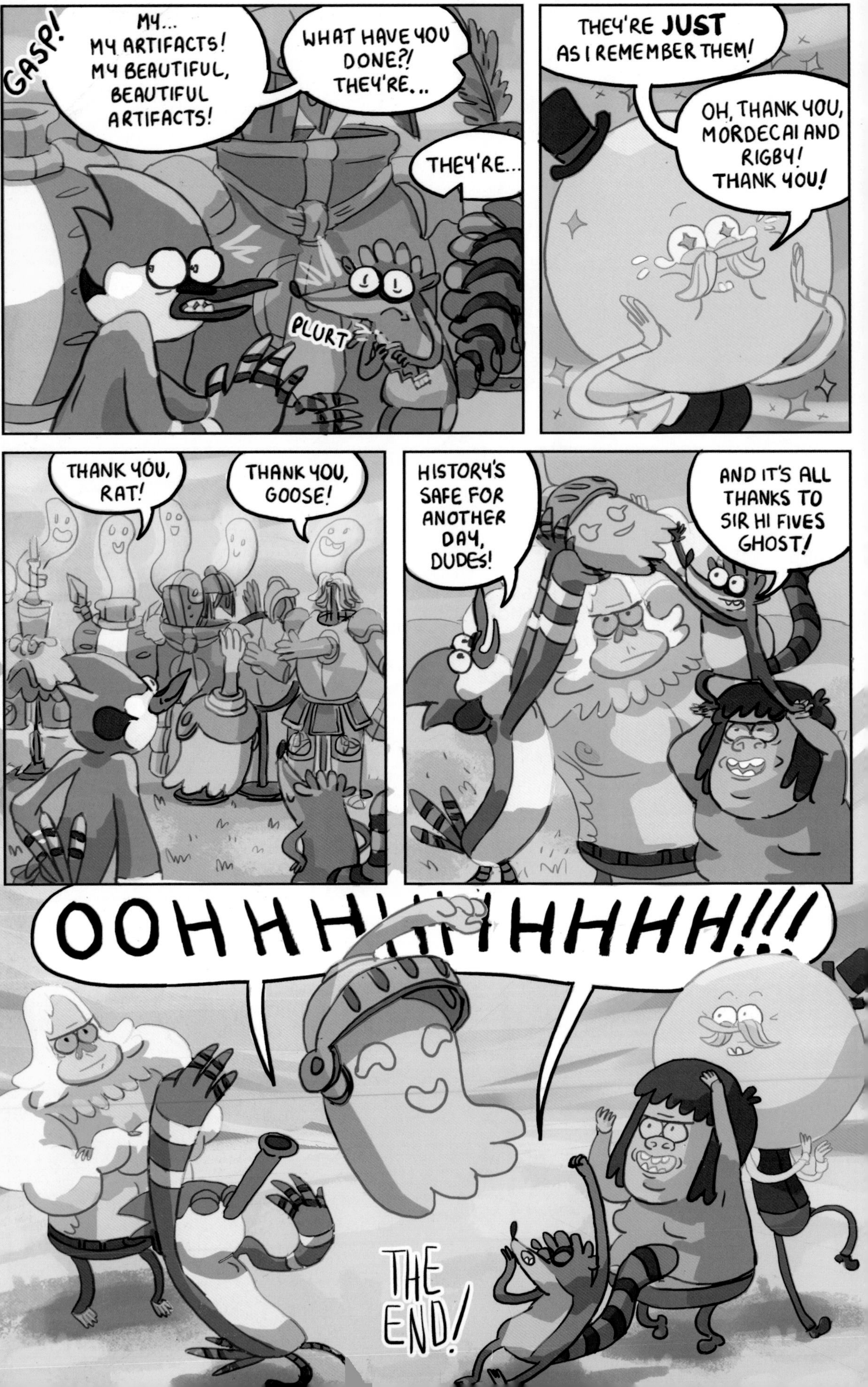
GASP!
MY... MY ARTIFACTS! MY BEAUTIFUL, BEAUTIFUL ARTIFACTS!
WHAT HAVE YOU DONE?! THEY'RE...
THEY'RE...
PLURT
THEY'RE JUST AS I REMEMBER THEM!
OH, THANK YOU, MORDECAI AND RIGBY! THANK YOU!
THANK YOU, RAT!
THANK YOU, GOOSE!
HISTORY'S SAFE FOR ANOTHER DAY, DUDES!
AND IT'S ALL THANKS TO SIR HI FIVES GHOST!
OOHHHHHHHHH!!!
THE END!

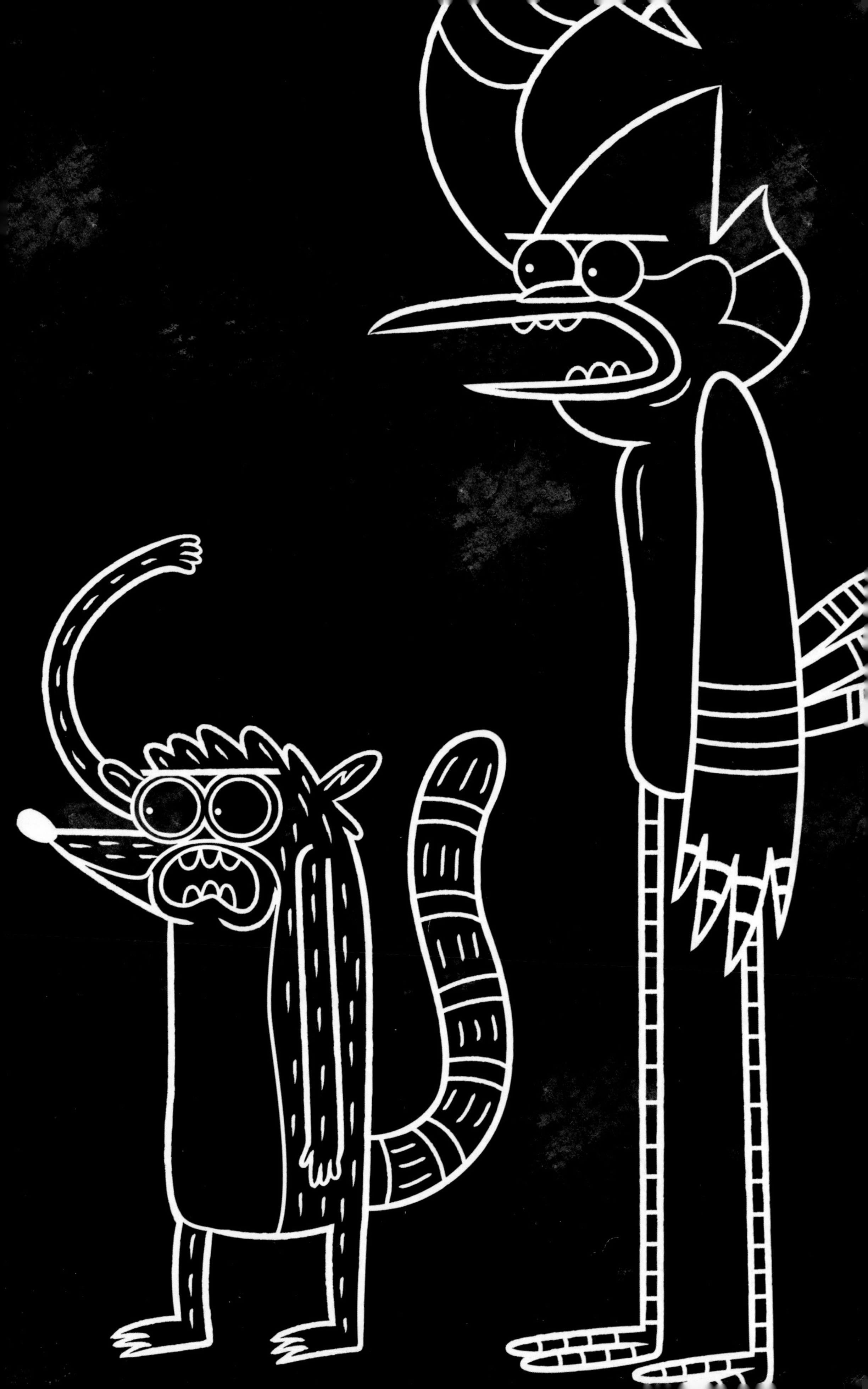

"MORDECAI AND--"

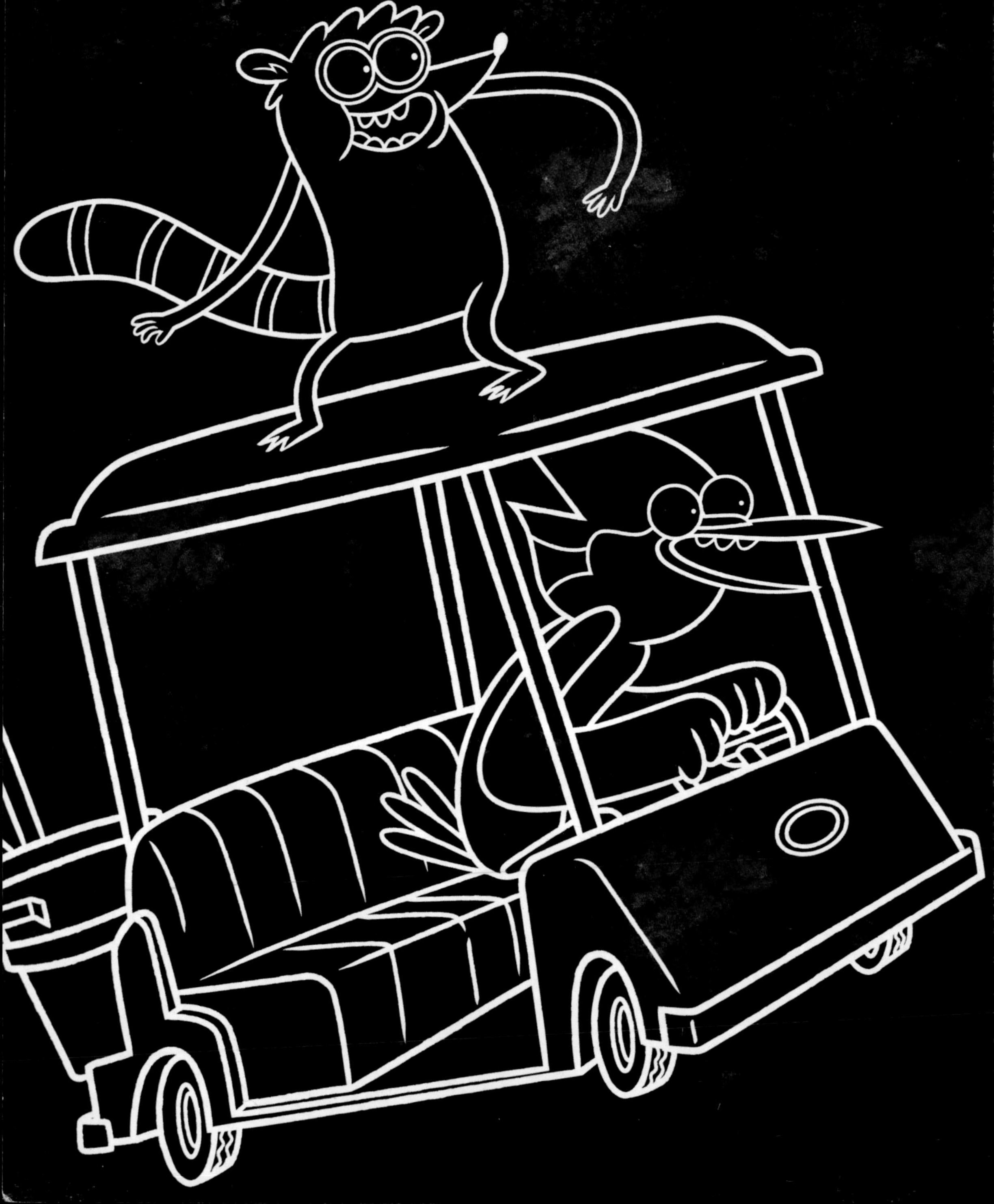

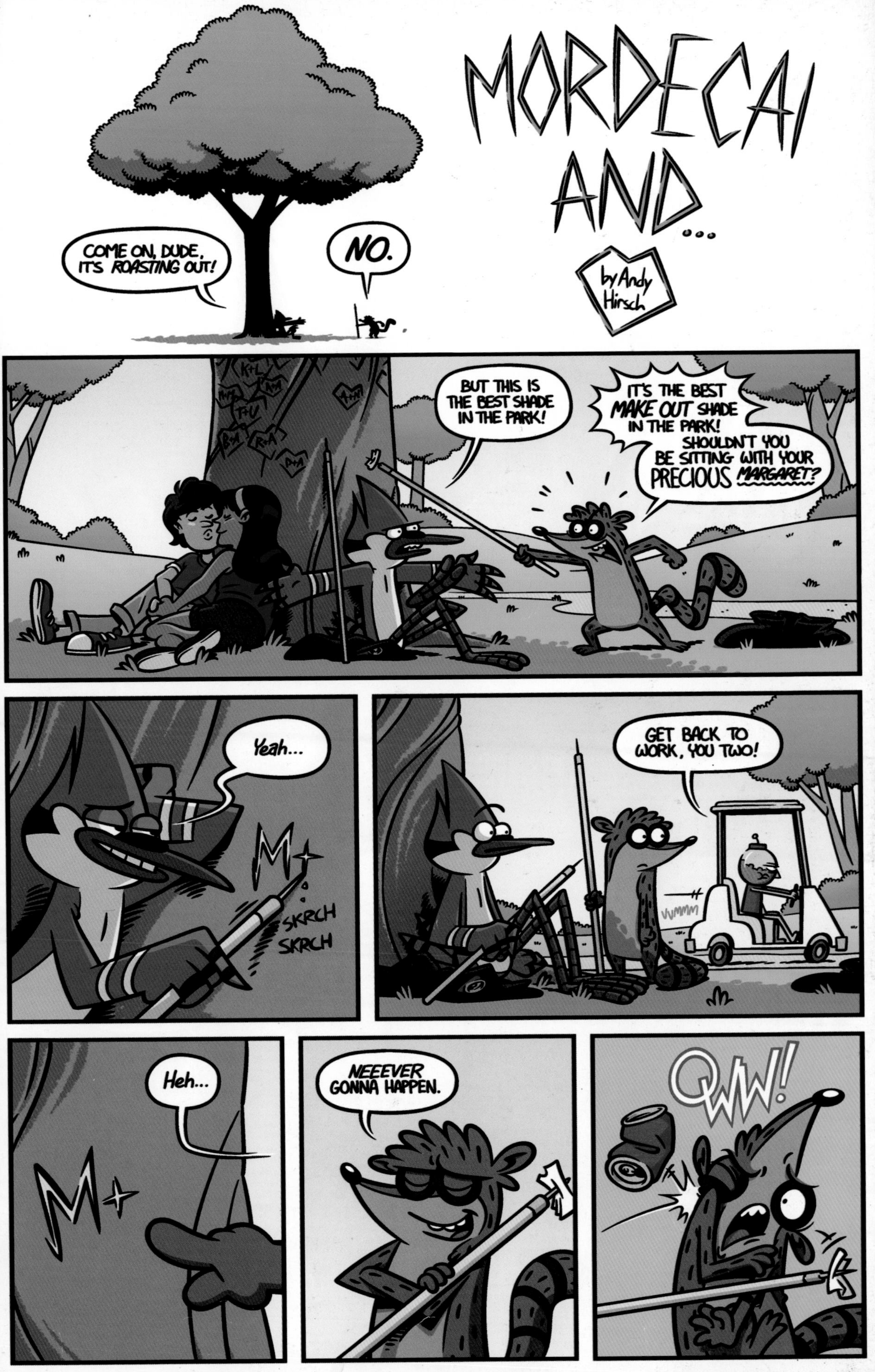
MORDECAI AND...
by Andy Hirsch
COME ON, DUDE, IT'S ROASTING OUT!
NO.
BUT THIS IS THE BEST SHADE IN THE PARK!
IT'S THE BEST MAKE OUT SHADE IN THE PARK! SHOULDN'T YOU BE SITTING WITH YOUR PRECIOUS MARGARET?
Yeah...
SKRCH SKRCH
GET BACK TO WORK, YOU TWO!
VVMMM
Heh...
NEEEVER GONNA HAPPEN.
OWW!

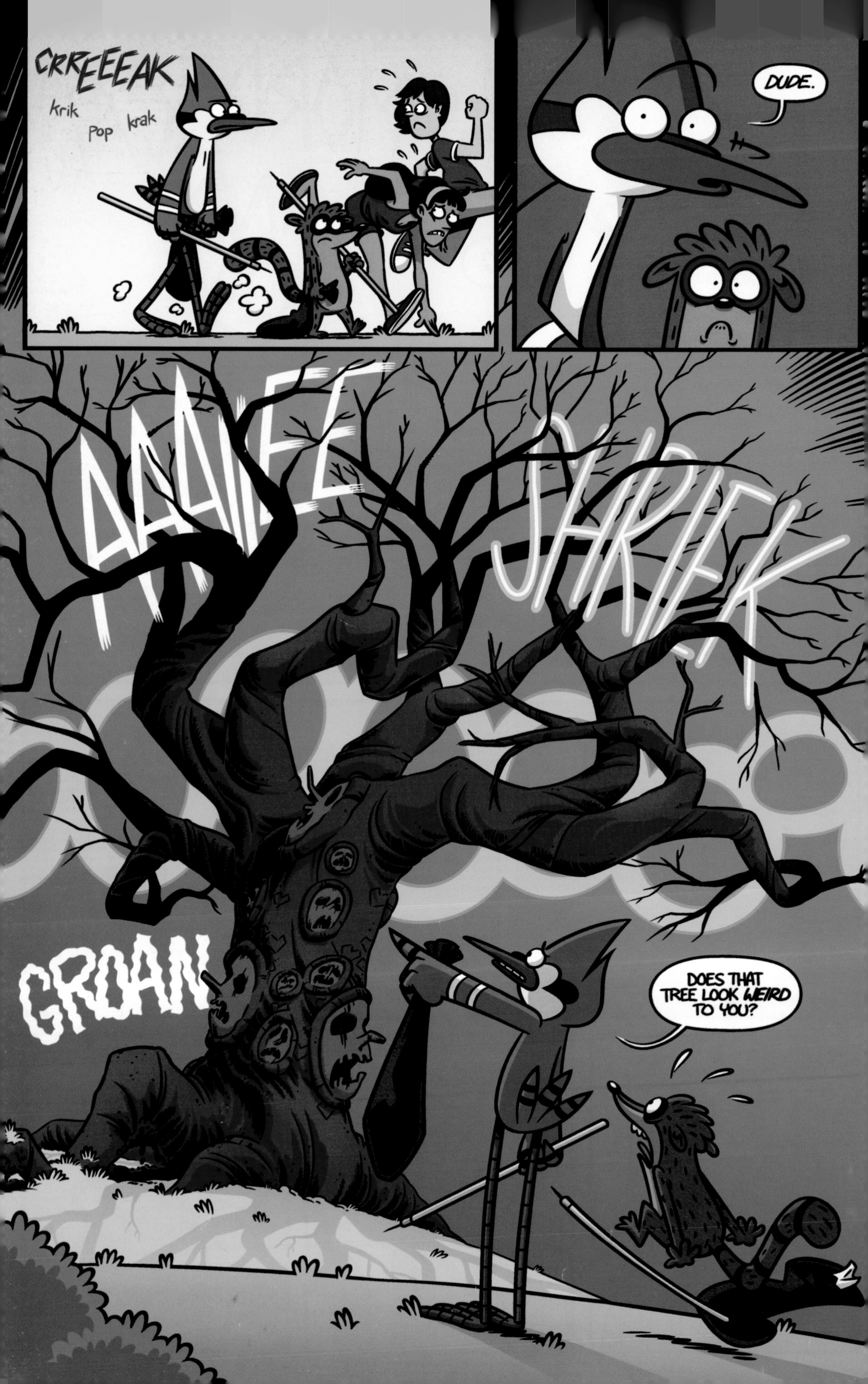
CRREEEEAK
krik
pop
krak
DUDE.
AAAIEE
SHRIEK
GROAN
DOES THAT TREE LOOK WEIRD TO YOU?

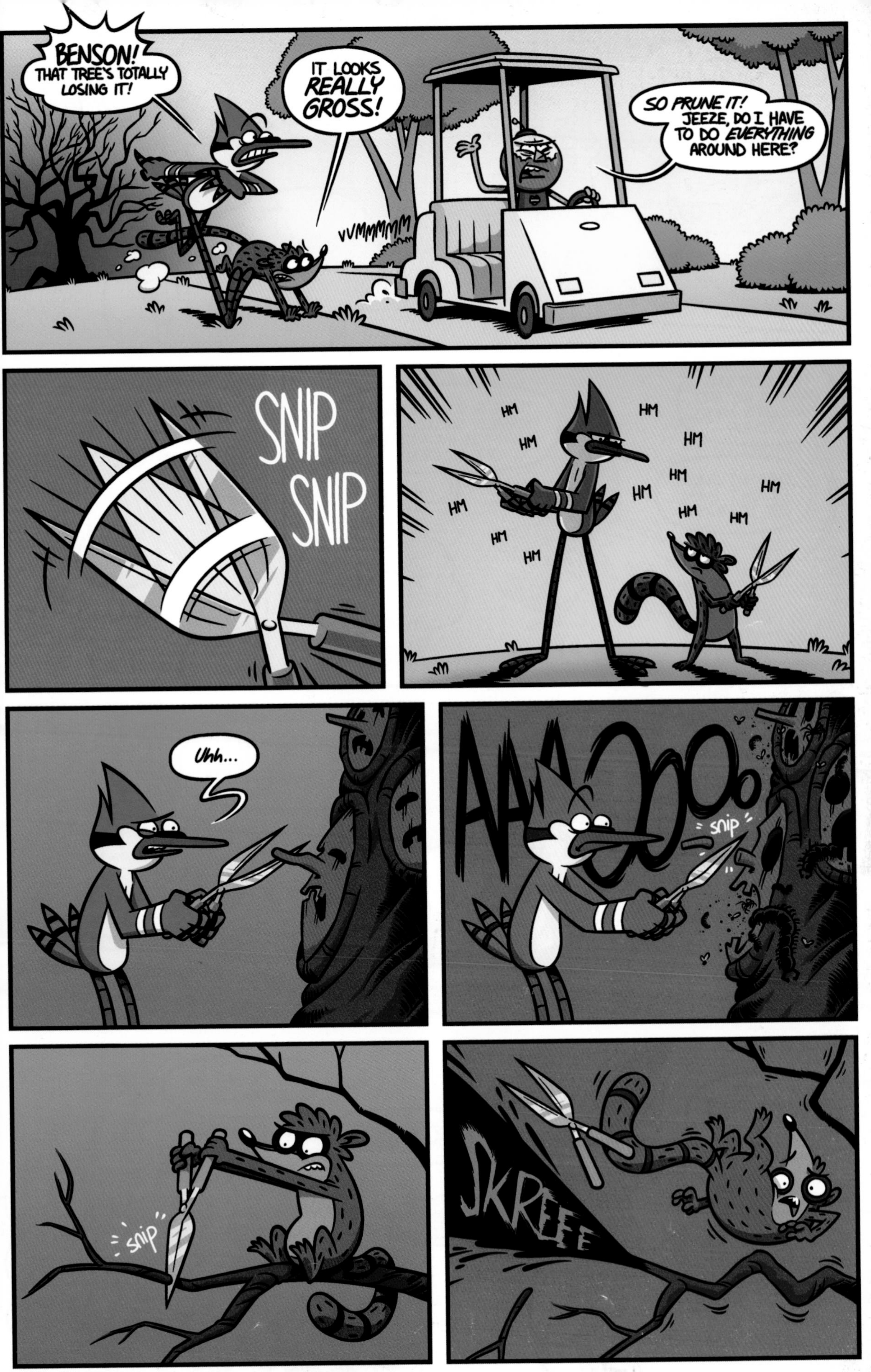
BENSON! THAT TREE'S TOTALLY LOSING IT!
IT LOOKS REALLY GROSS!
VVMMMMM
SO PRUNE IT! JEEZE, DO I HAVE TO DO EVERYTHING AROUND HERE?
SNIP SNIP
HM HM HM HM HM HM HM HM HM HM HM HM
Uhh...
AAAOOOo
snip
snip
SKREEE

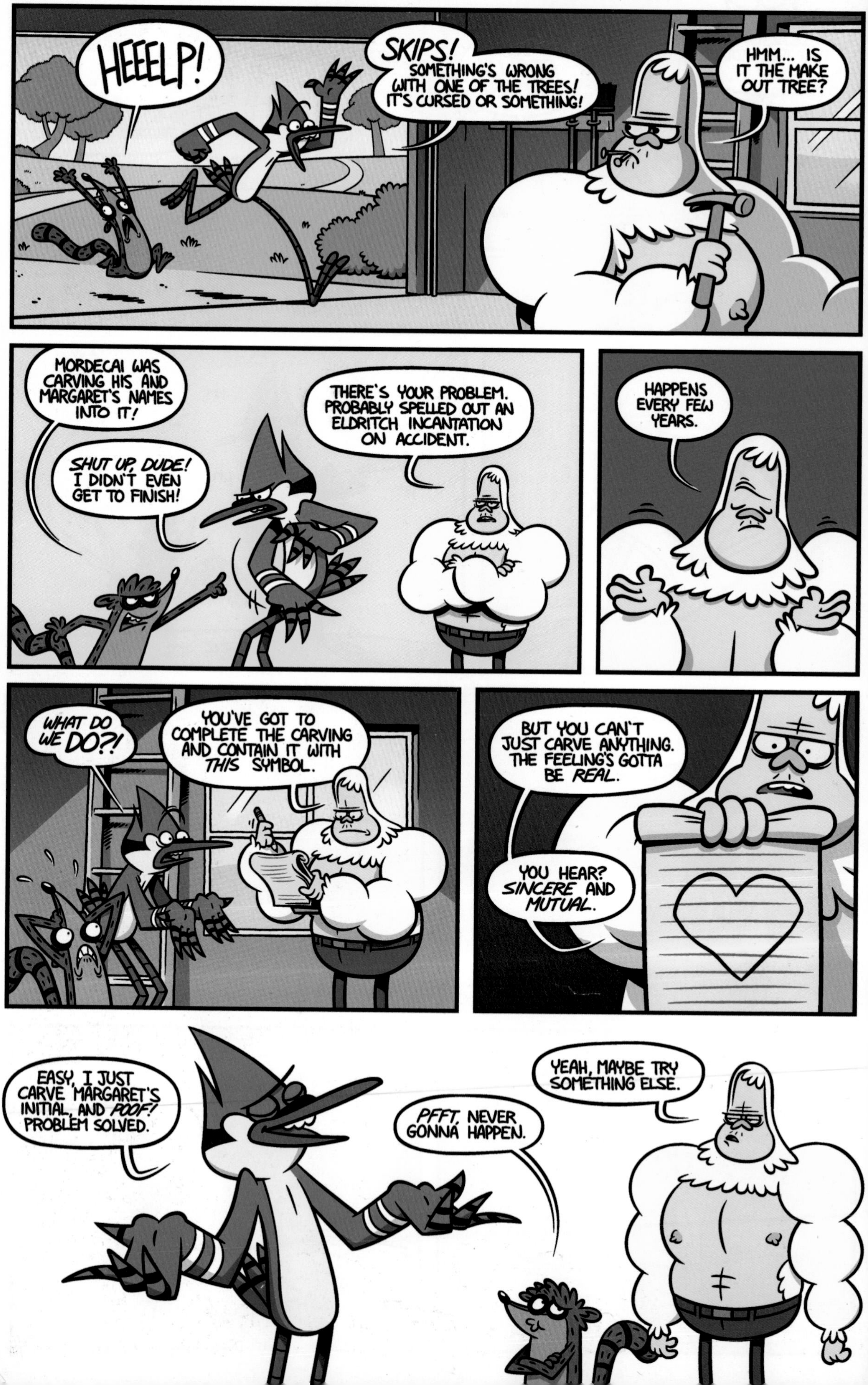
HEEELP!
SKIPS! SOMETHING'S WRONG WITH ONE OF THE TREES! IT'S CURSED OR SOMETHING!
HMM... IS IT THE MAKE OUT TREE?
MORDECAI WAS CARVING HIS AND MARGARET'S NAMES INTO IT!
SHUT UP, DUDE! I DIDN'T EVEN GET TO FINISH!
THERE'S YOUR PROBLEM. PROBABLY SPELLED OUT AN ELDRITCH INCANTATION ON ACCIDENT.
HAPPENS EVERY FEW YEARS.
WHAT DO WE DO?!
YOU'VE GOT TO COMPLETE THE CARVING AND CONTAIN IT WITH THIS SYMBOL.
BUT YOU CAN'T JUST CARVE ANYTHING. THE FEELING'S GOTTA BE REAL.
YOU HEAR? SINCERE AND MUTUAL.
EASY, I JUST CARVE MARGARET'S INITIAL, AND POOF! PROBLEM SOLVED.
PFFT. NEVER GONNA HAPPEN.
YEAH, MAYBE TRY SOMETHING ELSE.

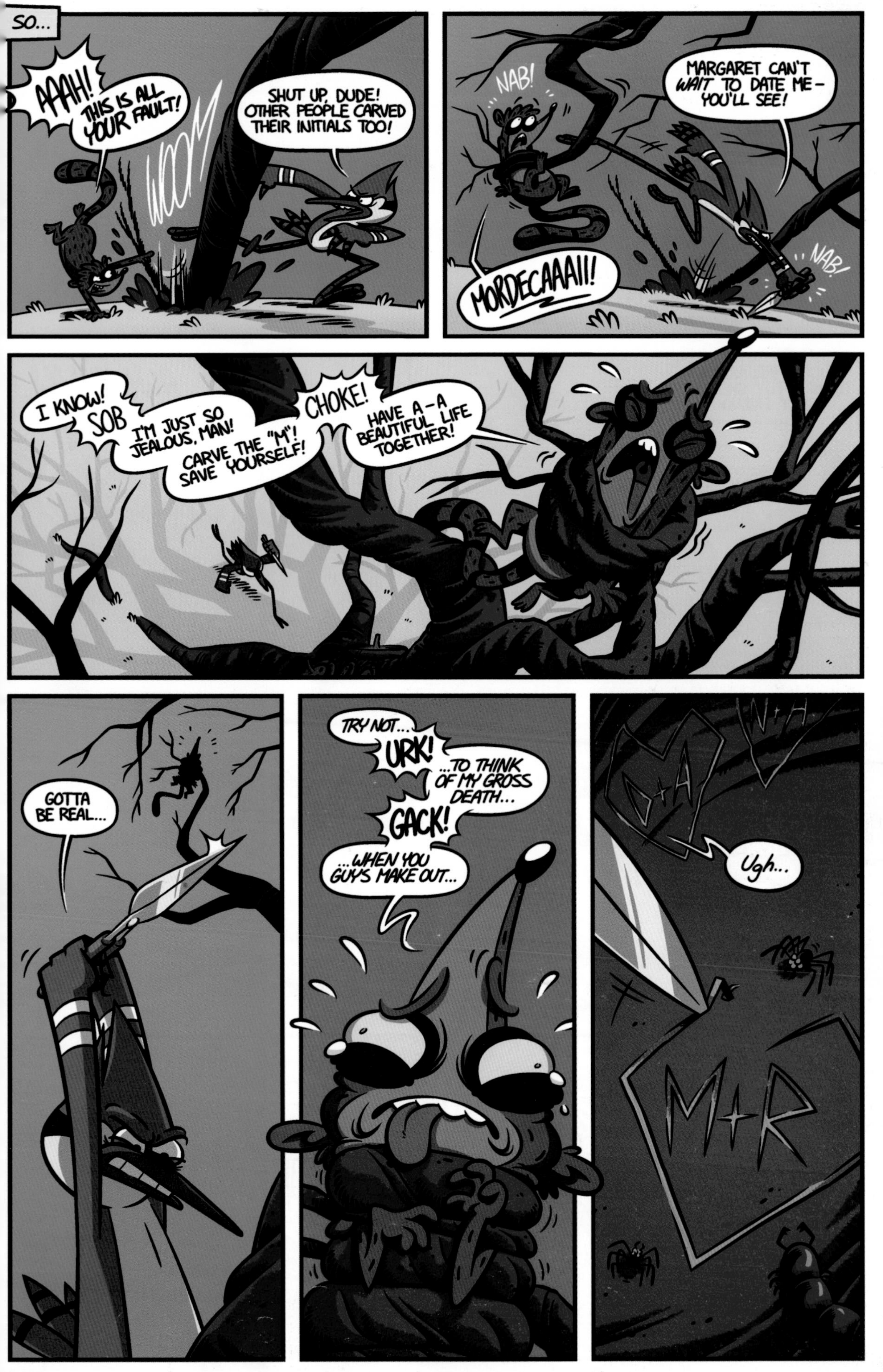
SO...
AAAH!
THIS IS ALL YOUR FAULT!
WOOM
SHUT UP, DUDE! OTHER PEOPLE CARVED THEIR INITIALS TOO!
NAB!
MARGARET CAN'T WAIT TO DATE ME— YOU'LL SEE!
MORDECAAAII!
NAB!
I KNOW!
SOB
I'M JUST SO JEALOUS, MAN!
CARVE THE "M"! SAVE YOURSELF!
CHOKE!
HAVE A—A BEAUTIFUL LIFE TOGETHER!
GOTTA BE REAL...
TRY NOT...
URK!
...TO THINK OF MY GROSS DEATH...
GACK!
...WHEN YOU GUYS MAKE OUT...
Ugh...
M+R

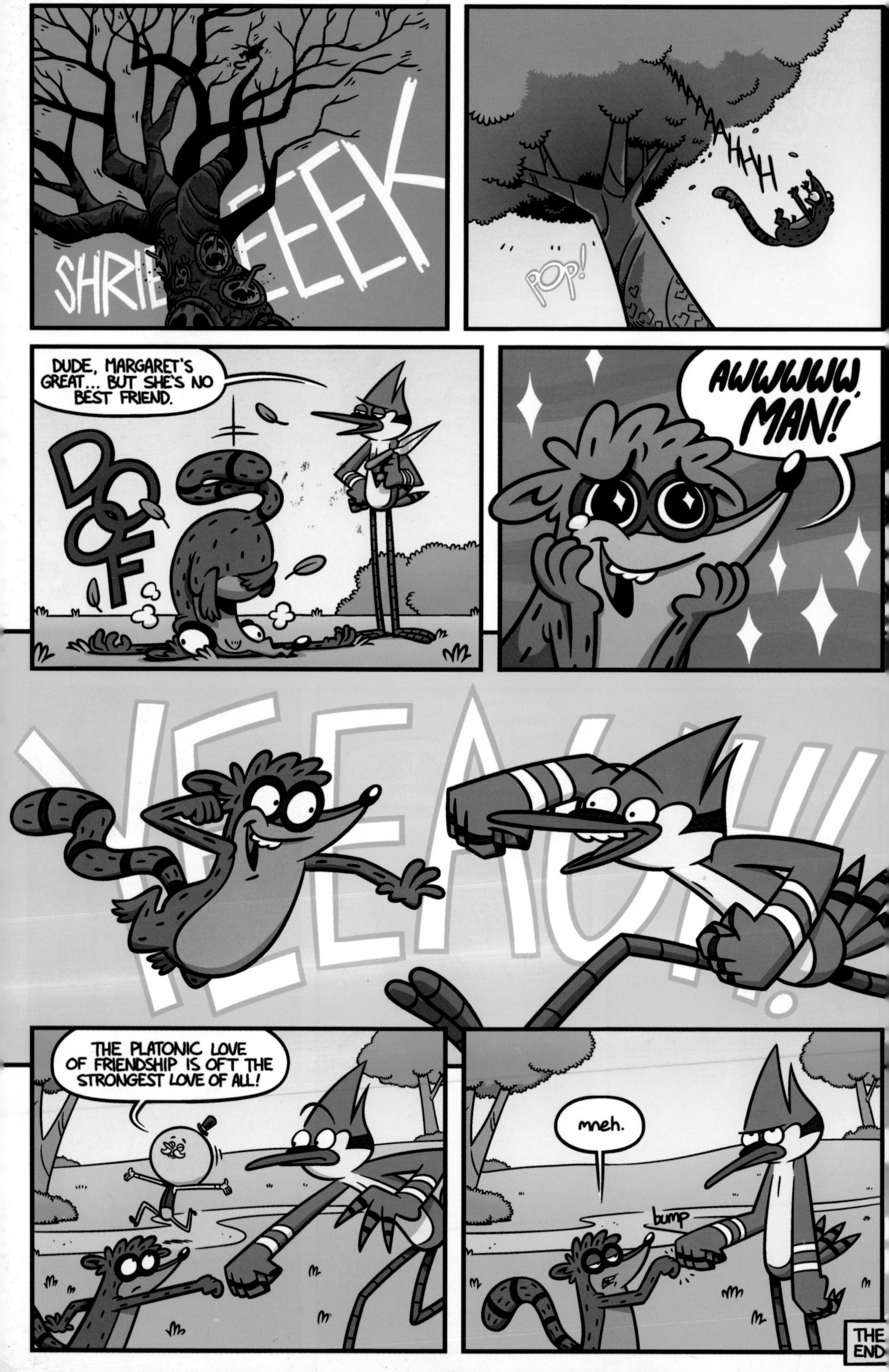
SHRIEEEEK
AAAAAAAAHHHH
POP!
DUDE, MARGARET'S GREAT... BUT SHE'S NO BEST FRIEND.
DOOF
AWWWWW, MAN!
YEEAGH!
THE PLATONIC LOVE OF FRIENDSHIP IS OFT THE STRONGEST LOVE OF ALL!
mneh.
bump
THE END

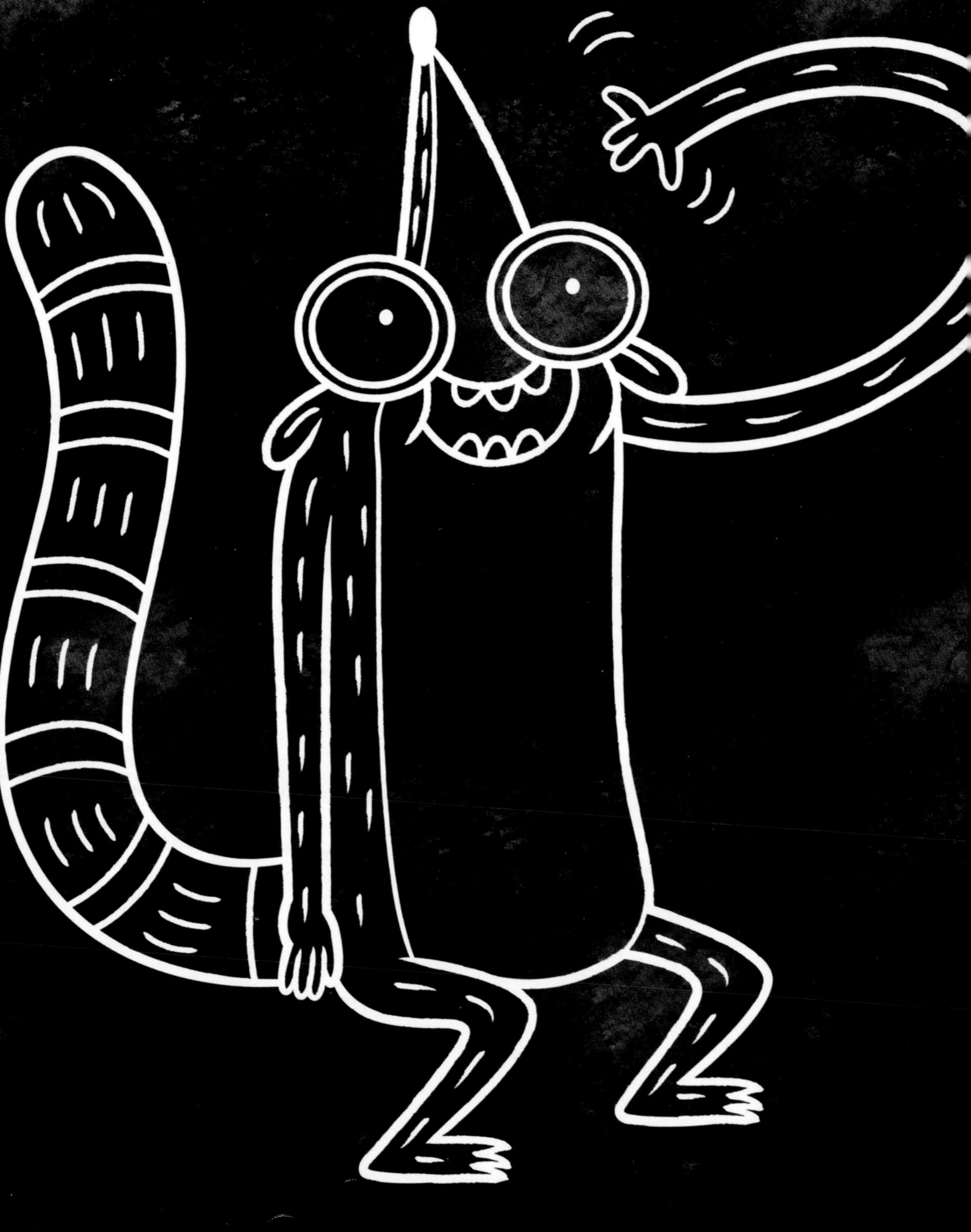

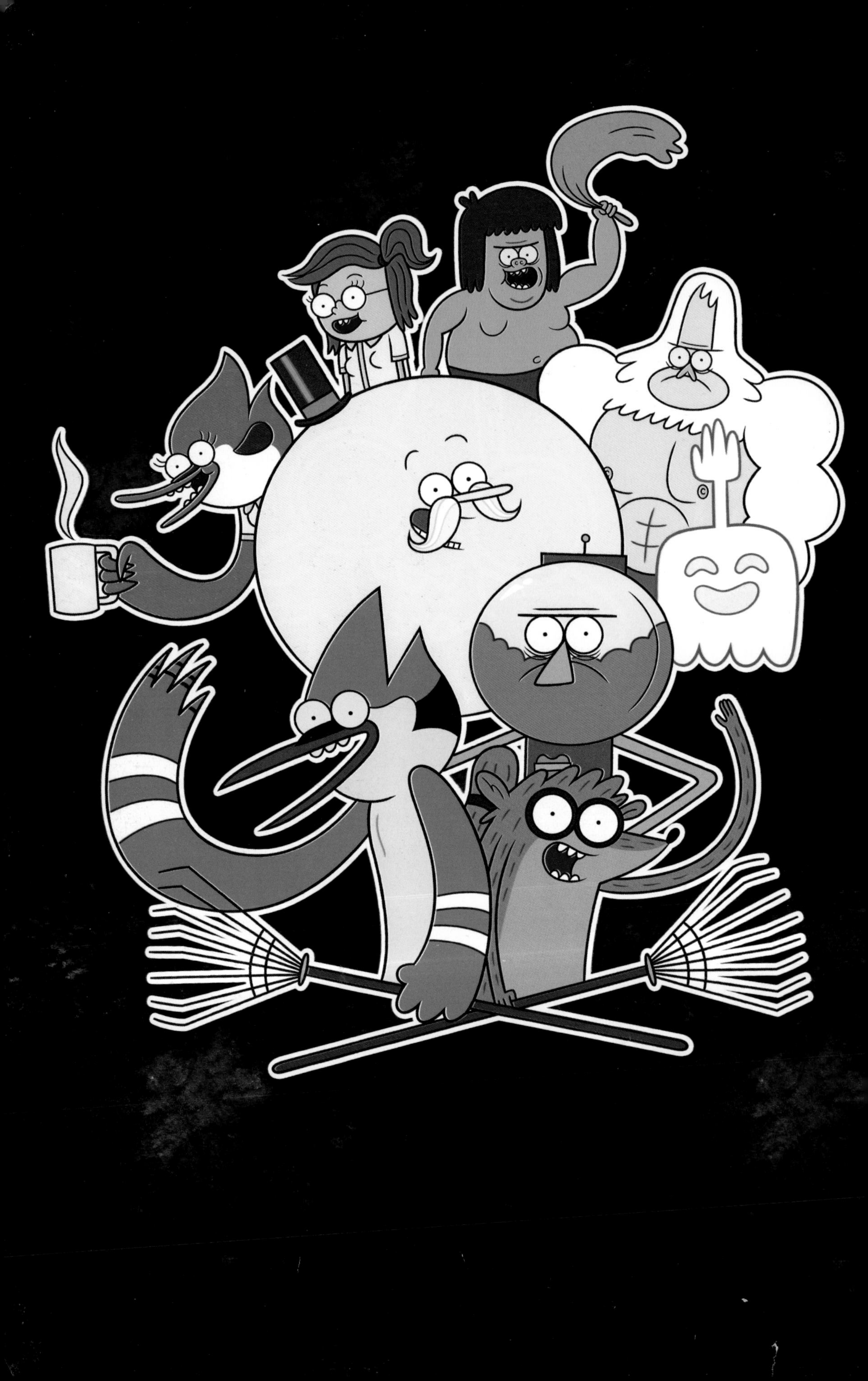

COVER GALLERY

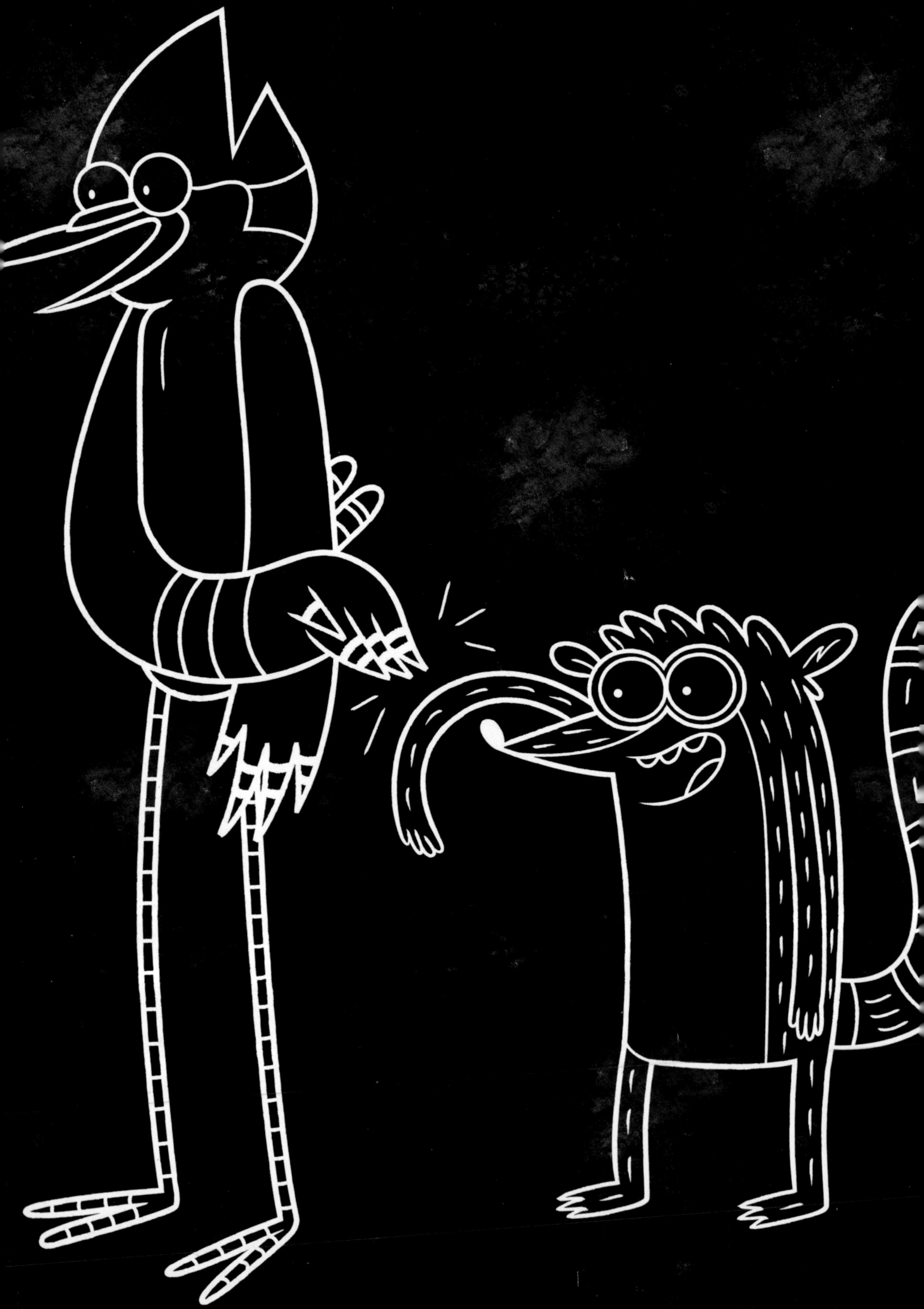

ISSUE THIRTEEN Main Cover
ANDY HIRSCH

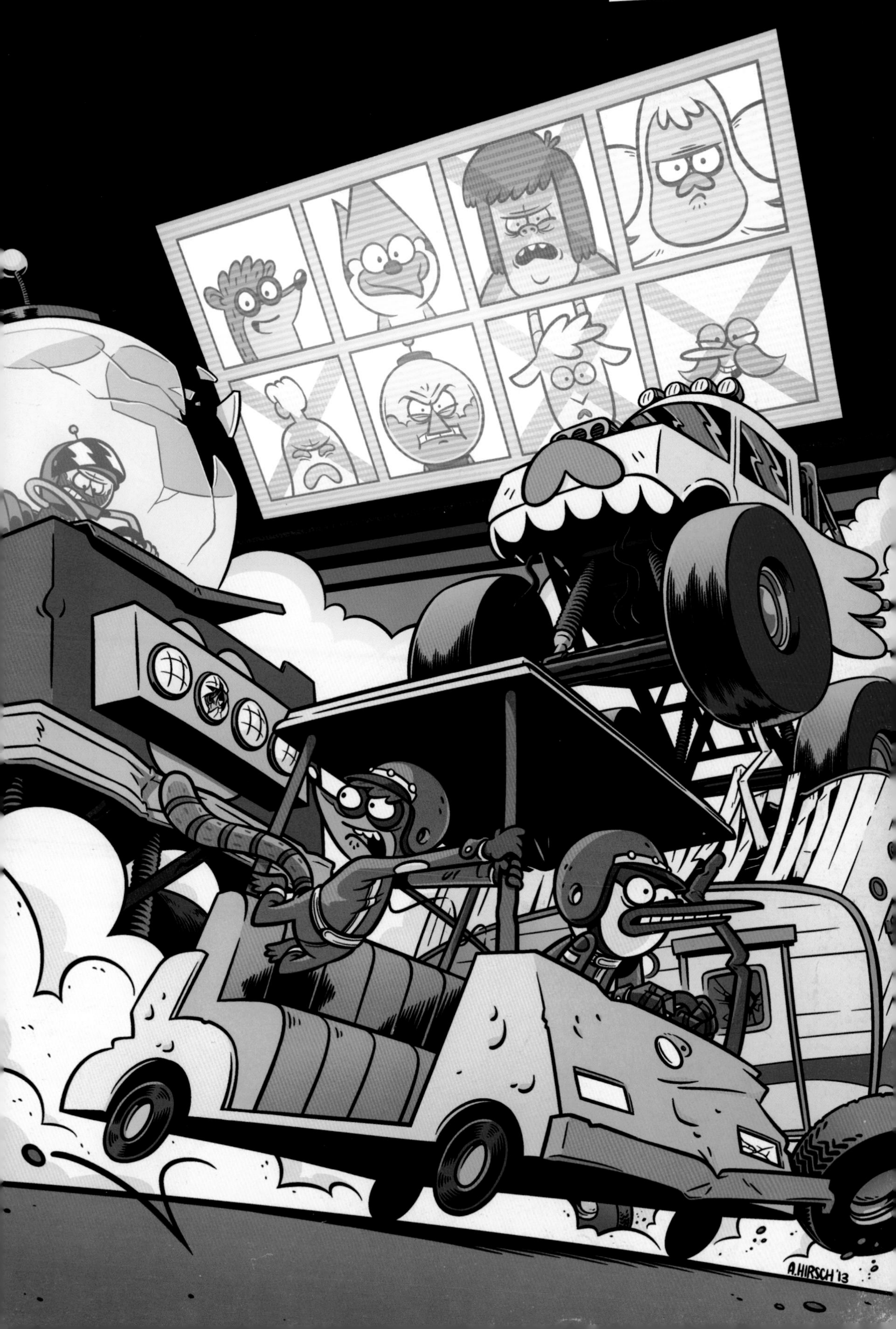
A.HIRSCH '13

ISSUE THIRTEEN Subscription Cover
COLE CLOSSER

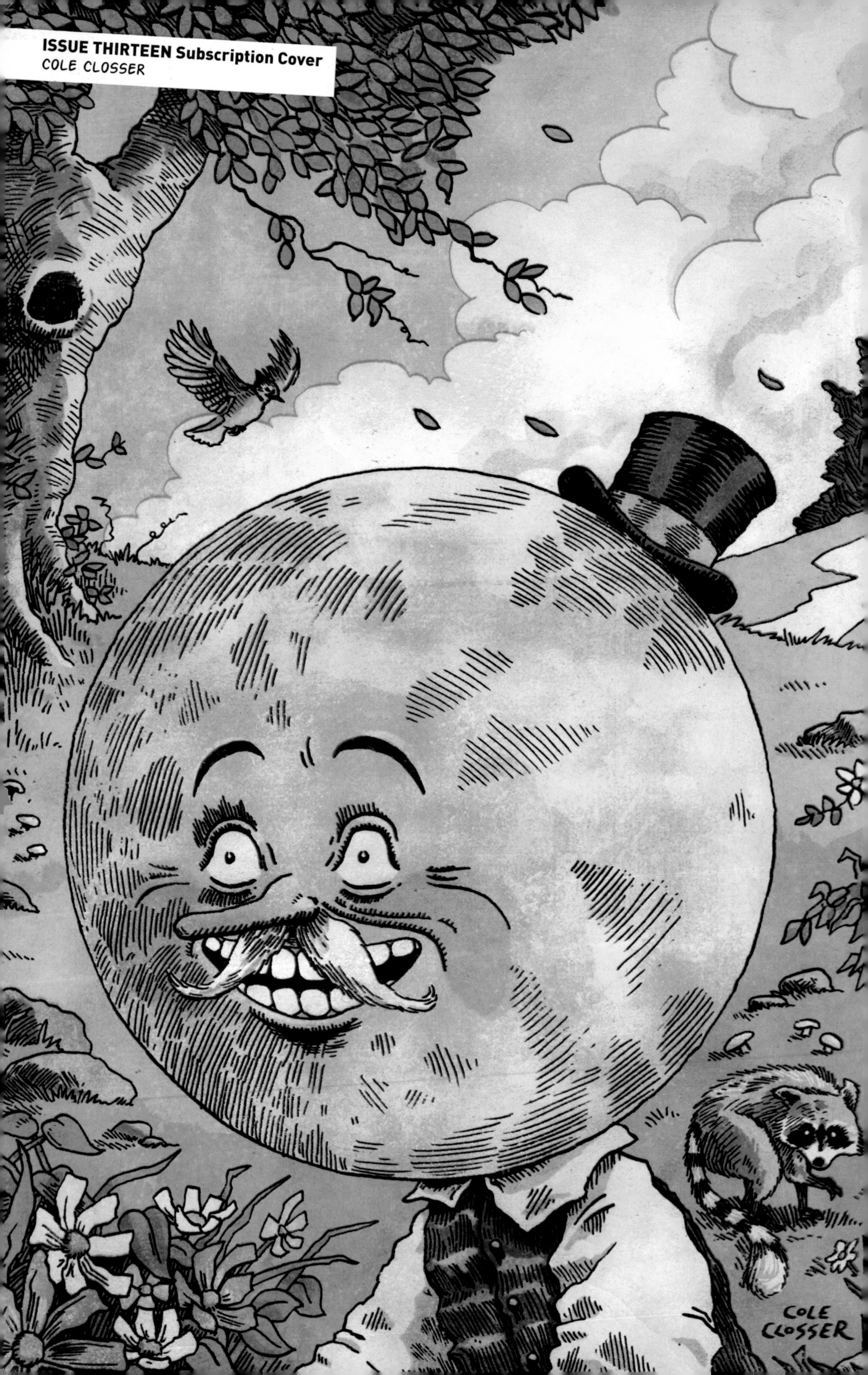
COLE
CLOSSER

ISSUE THIRTEEN Variant Cover
FELLIPE MARTINS

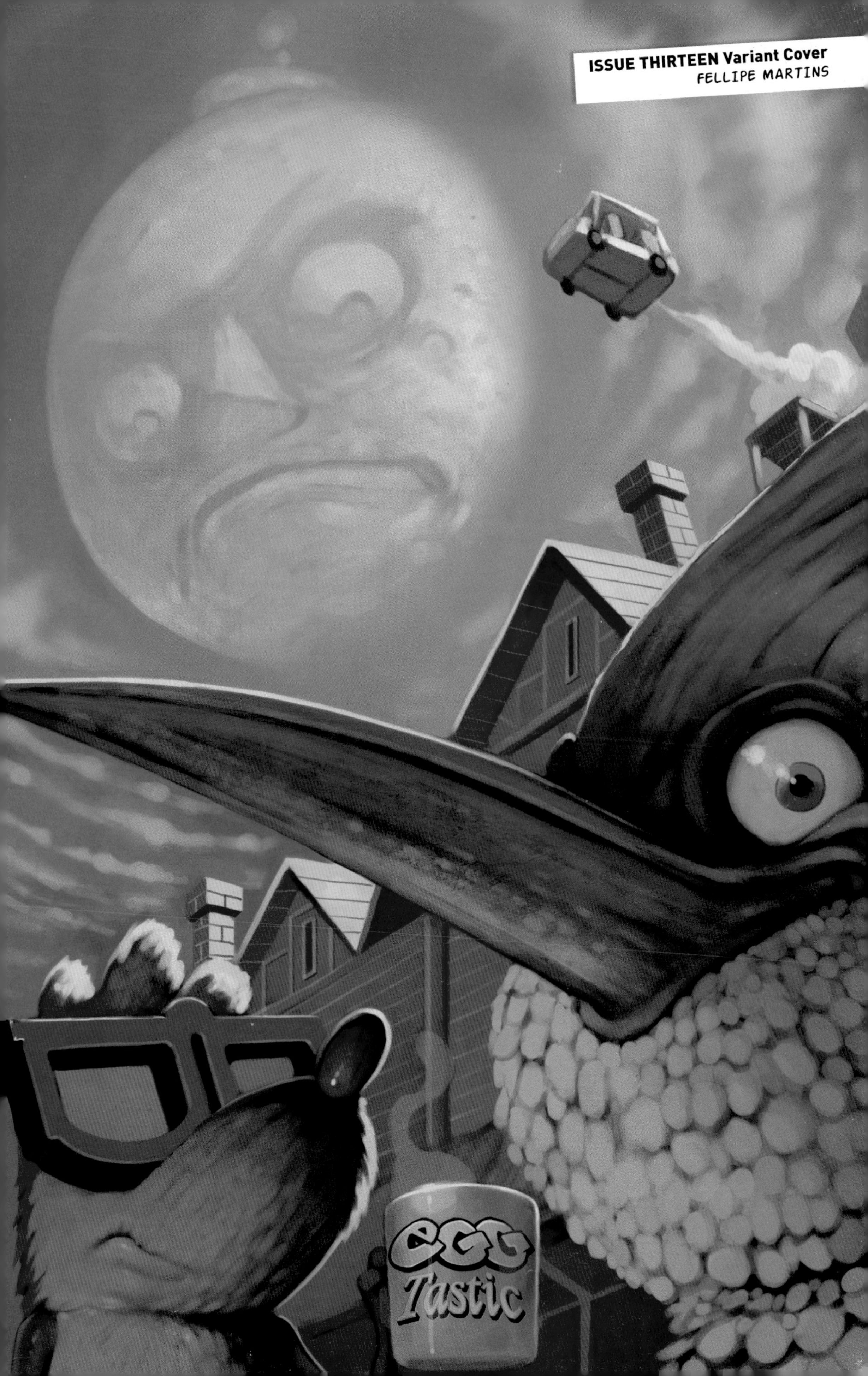
EGG
Tastic

ISSUE THIRTEEN San Diego Comic-Con Exclusive Cover
COLEMAN ENGLE

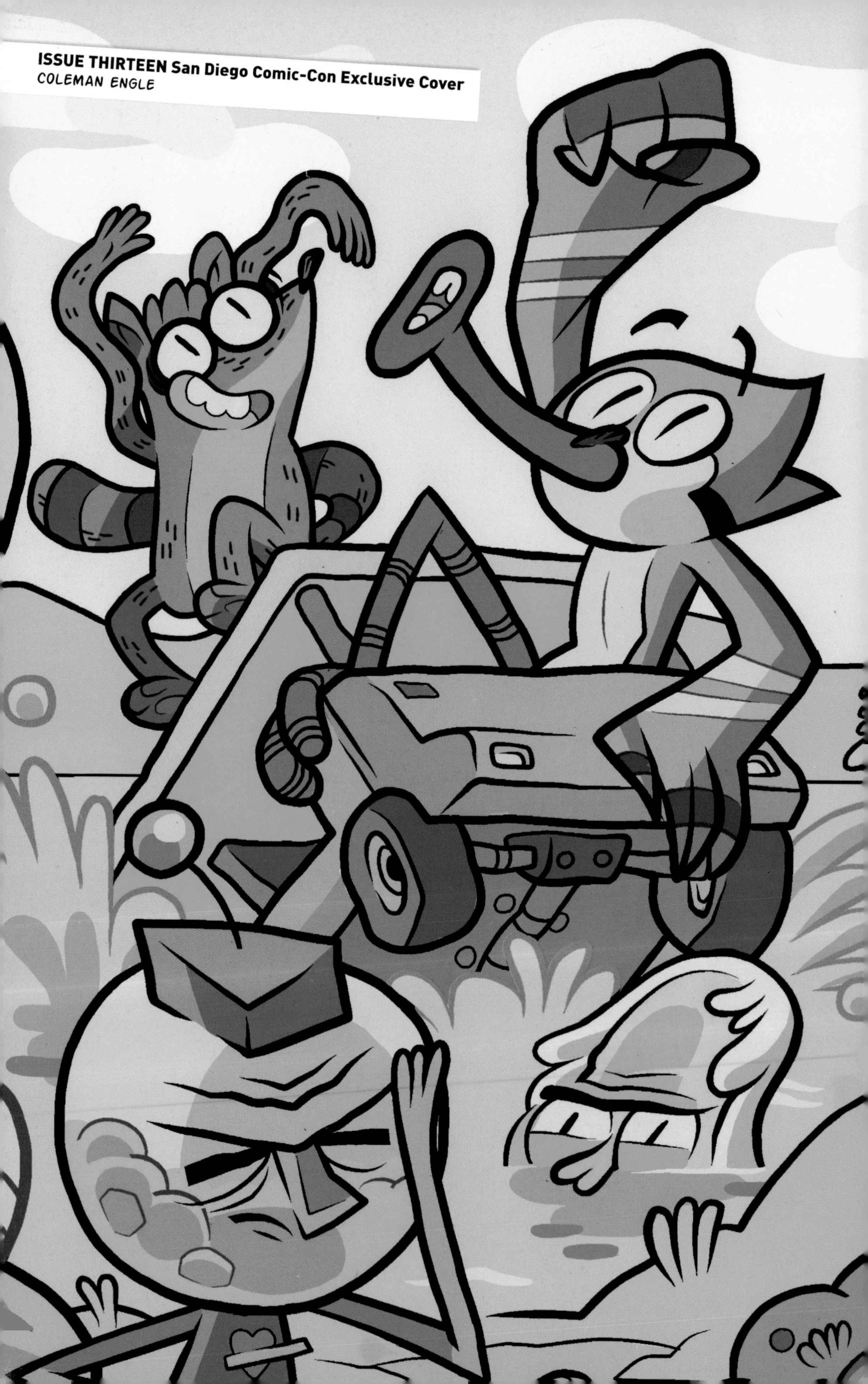

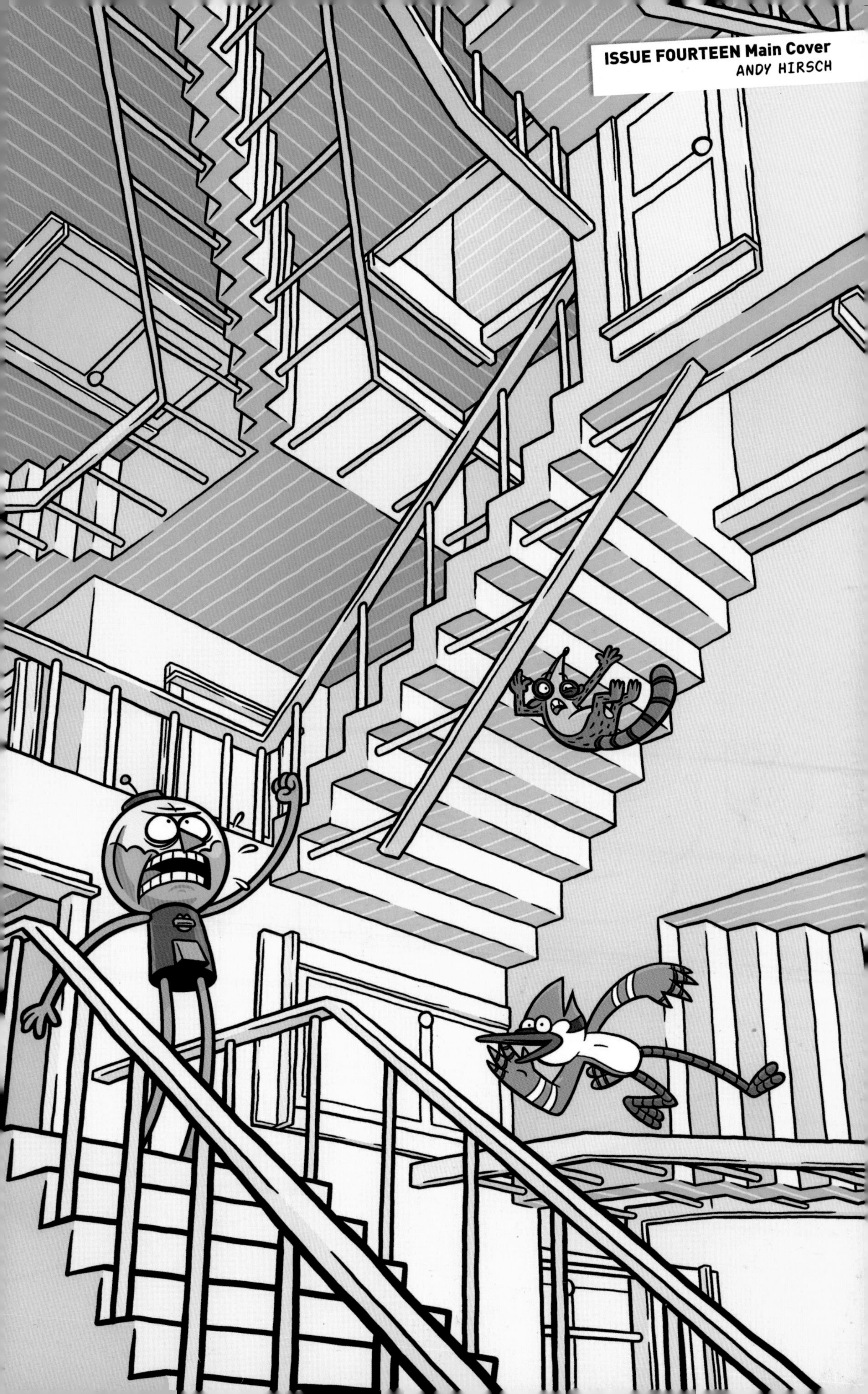

ISSUE FOURTEEN Main Cover
ANDY HIRSCH

ISSUE FOURTEEN Subscription Cover
CHELSEA MCALARNEY

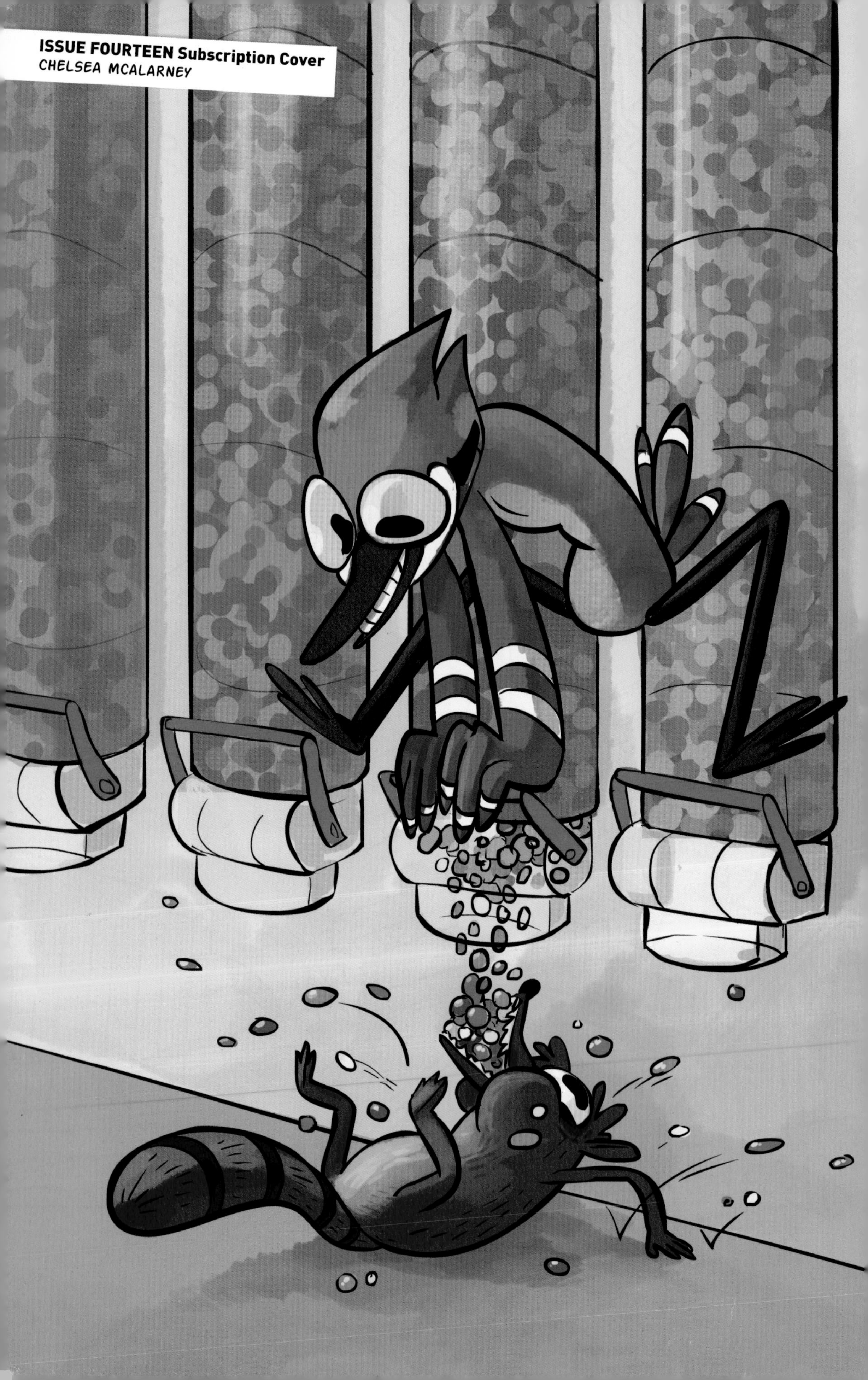

ISSUE FOURTEEN Variant Cover
JAKE WYATT

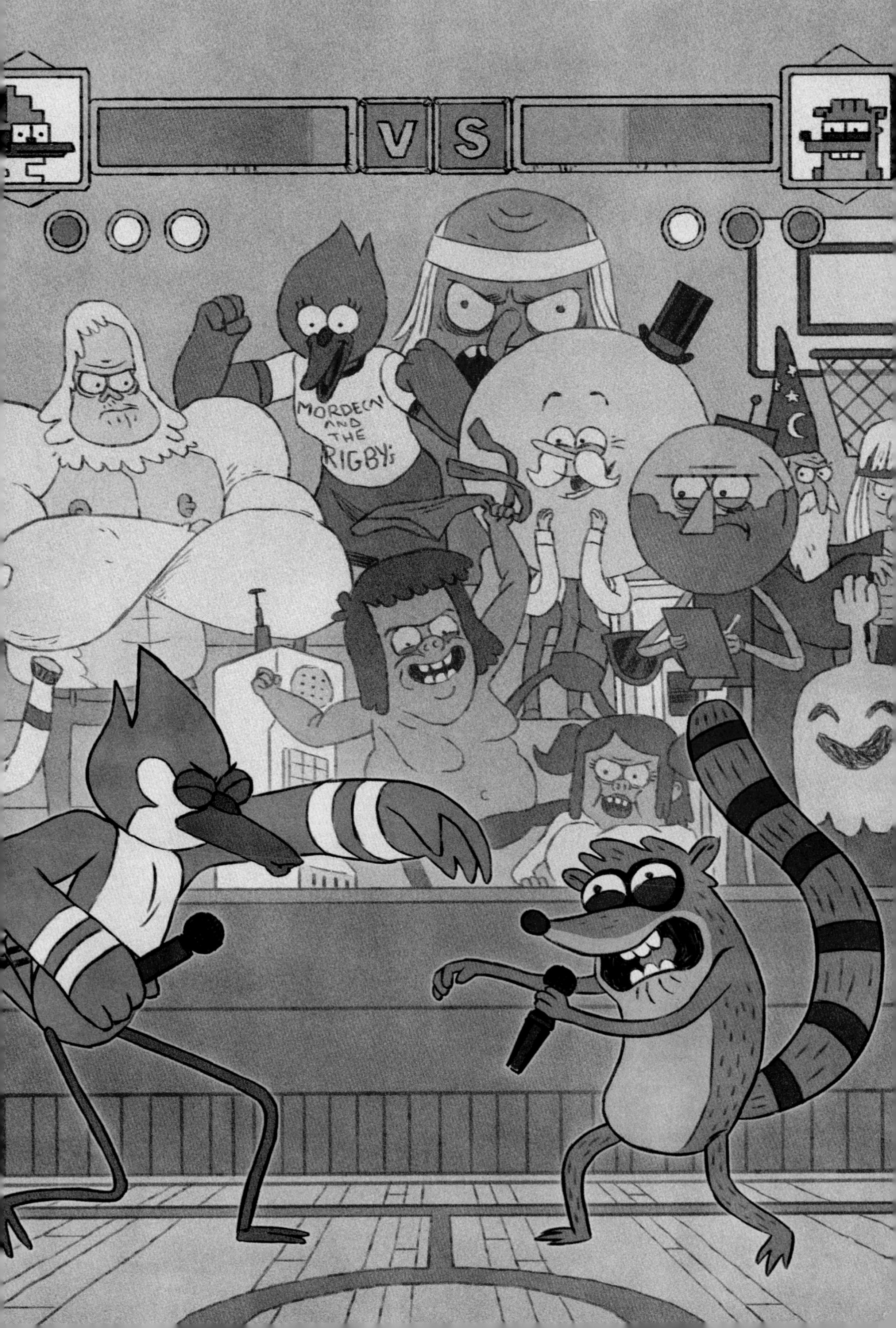
VS
MORDECAI AND THE RIGBY's

ISSUE FIFTEEN Main Cover
ANDY HIRSCH

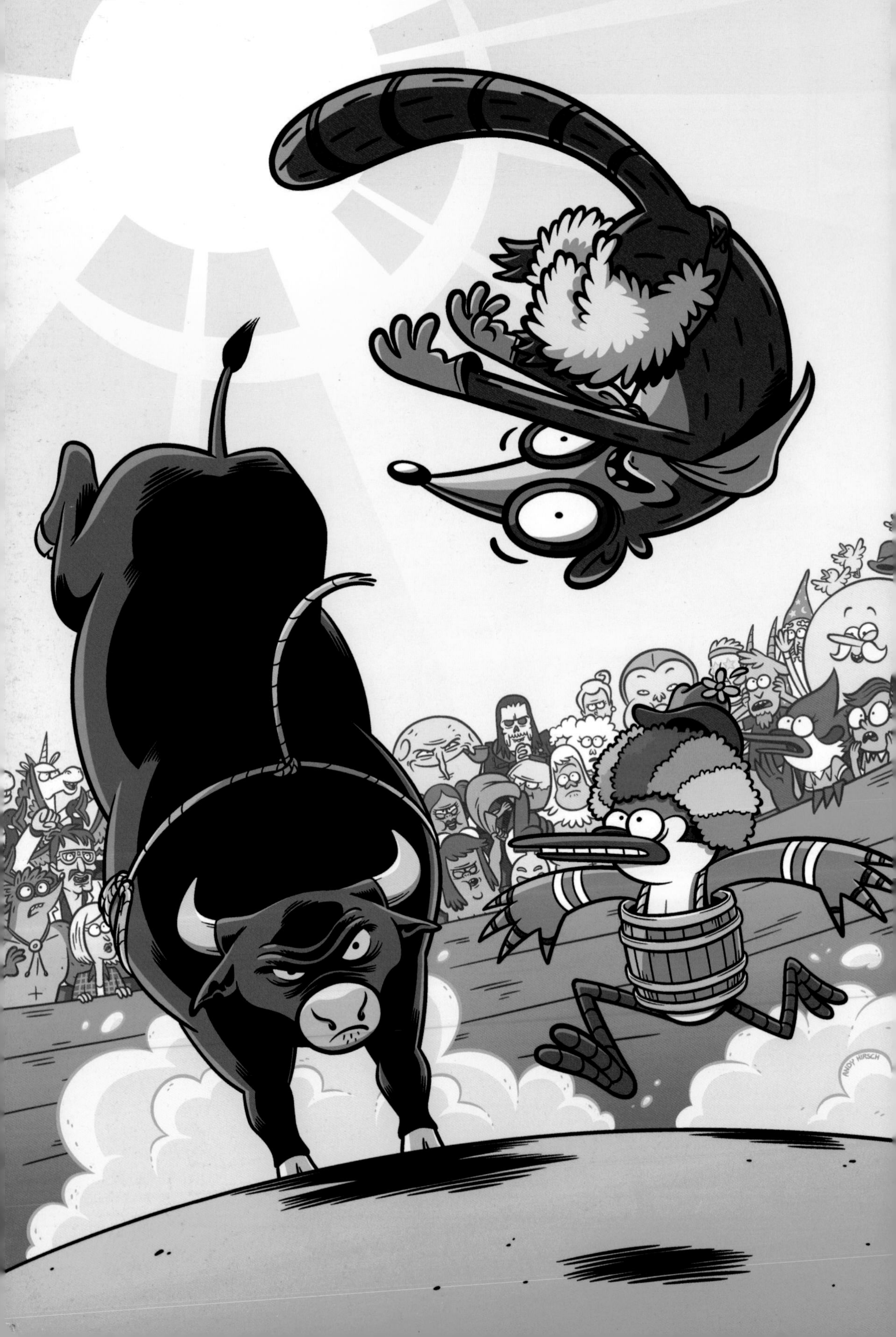
ANDY HIRSCH

ISSUE FIFTEEN Subscription Cover
KATIE MCDERMOTT

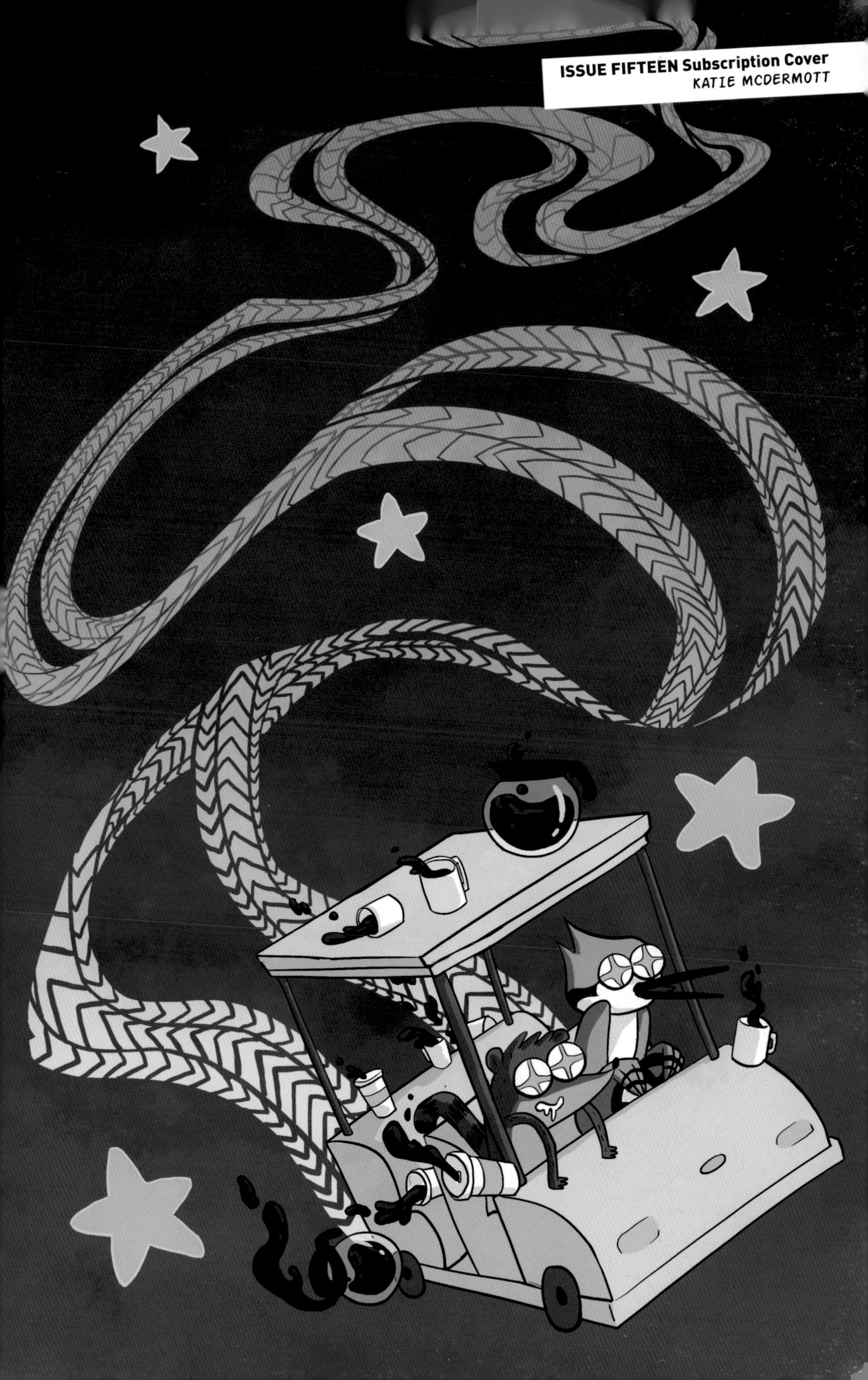

ISSUE FIFTEEN Variant Cover
T. ZYSK

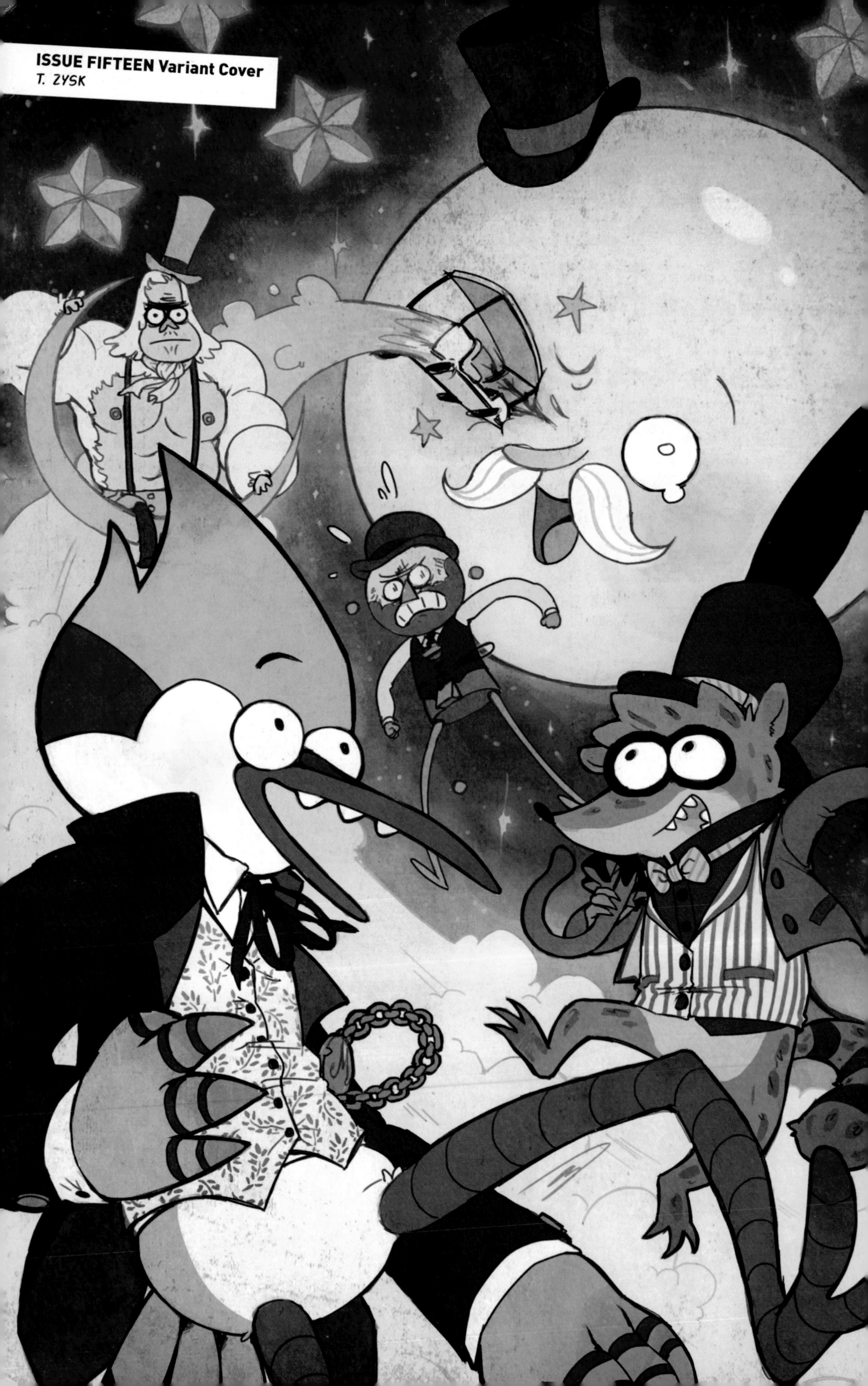

ISSUE SIXTEEN Main Cover
ANDY HIRSCH

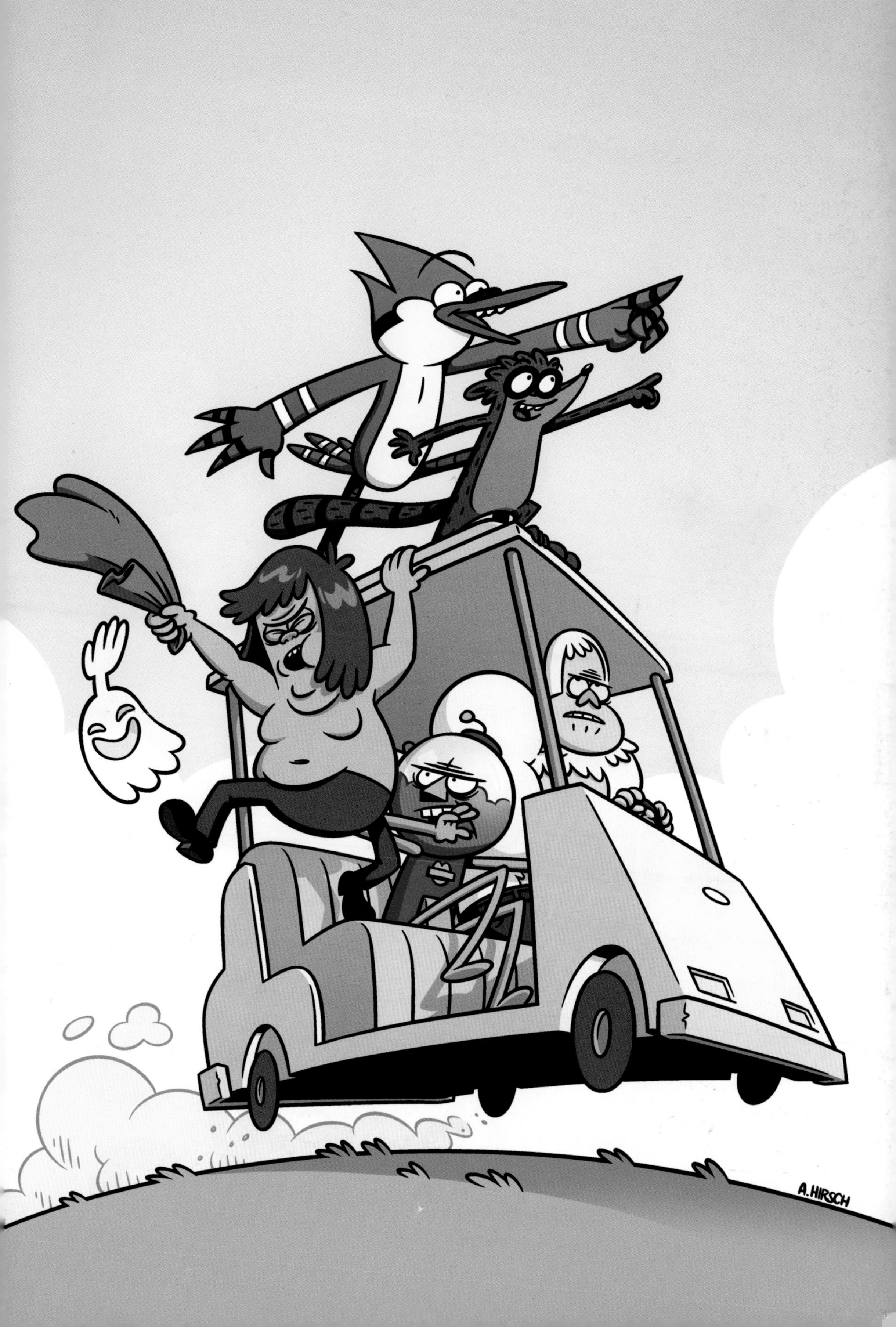
A.HIRSCH

ISSUE SIXTEEN Subscription Cover
KYLE FEWELL

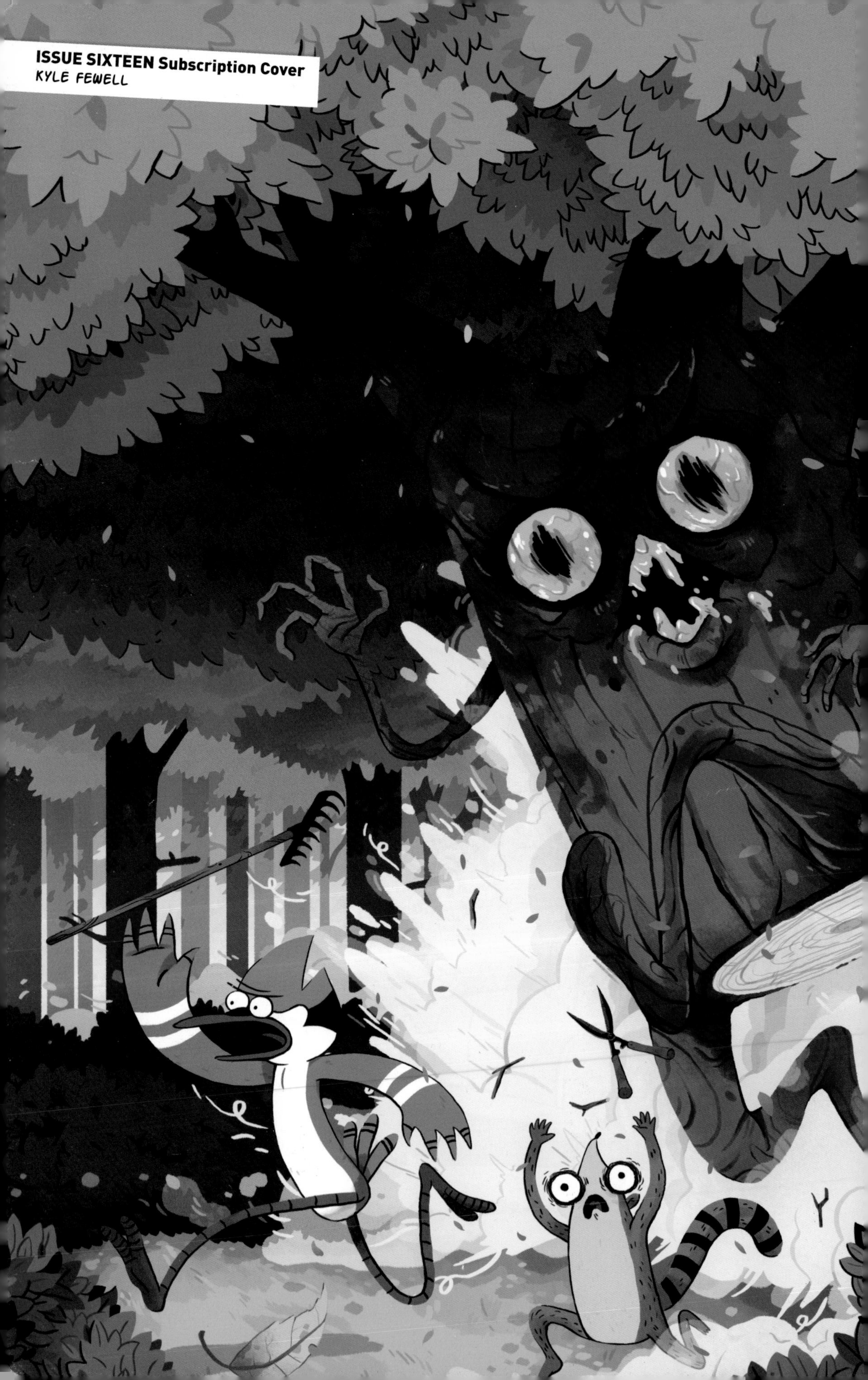

ISSUE SIXTEEN Variant Cover
LAURA MÜLLER

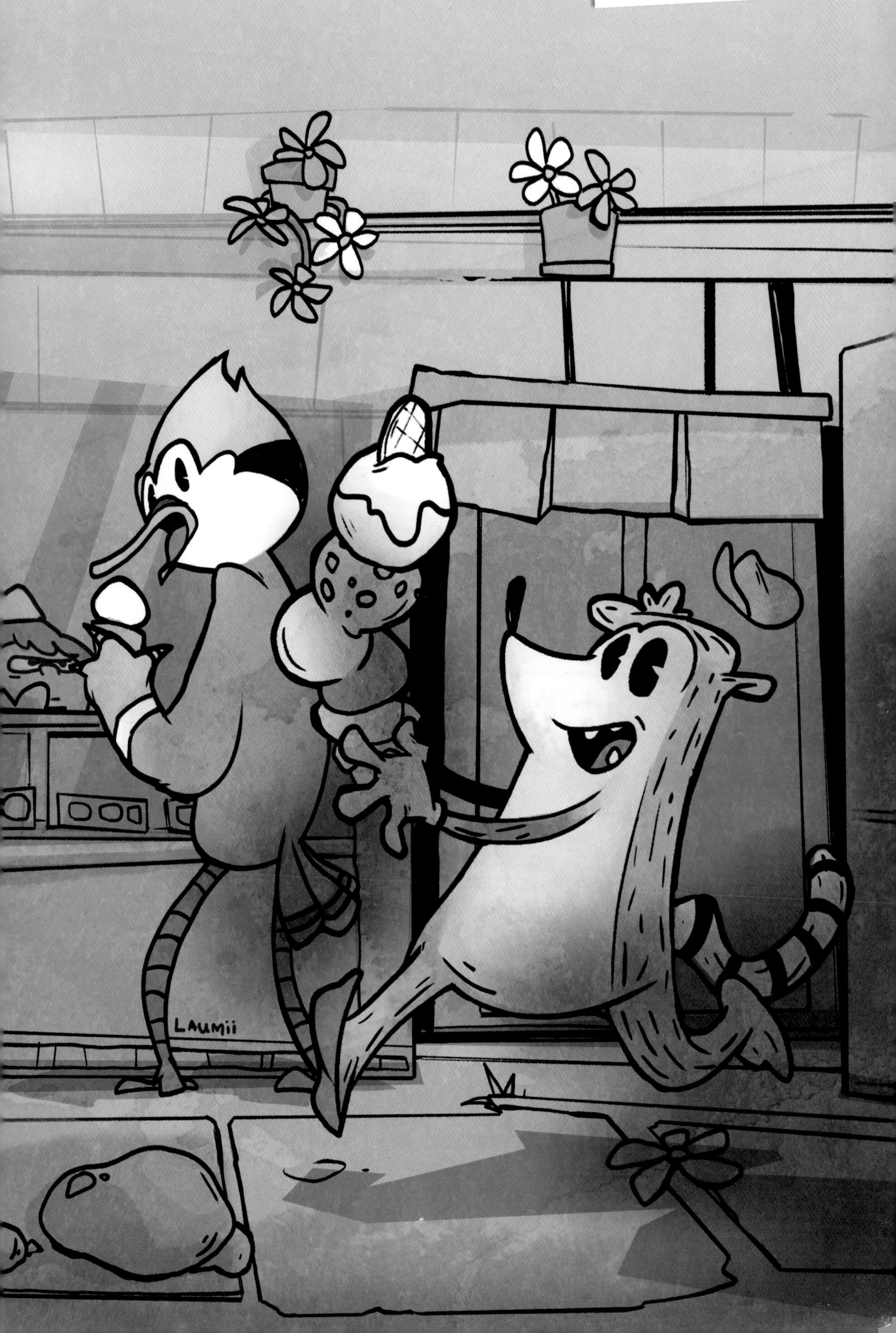

ISSUE THIRTEEN Unlocked Retailer Exclusive Cover
DUSTIN NGUYEN

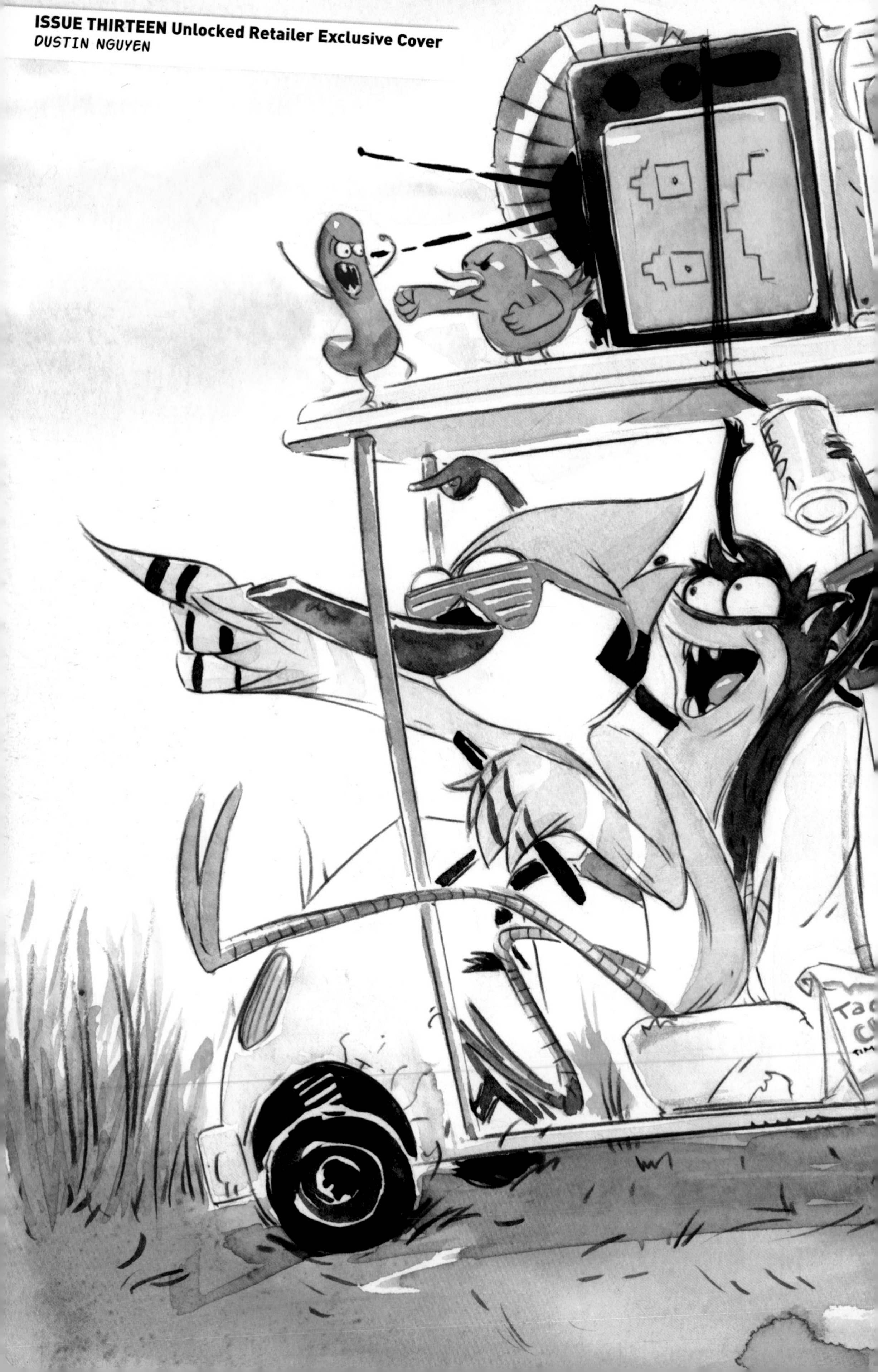

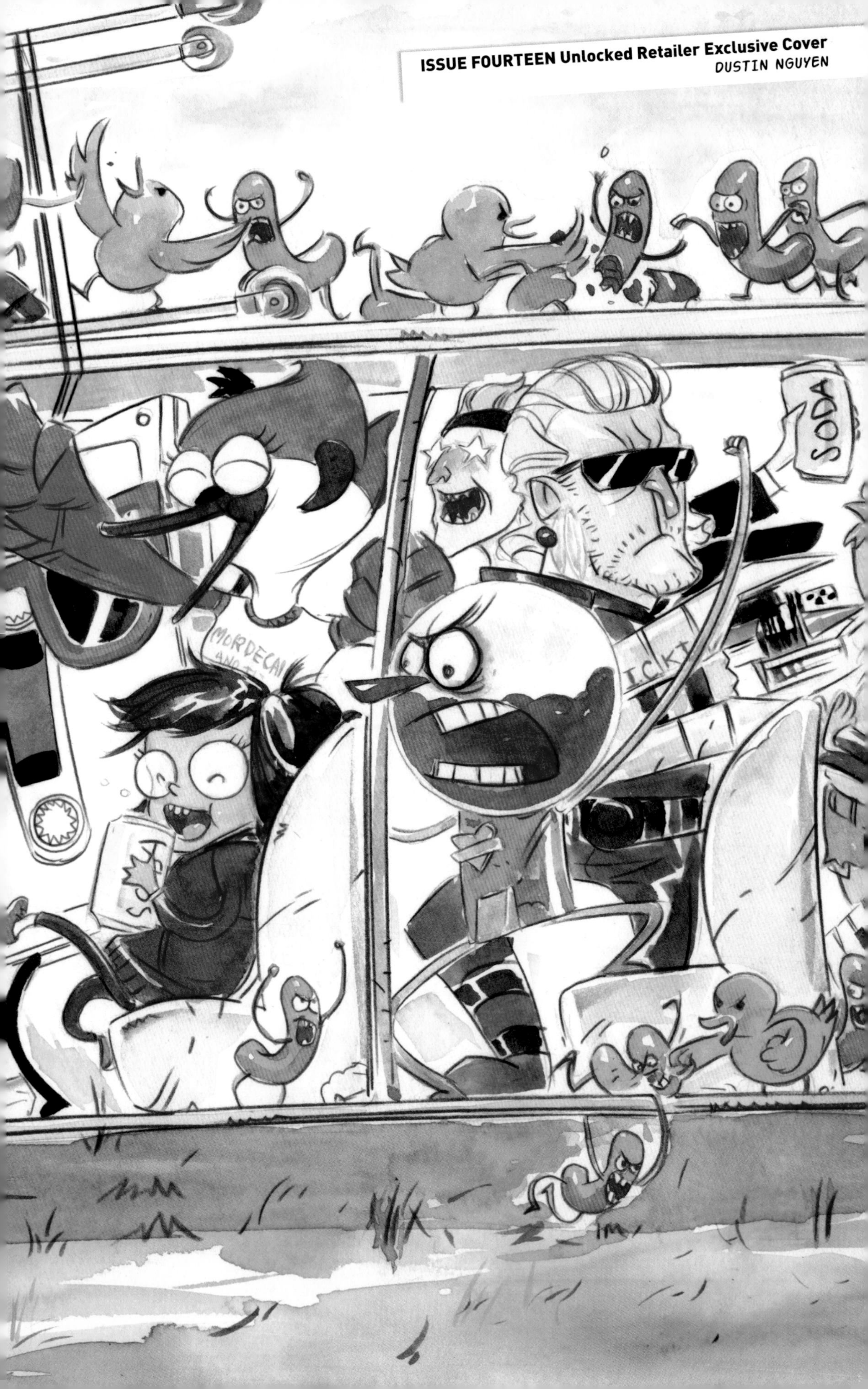
SODA
MORDECAI

ISSUE FOURTEEN Unlocked Retailer Exclusive Cover
DUSTIN NGUYEN

ISSUE FIFTEEN Unlocked Retailer Exclusive Cover
DUSTIN NGUYEN

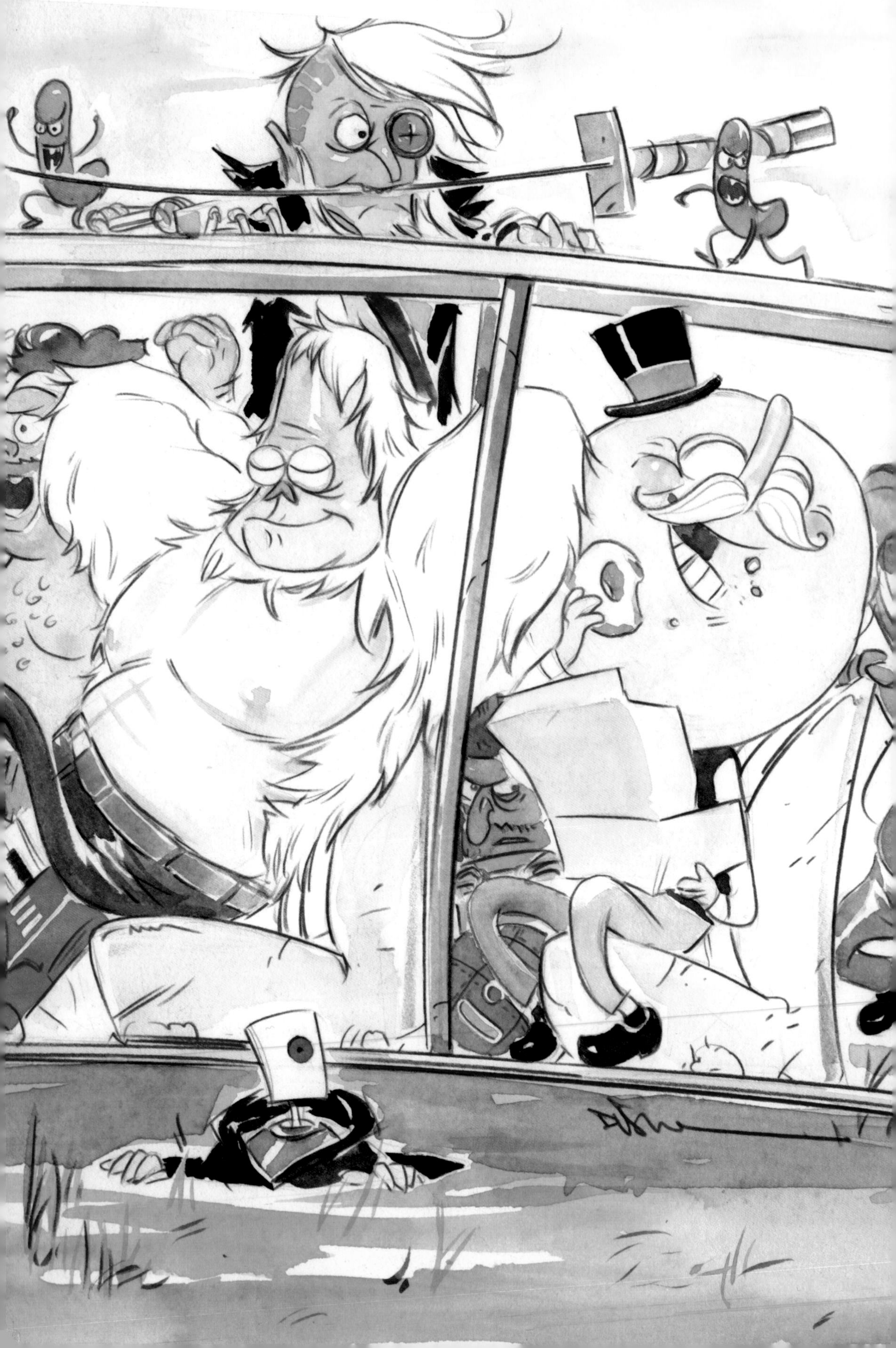

ISSUE SIXTEEN Unlocked Retailer Exclusive Cover
DUSTIN NGUYEN

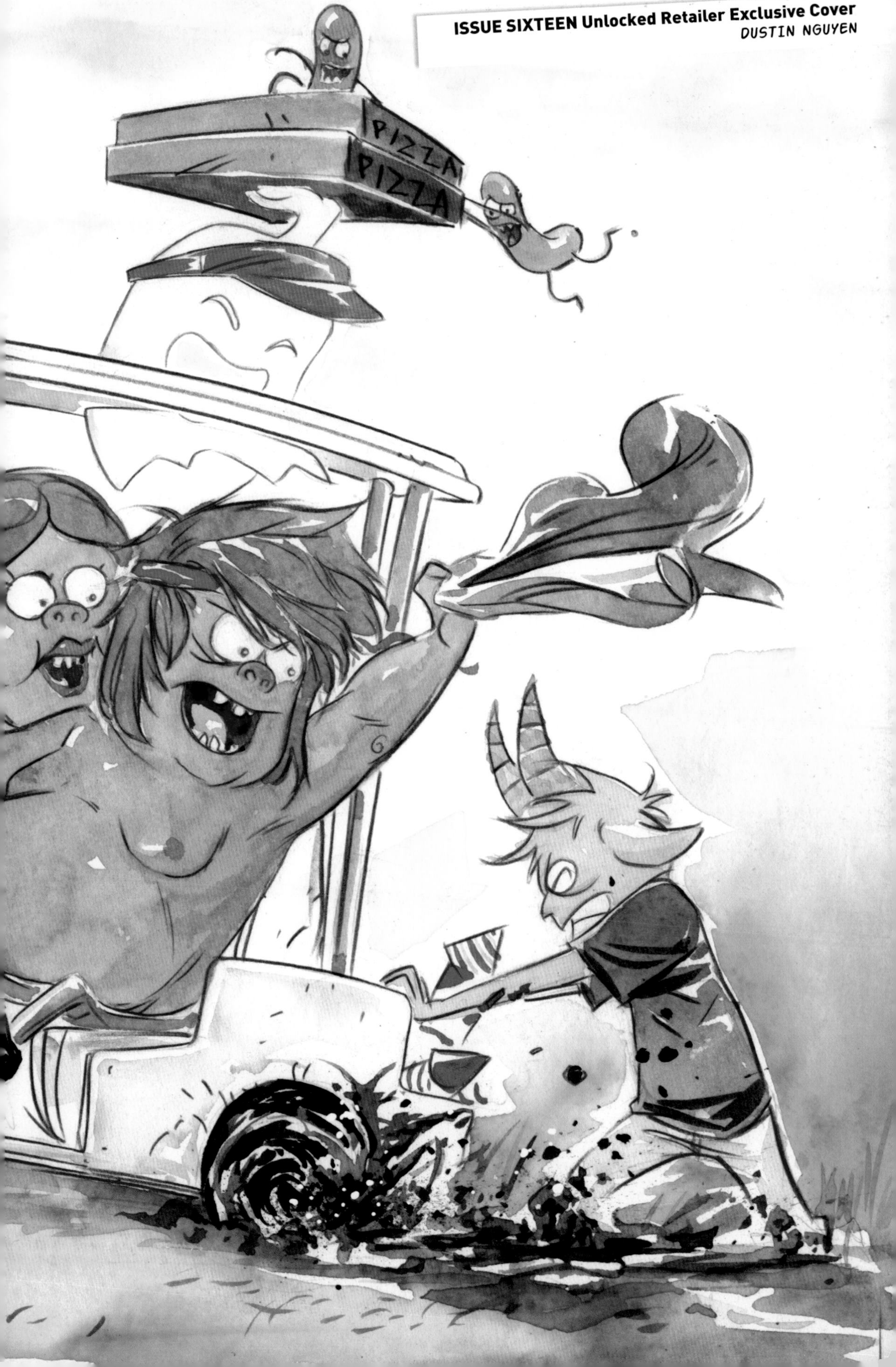
PIZZA
PIZZA

Unlocked Retailer Exclusive Connecting Covers
DUSTIN NGUYEN

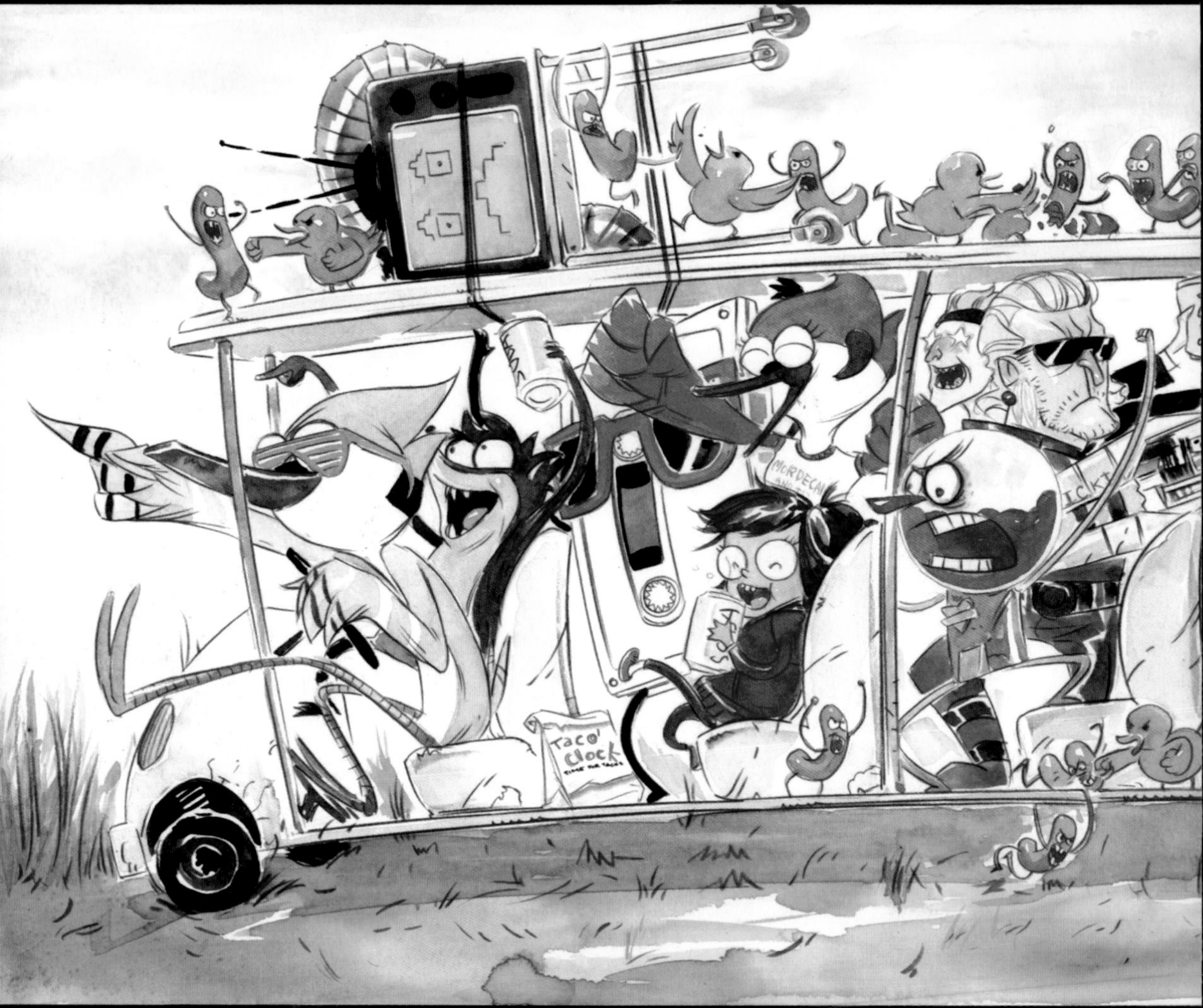

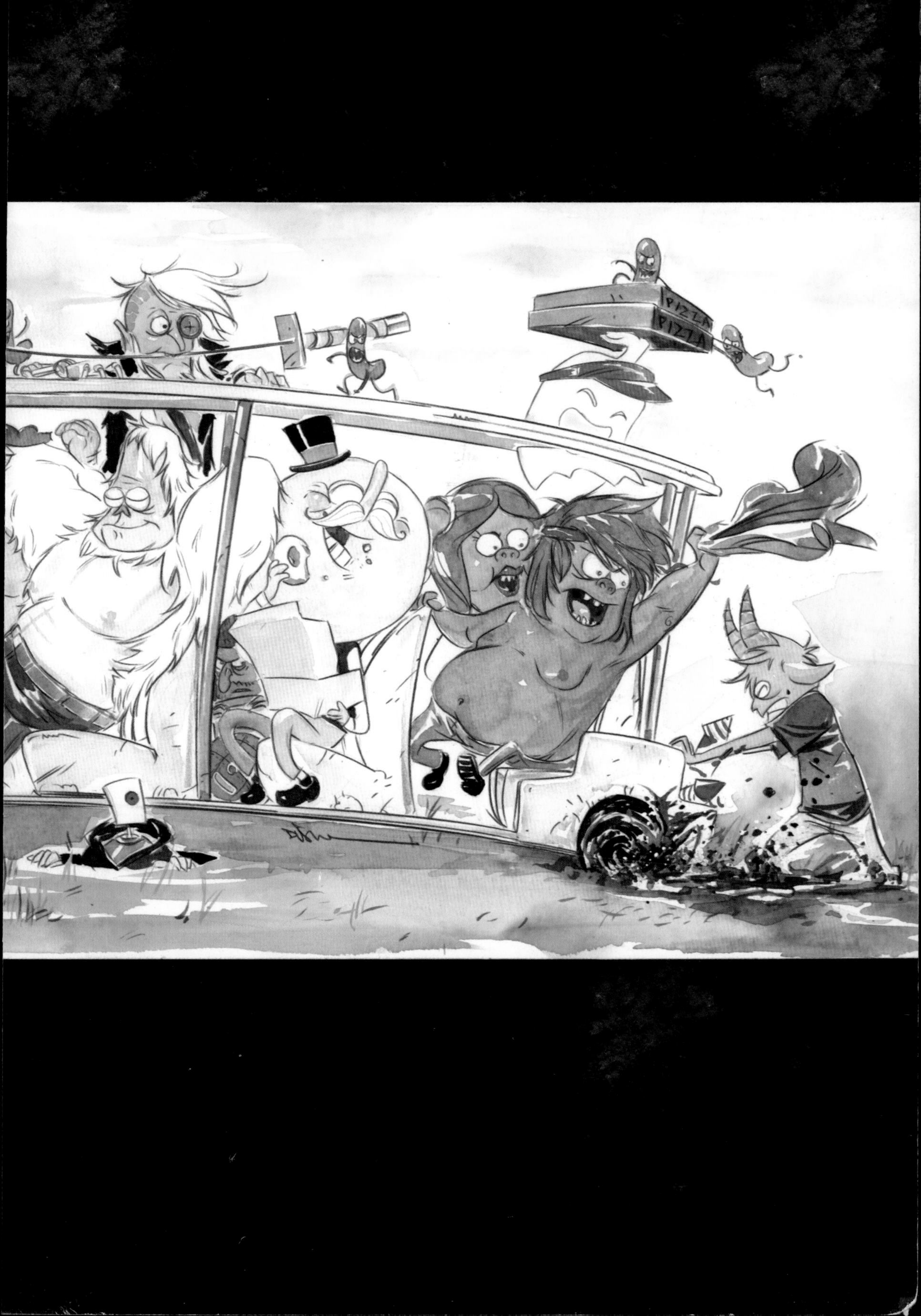
PIZZA
PIZZA

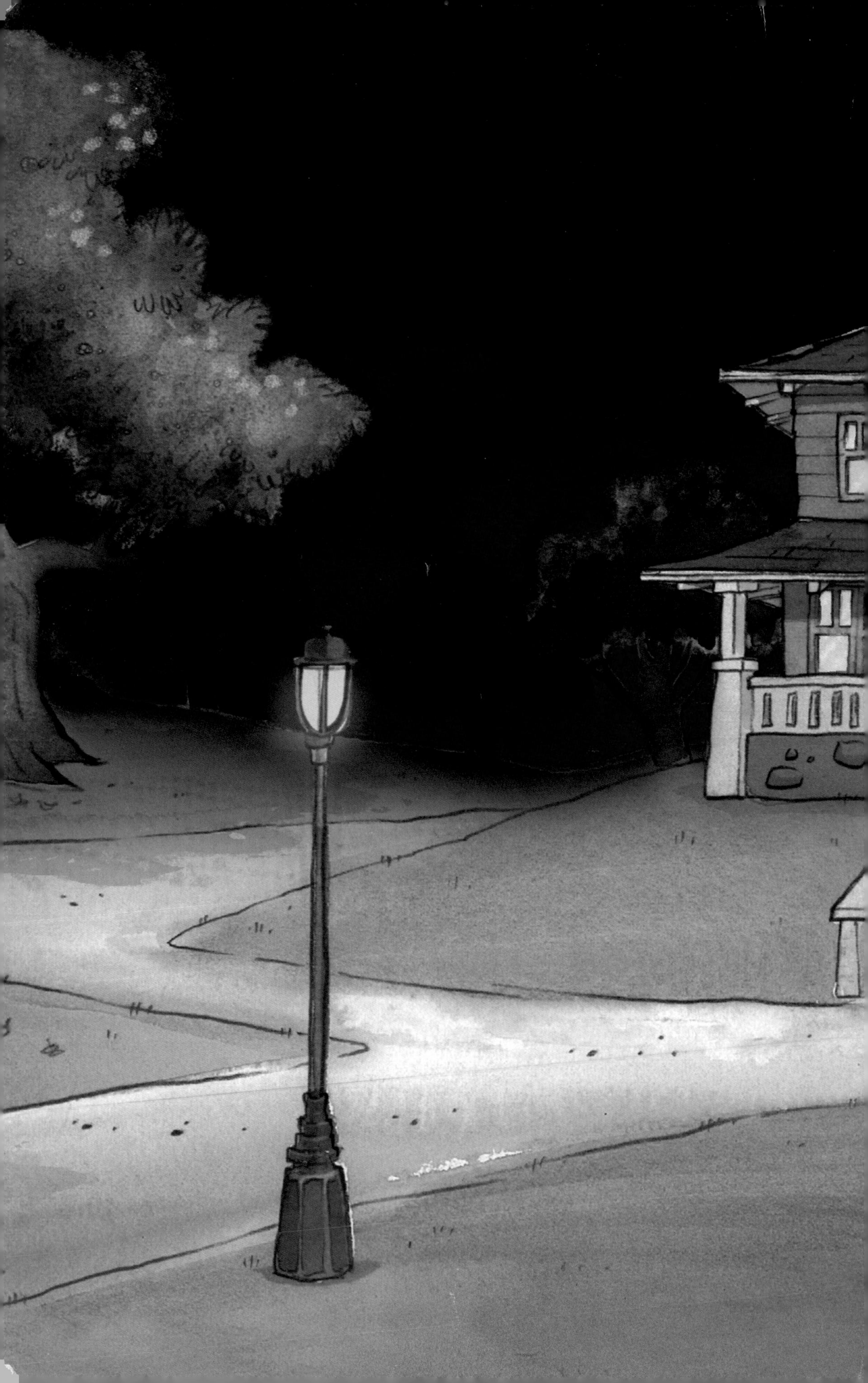

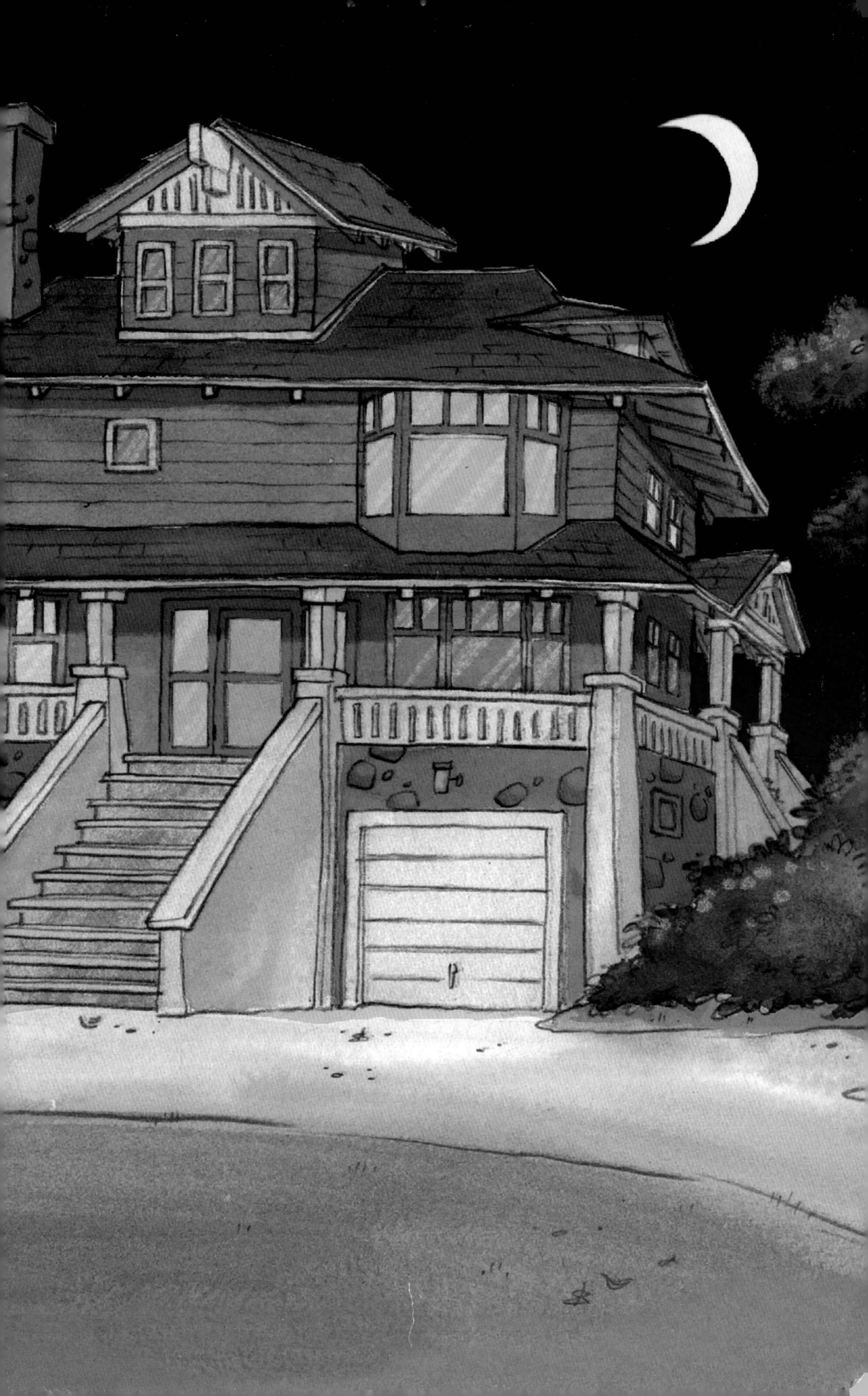

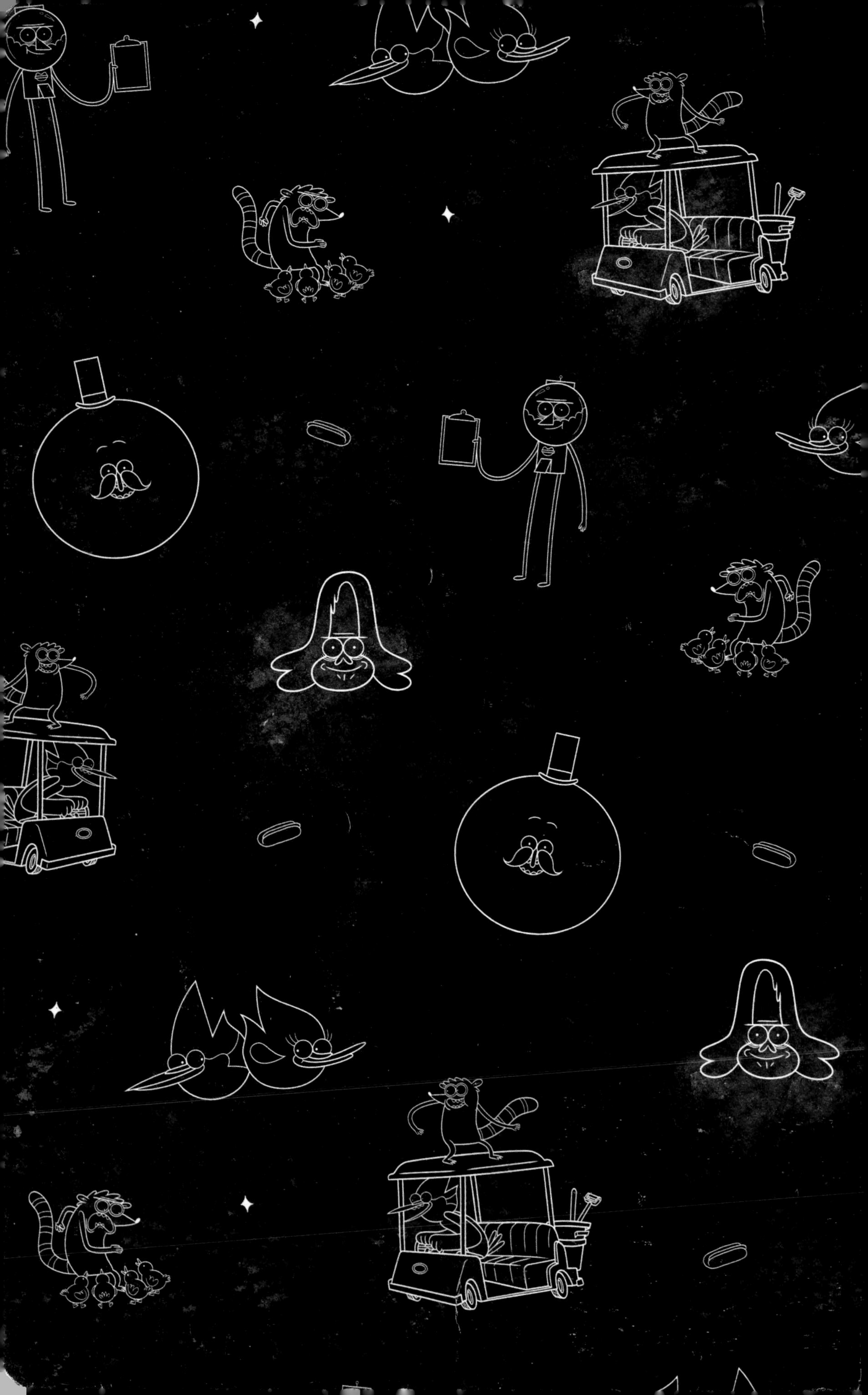